Tendu

DANCING IN THE CASTLE

Ailish Sinclair

GRAUPIUS

Tendu contains graphic sex scenes, violence, trauma and adult language.

For Charlotte

Part One

College

Chapter 1

THE CONFUSING TANGLE OF limbs and hands came to an abrupt and neat finish, almost as if it had been choreographed. The instigator of the collision held out my to-go cup of hot chocolate with an understated flourish, like a man presenting a gift. I reached for it, stared directly up into his eyes, and then the usual inner cringe never came. Obviously I was too incensed. How dare this unexpected person crash into me, steal my chocolate, and then behave as if he was being, in some way, magnanimous?

The rest of the morning was suddenly enraging too: London had been doing its special drizzle, the kind that looks like nothing but leaves your clothes damp and clinging in an itchy way. The other commuters had been so slow moving, I'd ended up catching my hair in the tube-train door. And then, once we'd finally reached college, there'd been a threat of expulsion, though only half spoken so as to confuse. People and their insinuating ways! And it had all made us late for class.

The red mist of rage cleared as I spied Justin through it. Justin Bevan: my Puck, mischief maker and beautifully outspoken best friend. He had one eyebrow raised, so: quizzical, possibly amused.

"She's sorry," he called after the man, who had continued on his way.

"I'm not sorry," I said. "If anyone should apologise—"

"Phi! Keep your voice down, or he'll hear you. And you realise this is exactly the sort of thing our esteemed leader was going on about?"

"I'm just so furious," I told him, the air reddening again as my hands formed into tight fists.

"Really? With him? Don't you think that's a bit misplaced? Madame's surely the more deserving focus for your anger with all that ignorant autism talk."

I stated facts. "He barged right into me. And he didn't say sorry."

"Actually, you were walking backwards to speak to me, and then you spun round, and you both sort of..." He crashed his hands together in lieu of finishing the sentence. "It was impressive how he caught your cup."

"You mean stole." I was almost hyperventilating with fury.

"Now, Miss Treadwell," drawled Justin, his slim form taking on the mannerisms of the not-really-so-esteemed Madame. "You must be sweet and demure and conduct yourself with perfect decorum at all times. If you want to stay in my school, that is."

The tension broke, and laughter replaced rage.

"Nice meet-cute, though," remarked Justin as we continued down the dark and narrow corridor towards the light of the stairwell.

"There is nothing cute about being rammed into."

"Watch your wording, darling. I'm blushing. However, if there's a whiff of gaydom about him, he's mine. Lovely hair." He patted his own dark curls and flattened down the sides absent-mindedly as he spoke. "Well-muscled arms, bet he has washboard abs, ballet boy with that stance, not British, had that sexy Slavic look about him, well packaged in the trouser department too."

"How can you possibly have noticed so much in so short a time?"

"How can you not? He had that 'Look at me, look at me!' stage-presence thing going on."

"I only saw his eyes. Brown. Like this chocolate that will now be cold."

"Actually," mused Justin as we climbed the stairs. "He might be nice for you after the nightmare of last term."

"Men don't like me," I reminded him.

"Untrue."

"Not once they get to know me."

"Nonsense. He looks classy and cultured. You would have shared interests. He might like literature, art, Shakespeare. You could discuss plays. Acting, Phi. You love acting. And then, of course, there's ballet. You could spend hours dissecting that: over dinner, under sheets..." Such speculation lasted all the way to the studio.

As if to demonstrate the chaotic result of being late, our classmates' bodies littered the beechwood floor in a bewildering mass of multi-coloured legs, sore feet and ice packs held on knees. Some discussed the latest diet fads, two stretched at the barre, and others stared with dismal inevitability at the biggest personality in the room: the mirror. Lining one wall, this most critical of daily companions reflected back our worst points, our weaknesses and errors.

I sat down beside it to reconstruct my bun with what pins were left, realising I'd stood in front of Madame with half-up-half-down wet hair. But it was the brown eyes that I remembered. They'd seen a girl with the dark and deranged locks of Medusa, and that thought let the cruelty of the looking glass through: breasts too big for ballet, hips... well... the oft-repeated mantra of 'lumpy-bumpy' surfaced, but was quickly quashed. The mirror existed to assist with technique. That was all. It was merely a useful tool, helping me in my quest to be the best dancer I could be. The new school year might bring new mistakes, but it was not a time to indulge old ones.

Justin's chatter had moved on to the subject of rock-hard thighs: who had them, who didn't. His own frame remained whippet thin regardless of what he ate, a fact that was reflected in his healthy relationship with food, and the mirror.

In came Simone. No sports bra required, the sexiest strappy leotards adorned her pre-pubescent boy's physique every day. The mirror smiled her way and gave a rousing speech: so perfect, so skinny, hair like spun gold, the longest of legs and such a neat little nose. The corner of Simone's mouth raised in a sneer as she glanced at us, but at least she didn't speak.

Our teacher arrived with an arm flourish which was at once a greeting and a call to stand ready. Peter had taught me since I was six years old, and his attitude had always been that of a somewhat judgemental father.

"You look unusually full of inspiration today, Amalphia," he said, walking over and placing his palm on my cheek. "Let's put it to work."

At the barre everything was simple. You were right, or you were wrong. You were good, but you could get better. Having missed my usual solitary pre-class warm-up and stretch, I needed the grounding strength of the barre more than ever. Peter always used set routines, allowing focus to be on the improvement of form rather than remembering choreography. The intricate and slow adagio sequence was designed to develop height and control. This type of work typified perfectly the continual improvement possible through perseverance, so I was not pleased to have it interrupted by late arrivals into the room.

The mirror stretched to accommodate Madame Genevieve, the head of our school. Once a great ballet dancer, she had since become a powerfully beautiful plus-size woman. Her confidence and poise allowed her to wear outfits that anyone else would have looked ridiculous in. Today's flowery purple dress with a monkey on the back, and green trainers adorned with ladybirds, called to mind exotic jungles and floral scents. But her earlier speech echoed. The official autism diagnosis had ticked a box that secured my scholarship. The recent removal of that diagnosis, a decision I had been assured would have no negative impact, actually meant no allowances would ever be made for me again. It was effectively a punishment for coping too well, or seeming to. Madame was just waiting for me to put an inappropriate foot wrong and then... She'd let it hang. The person behind her now, here in the studio, was dressed all in black which was oddly soothing, until I recognised his eyes.

Madame talked to Peter, and I inspected the chocolate thief. Justin was right. The man moved with a grace that meant ballet. The shape of his thigh muscles under the black jeans proclaimed the same, though his legs were not bulky like those of some male dancers. He sat down on a chair by the piano and ran a hand back through his dark blond hair.

I stared. He stared back, face expressionless, or perhaps stern. Could it be some sort of grumpy resting face? But no, he was actively looking at me. I waited for a sign of apology or recognition. His gaze moved off round the room without offering a hint of either. Only then did I notice the other intruder in our midst. Standing beside the brown-eyed man, the woman wore the most unpleasant array of red colours. I detected a strong and expensive perfume too. That had to be coming from her. This wearer of cloying scent and clashing shades was looking right back at me, her red lipsticked mouth turned up ever so slightly at the sides: mocking, thinking she knew something.

Well. I didn't look their way again for the rest of the twenty minutes they remained in the studio, instead pouring vigour and energy, possibly more than was warranted, into each and every exercise. My legs had never been higher. All jumps were at maximum velocity. It felt good. My eyes flashed big and dark and dramatic in the mirror, and then my hair fell down. But the man in black, and the woman in red, had already left with Madame.

Simone led the post-class discussion. "Do you think he's looking for students?" she asked the room in general. "His new school in Scotland is meant to be amazing. For starters, it's in a castle and has the biggest dance studio in Britain. It's got a swimming pool and a theatre. It's just amazing!"

"Who is the amazing one, exactly?" asked Justin.

She gaped at us in disbelief. "Do you two actually live under some sort of special-needs rock somewhere?"

Justin opened his mouth to retort, but Simone spoke gratingly on.

"Aleksandr Zolotov? The great Ukrainian dancer? He's amazingly famous! Any dance publication would tell you this. Honestly!" And with a toss of her golden head, she flounced from the room.

Justin took a bite of toast as we stood in our small 'must buy chairs' kitchen the next morning. He looked out the window at the damp grey day and bemoaned the fact that the only thing his father had ever given him was the flat we both lived in.

"Well, that and my Indian Ocean good looks, of course."

"You are very beautiful," I agreed.

"But have I ever met him?"

"No," I said, knowing my lines in this role by heart.

"How often do I get to soak up the sun in Mauritius while visiting him in his beautiful house?"

"Never."

"I could be there now, Phi," he said, gesturing at the weather. "My Mauritian blood doesn't like the cold."

"You'd be missing college."

He looked at me, possibly irritated by my deviation from the usual line of plain agreement. "Like you, today," he said and sighed. "I'd bunk off with you if you'd do something more fun."

But I was quite happy with my plans. College wasn't somewhere I wanted to be on Tuesdays, despite the trouble that the absences incurred. I sought other dance floors and companions once a week, the break allowing me to cope better with the usual routine when I returned to it.

Walking into the flat that evening, after my refreshing day of fun, I found Justin lying on the sofa with his legs propped up on a pile of cushions. A damp washcloth on his forehead completed the look of abject misery.

"I take back every trouser-packing, nice thing I said about him," moaned my friend, raising his head and removing the washcloth. "Sexy and Slavic he may be, but he's a sadist. He doesn't explain his planned sadism properly and then makes you feel stupid for getting it wrong. You're for it tomorrow; he was most upset that you weren't there. 'You are living with Amalphia?' he asked me. I said yes, as if I was straight and dating you, or something. I don't know why. Why do I do that? He is by the way. Totally. No gay man could dream up such torture."

We'd been moved into the Ukrainian dancer's new morning ballet class for what was to be a term-long audition for his school in Scotland.

"But we haven't said we want to try out for it," I said. "Shouldn't an audition be a choice?"

"Exactly," agreed Justin. "Madame's whims gone awry again, and we get shafted. Not in a wholesome man-up-your-bum way, you understand. And then there's the woman in red. She looks at you like you're dirt. Dirt, Phi! And then she smirks and writes stuff down."

"Well, I'm not going."

"D'you really think that's wise? With all that the mardy old bag said to you yesterday?"

I did a fact check. "Peter's class is good. This new one isn't. If Madame's looking for an excuse to expel me, it's going to happen anyway. I might as well stay with Peter as long as possible."

And that is what I did, heading straight for Peter's lesson the next day. As soon as I arrived in the studio, it was clear that our old teacher was irritated by the decimation of his class. All the best dancers, bar me, and I warmed to him for saying so, were gone. Those of us who were left got more individual attention, and there was plentiful room at the barre, so no need to turn to avoid kicking anyone. But despite these benefits, there was a sense of missing something, of an opportunity passing by unnoticed.

The next lesson on my timetable, pas de deux – partnering class – was also taught by Peter, so I lingered by the small upright piano, grinding my feet in the rosin box, pondering the wistful sadness that had pervaded the day. Had I been too quick to dismiss the new teacher? If he was starting a new school, and I was being ousted from this one— The thought stream was interrupted.

Will Hearst, the most annoying student in college, appeared in the doorway wearing his trademark trackies-and-socks combo. He constantly flouted the school's dress code. I'd never seen him in tights or ballet shoes. His insistence that we were friends because we'd known each other when younger was only matched in idiocy by Peter's insistence that we still partnered one another in this class.

As the only two students doing the teacher program in our year, we were often flung together, and I suspended annoyance to help him with the resulting paperwork as that part of the course gave him some difficulty. Today, however, his grin told me he was on top form, short brown hair all spiky and irritating as he strolled across the studio.

"You're in so much trouble," he sang, and I saw that he had the morose Ukrainian in tow, all in black again, and bee-lining for me.

"You are to be in my class," stated the stern man. "Why are you being here?"

"I decided to stay in this one," I said, interested by his unusual vowel pronunciation. I liked the way he spoke. I liked the odd little dent on the bridge of his nose, the imperfection somehow smoothing away the intimidating effect of his haughty demeanor.

Peter had been listening. "And she was right to stay here. You can't just waltz in and interfere with the training schedule of my dancers, Zolotov. It's clearly not in their best interest."

They faced one another, and the air grew charged, prickly and unpleasant like Will's hair. Zolotov – I only just resisted the temptation to say the name out loud, to experience the pleasing repetition of sounds again – was the taller of the two men, looking down at Peter from on high.

"Surely they should train with many different teachers, learn more methods, be pushed in new ways?" he countered.

"But you're not a teacher, are you?" remarked Peter. "Being a dancer does not automatically qualify you to teach. I don't believe this sort of experimentation should be allowed on our students."

"You were a dancer," I said to Peter, feeling the need to point out hypocrisy.

"Yes, Amalphia, but I am an experienced teacher now."

"You weren't when you first taught me."

"It is the now we are concerned with here," he snapped. "This is not straightforward guest teaching. The new school is a research facility. It all sounds decidedly suspect." He turned to Zolotov. "You're just the front name, chosen to lure susceptible young people in."

"This? It is simply not true," replied Zolotov. "Some scientific study is to take place for funding, yes, a small amount each day. I am concerned only with the teaching of ballet, to the highest standards, to those with talent." He turned to me, his eyes, which apparently I was looking directly into again, seemed to smile, though his mouth remained serious. "Please, it is your choice. Do one class to try."

"And what about your girlfriend in red?" I asked. "Is she also concerned with teaching ballet to the highest standards?"

"My colleague," he corrected, "runs the research. She is now back in Scotland with her studies."

Facts: it was my last year of college. Then, much as I didn't like to think about it, there would be big changes. Performing, if I could get Madame to arrange an audition for me at the company associated with the school. And if I could cope with the stage fright. Teaching, if I couldn't. Acting, maybe? I didn't know what work I would eventually manage to get and do, but this different and new teacher might help prepare me for it. He might help me be as good as I could be.

"You should totally do it, Malph," said Will, barging into my thoughts for the second time that day. "We've done lifts this morning, and I've got that fat girl." Annoying. "Bevan's got Simone. That's worth seeing." Interesting. "I'm Amalphia's partner," he told Zolotov, and my patience for his interruptions ran out.

"Well, there's a good reason not to do it," I blurted. "Three pas de deux classes a week with you is plenty. The constant chat is bad enough, but the smell... no. It's too much."

I'd gone too far. Will strode away to the other side of the room wearing his 'shut off from everyone' expression and began to warm up, surely a pointless exercise given that he'd just done class.

Aleksandr Zolotov took my hand in both of his. "Ah, but you will work with me. Everyone else is already in pairs, and I do not think I am smelling so bad? You would have noticed this on the day we meet, the day you are not saying sorry for banging into me?"

"Why would I apologise for something that wasn't my fault?"

He inclined his head as if conceding the point, then turned swiftly and left. The assumption that I would do his class was clear, and correct.

"Don't let yourself be swayed by a handsome face and charisma," Peter urged. "He's very keen to get you into his class. He has quite a reputation, you know. He'll be steering you in the direction of his bed next."

I decided it best to walk wordlessly away from such extreme nonsense and headed across the studio to Will, no longer the most annoying man in the room. I laid my hand on his arm, apologised for the inappropriate blurt and explained that it was only salt-and-vinegar crisps he smelled of. "Maybe a mint would help?" I suggested. "I'm surprised one of your many girlfriends hasn't mentioned it to you before now."

"Never gonna let that drop, are you, Treadwell?"

He returned to true form with a grin and talked incessantly for the entirety of the class.

Chapter 2

I WATCHED HIS FEET. I listened to his brief instruction and was left totally confused. The barre section of class had been difficult to follow, though it had contained a fascinating talk on the importance of the exercise of battement tendu, and how its proper execution stretched us in all sorts of ways. It was far more than a simple point and close. The pressure of the instep against the floor was proclaimed as the most important part of class, or perhaps even life. Will had interrupted the talk by whispering, "Dude, no it isn't," loudly behind me.

But the fast amalgamation in the centre was utterly incomprehensible. I put up my hand to query it, but Aleksandr Zolotov didn't notice, focused as he was on marking, or walking through, a complex end sequence. I stepped forward and touched his arm. The tall man spun round in surprise, confirming my suspicion that everyone else had been too much in awe of him, or too afraid of looking stupid, to question anything yesterday.

"Could you demonstrate more slowly, Mr. Zolotov? I can't pick it up from this."

Simone sniggered, but Aleksandr Zolotov touched his chest and said, "Is Aleks," and demonstrated the combination again. He kept checking with me after that, even for the simplest of stretches: "You have it?"

It didn't take long for a little awe of my own to form. Aleks's stance, the movement of his arms, and even his roughly marked footwork, had a quality I'd never been in the presence of before. And when he danced alongside us in encouragement, I wanted to stand still and stare, to applaud, and to ask, 'Why are you here? Why aren't you on a stage somewhere, wowing your fans, enchanting the masses as you are me?'

The time between his classes dragged. He was intense and demanding: our stamina increased, and our brains learned to memorise at great speed. His face transformed for a few fleeting seconds now and then when he smiled, crinkles appearing round his mouth and eyes.

His early arrival in the studio each morning effectively did away with my daily quiet time. He always got there first. He always played the piano. He'd always been smoking. I could smell it, but didn't experience the usual revulsion. Instead, the smoke mingled with the aroma of my hot chocolate in an earthy and thoroughly pleasant way. Aleks was the sight, sound and scent of the morning, the provider of contrapuntal melodies to stretch through, his wordless presence in the corner, strangely nonintrusive.

Will's plump partner arrived, along with Simone. They looked at me as if I'd been up to something nefarious. Things weren't going at all well for Simone in the new lessons. The speed of the combinations threw her, and Justin dropped her. I, on the other hand, suddenly had the best partner in the world. Over the years, my partnership with Will had become familiar and easy, but we still wobbled when faced with something new. Nothing was new to Aleks. All he had to contend with were my off-balance moments, and he was adept at catching and correcting those before they went too far.

We worked on arabesque penchée. Standing on one leg, the other high behind, fingertips almost touching the floor, the world seemed to stand still around me in a perfect moment of balance and extension. Aleks obviously thought something good had been achieved too, and he summoned the others to look. With ill grace, they did.

"See the line," he said, running a finger between my fingertips and toe. "Is perfect. Elongated in two directions. Everyone go do just like this."

They scurried off. He took my hand and raised me. "This, the arabesque, it shows much about your character, Amalphia.

You must go straight for what you want. Never let anyone else be telling you what should be."

Simone glowered at me. I glowed at Aleks.

After class, once Aleks had left the studio, Justin had plenty to say. "That wasn't about the arabesque. He was holding your hand very close to what he wants you to go straight for, darling. He has a reputation, you know. Now..." He held up a hand to quell protestation. "I know you have a little crush."

"I don't do crushes."

"Okay, well, he's your new special interest, then. I know you've been watching videos of him online."

"Yes. To get the most out of his teaching."

"You look him right in the face when he speaks to you."

Granted, that was unusual. "But, you see," I said, trying to find sense in that too. "His face is pleasing. The line of his nose fits the angles of his cheekbones so well. It's really quite lovely."

"No, not lovely," argued Justin. "Try, really quite old. Thirty-eight. Exactly twice your age. His cheeks wrinkle up when he smiles."

The beginnings of rage pulsed red behind my eyes. "Justin, I'm an adult, and I can make my own choices."

"He's your teacher."

"So?"

"Any relationship or naughtiness with him would be against college rules."

"Oh, and you're such a stickler for those?"

"Well, more than you, Phi. I mean, this isn't the first teacher that you've—"

"Nothing like that is happening," I said quickly.

"Read up on him," advised my friend with a sigh and an eyebrow raised in scepticism. "He's not for you, my sweet. There's an angry woman writes a blog about him."

"I don't want to look him up online, other than in ballet videos. How can you tell facts from bitter rubbish?"

"Read some of it, Phi, even just the wiki, about his injury and stuff. He's not the delicious forbidden fruit that you think he is."

That night I sat in bed with the laptop. It wasn't injury that had ended Aleks's career, but rheumatoid arthritis. The new school was mentioned in an article. One of its aims was to provide help for injured dancers.

There were many pictures of formal events. The various glamorous women on his arm made me feel inadequate and ridiculous. I was dark to their blonde and awkward in comparison to their obvious confidence. But I was glad that the woman in red didn't feature. I didn't like her. Sleep came amid clips of gravity-defying leaps and perfect pas de deux.

Friday brought panic. The internet had done nothing to slow the course of the headlong crush/special interest and two days of no Aleks stretched ahead. He sat at the front of the studio writing notes as the students began to leave after morning class. I lingered over my bag, and Justin stuck his head back round the door.

"What time you finished with your sprogs tonight, Phipot?"

"Seven." Teaching the college's part-time young students always made time fly, and would fill up some of Friday evening and much of Saturday.

Justin's smile was mischievous, and his voice was loud. "It's been too long. We need to quiver with desire and experience bliss mingled with fear. Meet me there at eight."

"Where?"

"Sweetheart." He came back into the studio, feigning horror. "It really has been too long. Natural appetites have clearly been oafed out of you. A Wonkies is long overdue."

"Oh, good idea." More time filled.

"We've got those teaching forms to do, Malph," said Will.

"Make it eight-thirty," I said to Justin.

"Can I come?" was an unusually daring request on the part of Will, given that he was always rebuffed, often in a brusque manner.

I patted his cheek, enjoying the gentle humour of the moment. "You're too young for such things." He was ten months younger than me.

"But what is it, this wonky thing? You always make it sound like sex." He aimed this at Justin. "But it's obviously not that."

Justin clapped a hand to his chest in more feigned horror. "Hearst! How dare you speculate about our private lives? This is how rumours start. Yes, we've heard them. What takes place between consenting adults in the heart of Soho... stays in the heart of Soho. Don't be late, Phi."

"I can just imagine it," scoffed Simone. "The three of you on a night out: dyslexic, autistic, and..." She paused, thinking carefully before including Justin in the sentence. "You must be something," is what she finally decided upon.

"Indeed I am, Miss Conner," he said. "Like my friends here, I am a gorgeous and gifted indigo child."

"What does that even mean?" she asked.

Will started to reply: "Oh, that's just Bevan's hippy way of saying—"

"That we're better than you," Justin finished, and Will laughed.

"Or," Simone said slowly, smiling but not meaning it, "it's the real reason you're in this school. We're not supposed to speak about inclusion policies, but they're a real thing." She waved a hand at me and Will. "Neurodiversity. That's the woke expression, isn't it?"

Justin laughed. "Oh, I call bullshit. The two of them are way more talented than you. They're total stars."

"You're a star too, Justin," I said.

He shook his head. "Not in ballet, I'm not."

"But you are," I insisted. "You talk about other people having stage presence, but you bring it to everything you do."

"Do I, Phi? That's so sweet of you to say."

"Umm, guys," interjected Will. "She's gone."

"Aww, bless," said Justin. "So little stage presence that we didn't notice her leave. Come on, Hearst. I'll explain Wonkies to you, man to man." And they left too. Will was undoubtedly about to have his head filled with some completely fabricated nonsense.

And then there were two. Myself and Aleksandr Zolotov. He sat beside the piano, engrossed in his notes, his body cutting a perfect shape against the window and the swirling grey clouds beyond. And, unlikely as it seemed, he appeared left out and alone in the corner.

"Bye, Aleks."

An unexpected smile lit his face as he looked up and spoke. "Enjoy your bliss and fear, tonight."

"It's a Chinese restaurant," I explained.

"Ah. I think I know this place. Good food. Angry waiters."

"Yes," I said, completely delighted that he knew it, that he had been where we would be. I wanted to say lots more but stopped myself, afraid of boring him. "Anyway, see you Monday."

"Oh, and, Amalphia?" he said. "I hear small bits of this conversation you are having. Competitiveness between dancers can sometimes be a healthy thing, but there is only one reason I chose anyone to be in this class: talent. And the most talented of us are usually differently wired in some way."

There was a pause while I tried to work out if he meant what I thought he meant, then I just asked. "You?"

"Yes," he said, nodding. "When I was small everyone is asking, what is wrong with Aleks? Why is he so berserk? One doctor, he watches me climb on his bookshelves and says, 'He has too much energy, but good balance. Try him in a dance school.'"

"Wow," I said, examining his face for signs of untruthfulness and finding none, and then not knowing quite what else to say. "Monday."

"I will look forward," he said and gifted a golden smile to last the weekend.

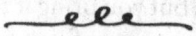

"Now," said Aleks, sitting down at the piano near the end of Monday's class, having dismissed the pianist early. "I play. You close eyes, listen, then dance. Forget your feet. Just be the music.

A deaf person should see the melody, the tone of the composition, in you."

The music flowed rather like his voice, his accent, thick and vibrational in unexpected places. It was similar to the previous pieces I'd heard him play, but much sadder. A cold and lonely tune filled the studio, evoking feelings of solitude and abandonment, and snow, snow everywhere.

Eyes open, I stepped out before everyone else, slowly moving through the sound, gliding across the ice. All was bleak with no hope of future happiness. The world was painted grey, yet a familiar energy lurked, warm and enticing for a second, and then it was all over. Music and class ended simultaneously.

"Amalphia, stay," commanded Aleks as the others exited. "Tell me what you have discern in the music."

"It was about being cold and alone. Everything hopeless. What was it?"

He got up from the piano stool and looked down at me. "Oh, things I feel, have felt. You had it. The only one to get it right."

"That was about you?" I asked, shocked.

He gave a half shrug, half nod.

It was unbearable, unthinkable and terrible that he should ever feel those things. I hugged him, wrapping arms around his body and pressing the side of my face into his chest. There was a tiny pause before he held me back. This was only warm and good. This was all he should ever feel. Not that music. Not that sadness. This was the opposite of alone. My arms tightened, and his hands moved slightly on my back. A mild soapy scent mingled with musky sweat from class, and the embrace sexualised.

I pulled back. "I'm sorry, really sorry." I'd just behaved so inappropriately, and where was my bag? I grabbed it, but his hand on my shoulder halted the dash from the room.

"Don't be run off, Amalphia. I am wanting to know. How does a young woman, surrounded by friends as you are, understand such emotion?"

I felt alone like that whenever I was in a crowd, but embarrassment about what had just happened was preventing me from expressing anything other than a practical fact. "I have to go. Class. Another class."

He held his hands wide with a forward movement as if to release a slow and stupid creature. I forced my feet not to run.

Chapter 3

T UESDAY DELIVERED A QUANDARY, but I had high hopes of solving two problems at once. Turning up to college at the very last minute would give Aleks no time to ask about the embarrassing moment of yesterday, and other difficulties would hopefully be avoided too if I sneaked out and away right after class.

The plan failed almost immediately. Just as I reached the studio door, my arm was gripped from behind.

"Not skiving today, then?" asked Gavin Tuesday, teacher of commercial jazz, ex-boyfriend, reason for non-attendance on Tuesdays and purveyor of general unpleasantness. He was hurting my arm.

"Still not speaking?" he noted. "I need to talk to you, Treadwell. Sort a few things out." His grip tightened and became more painful. As I tried to pull free, he started to get angry. A red spot appeared on each of his cheeks as if to match the new – ridiculous – red highlights in his dark hair. "You're going to listen to me," he said, pointing a finger into my face.

Another hand, this time on Gavin's arm, froze time and scene. "Amalphia has class with me now."

I was released.

"You missed your warm-up," said Aleks, now standing between Gavin and me. "Go do now."

I darted into the studio and over to the barre. Justin's raised eyebrow conveyed enquiry and concern. The mirror showed a red mark on my upper arm. Uncomfortable memories surfaced, things I didn't want to think of or acknowledge as having been part of my life. I marked the first combination Aleks set us and formulated a getaway plan. The pianist played, my legs bent and stretched, and the familiar exercise gradually overcame unpleasant thoughts.

I had finished. The others were in the middle of something much more elaborate than I had been doing. Hand flew to mouth as realisation dawned. I had just completed one of Peter's old set exercises.

Aleks must have noticed but had made no correction. He placed gentle hands on my shoulders. "Take a minute. Breathe. You will be right on the other side." His hands and voice were grounding, and my heart calmed. I watched Will to learn the combination, knowing that he always picked things up quickly, and calmed further.

We turned. Aleks adjusted the position of my shoulders and walked off. I focused all attention on his voice and instructions until the final second of the curtsey/bow of révérence. Then clothes were pulled over dancewear as fast as possible, and Justin's questions were dealt with in a similar manner.

"Shit, honey," he said. "I didn't think you were coming in, or I would've waited for you."

"It's okay."

"Was that Tuesday?"

Nod.

"So what did he want? I thought he'd stopped all that stalkery stuff."

Shrug.

"Listen, Phi, there's a thing. Baby Jesus, you know, Luke, was in roll call. Everyone fawning over him. Remember how they all bitched before? Different now he's a success, isn't it?"

"Justin, is there a point to this story? Because I have to go."

"Yes. Yes. He gave me – us – tickets for his show and after-show thing. He wants you there cause he still 'wuvs you so much.'" He said the last part in a baby voice.

"Justin," I warned, and was about to launch into a tirade against patronising the very young-looking Luke, whom I had once coached in a Jesus related song for an audition, resulting in the nickname, but something was wrong with the alignment of Justin's mouth.

"He said Edward told him to make sure I got a ticket," he told me. "What does that mean?"

"I don't know, Just. Maybe nothing."

"But, maybe something?"

"Well..." I acknowledged, silently believing that Justin's on-and-off boyfriend Edward never meant anything good, and wishing he didn't mean so much to my friend. The ever-changing status of their relationship was confusing to me and, though he never admitted it, I knew it was quite devastating to Justin.

"Would you be willing to come with me, Phi? I don't want to pressure you, but it might look funny if I don't go now."

He'd gone shrill. I put my hands on either side of his face and massaged his temples. "We'll go. We'll be fabulous. I mean we know the Baby Jesus, so how can we fail? I'll see you back at the flat tonight, but I have to run. He'll have a break now and—"

"You are leaving?" For once I had forgotten Aleks was there. "The angry man, he is interfering with your training? This, you should not be allowing, even a small bit."

Honesty, as ever, came immediately. "I'm only missing his useless commercial stuff, then tap and singing. I go to a better class somewhere else every Tuesday."

"I could manage some fruity jazz this morning," Justin put in hopefully.

"Advanced ballet with Olga today."

"No! Darling, you've had a nasty start to the morning. Do something fun, not that old bat's class. She's mean. Very rude to me, she was. I don't actually know what she said, but it wasn't nice."

"You didn't try hard enough in her lesson. I think she was saying you weren't to come back."

"Like I would."

Aleks asked, "Olga?"

"Primakova."

"Ah. Much is being explained. I can come, watch, no?"

I could find no reason to refuse other than a practical one and found myself being blatantly honest about that too. "Well, yes, if she allows it. But I was just going to climb out the bathroom window and go down over the roof."

His mouth twisted in humour and confusion.

"There'll be someone downstairs on the desk," I explained. "We're forbidden from doing classes elsewhere."

"Is no problem, come."

I was aware of the exaggerated height of both Justin's eyebrows as Aleks and I left the studio together and told myself that at least this disturbing development was doing some good. It had taken my friend's mind off his own problems.

Aleks kept his hand lightly on the small of my back as we walked down the stairs, only removing it at the main door. No one queried our exit, and we were soon in a taxi and on our way to Covent Garden.

"This one," said Aleks. "The angry man. He is your boyfriend?"

"Not anymore."

"He wants to be your lover again, I think."

The word 'lover' from Aleks's mouth made me feel warm, but it did not describe Gavin. There had been sex, yes, but it had never felt loving. "No, he's just angry," I told Aleks. "He's generally pretty angry."

"So, he is not good enough for you, and you walked away. This is right."

"Yes," I replied, turning my head to look straight into his eyes. "Ran away actually. Literally."

Gavin had chased me down several streets before I evaded him, but why was I telling Aleks? I hadn't even told Justin.

"Why did you hold me, after class, yesterday?" he asked.

"Because I didn't want you to feel that way," I answered at once, quickly adding: "I sometimes have trouble behaving appropriately. I'm sure you've been warned."

"I found it appropriate," he said, then looking out the window and changing the subject. We talked about London for the rest of the journey. He knew it well, though he inhabited an entirely different level of city life to me. His social scene was dazzling. He'd been to so many events and places. Tall buildings took on a shinier hue as I imagined Aleks partying in them, and we soon reached our destination.

Olga looked Aleks up and down then said a few sharp words in Russian.

"I am not permitted to watch, must take class," he explained and, in his black jeans, he did.

He was phenomenal, but Olga didn't seem to think so. In a room where he was so clearly the star, he was singled out for a lot of abuse. She slapped his knee back and squawked at him. I received encouraging smiles and corrections involving my stance: my shoulders, arms, head up and smile, always smile. I no longer felt like smiling at her.

"She is want to see what we have been working on together," Aleks told me as the other students left.

We had actually only done relatively simple lifts, presumably due to the wide range of abilities in the class at college. Simone would not have been safe with anything too high, Justin never having taken a pas de deux lesson in his life. We worked through what we had done and then moved on to supported pirouettes, the last of which caught me up short facing him. I grabbed his shoulders fast for balance and laughed. Then, sensing we were done as Olga and Aleks began to speak again, I went to change.

"I'm sorry she was so mean to you," I said as we wandered down the thin cobbled street afterwards, and through dark shadows between buildings. "Justin's right. She's an old bat, isn't she?"

He sighed. "She is right. I have let much go."

"But you're completely wonderful. I've never even been in the same room as such an incredible dancer before. You're..." I trailed off, seeing lines of distress on his face.

"No longer," he said. "But there is no excuse. In my home is both studio space and weight machines. I should get back to it."

I wondered about his condition but couldn't pry. He didn't seem remotely arthritic, though obviously doing one class could not compare to the slog of daily rehearsals and performing.

"Where are we going?" he asked.

"I always get cake after here, down in the Piazza. You don't have to come."

"Sounds good," he said, somewhat to my consternation. Coming to a class was one thing, but sticking with me for the rest of the day? What would we talk about? It would probably be horrifically boring for him.

I took a detour round by the majestic white Opera House, stopping by the bronze statue of the little dancer tying her shoes. "Don't you just love her?" I asked, touching her cold smooth hands.

His face suggested that he didn't like her at all, and I worried that I'd made a terrible mistake. Maybe the place had bad memories or connotations for him? I glossed past the odd moment, assuring him that he would love the cake, and led the way downhill towards the high columns of the Piazza.

A silver living statue sprang to sudden life, causing a passing woman to scream. "It's Amalphia Treadwell!" the statue announced to the street, arms wide.

"Jordan," I said, recognising a former student from college under the metallic face paint. He waltzed me round in a circle and turned to Aleks. "And would your – shit – really famous friend like to dance too?"

Aleks shook his head in strict refusal.

"What was it you said?" I reminded him as we continued down over the cobbles. "We should all train with different teachers, learn more methods, be pushed in new ways? I mean, have you ever danced with a living statue?"

He shook his head again and almost laughed which I considered an achievement.

We sat outside my usual café in the Apple Market with coffee and slices of many layered chocolate cake. A rainbow of scarves fluttered in the breeze on a nearby stall, while the sound of a busking flautist echoed and bounced off the high glass ceiling above. Aleks was very quiet, but it was a comfortable quiet with no need to make mundane conversation.

"You haven't eaten much," I said.

"I am not so hungry for cake."

"I was, but then I didn't have any breakfast. There was no food left in our flat. Have you been to the puppet shop?"

"No," he said, as if to an absurd notion.

It instantly became a challenge. "Oh, you have to see it. There's ballet things. And historical theatres – they're so beautiful – little puppet ones, you know? Replicas of old staging? Come on." I got up and pulled at his hands. "You'll love it, I promise."

He laughed and let me dance along in front of him, still holding his hands, until even I became aware of the unseemliness and walked sedately beside him.

He found a set of Matryoshka nesting dolls, in the back of the shop, that were painted like dancers. "Is like you," he said, opening the toy up. "The many layers of the woman. Look: the dancer, the most sensuous of lovers, the mother, and the childlike delight of the smallest." He bought the set and handed it to me.

"You don't have to buy me things," I said, unsettled by the expensive gift and the 'sensuous lover' thing. Was the day turning into some sort of date? Of course not, I told myself sternly, recalling the sophisticated beauties seen on the internet.

"I want to. This is a good day," he said as if such a thing were rare. The urge to hold him was strong again but gallantly resisted. He was, after all, just being polite.

"Thank you," I said. "It's always lovely here, sort of like a break from everything. The rest of life should be more like today, more like Covent Garden, don't you think?"

"Yes," he said very definitely.

"I need to go the candle shop too," I said, returning to practical matters. "We've run out."

"You are paint a grim picture of your living conditions. Is sounding Dickensian. No food, and lit by candles? I want to rescue you from this."

"Candlelight makes everything more beautiful," I told him as I bought a few pillar candles. I gave him one, evening things up a little on the buying front. As the long wax shape changed hands, the phallic appearance of its design became obvious. I blushed and it was a relief to turn my head away to read a text from Justin.

"Oh, I have to go," I said, disappointed to be bringing the afternoon to an end. "There's this thing tonight..."

"We get you a taxi."

"No, it's only a couple of stops on the tube."

He walked down onto the platform with me, where the gusting wind from the approaching train already blew. I turned to him, wanting to do something wildly inappropriate, but modifying just in time.

"Thank you for today, Aleks. It started badly, then it was nice." I stood on tiptoe, or demi-pointe, and kissed his cheek, acutely aware of my lips against his skin and the faint soapy scent of him like the day before in the studio.

I stepped onto the train and looked back round into dark brown eyes. His hands held my face as he placed two soft, lingering kisses on my mouth.

He stepped back onto the platform. The doors slid shut. There was a wolf whistle from further up the carriage. I stared out at him, hand pressed to the cold glass of the door as the train pulled away all too fast. I could feel the blood pumping through my veins. The abdominal lurch I'd experienced at the touch of his mouth reverberated round my body. His voice, his words, 'the most sensuous of lovers,' resounded in my mind as he vanished out of sight.

Chapter 4

Leaning against the inside of the flat's door was a relief. Outside had been so overly stimulating. I was too aware of everything: shoes, socks, feet and the hard pavement beneath them. I was acutely conscious of the breeze on my face and even my face itself, cheekbones under flesh. Skin, muscle, bone, blood.

Even within the safety of home, the door against my back was made of wood, wood that had been trees, growing in a forest, a forest full of sounds and smells and—

"You've been shagged senseless."

"No," I said. "The opposite."

"What is the opposite of that?" Justin asked, sitting me on the soft, soft sofa in our brown, and ever so fluffy, sitting room.

"I think I'll get my diagnosis back, but I'll be further on the spectrum than before. I've read about people suddenly becoming overly sensitised to stuff." The furry cushion was nice, though. I pressed it to the side of my face.

"Are you sure you're not just peopled-out?"

"No," I said, having a realisation. "He didn't people me out."

"You spent the entire day with Zolotov?"

I nodded.

"Well, good, that's three people in the world you can stand to be around now, Phi. But spill. The events leading up to said sensitisation?" He listened intently to the tale of the day. "I don't think it's an autistic thing," he said. "This is sexual awakening, and not before time. I wouldn't have taken you for a granda-grabber, though. Nothing wrong with going after a silver fox, or one that will be silver long before you, but does it have to be him? Choose one that's going to be nice to you. That's the whole point of them, isn't it?"

"It's not like that. And he was very nice to me." It was difficult to express the magic of the day to someone who was determined to view it through a filter of scepticism.

"A veritable eighties montage, darling. The dolls are a bit creepy, and the train snog? Cliché."

"It wasn't a snog."

"Whatever. It's cheesy, like the end of a bad movie."

"No, it was..." Memory of the soft pressure of Aleks's mouth made my lips tingle. Would that happen again? It felt very vital that it should but... "D'you think he kisses everyone like that? Maybe that's how they say goodbye in Ukraine?"

Justin shook his head. "If it was, I would know and might be living there now. He gives off a vibe around you but, as far as I can determine, he doesn't tend to go for younger women. I suspect he wants something new, a short blast of fun. What you've got to decide is whether you can work like that. I don't want you to get hurt, Phi."

I squeezed his hand and thought of how Edward's out-of-the-blue departures always hurt him. Edward was successful and professional and eight years older than us, though hardly silver. And he might be at the event tonight. "Let's do this thing, Just."

That night I had a vivid dream about Aleks. It involved the impossible scenario of him coming straight over to me before class and lifting me up against the barre. It was rough and mad and sexy, and I woke sweaty and aching and unbelievably alive. The tactility of the world was strangely exciting: the crumpled cotton sheets, woven carpet and cold metal door handle were all sensory adventures. Hot swirling tea in a pure white cup was an enchanting and intoxicating liquid that I had never properly appreciated before.

And then later, before class, he really did walk straight over to me at the barre. My heart rate increased. He then enquired politely about the show the previous evening, and I basked in his radiance.

Justin took it upon himself to answer. "We found ourselves in a room full of pretentious people who were looking to see what they could get out of each other: users, philanderers, and the odd innocent who didn't realise what was going on."

"Is sounding familiar," said Aleks with a small, not as golden as usual, smile.

"I have no doubt it is," replied Justin.

Edward's absence had been a bitter disappointment.

"The performance was good, though," I reminded him. Luke had been especially impressive in his unlikely role as a teenage super hero from space.

Aleks set our first plié combination, the pianist started to play, and I placed my hand on the barre to begin. The wood was polished smooth by years of exertion. I could feel the inner workings of my body, especially when Aleks stood near or gave a correction. My heartbeat was so loud, I worried that other people could hear it. Get a grip, you stupid girl, I instructed myself. Someone so beautiful would never want you. It was just a kiss to him, nothing worthy of note. The mirror's icy face agreed and pointedly displayed my many deficiencies to prove the point.

"Your révérence is sad today, Amalphia," said Aleks of my curtsey. "What is happening?" His voice was deep and gentle, and it made my whole body flush. "You will wait behind a minute?" he asked.

Oh no. He was going to explain that the kiss meant nothing, and I didn't want to hear him say the words. It would be entirely preferable to just never mention it.

Will was on hand to delay the dreaded moment with some nonsense. "Malph, you know that song you did last year with Bevan?"

"No."

"You do; soppy, romantic thing. It's up on the college web-site. It's awesome, totally awesome, but you need to go look at the comments. There's like a million. I left one," he said as if bestowing a gift.

"I think I'll give it a miss, thanks, Will."

"Our Phi is somewhat resistant to looking at things on the internet," said Justin rather loudly. "Even when they are pointed out as essential reading. I, on the other hand, read avidly." I overheard him enquiring as to whether there were any comments about him on the website as the two of them walked away down the corridor.

Aleks shut the door. Doom was upon me.

His face was appropriately sombre. "Have dinner with me."

I stared stupidly. He stared back. I looked at the mirror, but it had little to add, other than to draw attention to the incongruity of the words and the characters.

"Yesterday was good, no?" said Aleks. "You say is nice. I am much enjoying your company and am thinking, it is how two people connect that is important. Age, it is not mattering. This is what I feel."

Even his mouth moved beautifully. It was hypnotic. I very much wanted it to touch mine again.

"Just one dinner," he continued. "If you are not liking, is fine, is your choice. And you can always climb out the bathroom window if it is really bad."

That made me smile.

"You will come?"

I nodded and was at once immersed in the golden light of his smile.

"I pick you up at eight?"

I gave another nod.

He laid his hand on his chest which I knew was warm. The veins on his hand extended up his arm, pulsing with life and strength. "I feel much, Amalphia."

"So do I." This was an understatement of huge proportion. An abbreviated list: the throb of his pulse under my fingers as he took my hand, the cling of my leotard and tights; the need to kiss him might have even been fulfilled had the door not burst open.

"Amalphia Treadwell! Don't you have another class to get to?" For a woman dressed in a neon-pink jumpsuit and wearing boxy platform shoes, Madame Genevieve certainly moved with stealth.

The sensual euphoria of the day was gone by seven-thirty. Justin contributed to its demise. He wouldn't let me wear my strappy dress, declaring it too sexy.

"But I want to look sexy."

"Well, you shouldn't. It'll give him the wrong idea."

"It's not the wrong idea. I really like him."

"Just because he buys you dinner, doesn't mean you have to sleep with him."

"I know."

"Look, Phi. Oh, I don't know. I'm so conflicted. I suppose the best scenario is one that's over quickly. Shag him tonight, and it'll all be finished with tomorrow before anyone gets hurt. Worst case: it goes on a bit, and then you don't just get hurt, you get squished. Don't give him that power, sweetheart."

We compromised on a skirt and top.

"It's perfect," declared Justin. "It says: 'I have lovely tits but am not showing them to you.' And the skirt is very, 'My, don't I have nice legs, but I am fully capable of keeping my knickers on and returning to Justin in a chaste condition before midnight.' No," he said to delicate heels. "Wear your lace-up boots, nothing quick to kick off. Are we thinking make-up?"

"No."

"Good, no changing yourself for him. That's good."

"But can you do my hair in that roll thing that doesn't need hairspray?"

His eyes narrowed, but he obliged. "Rethink the stockings, no need for them. Haven't you got some thick woolly tights? I should have knitted you some. Or, you know, learned to knit."

The door buzzer sounded. "It must be him," I said, resisting the urge to jump up and down in excitement. "Let him in. I'll finish doing up the boots and be through."

Out in the hall, moments later, Justin had obviously just answered the buzzer and was replacing the handset.

"Is he coming up?" I asked.

"Told him to wait down there."

"That was a bit rude."

"Keep him standing on the doorstep, good for him, taste of things to come." He gripped my wrist as I exited the flat. "Remember, he's years – many years – ahead of you in experience. He's a ballet king, a diva, used to getting his own way. God only knows what diabolical proclivities he may have developed. Keep your wits, and your clothes, about you at all times."

I kissed his cheek and tried to reassure. "It'll all be fine," I said and pushed him back inside. However, without him there to debate, his point rather won. Of course I would be completely out of my depth. Yesterday had worked out okay, but this was completely different. On an organised date, I would be expected to be, what? Sophisticated and witty? Oh dear.

The walk down the stairs was littered with doubts, though they lessened a little when I saw him standing outside looking similarly uncertain. We smiled at each other through the glass as I opened the door.

"You look beautiful," he said and handed me a white rose. It was the most romantic event of my life so far. "Is different to see people outside class, no?"

"It is," I agreed, touching his white-shirted chest briefly, noting the smart jacket and trousers.

There was no time to dwell further on the scarily grown-up nature of the night as he whisked us down the steps and opened the door of a shiny black car. The depth of the plush leather seat demonstrated the depth of trouble I was in. He'd booked four restaurants for me to choose from. They all had chocolate cake. He'd checked.

Smiling, intimidation temporarily forgotten, I chose Ukrainian. "I've never had that before," I said, and then worried it sounded like an innuendo.

If it did, he didn't react. He started the car, and we set off at an alarming speed. "Is good, this choice. Better traffic. Do you drive, Amalphia?

"No."

"I think you would like."

He took my hand, and linked our fingers over the gear stick as he drove. The experience was hugely erotic. He continually stroked my little finger with his thumb. We sat in happy finger-thumb-dancing silence for a while, and then we were there, and he opened more doors. In the restaurant, he took my coat and pulled out my chair. It was a little overwhelming, but not bad, not intimidating.

I settled back and stared around at the lavish cream and gold interior of the place. There were tapestries and embroidered cushions. Glass crystals hung from lamps large and small, making the place glitter. The walls displayed ornately framed mirrors between clusters of plates and pictures, some of famous patrons, including one of Aleks himself.

"It is good we come here," he said with a smile. "Makes me look impressive. Is all right if I order for us? I am knowing what is good."

"Yes, but I don't eat meat."

"You don't eat meat?" He laid down his menu as if I'd said something shocking.

"I'm a vegetarian."

"But you eat chicken? Fish?"

"No."

"Amalphia, is very important for a dancer to get the proper nutrients."

"Are you joking?" He clearly wasn't. "Do I look nutrient deprived?"

"No."

"Because I'm not. Oh no..." I looked down at the list of dishes. "Is Ukraine like France? I spent a holiday there living mainly on bread and cheese. No, it's fine. There's lots of things I can have. Potato pancakes sound good."

"You will be finding it disgusting if I have meat?"

"No," I said, annoyed. "It's not me who's passing judgement on the food choices of others."

"Ah, Amalphia, I am sorry. We start again. You will forgive me?"

He looked so comically sad, how could I do anything else? And everything was nice again for a short while, until he asked me about college.

"It is not the best," he said. "You are in the top class, the best dancer there. What can it offer you? How can it stretch you?"

"I can't go to the best. I don't have the perfect body type."

"You are completely perfect. Why did you pick this school?"

"Peter suggested it."

"He was your teacher and wanted to continue teaching you. And this, about your body, it is from him?"

"No. He never said anything like that. But Peter was right. I didn't want to narrow my options to only ballet. I love acting too. I mean, really love it. The drama teacher is off this term, and I miss it terribly."

"But you are made for ballet. You are beautiful doing anything – I see you with Justin on the college website – but is a waste. Your potential is not being recognised. Your training should be exclusively classical."

"You're a ballet snob, Aleks."

He hit his palm to his forehead. "Ah no, I am do again. I am being nervous, is giving me the foot-in-mouth disease. I will go bathroom," he said. "When I come back, there will be no snobbing or judging. Truly this is not what I feel. If you were not at this school, I would never be seeing you, and you are complete loveliness to me."

I didn't know what to do with that. A sarcastic 'ok-ay' didn't seem right, and I wasn't brave enough to tell him he was complete loveliness to me too. Self-effacing humour was surely the best idea. "Maybe you need glasses?"

He laughed in misunderstanding. "You are not to be letting me off so easy, I see. Is okay, I deserve."

He went. The food came. I waited, and then wondered if he had climbed out the window to escape the mad vegetarian, and decided to start eating anyway. If I were to be bankrupted by the meal, I might as well enjoy it, and the pancakes were delicious.

He returned. "Alas, I am to be everything wrong tonight. The tap is spraying me, is not work right."

Both his trousers and shirt had taken quite a soaking, and I couldn't help laughing. He was reflected in several mirrors as he stood in front of me, which only seemed to multiply the misfortune.

"If you are wanting to go, I will understand," he said. "I do not wish to embarrass you."

"Would I be friends with Justin if I embarrassed so easily? But if you're cold and uncomfortable..."

"See? Complete loveliness."

He sat down, leant his chin on one hand and smiled at me. Then he moved his hands down and somehow caught his watch strap in the opposite sleeve and was stuck. He really was nervous. I reached forward and untangled him.

"Is never happen to me before," he said and closed his eyes. "I am just to say unfortunate things all night."

"It's actually quite nice," I told him. "I was worried you would be intimidatingly sophisticated, and that I wouldn't know what to do or say, and it isn't like that at all."

His smile was too small to be golden.

"Eat up your lump of dead animal," I advised. "And you'll feel better."

Everything became more relaxed after that, and by the time we had the lusciously layered chocolate cake and ice cream in front of us, his body language was completely open. He leant back, one hand behind his head as he spoke of his childhood. He told me about the place he'd been born, how his mother had died when he was five and then his father when he was eight, just after he'd started ballet school. "I am not sad for it now," he said as I looked at him in horror. "Please eat." The school he'd attended had been harsh. He was cold much of the time and beaten with a stick.

"Please tell me you are making this up," I said.

"This is just how it is."

"Poor little boy. I want to give him hot chocolate and cuddles."

"Is appropriate, I think."

Chapter 5

THE PREDOMINATING CONCERN, ONCE we were back in the car, silly as it was, was that we hadn't kissed. Maybe we weren't going to? Uncertainty returned as Aleks walked round to the driver's side. Was he going to take me home, and that would be it? He considered the evening a disaster and was glad it was over? There'd been opportunities. His face had been very close when he'd helped me on with my coat, and again when I climbed into the car.

"Amalphia," he said as he sat down. Here it came. "I am wanting very much to show... to have you see..." He looked directly at me. "The foot-in-mouth is still with me. There is no way to say without sounding wrong."

"Whatever it is, just blurt it out. Fast like a plaster, you know." I mimed ripping one off my arm.

"I cannot." He seemed to wilt with sadness.

"I really want to know now, even if it's really bad." Despite expectations, I couldn't help but be funny and encouraging to him, and an idea struck. "Tell me in your own language."

He held his hands up. "But you will not understand."

"I would like to hear it anyway. And maybe it'll help clarify things for you."

"You are a very unique woman," he said thoughtfully, and I hoped 'unique' wasn't a euphemism for weird or unfortunate or repugnant.

He talked. The words were beautiful, his voice deep. At first it was all very solemn, then he leant sideways against the seat and smiled.

My face responded to his change of expression, joining him in the smile. I felt my eyebrows rise at subtle nuances in tone and inflection. I almost leant forward and kissed him at one point, but reined it in at the last moment.

He awaited my response.

I thought about it. "You seemed concerned for my wellbeing. Is that right? I don't know."

"Is right. I want you to have no worries, to be completely comfortable."

He paused, and it occurred to me that his criticisms of me in the restaurant hadn't really been that. He'd been questioning whether things were good enough for me, and that was different. He was different.

"Is really quite simple," he said. "I see yesterday, in Covent Garden, how you are appreciate beautiful things. In my home, I have a painting. I know you would like it. But I do not want you to think, if you accept to come..." He shuffled his shoulders in a dancey way as he sought the right words. "I do not want you to think that I am expecting or assuming anything from you. You see my home, we talk, have hot chocolate – I know you like this – and then I drive you back to your friend who is pacing and looking at watch, no? Yes? Maybe?"

"I would love to see where you live," I said.

"I know you will like," he said, bright and happy once more.

Justin would say I had fallen for a line, but Aleks seemed sincere. And did it really matter? My only reservations about this stage of the evening were based on another time, and another man. It wouldn't be the same. In fact, I suspected it would all be rather delightful.

He chatted on easily, telling me how he had bought his flat many years ago and done it up. We drove past the expensive designer shops of Sloane Street and up several side roads.

"Ooh, you can see the top of the Shard from here," I commented, impressed by the skyline.

"Upstairs is much better," he proclaimed, drawing in to a parking space and pulling on the handbrake. "I have the seventh floor apartment, the only one with balcony."

The red brick walls of the building looked warm, and the white painted windows, bright and clean. The plush blue carpets of the entrance hall only confirmed the elegance of the place.

"I am very hoping you like," he said, pressing a button on the wall. "Here is the elevator."

I leant back on more cushioned softness. "What a lovely apartment," I said. "Small, obviously, but the carpet on the walls is a nice touch." Making him laugh was a sweet joy. It made my tummy feel tickly inside.

We reached the top floor and stepped out into a small hall. He unlocked what was presumably his front door and ushered me into a long corridor with wooden floors. I immediately liked the place. Although the area was devoid of anything but an old-fashioned, three-legged coat rack, it felt homey and welcoming. We passed through another door and I gasped.

We were in a huge room like a ballet studio, complete with barre and full height mirrors on the wall to the right. A grand piano sat in front of floor-to-ceiling windows that overlooked the sparkling city. Two large black leather sofas occupied the middle of the space, a glass coffee table between.

And to the left? "A wall of books!" I ran my fingers over the spines, some very worn, many titles in Ukrainian, but some English ones too. "Have you read them all?" I asked, still exploring the library. The books, like the windows, were ceiling to floor. Not doing things by halves was a definite theme in the place, or maybe the man.

"Most. Some I buy and never get round to."

"I do that too."

"Look," he said, flicking a switch on the opposite wall and illuminating a painting. A beautiful theatre was viewed from the back of the stalls; the scene in front stretched on and on across the brightly lit stage.

"It goes on forever," I said in wonder.

"You think this, but no, everything ends, is unexpected. There." He pointed to the backdrop of scenery. It was confusing.

I stepped back and inclined my head to the side trying to work it out, then gave up. "It's beautiful. There's no point trying to understand it," I mused as I stared out over the painted stage.

"This is the first thing I thought when I came home yesterday. She would like this, and I wanted to show it to you. Is very odd."

"Why is that odd?"

"Because I am not so good at sharing my toys. Usually. Now, I promise you hot chocolate. But you must guess where the kitchen is."

I looked round. "Presumably not out there." A balcony lay beyond the large windows. "So it must be back through..." I indicated the door to the hall.

"No."

There were no other visible doors. "Not the books? Do I have to press the right one, because that could take a long time?" I walked along and pushed the shelves in several places until a block in the middle gave way and swung inwards. "It's very dark in there."

He leant past me and switched on the light, revealing a small but well-applianced kitchen.

"Oh, and there I was expecting a dungeon," I said. "This is very disappointing."

"There is a dungeon in the castle," he said.

My look was blank.

"The school in Scotland," he explained. "The biggest studio is below ground level. We call it the dungeon."

"Creepy," I said, suppressing a shudder. "Where's your bathroom, or is there a secret entrance to that too?"

"Is first door across hall. Look around everywhere else if you like."

I found the bathroom quickly and discovered that it was dominated by a gargantuan marble bath. It was impossible to look at anything else in the room. I descended the five white and grey steps into what could have been a small swimming pool, and the phrase 'out of my depth' repeated. Was it a sex bath? It could play host to an orgy. Justin had read things, and said things, and hinted at more. Why did he have to do that?

Twitchy and nervous, I returned to the big studio, strongly resolved to leave as soon as possible. Aleks was in the tiny kitchen, looking all domestic and innocent and sprinkling something chocolaty on top of frothy drinks.

"Ooh, what's that?" I asked, sex bath forgotten.

"Hot chocolate. I make this, you cuddle me. This is right, no?"

"No." Laughter danced through my words. "That was hypothetical. It involved you as a small child, remember?"

"He is still in here." He put a hand on his heart. "And no one holds him. Except you, other day."

Out on the balcony, I laid my mug down on the table to better take in the panoramic view of London. Spread out below us, the city sparkled and shone as if announcing the glittery arrival of a special event or holiday.

Aleks stood behind and pointed out landmarks and colourfully lit buildings in the distance: the Gherkin, St. Paul's Cathedral and some places that I didn't know. I was aware of two things, two temperatures: the cool balustrade pressing my abdomen and the warmth of his body, close but not touching. It would have been nice to be touching, to be familiar enough to lean back against him and look up into his face. But I could be polite and appropriate sometimes.

"I've never seen the city look quite like this before. It's beautiful."

"Very beautiful," he echoed. "Malphia, your hair. If this clip comes out, it all come down?"

"It should do."

He unclipped the hair slide, and it bounced off the side of the balustrade and down to the dark street far below. I laughed, but he was crestfallen.

"I have lose the ability to be clever in any way. Between us maybe there should be only truth."

"And what is the truth?" I asked.

"I want to kiss you."

"I want to kiss you too."

We were tentative. Noses brushed, breath mingled, and then: two soft kisses like on the train. They had the same enlivening effect. I kissed Aleks back with a crazed sort of desperation. I was aware of myself clutching at his back, and then his hair, before a violent shiver ran through me.

He pulled away. "Cold?" he asked.

I shook my head.

"Do not be afraid, beautiful Malphia. I know that making love to you, if it were to happen, and I do not assume, will be one of the most exquisite experiences of my life. But it will not be tonight. I want you to be completely at ease with me. Ah look, the chocolate is get cold. Let's sit."

Somewhat stunned by the blatancy of his words, I sat beside him, feeling both at ease and a little petulant.

"See the chocolate hearts," he said, indicating the chocolate. "They have melted, only gold stars are left."

The shiny stars looked surreal on top of the chocolaty froth. The drink tasted lovely, thick and sweet and creamy, the melted chocolate dots dark and rich on my tongue.

"You look different with your hair this way. I don't know if is younger or older?" He tucked some hair behind my ear, the touch of his fingers sending little shocks down my neck and spine. "Timeless, ageless beauty," he concluded. "Please be not having offence," he said, "but I am seeing in your timetable that you have classes alone with, this one, Peter?"

"Private lessons, yes. Three a week."

"I want you to have these with me too. I think is important we work together more. Olga, she has say this also. You would like, Amalphia?"

I liked the way he said my name, the second and third syllables extended as if they mattered, as if I mattered. "Of course. You asked how college stretches me? Your classes do that."

"I am still feeling my way, as you know, learning how to teach and explain. But I have knowledge of much that will be good for you."

"What else did Olga say?"

"Come, I show you. Will be better."

He didn't kiss me, despite my upturned face, but walked back inside to the piano. It was nice to sit on the cushioned stool with him as he opened the lid. Our thighs touched.

"This," he said, "is you." He played a tune on the higher notes, all light and tinkly and frivolous.

"I sound like an animated squirrel jumping through the tree-tops. I have to tell you, I rarely do that."

"Yes. There is so much more." The lower, sensuous melody didn't seem very like me either. Loud discordant crashes were even more confusing. "Hidden underneath," he explained. "And here I am." He played low and slow.

"That's not you. It's a funeral march!"

He gave a small laugh. "Sometimes this is me. But together..."

The squirrel danced through the melancholy tune, and the two threads blended to create a new and rich composition. Eyes shut and head against his shoulder, I lost myself in the music, his music, his interpretation of us. Us together, wound round and through one another...

He had stopped. I felt his breath in my hair and then we were kissing again, more slowly this time, luxuriating in the experience. His thigh muscles were hard beneath my hand. It took determined restraint to keep my fingers there. A depraved being had replaced timid Amalphia, and she wanted to run her hands all over Aleks.

The phone rang and he got up to answer it.

"I have to take," he said. "Will not be long. Please be completely at home. Do anything you wish." He walked into the hallway talking into the phone in a grumpy voice.

There was a laptop on the coffee table and, in the name of making myself at home, on it went. The screen opened to the college website, the fifth page of comments on the song Justin and I had done together last year. It didn't take long to work out that my breasts were the main topic of discussion, and what people would like to do to them and me. I laughed at the stupidity, then realised Aleks had been reading it all, and that wasn't so amusing.

The contribution from 'sexyWilliam222' was infuriating: "even better when there pressed up against you, beleve me." Bastard. Dyslexic bastard. But I had a defender, a furious one, who had triggered a heated debate about women and respect. He came back into the room and closed the laptop lid.

"You should not be look at this," he said, sitting beside me on the sofa.

"The internet's full of idiots. You didn't need to get so upset."

"But they shouldn't say these things. They shouldn't even be look at you." He turned away, distressed. "It spoils the evening, another thing to go wrong."

"No. No it doesn't, it isn't. Don't be sad, Aleks."

He shouldn't ever be sad. If anything was wrong, that was. I started to kiss away the sorrow, and everything went frantic. His mouth felt harder. I loved it on my neck. It wasn't until he spoke that I noticed the outsides of his legs were pressed against the insides of mine. At some point I had sat on him.

"I should take you home," he said. "I have genuine meaning to do this."

He was clearly determined not to have sex with me, making my out-of-character behaviour not a little humiliating. I started to back off, but his hands held me in place.

"Be not misunderstand, Malphia. You are a beautiful, natural woman, a very young woman. I am try not to be a sleazy old man to you."

"You're not. How could you be?" Embarrassment forgotten, I leant forward to kiss him again.

"You understand what I am saying?" he said into my mouth. "Every instinct is telling me to carry you to bed."

The contradiction of being very warm all over but also covered in goosebumps, caused me to tremble.

"See this, no," he said. "I want you to know that you are safe with me."

"I do."

He brushed the back of a finger over my arm, worsening the situation considerably: my tremulousness, his concern.

And then I knew how to fix it, how to lift him and take the worry away. "I'm not shivering because I'm frightened, Aleks. But if you are, if you're not ready, that's fine. I can wait as long as—"

Chapter 6

IN WHAT SEEMED LIKE seconds, we had travelled down the hall, into another room with floor-to-ceiling windows, and onto a big white bed.

He undressed me with great care, always returning to kiss my mouth between other places. I was kissed more than I had been in all the rest of my life put together. He told me I was beautiful more times than I could count.

He had to remove his own clothes, the grown-up man belt and trouser fastenings being beyond my skill. His legs were hard and muscular; my fingers explored the contrastingly soft blond hairs. I examined his smooth chest, his shoulders and arms. I was used to seeing boys at college in a state of half undress between classes, but Aleks was different, as if life had sculpted and honed a more finished and well-defined version of masculinity.

The muscles in his shoulders moved against each other like small and perfectly aligned ropes as he knelt in front of me, and then the fullness of his black trunks became the obvious focus. The one piece of clothing had been left for a reason. I could still say no.

I stretched the elastic out and down over his erection, setting it free, and was instantly fascinated. It was big and long and pointing up, friendly and happy. The combination of hard flesh and soft skin was inviting. I had to at least kiss it. I barely got to do that, we tumbled back so fast. His mouth found my breasts, and I was overcome by chills and warmth and life and everything.

He hadn't lost the ability to be clever at all. His tongue was doing things I'd only read about in books, and it was too much. I fought against the extremity of sensation and couldn't bear it.

"Aleks," I begged.

His face appeared by mine at once.

"I want your penis inside me," I told him, knowing I'd said something blurty and blatant, but not caring a bit.

"Oh, my darling, my angel, you can have, is yours."

I had it in my hands, the object of desperate, aching want... but where was he going? He leant away, reached into a drawer and produced a box of condoms, shiny and sterile in unbroken cellophane.

"I'm on the pill. And I don't have anything. I mean, I was tested in the summer." Was I ruining the moment? Making everything clinical and cold?

"Ah, me too. I am clear," he said, matter of factly. "But I can still..."

My head made small instinctive negative movements. He dropped the box on the floor, and kissed my mouth and my nose and my mouth again.

"Is sacred moment," he said. "This, our first time. I will never forget."

I loved the way he watched my face. I loved the feel of him within me, and his eyes above me. I loved it all. Aleks was inside me and it was absolutely the best thing that had ever happened to anyone, ever. We were like the music. Two people, two rhythms, woven through each other and into more: a greater harmony, a new melody.

Lots of new things were happening. I couldn't be quiet, couldn't be still. My hands were everywhere. I arched under him, and the capacity to feel and experience grew bigger and wilder.

Every nerve ending directed itself at Aleks, for he was the source, the catalyst for what approached. He'd been right to place import on feeling safe, for it allowed me to let go, to give myself up to all that was happening and relinquish control. I screamed and cried, and that was part of the joy of it, to be so released from appearances and concerns, held and connected, yet free.

I felt the vibration of his deep voice as he spoke reassuring words; it buzzed within me. I felt his orgasm as a desire answered, a craving met. I'd needed to feel him lose his own control with me.

His eyes were dark as he moved to look down at me again. "Malphia, my beautiful Malphia."

He kissed a line across my face, and we became still, together, breathless and recovering.

"Are you all right?" he whispered, rolling us onto our sides.

His body left mine and I was cast adrift: a stretchy, relaxed thing, all languorous and floaty. I touched my lips and found them quivery and strange. I couldn't speak.

He stroked my hair. "You are a revelation."

I pointed a finger into his chest. He was the revelation.

"You will stay?" he asked. "Sleep here tonight? I very much want this."

He smiled at my nod. The idea of leaving was abhorrent. To miss sleeping in his bed with him, and maybe getting to do it all again?

"I get us water," he said and, without pausing to put clothes on, disappeared out of the room.

It was good to discover an ensuite bathroom, a nice normal one. There were discarded clothes on a chair, a towel on the floor, and shaving foam on the sink. I liked the foam. It smelled of Aleks.

I walked round his bedroom and admired the free-standing wooden drawer units and wardrobe. Catching sight of my naked self in the mirrored wardrobe door heralded the return of self-consciousness. By the time he came back, I was modestly clad in a T-shirt from the bathroom and my own underwear.

His face elongated in sadness. "I want to feel your skin against mine as we sleep."

"Oh. Well..." I looked down at myself.

"You are being shy now?" he asked, and lifted my chin. "I see you. You are like the sky on a summer's day showing different colours at different times. Sometimes pulls clouds across, hides beauty." He tweaked the shirt.

A small smile was my only answer to the odd speech. He was talking like... I didn't know what he was talking like. I had no suitable point of reference.

"But then, it is night." He switched off the lamp, plunging us into darkness. "How is the starlit sky?"

I laughed at his continuance of the metaphor, and there were more kisses, soft and sweet. Clothing dispensed with, we faced each other under the blankets.

"You're cold," I realised and tried to rub warmth into his back and arms. "Your feet are like ice." I sandwiched them between my own. "See, this is why people wear clothes."

"In the arms of my angel, I am warm."

The last sense to be stimulated before sleep was that of scent. He smelled like almonds. Marzipan. Christmas cake. Aleks.

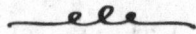

Everything was gloriously right and as it always should be. I recalled talk of angels, and it was if they were singing: 'Yes! Yes!'

His arm was stretched out under my neck as my eyes opened to take in the scene. His other arm was flung wide as were his legs. I was curled in the corner of his great big X shape. He was obviously used to having the bed to himself. His face looked younger in sleep but still as beautiful, the unshaven chin and tousled hair enticingly male and sexy.

I woke more fully. Of course he wasn't used to being alone. Justin's warning replaced the heavenly singing: it'll all be over by the next day. Then I recalled Aleks's own words: making love to you will be one of the... one of... one.

We'd shared an incredible experience, but that was it. Tears threatened. I had to go. The thought of him telling me, 'I'll see you around,' or whatever got said in these situations was excruciating. The fact that my ballet shoes, and everything else required for college, were at home became a neutral fact to hold on to, a practical and non-emotional reason to leave.

I allowed myself one last look, but no kissing or touching, and I tiptoed out of the room, clothes in arms.

Quick dressing took place in the large studio room, interspersed with vibrant memories of the night before. The balcony. The piano. The theatre picture. I clutched my white rose and took one long and final stare into forever.

"You are leaving?" His deep voice was at once a shock and a relief. "I thought we would find each other again in the dark, angel. Instead I do this unheard of thing and sleep all night. You can be forgiving of me and stay?"

He kissed my ear and tangled his fingers through my hair, banishing sad thoughts, though one inconvenient fact remained.

"My things for college are at home."

"Ah." His frown quickly became a smile. "Justin can bring! You phone him, and I get breakfast for us."

He headed for the kitchen, and only then did I notice he was still entirely without clothing.

"Your feet'll get cold!" I called.

His laugh carried back from the small room as I sat on the sofa and discovered a dead phone battery. He returned with what looked like a large pot of chocolate mousse and handed me the landline from the coffee table.

"My little Phi, all grown-up and slutting it about town with the best of them," commented Justin. "It fair brings a tear to my eye."

I had exited the delightfully snuggly taxi on seeing my friend, after telling Aleks that it would be better if we didn't arrive at college together, given the rules about relationships between students and teachers.

Justin went on. "So, to continue the unfulfilling conversation from, may I remind you, five-thirty this morning – I thought someone had died! – how was the one-night stand?" He handed over the heavy bag, which was overstuffed with various items of dancewear and possibly bricks.

"I don't think that's what it was." The concept of 'one night' had evaporated in the presence of Aleks, but it crept back a little in the grey concrete street.

"Don't get your hopes up, sweet pea. I read up some more on him, so I'm in an expert position to guess the night's events. Did you go to a hotel?"

"No. His flat."

"Really? You're sure?"

"Yes." I described the property in some detail.

"Whoa. Odd. There's this bint with a blog, shagged him for some time, never once got invited to his house. Very upset about it she is, too. But he took you there." His voiced slowed. "We could have a force-ten dating alert here, Phi. I've seen this somewhere." He thought for a moment. "Yep, got it. Documentary. Straight ballet people: mating habits of."

"You're making that up."

"Okay, so it was about birds, but same thing really. Excited little male robins? Finches? Wrens? I can't remember. Anyway, they show the females their nests, and the girls pick the best one. And that was some nest. I would mate him."

Rolling my eyes didn't stay the roll that Justin was on. He indicated body parts as we walked. "Pretty little face, child-bearing hips, breast-feeding tits. He's old. Ready to settle down. And what's with the T-shirt? Putting you in his ballet pro-mo things? Territorial, that is: marking you as his."

"I didn't want to look like I hadn't been home. He said I could take whatever I wanted."

Justin was still developing the mating-ritual theory when I left him outside the second-floor toilets to get changed. "Those dolls he got you. Didn't he say one was a mother? Phi, you need to be very wary now. He'll have you chained to that apartment, pregnant and barefoot." His own trendily trainered foot propped the door open for a moment. "Or it was a one-nighter, so no hopes either way now. You hear me?"

Aleks wasn't in the studio when I went through, all changed and ready for class. Justin stood by the barre. Will sat in the middle of the floor with his back to the door, scrolling through something on his phone. A small detour allowed an 'accidental' whack of his head with my bag.

"Oi," he said, rubbing his head. "What's up with you?"

"Your stupid head was in the way, Hearse." He hated the nickname of Hearse – in a particularly bitter moment, I had once said it was based on wishful thinking – and 'stupid' was a line I never usually crossed.

His side of the mutual glare shifted from anger to understanding. "You saw my comment on the website." He rose smoothly off the floor. "It was meant as a compliment."

My glare continued unabated.

"I'll delete it," he said.

"Bit late for that."

"Er, Phi?" Justin interrupted, and then kissed my neck from behind.

"Hey!" I cried in shock. "Boundaries, Bevan."

"See, things like this are why there's rumours about you two," Will said with an annoying grin.

"There's chocolate on your neck," said Justin. "Been eating in bed, have we?"

I struggled to keep my face neutral, recalling how Aleks had said he'd wanted to feed me chocolate with his fingers since the cake at Covent Garden. If someone else had made such a comment it might have sounded sleazy, but from him it was just so sexy and romantic and delicious. "Umm..." I said to Justin. "Must have lain on it, or something. I did have a shower afterwards."

It wasn't clear at what point the purpose of that shower had ceased to be the removal of chocolate mousse, but there was no stopping the memory of Aleks lifting me up against the tiled wall. Or the way his wet body had felt, his firm chest and arms, my limbs wrapped about him, the water cascading off us both...

"There's going to be a proper debriefing later," Justin began, only to be cut short by the striding arrival of Aleks who handed me a piece of paper.

"Is arranged," he said. The paper bore the times of my tap classes. "This one," he said, pointing to Tuesday afternoon. "We do in my studio. Is better, no? First one, now, is today, right after morning class."

Official information given, our teacher paced briskly to the front of the room. Was that all he was now? We hadn't made any plans to see each other again, other than the official written ones in my hand.

Barre. Focus. Breathe.

Even in the lifts at the end of class my concentration remained on technique, extension, balance. Not the strength of Aleks's arms, not the attentiveness of his eyes.

Then it was over. Class, and maybe everything else too.

"Treadwell?" Will paused at the door. "I'm sorry."

A shake of my head dismissed him. What did it matter now?

Aleks closed the door. I braced myself. How could I be here again? Day after day, facing the same, or similar, end-of-class doom? We'd been so close, so intimate, and now—

"Tonight, I will pick you up earlier, and cook for you?"

My vision blurred.

"Ah, I have say something wrong again. I make assumption, so stupid. You are already busy with other things and people?"

"I didn't know..." Was I really going to tell him this? "I didn't know if it was a one-night stand."

"A one-night—? This is what you wanted?"

"No, I..."

"Did I do something to make you feel this is what is happening?"

I shook my head, worried that I'd offended him. "Justin. He said probably. He was just trying to protect me."

"Malphia, come, sit."

There was no pianist for the private lesson, so I sat on the recently vacated piano stool.

Aleks crouched beside me and took my hand. "Between us there is... is wrong to say sparks, more like big, big fire. We have to explore, see where we go. Is something very special here, to me this is how it is feeling."

"To me, too," I said, looking down at him. "But..."

"But?"

"I've already been warned about behaving properly, and obeying the rules, by Madame this term. So, we'd have to keep it a secret."

He smiled. "A secret could be fun, no?"

I nodded. I suspected it could.

"So, I will pick you up at six? You bring your things this time?" A smile flickered back and forth between us. "But, no, this is terrible," he said, standing up in horror. "We are talking through your lesson time. And it is to be the best you ever had."

It was.

Chapter 7

Aleksandr Zolotov quickly became my whole world. The following day, I went straight to his flat from college. The day after that, I let myself in with my own key. I loved running in to find him, wherever he was, the hours apart having felt like weeks. And my need was shameless. If he was on the sofa, his neck and face were kissed from behind as my hands felt their way down into his trousers.

He flipped me over onto the cushions and pinned my arms back behind my head.

"I have never meet a woman who is so much enthused for... me."

The statement couldn't be true, but the enthusiasm was. The study of Aleks was an all-consuming project. I loved his hands, so much bigger than mine. Kissing each of his flat fingertips became a nightly ritual. He insisted they were that way due to being hit with a ruler in piano lessons. I couldn't tell if the stories of childhood beatings were true or just cuddle-seeking jokes.

I laid my cheek against a hard hip bone and watched his erection grow. No part of him went unkissed, including the long vertical scar on his knee. The first time my lips touched it, I was sitting between his legs in bed, having thoroughly explored long man toes, high arched feet and impressive calf muscles. My fingers traced the dark red mark and I kissed it gently, glancing up to find a hitherto unseen expression on his face.

"Aleks?"

"You are so very real," he said with aggressive intensity. "There is no affectation in you, no pretence."

I blinked, unsure as to whether this was a good or bad thing.

"And now I have embarrass you again. Is good I know the cure for this," he said, kissing me and chasing confusion from the room.

I didn't ask him about the scar, and he didn't ask me about certain things. He deleted Gavin's number from the new phone that he bought me, without a word. There, though, lay a slight discomfiture: all the gifts he kept buying. Hardly a day passed without something waiting for me on the sofa or in the bedroom. Telling him it was unnecessary only encouraged the habit.

"You are not used to being treated well," he said.

"But it's not fair. I've hardly bought you anything."

"You are a student, and what do I need now I have you? You are everything. This, I completely mean," he added, seeing my sceptical look.

I did give him some thick warm-up socks to keep his feet cosy, one pair for every day of the week. He delighted in wearing them and nothing else, and advising me to do the same. "You are not shy when we make love," was pointed out many times. Pulling the sheet up over my breasts or attempting to wear anything in bed caused his eyes to widen and mouth to turn down, a look that was impossible to refuse.

I gradually accepted that he found me beautiful. The mirror became silent as I became more comfortable in my body, once thoughtlessly walking out onto the balcony in just underwear. He wrapped a towel round me. "I would like is just for me, angel."

And when I wasn't with him, I was thinking about him.

"You're not bloody well listening, are you?"

"Sorry, Justin. Tell me again."

"What's the point?"

"I'll be home this weekend. We can spend some time together then."

"Not happening, Phi. I'm going to Mum's. I need pampering after all these weeks of brutal ballet."

But before we got to the weekend, I almost wrecked everything.

Aleks had been lifting weights when I arrived at his flat after college. He went to have a shower, leaving me in the small workout room. His phone rang. I looked at it.

I could feel the downward spiral into badness begin as I sat on the padded black seat of the weights machine and studied the very red picture of the very red woman on the phone's screen. I hadn't noticed her mass of blonde hair before. It hadn't been loose before. And, though she was still wearing red, in this picture it was a nightdress or some sort of shiny lingerie that she wore. Had Aleks taken that photo?

The phone alerted me to a new voice message. I automatically slid my finger across the notification and, knowing his passcode, clicked through to listen to a posh voice with a small hint of Scottishness about it.

"Aleks, you naughty boy, are you avoiding me? I think a good spanking is in order next time I see you. Call me back."

Without thinking, I deleted the message and laid the phone down on the seat exactly where it had been. And then I just sat, trying to fit facts around the event.

I was still doing that when Aleks returned.

"We never said we were exclusive," I said, stating fact number one that had come to me.

He ran his hands back through his damp hair. "We can have that conversation now."

I shook my head. "This is all too intense. I can't cope. I have to go." I could hear my heart beating in my ears and was acutely aware of two terrible things: the invasion of privacy that I'd just committed, and the other, the posh Scottish other.

"Malphia, have I done something?" seemed a nonsensical question. We both knew the things we'd done. "Or said something?" he added.

"You haven't said anything."

I walked out of the room, down the hall and into his bedroom where my bag was. The sky beyond the huge windows was a mix of reds. The great domes of the city reflected the colours of the sunset, all natural hues that went well together. My eyes perused the beautiful view a final time, and then I left.

He didn't make it easy, following me out into the hallway. "You will let me drive you home?" His voice sounded different, cross and short.

"No."

"I will call you a taxi?"

"No," I said, stepping into the elevator.

"You will let me know when you get home," was not a question so I didn't answer, and then the doors closed.

"It's over," I told Justin when I arrived back at our flat.

He pulled the details from me. "I don't see it," he said. "Her and him. That first class you missed, right back at the beginning? He was pissed off that the woman in red was there that day, and pissed off that you weren't. You need to talk to him. Get clarity."

It was true. I did need to tell him that I'd both listened to and deleted his message. It was a hot and itchy thought, and it made me cry as I took my phone out to send him a text. I couldn't type the terrible thing I'd done. I needed more time to think how best to speak about that. So I just sent: *home*.

"He asked me to tell him," I explained to Justin's eyebrow.

"Really? You're having an argument, and he asked— Oh! Why did I not see this before? I thought you had some sort of thing for teachers, but no: you've got daddy issues!"

"I do not."

He started counting points on his fingers: "Older man, caring, knowledgeable, wanting to know that you're safe. Not things your own parents are known for, so he's meeting an unmet need. Maybe it's better you end it, Phi. I don't think it's healthy."

I pressed my face into the fluffy cushion and cried. A place in my chest hurt and made it difficult to breathe. I went to bed and planned my words for the next day, a day that arrived all too quickly.

⁓ll⁓

"Aleks, I did a terrible thing last night," I told him in the bright studio before class, but that's all I got to say because: Madame. She clod-hopped into the room wearing wooden clogs, a woven dress with windmills on it and a tiara of tulips, and demanded to know why I was there. She then commandeered Aleks in a quiet conversation, that I couldn't hear, while I warmed up.

He was sweet to me during class, correcting my tendu but saying that nothing was so terrible we couldn't work past it. And when I finally, during our own private class, got to tell him what I'd done? He laughed.

"This is all?" he said, then sobering. "Michelle is a colleague only. She has a way of speaking that is rude and inappropriate sometimes. I am sorry you have heard this and been distressed. But she is right about one thing. I have been avoiding her calls. I do not care that I missed the message. I do not want it."

Inappropriate, I got, but: "Aleks, I'm shocked at what I did. Aren't you?"

"No," he said at once. "I am glad."

Totally confused, I examined his face for sarcasm or humour, but found none.

"You have behaved in a possessive manner," he said, and I cringed. He went on. "This shows your depth of feeling. When the emotion is large, these things? They happen. Believe me when I tell you that I would have done much worse in the same situation."

"No." It was my turn to laugh. "You're just being kind to me."

"I am not," he said, serious. "When I am jealous or threatened, my behaviour? It is not good." He paused, looking down, thoughtful. "There are words we need to say to each other soon, but too much, too early, is frightening. I don't want you to run away again. You will stay with me this weekend?"

His big brown eyes beseeched. It was difficult to say no, but I did so with an unfortunate blurt: "I can't. I'll have my period."

He didn't flinch. "But you can still stay. I will look after you. Make soup."

"I'll be in a lot of pain and a very bad mood. I don't want you to see me like that."

"I understand. But, did you know orgasm can help with this particular pain?"

"Really?"

"I read this. Maybe can do for you, no?"

Resistance crumbled in the charm of his playful look. "But..." The idea contradicted my previous relationship experience. "Wouldn't that disgust you?"

"No. Why you think this? Is like a magical power, the ability to create life. So many times we are making love these last weeks." He splayed his hand wide over my abdomen. "If we were cavemen, already my seed would grow in you." My eyes met his in surprise as he went on. "So: chocolate, pain killers, hot water bottle. This is to be my shopping list?"

—— *ell* ——

Friday and Saturday proved too painful for any orgasmic experimentation, and rolled over into Sunday evening when I woke feeling terrible. It was the opposite of that first time I had awoken there in Aleks's flat, the feeling of rightness now replaced by a horrible wrong. The air was thick with sweat and... what? Itchy and uncomfortable, everything felt out of place, like nothing fitted in the world.

I turned over in the bed and found Aleks, awake and grey-faced, hair damp against his skin. His forehead was hot under my hands. "You've got a temperature," I noted, sitting up to inspect him, my own malady forgotten.

He sat too, repressing a groan.

"And you're in a lot of pain." I hesitated to touch him further, sensing aches everywhere.

"It happens." Voice hoarse, he leant back against the headboard, and I understood he'd rather I wasn't witnessing this. It was Will and his dyslexia in a different form, and I knew just how to be.

"See, you ballet boys are all the same," I said in a totally unsympathetic manner that shocked him into looking at me. "So precious about yourselves. You think you're the only ones who ever have problems or feel pain." Considering the way he'd cared for me over the weekend, and that Will had covered my Saturday teaching, the declaration was grossly unfair, but kindness that could be interpreted as pity had no place in the situation. I knew that well. "They gave me the pill and Paracetemol to control my medical condition. But you've got something far superior. I've seen it in your medicine cabinet, and that's what you need now, isn't it?"

He nodded, still somewhat taken aback by my speech.

I fetched the pills and a glass of water and held out the prescribed two.

"Four," he said.

I popped two more out of their foil, and he knocked them back.

"Do you need anything else, Aleks?"

He lay down, slowly, carefully, completely unlike his usual self. "Sleep," he said. "You."

The place in my chest that had hurt before squeezed as I rested my face near his and smoothed back his hair. His features relaxed once he was asleep, but his breathing was disturbingly ragged. How often did this happen? How had it been when it first began? Had it been worse than this? It must have been, to end his career like it did. The thought of all the pain he had been through dismayed me, and all it had cost him. My lovely, lovely Aleks, who was so good, so kind and so perfect. I wanted to wrap him up in love and keep him safe and well forever.

Morning arrived with a fanfare of sunshine and normal temperatures. I turned under his arm to examine his sleeping form, and was relieved to discover easy breathing and a healthy looking pallor.

Returning from the bathroom, I found him sitting up, arms hooked round his knees, sheet over his legs. He regarded me with some wariness, possibly wondering if more meanness were to be levied his way.

"You look better," I said, sitting down and assessing the mean/nice requirement.

"Yes." He shrugged, obviously not wanting to talk about it. "And you. You are better?"

"All cured by a magic pill."

"This is the reason you take? You said last night, you have a condition?"

"Polycystic ovary syndrome. And you thought I was just wildly promiscuous."

He smiled. "This, I am never think." The happy mood evaporated. "Malphia, when this drug I am taking, it is making me... It has side effects." There was a pause during which I worried about what other suffering he had to endure. "I won't be able to make love to you, maybe not even tonight."

"Silly man." The words came out more gently than intended, and I kissed him to hide it. His mouth tasted odd, bitter from the illness or the drug.

He sighed. "You are to see all bad things of me today, angel. The medication leaves me like hangover, certain food I must eat, and also I very much want to smoke. I go outside."

I got dressed in the bathroom, sensing his unusual need for privacy. Then, feeling the chill breeze from the balcony doors, I took a sweatshirt out to him. Sure enough, he was insufficiently dressed in vest top and trackies. Cigarette in mouth, he leant forward on the balustrade, stretching his calves.

"Sit upwind," he suggested, indicating the chair to his right as he sat on the other.

"It's colder today," I observed, wrapping the jumper round his shoulders before sitting down and looking out at the city coming to life. The dome of St. Paul's glowed with the first golden light from the sun. The lines of cars, with their red and white lights, were not so serene. They seemed an unnecessary and noisy addition to the morning. "I wonder where they all have to be at this time?"

"Takes long while to drive through the traffic. They go early, make coffee in office."

"Do you want coffee, Aleks? I'll make it." His hand felt very cold in mine.

"No, I will do," he said with a small smile. "I want it to be good."

My face wavered between laughter and offence.

"You are the most surprising and delightful woman I have ever met, but you cannot make coffee. And I love how you still cannot accept a compliment."

"Am I allowed to make toast?"

"Yes. I love the way you make toast."

We had arrived at our game.

"I love the way you hide your cigarettes from yourself," I said, watching him replace the packet behind a loose red brick.

He continued on in the kitchen. "See, I love this you do with the toast, the one side burnt. Is the English way, no?"

"I love how you think disgusting food is nice," I said, eyeing the mixture of eggs and vegetables, to be topped with caviar, in distaste.

His mobile rang. I stirred the eggs. He had a brief phone conversation in the studio before returning to switch off the burner.

"This afternoon," he said. "Michelle is coming to assess who of my class has right attributes for her research. Such short notice. Always she is like this, obsessive, and blind to any consideration but the work."

"Oh." I tried to sound neutral at the mention of the red name, then thinking his words through. "So this is the real audition?" I asked. "We won't all be going to the new school? I might not be going."

He tipped my face up to look at him. "A point has been reached now where this is not thinkable."

I shivered as a gust of wind blew in from outside, suggestive of how cold and empty life would be without him. I could see myself standing in this small kitchen, alone and longing for Aleks, and it was a deeply distressing vision.

"So. Is simple." His fingertips danced through my hair and settled low down on the back of my head. "This is the place where discomfort is to be felt in suitable candidates. You will do Amalgamation C, a strange combination of movements, very bad choreography. But it stimulates the brain in some people. First time I do was like, ahh..." He put his hand to his own head as if in unexpected pain. "Is only hurting first time. Don't worry. And is only for funding. The teaching, the part that really matters, it will not be affected by this."

"So, if it doesn't work on me, this amalgamation thing, you're suggesting I fake it?"

"I love that this is so unnatural an inclination for you..."

Chapter 8

I GAVE JUSTIN THE information about the amalgamation before morning class, so he could fake it too if he wanted. Then I found myself blurting it out to Will as well while we waited in the studio at four. The ensuing, "But how do you know..." conversation petered out as Madame Genevieve, in a newsprint dress and sunflower-bedecked boots, came into the room accompanied by the horrendous colour clash of Michelle.

Posh Scottish Michelle stood tall in shiny red stilettos, her petite figure flattered by a tailored red skirt suit that was slightly lighter than her shoes. Her long blonde hair was elaborately twirled on top of her head, and perfect make-up was set off by cherry-red lips and nails the colour of congealed blood. The smell of her perfume caught my throat from across the room, just as cloying as before, probably originating from an expensive and perfectly formed red bottle.

Aleks and Michelle greeted one another with cheek kisses and friendly smiles. The mirror chuckled.

Class commenced with a short barre. I felt scrutinised and judged, and was three times corrected by Aleks. "Eyes up, Amalphia. Where is your confidence today?"

"Let's do it," said Michelle, licking her lips in obvious excitement. "There can be some disorientation or mild discomfort when you first try this," she told us. "Though, as dancers, you are prime candidates to work with the technique. Listening to music uses the whole brain, and you do that all day long. The specialised choreography of Amalgamation C will enhance the abilities you have already developed and, with you all being so young, I'm hoping for spectacular results."

Justin raised two eyebrows.

Aleks took us through the strange dance sequence. It reminded me a little of the brain-gym classes I'd done as a child as my mother attempted to 'fix' me. There was lots of crossing the midline, and changes of direction were complicated by the accompanying arm exercises.

"Is very quick with the music," Aleks explained. "No worries if you don't get it right first time."

The sound from the studio speaker was unusual and very loud, a deep resonant hum running below the melody. I had picked up the complex routine perfectly, as had Justin beside me, but we didn't quite reach the end. The final turn went black. The base of my skull felt as if my brain were swelling under it, the pressure excruciating. When my eyes cleared, I found myself crouched on the floor, Aleks and Michelle filling my field of vision and focusing my thoughts.

And my thoughts were fast. In the few seconds it took Aleks to bend down and put his hand on my shoulder, many dots were connected. I'd wondered about the two of them, today, and before, and now all those little moments were available for inspection and deduction. I re-ran every look, smile and kiss of the afternoon. I scanned all the times he had mentioned Michelle in conversation, noting the tone of his voice, his facial expressions, the brief avoidance of eye contact. Then there was the red nightdress picture, a photo he had assigned to her name, a photo he had most definitely taken. The red around her in that image had been a pillow. Those facts melded into the present picture: her red nails like claws on his arm, her body turned towards him, so intimate, so familiar. And I knew. I absolutely knew.

I squinted against the bright light of the studio and pushed his hand off my shoulder. "Get away from me."

"Phi, why didn't you tell me?" asked Justin from where he sat on the floor, tearful and green looking. "Why didn't I ask? I mean, I did think.... You were so quiet. Something brutal went on with Tuesday, didn't it?"

I nodded. "I ran away. He didn't get me. I ran away."

"Gonna puke," said Justin, retching and trying to stand.

"You do seem to be having impressively strong reactions," said Michelle, her red shoes uncomfortably close to me, alongside Aleks's black ones.

"What have you done to Justin?" I shouted at her, standing up as the air became red and cloudy. "And to the rest of us?" Some of the others were clearly in distress too.

She smiled, showing brilliant white teeth, and a quiver of exhilaration ran through her body.

"Amalphia. What is it you are feeling?" asked Aleks, feigning big brown puppy-eyed concern.

"I'm seeing the truth," I said, then shoving him back. "You. You're playing a game with me."

Justin spluttered again, and I put my arm round him. Will went under his other arm to aid our escape, but the way was barred.

Madame Genevieve was furious. "Amalphia Treadwell! Apologise this instant! You do not speak to visitors in my school like that!"

My voice was loud. And rude. "Me apologise? Me?"

"Your scholarship is on shaky ground as it is, young lady."

"You should be worried about litigation, Genevieve," I told her, truth still with me. "You're negligent for letting this experimental, and potentially harmful, activity go on in your school."

I turned to Michelle, the need to unleash pure facts on her, too great to be resisted. "None of your reds match."

Her smile wavered.

Will and I helped Justin down the corridor to the toilets, leaving Madame, Aleks and the many tones of red staring after us.

Justin hung over a sink in the grey light of the bathroom.

"I kneed him in the nuts," I told him. "He dropped like a stone." That, at least, was a satisfying memory.

"You should have told me, reported him, something..."

"Zolotov did something?" asked Will. "He hurt you?"

"Yes," I said. "But, no, this... This thing was someone else. It doesn't matter. Are you all right?"

"Yeah, babe," said Will. "It's you that's crying."

I touched my wet cheeks and tried not to think about why they were that way. "I've got to go. I can't take any more from any of them today. You coming?" I asked Justin and opened the window.

"Not out a window, I'm not. We're on the second floor, Phi."

"It slopes down to the street," I explained. "It's easy enough. Will, I need you to do something for me."

"Anything, Malph. You didn't see. You see, I didn't..." He trailed off, presumably full of his own weirdness from the class.

I gave him his instructions. "I need you to tell Aleks that Justin's being sick, and we'll be back through in a bit. And get my bag for me. Say I need something out of it."

Will returned quickly from the task and was upset that I wouldn't let him come with us.

"Don't screw up your scholarship too," I advised, and he nodded.

Getting down over the roof was easy, despite the loud fuss Justin made about the possibility of us falling to our deaths. However, as we slipped over the low end wall, we were met by Aleks in the street.

"Your old friend does not lie so well," he said.

"Not as accomplished as you," I muttered, walking away holding Justin's hand.

Aleks kept pace with us. "What is this? Malphia, what has happened? I didn't know anything so bad could go on. Michelle thinks your youth is enhancing the potential— Making things worse," he corrected.

"Michelle, whom you dislike so much?"

He sort of shrug nodded.

"Give it up, Aleks," I said. "It's over. You. Here. Everything."

"You will tell me what this is about. Now."

"You're sleeping with her. But you already knew that. I know too, now. It was completely obvious."

His face paled. "Ah, no..."

"Don't lie to me again."

I turned and ran away from him, pulling Justin along in my wake. At the tube station we bent over, completely out of breath.

Aleks hadn't followed.

Justin and I hugged under the sofa blanket, the fluffy cushion squashed between us.

"He's mad if he prefers that cold tit-less cow to you."

"She's beautiful."

"Cake of make-up, long hooked nose. She's not even pretty."

"You're gay. You wouldn't find her attractive."

"I know the straights like voluptuous. Me, I like a flat body and a big cock, but each to their own."

I burst into tears again, wondering if it was all a nightmare. How had everything changed so fast? It had all been so good this morning. The love words. The eggs and the burnt toast.

"D'you think he's with her now?" I asked, chest constricted and aching in a stabbing way.

"Stop that. We need to find you a better man, no more dancers. Time for a nice bricklayer with hands that could ladder your tights."

"No. No more relationships. No more men. They don't love me back, or they shove me about, or they're lovely and it's all a lie."

He tightened his hug. "Did Hearst call you, 'babe?' In the bathroom?"

"Yes. He used to do that, you know, a long time ago. He was looping too, didn't you think?"

My phone rang. The phone Aleks had given me. It was him. I let it ring. Voicemail beeped. I ignored it. Justin and I stared at each other in the relative silence. It rang again.

"This could get old fast," said Justin. "I'll answer it."

"No. I'll switch it off. Or throw it away."

"You can't throw away a brand new phone."

"Watch me."

I took the phone over to the window, but he snatched it from my hand.

"I'll have it, if you don't want it. Might as well get what we can from the bastards, Phi. Top of the range this, isn't it?"

I returned to the sofa, defeated in all efforts to improve my lot.

Justin's own phone began its musical-theatre medley. "Your old number," he said, mystified.

"He has the sim card." I remembered how he'd used it to transfer contacts to my new phone.

"How very determined," said Justin and, to my horror, he answered the call.

I covered my face, then uncovered it and watched his reactions.

"Yes?" said Justin into the phone. "Not going to happen, matey, so you can forget that right now." There was a long pause during which Justin listened, rolled his eyes and sighed. "Okay, I'll tell her." He disconnected. "He's desperate to speak to you, like might come round and lean on the bell all night, desperate."

"He said that?"

"No, this is my assessment of the situation. You be quiet and listen. Two main points. He says you were right about him and Michelle, but it's in the past. There was this whole repeated thing about it being only you now, very keen to make sure I told you that. And you're not to worry about college. He's fixed it all with Madame, so you're not in trouble." Justin paused a moment to think before continuing. "I hate to stick up for a bastard man in any way, but, well, you've been with him every night for weeks. We can discuss the neglect of your best friend at a later date over apologetic gifts and cupcakes, but the fact is, he can hardly have had time to see her too. He sounded kinda broken, Phi."

It was all too confusing and terrible. Back in my small single bed, the solace of sleep wouldn't come. The scene with Michelle and Aleks in the studio replayed on a loop: how they'd looked, how they'd spoken, the cheek kiss and smile. An unhealthy amount of time was spent trying to work out what every little inflection and movement meant. The night sank into a void of blackness from which nothing good could ever come, and I wept.

I wept for Aleks, for though my mind had initially fixated on the facts of his relationship with Michelle, there was a darker, sadder truth too. The end of his performing career must have been terrible. I recalled that the research did have something to do with rehabilitation for injured dancers. If she'd been there for him, if she'd helped him, what right had I to condemn that?

Someone hammered at the front door. Justin didn't emerge from his room, and I peered nervously through the peephole. It was Allan, our neighbour from upstairs who often worked nights.

"Hi, Phi," he said when I opened the door. "There's a bloke sitting on the steps outside. Usually something to do with you, aren't they?"

"What bloke? Who?"

"Don't worry. I didn't let this one in, not that he asked. Blond guy."

So Aleks was near, but not bell leaning or demanding to be let in. I really wanted to see him, but also didn't. Because. Because what? Jealousy. Some form of instant clarity was still uncomfortably with me. A peek from the bottom of the stairwell to check that he was all right couldn't hurt, though, surely?

My socked feet were silent on the stairs.

He sat on the top step outside, head in hands. He looked round, and we regarded each other for a moment before we both approached the main doors. I nearly turned and fled, but instead opened the latch and began to sob as his arms came round me.

"I am so sorry," he said several times into my hair.

Unable to analyse the situation, I just held him. Everything about Aleks was comforting: his arms, his almondy smell, and the complete non-aloneness of hugging him.

"I should have told you," he said. "Of course I should, but I did not want to cause upset. And this thing with her? It was nothing, just a convenience at a bad time. For her too. It was not like us, how we are being. Don't think that. You are so perfect to me." He sank to his knees, holding my hands in his. "I love you, Amalphia. I completely adore you. I am begging you still to please not leave me."

I knelt too and examined the pleasing lines of his nose and cheekbones, the latter of which were more distinct in distress.

He went on. "But it is when one thing go wrong that you see what else is wrong. I know I am not so perfect. You are right to say is over; all is over for me. You have already seen I have the disease of an old man."

I shook my head. "Your hands are very cold," I told him. "You'll have to come up to the Dickensian hovel now."

We were soon cuddled and warm in my tiny bed.

"It was so awful," I told him. "It was like I could just pull all the clues together and see what was true."

"The amalgamations are meant to stimulate parts of the brain not usually used. I experienced only slight discomfort myself, nothing else." His tone darkened. "But I am feel the badness of the past too, angel. Each week in the staff meeting, I am sit near the angry man. Justin is sensing this today, no? Seeing that this man is hitting you?"

"He didn't hit me, not exactly. He shoved me around a bit. The worst thing was how he spoke to me." I didn't want to have Aleks hear the unfortunate tale, but truth flowed on. "It was like the opposite of how you speak to me."

"He is putting you down? Oh yes, I see him. He knows he is with a woman several leagues above. His only chance to keep, is to make you believe you are less than you are."

I frowned. That didn't seem right.

"Justin said something brutal happened," he persisted.

"We'd been at a party to do with Gavin's work. I'm not good with things like that. I can't make clever spontaneous conversation with strangers. He was drunk and angry. He strangled me up against a wall. I couldn't breathe. I thought he was going to kill me." I took a deep breath, reliving the emotions of that day. I'd felt used, dirty and pathetic. Not wanting Aleks to associate any of those things with me, I just told him of the surrounding thoughts and actions. "I knew he wouldn't seek medical assistance if I stopped breathing. I mean, he didn't even like me. I wondered how he'd dispose of the body. But then, I managed to knee him and run. I had to walk all the way home. I'd left my jacket in his house, and my phone was out of charge. He's been very keen to speak to me ever since, probably to tell me it was all my fault. Everything was always my fault."

Aleks's face was grim, though his hold had become more like cradling. "No one is hurting you like this again, my darling."

With my face nestled in his neck, it was easy to believe that. He was safety. He was love.

"You have had many other boyfriends?" he asked a few minutes later.

"No, none."

He lifted my face to his, as if disbelieving.

I sighed, more uncomfortable things about to be revealed. "I had an unrequited situation going on for a while, a long while, for someone who would never like me back that way. Gavin asked me out, and I thought it was about time so... But I wasn't properly attracted to him, and I think he knew that. But enough about me." I couldn't ask the same question. It wouldn't go well. There was one thought that might fester, however. "Michelle seems very cool and collected."

He stiffened. "She is pleased with how things go. Eleven of you with reactions, is more than she expect."

"I mean in general. I must seem like a mad, inappropriate creature compared to her."

He breathed out fast as if in shock. "Never be comparing yourself to this one. She is cold and obsessive. She is the creature. Everything she does is to manipulate. I went along with it for a while. But you... You." The pause was ominous. "Everything about you enchants me. You must know this. Your responses in love are so natural and so strong. You are not thinking of what shoes you are to buy the next day."

"What? Who does that?"

He shook his head and smiled. "You make me feel so wanted."

"You are." I pressed my mouth to his ear and whispered: "I love you too."

More words came out small and soft after that and continued on and on. It was the most whispery, talkative love we had ever made. 'I love you' was a happy novelty to say and hear, and trying to be quiet added the new element of laughter. But he was more than loved, more than wanted. He was needed, and that realisation had the potential to be frightening, but somehow wasn't. With Aleks, big feelings were natural, manageable, and even easy. The need was mirrored in him. It was there in his kiss, in his body and breath, sex a blissful confirmation of our continued togetherness.

A little later, there was knocking. "You all right, Phi?" asked Justin, fortunately not opening the door.

I cleared my throat. "Yes."

"Bad dream?"

"No."

"You should try and go back to sleep, sweetheart. It's early. And don't you worry. We'll be fine. Who needs men? Fuck 'em. Fuck the whole flaming lot of them. Now, there's a dream." He shuffled back down the hall to his room.

"Is nice, this relationship," commented Aleks. "You look after each other. This is how we are becoming too," he said, then getting out of bed. "Where is your bathroom?"

"Just through that wall. The first door."

Once he was gone, I pulled my pyjamas back on, thinking to go and make coffee. Or maybe he should make it, so it would be good. I smiled at the thought.

He came back into the room and closed the door, leaning back on it as if traumatised. "I meet Justin."

"Oh." I laughed. "See, another reason why people wear clothes."

"I will never be able to look him in face again."

"What did he say?"

"Good morning, Aleks."

Chapter 9

T HE RADIANCE OF JUSTIN'S smile shone from the kitchen, perfectly accompanied by the aroma of coffee. "Everything back to sweet goodness in your world, Phi?" he asked.

I beamed.

He shut the door and lowered his voice. "He's like a work of art. I mean, you can tell he's fit through his clothes, but pfwah! Does he often walk round in the buff like that?"

"Yes."

"No wonder you've got it bad."

"He's embarrassed. You're not to say anything about it to him."

"No, no. But listen, you make sure he knows it's fine. This is a broad-minded household. If he wants to dance around starkers at any time of day or night, that's perfectly acceptable."

"Justin," I warned, recognising his look of naughty intent just before it changed to accusatory.

"There really was no bad dream."

"No."

"Well, who could blame you? In bed with that? Plenty to keep you busy downtown, isn't there? I had to fight a strong instinct to fall to my knees."

"Justin! I'm opening this door, and we're going to behave."

That said and done, I sat on the worktop and sipped coffee until Aleks emerged, fully dressed, and joined us. A 'How do you like your coffee?' exchange took place, during which Justin smiled far too much. Aleks stood between my legs against the worktop, and I kissed him.

"Well, isn't this lovely?" said Justin. "Mummy and Daddy are happy again. I have a slightly better chance of turning out well balanced, and the sun is shining."

I rested my head on Aleks's shoulder and smiled at my friend.

"And I hate to be the one to bring it up, my darlings," said Justin. "But are we speaking about it? What happened yesterday, I mean, because, one: what the hell was that? We're all mystery-solving geniuses now? And, two: is it going to happen again? Because I, for one, am not up for it. I have no desire to be a crime-fighting-ballet-super-hero, thank you very much."

Neither did I.

"Is very bad thought for me also," said Aleks. "I have such a long and stupid life, many things I would not want you to know."

I tried not to think about that, about any of it.

"Well, you just have to get over it," said Justin.

We both looked round at him.

"Look at you, all sweet and happy together, aren't you? Well, everything you've been through, good, bad, stupid; that's what made you who you are, and put you where you are too. Accept yourselves and each other, and everything will be fine."

The speech was followed by a digestive hush which was eventually broken by Aleks. "I did not know you are so wise, Justin."

"I can be extremely insightful at times," he replied. "I should really write a book. *Justin's Little Book of Wisdom*, the perfect stocking filler to give the person with everything or nothing, the one you love, the one you hate... But, putting my perceptive talents aside for a moment, what are we going to do now? Class as normal like nothing happened? Not likely, is it?"

Aleks proposed a plan. We would drive over to college early, right now in fact, and try the amalgamation before anyone else arrived. He was sure there would be no repeat reaction, and it was so good to discover that he was right.

In the early morning light of the studio, we merely performed a strange combination of steps with peculiar music. There was nothing exceptional or frightening about it at all.

After we'd finished, and breathed our collective sighs of relief, Justin put a loud and orally euphemistic song on the studio speaker system.

The mirror and I gave him a look.

Aleks went downstairs to get coffee while I headed for the bathroom to be alone for a moment, to breathe and be calm.

Emerging from the sanctuary a few minutes later, I ran smack into Gavin in the corridor. He didn't seem so scary anymore either. He was just a stupid man who showed up on Tuesdays.

"Thought I heard the poofter's style of music up here," he said. "No, you don't, Treadwell. We're going to talk."

"Let go my arm, you belligerent prick."

"She speaks," he said with the smile that I used to think was handsome.

I was considering kicking him in the shin when he shot backwards across the hallway. Gavin was pinned to the wall, Aleks's forearm across his neck.

"You do not touch her!" Aleks roared, face twisted in rage.

Terrified that Aleks might get hurt, even though he was the taller and stronger of the two men, I put my hand on his arm. He loosened his hold for a moment, and Gavin broke free.

"You a bloody psycho, or what?" yelled Gavin. "Don't go getting any ideas. She might look like that, but she's a frigid little—" His head hit the wall with a crack. Aleks had punched him. Gavin held his nose and blood showed between his fingers as he backed off, muttering incoherently.

"Come near her again, and I will do much more," Aleks said in a cold calm voice as Gavin disappeared round the corner.

I started to shake.

"Are you okay, Malphia?"

"Yes. Are you?"

He held up his hand. "Is not so simple as it looks in films."

I led him back into the studio to study the injured hand in the light, aware of a silent and agog Justin at our side. Aleks bent and flexed his fingers as a range of different thoughts appeared in my mind. He'd protected me. I wanted to protect him. I loved him so much. He was my shiny knight—

"That," said Justin, unusually quietly, "was the most fantastic thing I've ever seen. I thought I heard voices, and was just coming out to see what was what, and whack! The way he went back, the sound of his head on the wall!"

"Whose head? What wall?" Will had arrived.

"Gavin Tuesday's!" Justin continued excitedly, back to full volume. "Zolotov hit him." He flapped his hands in hyperactive delight.

"Oh?" Will obviously wanted to ask more, but Aleks's presence deterred him. I watched my old friend try to read the interplay between us. It was time to put his quick mind to practical matters.

"D'you think we should get ice?" I asked, indicating the hand that was starting to swell, and resisting the urge to kiss it.

Will, as I'd hoped, was full of advice. "You hit him against a wall?" he asked.

Aleks nodded, but said nothing.

"See, it's the impact that's done it. If he'd just gone back, it wouldn't be as bad."

"You're an expert in such things, are you, William?" enquired Justin.

"I've hit a few idiots, yeah. You remember, Malph?"

I did recall an incident from long ago and nodded.

"Ooh, ooh," said Justin, clapping his hands. "This is a story from the streets, isn't it? Or some sort of ghetto?"

"It took place in a school gym a couple of miles from here," I said. "Will sat on a boy and punched him against the floor. Peter had to pull them apart."

"Yeah, well he said—"

A small shake of my head quelled the rest of Will's words. Aleks was listening very intently, eyes narrowed, and some things did not bear repeating.

Justin wasn't about to let it go, however. "But this was the class of bad boys? You got to go every week, didn't you? All that burgeoning, out-of-control testosterone in one room..." His face took on a dreamy quality as he spoke.

"Peter thought it was a good idea," I explained. "I was naïve and... stupid." I looked at Will, remembering how I'd inadvertently made fun of his reading difficulty. I'd gone to his school to apologise that day and ask him to come back to ballet.

Aleks removed his hand from mine and walked over to the piano.

"It's funny," said Will, looking straight back at me. "I was just thinking about, you know, back then, and about what a complete idiot I was. Am, even."

Justin gasped. "That's the most intelligent thing I've ever heard Hearst say. That amalgamation thingy really has upped our IQs, hasn't it?"

"An interesting assessment, Mr. Bevan," said Michelle, entering the room. "Tell me more."

"I've been imparting wisdom up, down, and centre stage," replied Justin.

"Really?" she said, amused as she turned to look at me. "And are you both feeling better today?"

I let Justin answer in the affirmative for us, aware that it would be appropriate to apologise for yesterday's rudeness but feeling utterly unwilling to do so. Her reds had changed. She wore a maroon dress and black shoes. The lipstick and nails matched each other, and were a very similar shade to the dress.

"I can see you two are going to be my star pupils," she said with a wide smile. "Good heavens, Aleks. You look rough."

How dare she? He was unbelievably handsome, all dishevelled and lovely. I wanted to go straight home to bed with him.

"Are you really okay now?" Will asked as Michelle commandeered Aleks, and the others started to arrive.

I nodded.

"Weird thing that," he said, but then class began.

It was easy, something we had become unaccustomed to since Aleks started teaching us. The mirror had an interesting and new story to tell as I gazed into it. Justin, Will and I were changed. We were better. So much better. It was almost unbelievable that such a dramatic improvement had taken place in so short a time. In less than a term, we had grown obviously stronger and more supple. But the biggest difference to be seen was in the way we held ourselves. Our stance and arm movements showed some of that special quality I'd noticed in Aleks back in that very first class of his.

And it wasn't just us three. The other students in the studio had it too. For a moment, I was overcome with emotion. I felt such love for Justin and Will; they deserved this opportunity so much. And the others too, though I didn't really know them. I knew we were all heading to greater things than we had been, and it was because of Aleks's teaching. My goal of being the best dancer I could be was actually happening.

And Aleks. My dear Aleks. He'd lost one career, but he had found another calling, another gift. He would do great things too.

I'd missed the explanation of the next exercise, but picked it up at once by watching Will. We were all much quicker in that capacity too.

In the centre, tight-lipped and tentative, we performed Amalgamation C, and it produced no results in anyone. There was a collective sigh of relief. Only seven of the students who had produced suitable reactions were still interested in continuing. The rest had returned to their normal classes today. And seven was a tiny number.

Michelle told us that we were being offered a once-in-a-lifetime opportunity. Our places were dependent on participation in the 'ahead of its time' research for which we would be paid a small salary. We would receive world-class dance tuition, concentrating on ballet, though there would be contemporary and other classes too.

"Drama?" I asked.

"There will be repertoire coaching," said Aleks. "Acting is always a big part of it."

"I could make the most of that," I said.

Michelle continued on as if we had not spoken, telling us that there would be regular teachers like Aleks and also other guest celebrities. The castle – yes, a real castle – boasted luxurious accommodation, outstanding views, and its own theatre. She made the whole thing sound like an all-expenses-paid, five-star holiday.

"See, I've always thought I should live in a castle," said Justin. "You know what this is? Manifesting!"

Michelle paused beside us as she handed out questionnaires and contracts. "Miss Treadwell. Mr. Bevan. I am particularly interested to know everything you two experienced yesterday. If there's not room on here, write on the back, or we can make an appointment to speak about it."

"There's plenty room," I said, looking at the two lines for text by that question. I intended to put what Aleks had suggested: 'I felt pain and something strange that I can no longer remember.'

She moved along to the others as basic input of information held my attention. Name. Address. Date of birth.

"It's your loss." Michelle's clipped accent sliced through the bureaucracy, and I looked up to see Will drop his forms at her feet and walk out.

I crossed the room and picked up the fallen papers. "What happened?" I asked Michelle.

"Mr. Hearst didn't want to fill in his details now, and I need them this morning. I don't think we'll miss him too much," she said with a laugh in Aleks's direction. "Have you glanced through this?" Seven student files sat on the piano, the thick one on top the source of her derision.

"You should have read it properly," I said. "You just humiliated him."

"Are you talking about the dyslexia?" interjected Simone. "Because I always thought that was a put-on to get out of doing stuff."

I struggled not to shout. "It is not a put-on."

"Dyslexia?" mused Michelle. "That could actually be interesting."

Disgusted, I stormed out of the room and stopped in the corridor, wondering and then knowing exactly where Will had gone.

"Amalphia, wait." Aleks had followed. "Ignore her inappropriate nonsense. Remember what is important. The training. Us."

"It's okay," I reassured him. "I'm going to find Will and sort out the forms. You could have a word with her about her attitude, though."

He sighed. "I will try. But you should not push your friend too hard. The tough regime at the castle will not be right for everyone."

"I think he can take it," I said. "Especially after your teaching. Aleks, you've done great things for us." I squeezed his non-hurt hand and then headed off to what was fast becoming a place of daily refuge.

In the bathroom, Will stared at himself in the mirror. I leant my head against his arm, a stance from long ago, and we regarded each other in the glass.

"You've got to come with me, Will." I felt an inexplicable level of panic at the thought of being far away in a strange land without him.

"Don't upset yourself, Treadwell. I'll come. Not impressed with the stuck-up cow, though."

"No one is."

We sat side by side on the cold lino floor and answered mundane and not so mundane questions on the form. It was like the old days, and yet actually the start of a new adventure. Stepping out into the unknown was surely easier with friends at your side.

The door opened. "Everyone is okay in here?" asked Aleks.

"Yes," I told him.

"This is good. Justin, he is very excited about the pool."

"There's a pool?" I asked.

"Is very big." Aleks stretched his arms out wide.

"Are you going to teach us those big lifts that you're famous for?" asked Will. "And the jumps, the massive ones that go all round the stage?"

Aleks shrugged. "I can show you this. So. It is Tuesday, Amalphia, and time for your class in my studio. Five minutes, we go."

Will's questions continued. "Are we all gonna get private lessons?"

Aleks raised his eyebrows, possibly tiring of the inquisition. "This could be discussed," he said, and then left with our forms.

"Watch out for him, Malph. He's got a reputation."

"Yes. Everyone keeps telling me that, thank you, Will," I said, cross, then softening. "I'm really glad you're coming, though, and, you know, that we're friends again."

"Always were, babe. You just forgot for a while."

Chapter 10

Twelve days later, I wiped a smear of chocolate from my cheek in Aleks's small kitchen and admired twenty-four perfectly iced cupcakes. They were an apology, not that it had really been my fault.

We'd had three more days of college followed by a week off. Time in bed had been interspersed with learning a sexy new pas de deux, and going shopping for food and yet more gifts.

"Soon it will all be different, so different," Aleks had told me. "This is our time. We must enjoy it to the full."

So I didn't complain as he did up a watch strap or undid new underwear. Life was a magical dream, hazy with love and autumn sunshine.

It was Friday before I stopped to wonder why nobody had phoned or texted me about the planned picnic. The get-together had been a good idea. Apart from Justin, Will and Simone, I barely knew the other students that were also going to the castle. The willowy girl with short dark hair was called Sun and in my contemporary class, but the shorter girl and the quiet boy? In the presence of Aleks, everyone else had only been seen peripherally, eclipsed by his brightness and beauty. I thought about what I did know about them as I looked for my phone. The quiet boy was black, handsome and an extremely skilled dancer. The short girl was plump, and not so gifted with dancing ability. She had been struggling through lifts with Will and finding Aleks's amalgamations very difficult. She was also a friend of Simone's, which didn't bode well.

I finally discovered my phone lying dormant on the coffee table. Once charged, it played increasingly irritable voice messages from Justin. The picnic had been on Wednesday, a good time had been had by all, and I was now universally resented and disliked.

"Ah, this. You must not be angry." Aleks assumed the sad, sorry little-boy expression that anger could never be directed at. "I put both our phones on silent. I wanted you all to myself this week. They will have you soon enough."

"But they've all bonded without me. They went boating on a lake together, and they all ate ice cream, even Simone."

"If you want to go on boat, I can take you."

"That is not the point."

He nuzzled my neck. "But we are to have this whole day and night apart. Really is two days, is so terrible. Then, because we are secret, only the night will be ours."

He drove up to Scotland on Sunday, partly because teachers were supposed to arrive before the rest of us on Monday, but also so he could have the car there. I spent the day packing and baking and imagining the two of us taking romantic drives against a backdrop of snowcapped mountains, dark forests and misty lochs.

I noticed Aleks's medication, forgotten in the bathroom cabinet, and popped it into the side pocket of a bag, though I wasn't sure if he needed it all. I'd never seen him take the anti-depressants.

There were leftovers in the fridge, and I invited Justin over to eat them with me.

"Can't," he said. "Busy."

"Sulking?"

"No. Well, yes, a bit, but no. Ed's coming over. I'll see you tomorrow."

So I spent a quiet evening with one of Aleks's books. There was a late-night phone call from Scotland. The castle was described as cold, grey and desolate.

"Text me when you are on the train," he said. "I will feel better knowing you are on your way."

"I don't know if I want to go anymore. It doesn't sound nice at all."

"Malphia, do not be joking about this. Is not funny."

The guard blew the whistle as I was trying to pull my case and bags up onto the train.

"No boyfriend to see you off then, Treadwell?"

"No."

Was Will's question hypothetical? If not, how deep did it go? Did he know about Aleks? He lifted my case with a humiliating lack of effort and rammed it into the luggage area.

Sun appeared and offered to take a bag. "Justin's been telling us about your boyfriend, Phi," she said as we joined the others in the carriage where a group 'hi' took place.

"Can't expect me to keep all your secrets, darling. Not after last week," said the informer with a grin, delighting in my discomfort as he played with his phone.

"Have to say, I was surprised," continued Sun. "I thought you were a totally chaste and devoted ballet girl."

I lurched into the seat opposite Will and Justin as the train moved off. Sun took her place by Simone. The other two, 'Short' and 'Quiet,' sat across the table from them.

A text from Justin put my mind at rest: *I didn't tell them who he was.*

"There have always been rumours," said Simone. "The ones about you two were patently ridiculous." She gestured towards Justin and me as she spoke. "But Gavin Tuesday, and now Aleks? Any truth in those?"

"None whatsoever," answered Justin, back on side. "My Phi is a good girl. Look at her." Everyone did. It was cringe-making. "Leaving her rich, well-endowed boyfriend to study ballet at the North Pole? That's dedication. Don't look so grateful, Phipot. I'm still a bit aggrieved."

"I made cakes," I said, pulling the storage box out of a bag, "to apologise for missing the picnic."

"Cupcakes!" Justin helped himself to three. "The ones with the icing inside too."

Will took a chocolaty bite. "You made these? Marry me, Treadwell."

The cakes passed to the other table. "Did you even attempt to make them low fat?" asked Simone. "You shouldn't, Sadie. Don't ruin your diet with cake that's probably not even good."

A-ha! I had a name for the short girl. "I have other things," I said. Out came the tubs of leftovers: pasta, curry, a box of cherry tomatoes and some cheese, most of which was claimed by Will, only the tomatoes making it to the other table.

"I didn't have any breakfast," justified Will.

"So lover-boy can cook as well," said Justin. "Life is just not fair."

"Have another cake," I said, taking one myself. "Did you have a nice time yesterday?"

"Mmm," he conceded, examining me. His hand waved up and down, indicating the new clothes, and then grabbed my wrist. "With a watch like that, you could at least have been on time."

"So, Amalphia," said Simone. "You went to Aleks's own studio for extra lessons? The one at his house?"

"Yes." Monosyllables might be best.

"Did you glean anything about him as a person?" she asked.

"Like?"

"Well..."

Sadie butted in. "Like, does he have a girlfriend, wife or significant other? It's what you wanted to know," she added in the face of Simone's obvious annoyance.

"He only talks about ballet in the lessons." That was true. The teacher part of Aleks was most focused, and actually quite stern, until the end of class. I didn't like lying and had planned to tell the truth whenever possible.

"Simone Conner," drawled Justin. "Are you all warm and squidgy for the Zolotov?"

"No," she snapped. "But he's going to be our main teacher, and we don't know much about him other than his career."

"We've all wondered what he's like in bed, of course," said Justin dreamily.

"I haven't," commented Will.

"Someone as good looking as that?" said Sadie. "Bound to be all about himself."

This nasty remark about Aleks caused me to examine the short girl in a slightly different light. Her hair was an unattractive colour of brown, so dull it appeared dark grey. It sat like a bowl over her unintelligent bovine features.

Justin gazed at me as he spoke. "Cock-centric, you think, Sadie? I wonder..."

"Aren't all men?" said Sun with a laugh.

"What do you think, Phi?" asked Justin. "Any thoughts, my lovely?"

"Yes. I think you and Sadie are going to thoroughly enjoy the new piece you'll be dancing together: the sexy, sexy *Sarabande*."

The statement attracted questions about the new pas de deux and the other partnerings that Aleks had planned, and most people were not pleased. I could see that Will was thinking Simone would be taller than him when she stood en pointe, Justin that Sadie was going to be heavy, and Simone was jealous that I was with Aleks. Sun and the quiet boy – I hoped someone would say his name soon – merely smiled at each other.

My phone rang. "Ah, you are travelling," said Aleks. "I hear the noise."

"Yes."

"She nearly missed the train," Justin said, leaning forwards towards the phone.

"Did you? This is very irresponsible, Malphia."

"I'm on it now," I said, getting up and walking out of the carriage to stand beside the train doors.

"You knew I was worried." He sounded different speaking from the echoey old castle, dismal and, as he put it: "Far away, you are so far away. I feel the distance like a physical pain, and it is so cold here."

Two people went past and into the small toilet.

"I'm getting closer all the time," I told Aleks.

"Yes, this is how I shall think of it now. I have allocated bedrooms. Yours is the best."

"That may not have been a good idea. I'm already unpopular."

"I will make it alphabetical."

It wasn't until I disconnected the call that the people going into the toilet cubicle registered properly in my mind. Back in the carriage, it was indeed evident that Justin and the quiet boy were absent. I confided what I'd seen to Will.

"No way."

"Well, that's what it looked like. I can't believe it. He was with his sort-of boyfriend yesterday, and he's always very devoted and true."

"Well, desperate times, though, aren't they? Could be cold and lonely for us all."

Justin returned. I looked out of the window and sucked in my lips to avoid laughing. It was no good. I had to blurt. "Justin, were you in the toilet with the quiet boy?"

"Ruaridh?" Halleluiah! "Yes," he said with some sadness.

"Doing what?" I asked, possibly inappropriately.

"Snogging."

"Wow," I said. "So, is this a thing now?"

"No. We have agreed. There's no chemistry. It's going to be a bloody long haul in frigging freezing Scotland."

"Will's thinking the same thing."

"Oh, yes. Sir William of Shagsalot. How are you going to manage?"

"What d'you mean?" asked Will.

Justin snorted. "We watched you shag your way round college. This is all you've got to choose from now." He gave a wave round our group. "Our girl here is taken, and Sunshine bats for the other side. Simone and my hefty new partner over there are the only available women."

"I didn't shag my way round anywhere."

"Sweet William, we saw. Well, I did. I trained Phi in the art of observation. Their broken-hearted little faces in roll call? You're a cruel man, Hearst."

"No," said Will. "It wasn't like that. I've just never done the relationship thing."

"Prince of the one-night stands?" asked Justin. No reply was offered. "Watch out, Willyboy. It only takes one girl to steal your heart and tame you. I've seen it happen to a king of the one-nighters recently."

"It's not going to be just us, though, is it?" I pointed out, wanting to direct the conversation away from Aleks. "There'll be other people about."

"Ooh, yes, men in kilts!" Justin was happy again. "Scotland's crawling with them. Isn't that right, Ruaridh?"

"Not really," Ruaridh said. "Best chance of seeing them is at a wedding."

I liked Ruaridh's gentle Scottish accent and friendly face, and was sure he was nicer than Edward in every way.

"Well, we'll just have to arrange a marriage," declared Justin. "Phi, if your current model won't step up, remember Hearst has already offered to take you off my hands for a cupcake." He inspected Will. "We can clean him up a bit. Put him in a kilt, maybe? He should have the legs for it, with all the ballet. Though I've always suspected he might be hiding some sort of..." – he lowered his voice to a whisper – "inadequacy, under those trackie bottoms. That could put a dampener on the wedding night."

"Hey," complained Will. "I'm equipped."

"I'd check that before you commit to anything, Phi," advised Justin.

"I'm going for a walk up the train," I said, having had quite enough of the bizarre discussion.

It had been my intention to spend some time alone, so it was annoying when Will chose to join me. However, he was relaxed company, and we soon stood in another space between carriages, looking out at another city as the train slowed to a stop. "What a shame there's not time to get out and look round," I noted. "We're only getting to see industrial bits of all these towns near stations. It makes me realise I've never been anywhere."

"Didn't you used to go on posh holidays with your parents?"

"We would fly somewhere hot and hang around a beach and pool for two weeks. I wasn't allowed to eat or have any sort of fun. You remember my mother?"

He laughed. "Loved me, didn't she?"

"Don't worry. She only likes vile people."

"What's she think of you doing this then, going up north?"

"Umm..."

"You haven't told her?"

"D'you think I should?"

He shrugged.

We stood to the side to let people on and off. The train moved again. I caught glimpses of a big station clock, a newsagents shop, and a mother dragging a small child along the platform. My parents did sometimes call round to our flat, always unannounced, always askance at something: the mess, Justin's pyjamas, or the fact I'd still been in bed at eight-thirty on a Sunday morning.

I braced myself and hit call. "Hi, Mum. Yes, I know, I've been really busy. No, he was a complete bastard. I explained that." I took the phone away from my ear and glared at it for a moment. She was still talking when I replaced it.

"Anyway," I said over the Gavin gush. "I've something to tell you. I'm going away to study at another school. Yes, a ballet school. Yes, a good one. Nothing. It won't cost you anything. We've been having lessons from one of the teachers already, Aleksandr Zolotov. No? Well, look him up." Perhaps that wasn't such a good idea. "Will and Justin are coming too." I held the phone back to avoid damage to my ears. It was hard to tell which boy she disliked more.

She set off on a disparaging rant about my bad taste in friends. I did a little dance with the phone, waved it around my head and out the window. Eighties-style disco moves twirled while Will laughed. I listened to part of a talk on my general irresponsibility and lack of concern for others, and then felt the buzz of a text. "Sorry, Mum. Have to go. Thanks for the support."

"She hasn't changed much then," said Will.

I read Aleks's text and struggled to maintain a bland expression. We would make love under the stars? Was that likely in somewhere so cold? I sent a question mark in response and pocketed the phone.

The afternoon felt cosy. Ruaridh and I read books, Sun and Sadie fetched tea and coffee for everyone, and Will rubbed my feet.

"You're good at that, Hearst."

"I'm good at a lot of things, Malph."

Green fields and cows whipped by. There was a muted 'ooh' when the choppy sea came into view and much amazement at the wild craggy bays and cliffs. Everyone grew quiet, lost in contemplation. A ruined castle struck a dark silhouette against the greying sky, but it wasn't the place of our destination.

The train hurtled along, unstoppable, and headed to, what, exactly? An adventure. I could do that. A new country. That too, was conceivable. But what were Aleks and I doing? The intensity of our relationship became terrifying as I watched the sky grow darker yet. I panicked. I curled up with my phone in the tiny bathroom cubicle and spoke to him.

He was comforting. He was kind. He assured me that living together as we would be at the castle would remove any confusion or doubt we might be feeling. We would have our own bedrooms for personal space. He said it would be quiet. He said it would be calm and good and wonderful. And I believed him.

Part Two

Castle

Chapter 11

Anticipation mounted. The journey felt slower as it got later, and it was a tired and disgruntled group of people who dragged their bags onto the platform in Aberdeen. We were greeted by a friendly seeming plus-size woman who talked gibberish, and a stick-thin man with receding, oiled-back hair. No Aleks. An hour's minibus journey lay ahead.

We followed the man and woman along the long platform. There were old wooden slats and riveted steel bars above, none of the modernity of Kings Cross. As we travelled through the open space of the main station, Justin screeched: "Oh my God! There's a bomb!"

Other passengers and a ticket inspector turned in alarm as we inspected the gold-coloured artillery shell. The old warhead was being used as a charity collection tin. Everyone relaxed and continued on their way towards the exit.

"Still," said Justin. "Who displays a bomb in a station? In this day and age? What sort of barbaric northern hole have we come to? I mean, Phi, I came to support you. You know ballet's not really my thing, but if it's going to be— Oh, thank God."

We stepped out of the station and into a very large, very bright shopping centre where Justin immediately wanted to buy a retro neon wristwatch, but it was established that there was not time for shopping. The bus was waiting. Or that was what I hoped the friendly lady had intimated with her unintelligible words and slightly more understandable gestures.

It was. Out in the car park, a white minibus awaited. We piled in and set off. We passed huge boats in the harbour, orange and blue and white. Then: grey streets, small shops, a view of the sea to the right, and finally we were out into the countryside. The bus windows displayed expansive but bleak spaces in an ever-darkening damp world. Justin's alternative rendition of *She'll be Coming Round the Mountain* did nothing to raise spirits. "Come on, join in," he encouraged us. "Anyone? Sun? She'll be coming with a woman when she..." No one was amused. "Simone? Who wants to come with Aleksandr when she—?"

I gave him a push.

The unintelligible woman turned round in her seat to look at us. "Fa's the veggie?" she asked.

We all looked at her blankly.

"The veg-e-tar-ian," she enunciated.

"Oh, me," I said, as if confessing a crime.

"Aye." She looked me up and down.

Simone giggled. "So much for vegetarianism being slimming."

The woman turned to her. "I'm een ana." But what that meant, nobody knew.

"How did you know?" I asked the woman. "I don't remember anything about food on the questionnaire."

"Yon Ukrainian manny telt me."

"Aleks?" said Simone, understanding something. "So, Amalphia. You didn't just speak about ballet with him if he knew that?"

"We did talk about food," I admitted.

"Maybe in his car?" suggested Simone. "That last Tuesday of term?"

The bus turned sharply through grand and ornate gates, fortuitously distracting everyone. The bright headlights allowed a glimpse of metal scrolls entwined with bunches of cast-iron fruit and flowers. Two majestic stone pillars, one topped with a mermaid and the other with a fearsome-looking bear, loomed large for a second and then were gone. It was properly dark between the densely packed trees that lined both sides of the single-track road. Everyone was quiet, looking ahead, awaiting the first view of the castle.

It burst into sight, all pink and floodlit at the end of the forest tunnel. The building was made up of various segments: a main square block, an imposing round tower at the back and a long flat part to the right. A familiar figure sat on the steps below the many brightly lit narrow windows and little gun-loop holes. He ground a cigarette out with his foot, and the intimidating grandeur of the place faded.

Vaguely aware of the scent of pine trees and wood smoke as I got off the bus, I wanted to run over for a hug, but couldn't. This was the first time that the secretive nature of our relationship had seemed problematic, or like a big deal. Forcing myself to look away from Aleks, I dragged my suitcase awkwardly over the gravel and listened to the others exclaim about the magnificence of the place.

Up the castle steps we went and into a huge entrance hall. The thick medieval door banged shut behind us, metal studs glinting in the light, and everyone was awed into silence. A wide stone staircase lay at the back of the room, winding up to who knew where. The ceiling was high and ornately corniced. Carved stone angels flew round the perimeter; some sounded trumpets while others held their hands wide as if offering blessings or protection. There were large double doors on either side of the foyer and an elevator at the back, providing transport to the top of a turret, perhaps? The black-and-white parquet floor looked like a giant chessboard and spoke of games, old and new.

"How was your journey?" enquired Aleks, having come in with us.

Justin answered him. "Boring as sin. Hearst asking Phi to marry him was the highlight of the day."

"A cake-related joke," I pointed out, but Aleks didn't smile.

"Aye, weel, ye'll get yer dinner in an oor," barked the friendly woman. "In there." She indicated the doors to the left. "Hae a winner aboot first, like. See yer rooms."

"Yes, indeed." The receding man spoke perfect English, though seemed even worse at eye contact than me. He addressed his words slightly to the left of our group. "Explore, and after dinner we'll have an introductory talk and get properly acquainted."

"Your rooms are all in tower, with names on doors," said Aleks, pointing to the stairway. "Mine too, as I am one of the research participants also. Just like you."

But no one was listening to him. At the mention of our bedrooms, my fellow students had all taken off towards the stairs at great speed. I shot Aleks a wide smile and then followed everyone else.

Up and round we walked, passing an open corridor to the left. The first door we came to bore a paper name tag: William.

"I have the shortest climb," said Will.

We all peered into the room. I walked over the plush blue carpet, then admired the large double bed and antique looking furniture. "I hope we all have one of those," I said, pointing to the ensuite bathroom.

I ran up the steps, passing many other labelled doors, including 'Aleks' just below my own at the very top. My room was much bigger than Will's. Thick red carpet gave way to a wooden floored area with a barre. The walls were rounded as was the barre. The dome of a ceiling was topped with a hexagonal window that showed black sky. It was mesmerising to stare up through the top of the roof, and Justin soon joined me in the activity.

"Two words," he said. "Preferential treatment."

"It's alphabetical."

"And what was with Zolotov making out he's one of us, downstairs just now. No one's going to believe that of a teacher."

"He was just being welcoming," I said, feeling quite defensive on Aleks's behalf.

"You've landed on your feet here, Phi," said Sun, coming into the room and ending the conversation. "Bit heavy on the male-power symbolism, though, isn't it, us all sleeping in a tower? And look at that!" She lay on the bed to better view the skylight. "No need for a weather app in this room."

"I want to see everything," I said, hoping to find a quiet moment with Aleks, and made my way back down the tower, peeking in on any room where the door was open. Justin's was furnished in red like mine. Round and down I travelled to Will's blue room where he was unpacking or, to be more accurate, tipping the contents of his bag onto the bed.

"Is it true you've got the best bedroom?" he asked.

How had word spread so fast? I admitted the fact as Justin came in.

"Sun is still lying on your bed," he told me. "All starry-eyed about that window. I'd be a bit worried if I were you."

"Why?"

"Let's review. We've already discussed the possible onset of sexual desperation. Then she comes out with all that male-power stuff in your room. What did she mean, anyway? That the tower looks like a cock? Odd thing for a lesbian to notice, surely. Can only have been to get your attention. I'm waiting for her to suggest a girl-on-girl pyjama party that Sadie and Simone will predictably refuse to attend."

"You're still jealous about the room and making no sense," I said. "Isn't Will organised? Unpacking already, look."

"Have you got anything interesting here?" wondered Justin, surveying the bed. "Straight porn's always a laugh. Wait, oh my." He lifted a brown jiffy envelope and emptied it over his head. "It's Christmas!" he shouted as a shower of condoms rained down over him.

I covered my mouth and laughed.

"William," said Justin. "I take my proverbial hat off to you. You had very high expectations of this escapade, didn't you?"

Will shook his head. "I didn't know if there'd be anywhere to buy them, or how long we'd be here. It's meant to be a year, isn't it?"

"Actually, that is very true," said Justin. "Well, we'll all know where to come if we're caught short."

"How many are there?" I asked in wonder, lifting up a handful and letting them fall back onto the quilted blue bedspread. Each ringed square signified future sex for Will. Will would wear... I forced the strange thought flow to a stop.

"Cheaper by the hundred," Will informed us.

"You shouldn't be laughing, Phi," said Justin. "Very important items these. It's an unacceptable risk not to use them. The pill isn't enough. You do know that?"

Not wanting to be called irresponsible twice in one day, I changed the subject. "Anyone else hungry?"

The two boys joined me in the quest for dinner downstairs. The previously indicated doors opened to a vast room with two lines of long tables at one end, and high Gothic windows at the other. The dark wood of the floor had been polished to a shine, and the fireplace to the left would have been big enough to stand in, but it already blazed with flames and warmth. An orange velvet sofa and three soft chairs suggested relaxed reading at the fireside in winter.

The ceiling was higher even than that of the entrance hall but pitched to the centre like a church. A wide serving hatch slid open on the far wall, transforming the room into a grand cafeteria.

Vegetable lasagne was plopped onto my plate by Holly, as we gathered the friendly and unintelligible lady's name was, and it looked creamily delicious.

Sun requested it too. "Time I bit the bullet and gave up meat," she told me. "Fits much better with my beliefs. Is it philosophical for you, Phi?"

I ignored Justin's raised eyebrow, and answered her. "I don't think about it too deeply. It just doesn't make sense that a life had to be lost for me to have a meal."

Simone laughed from further down the queue.

By the time we assembled round the hot fire after dinner, I was almost comatose. My eyelids felt dry and heavy. Squeezing them together only attracted a comment about how weird I looked from Simone. She had managed to flirt with Aleks all through dinner and was once again beside him on the sofa, while I sat between Will and Justin on the rug.

I barely paid any attention to Paul, the thin man, as he explained each and every detail of the shield-shaped coat of arms over the fire. He droned on and on about the relation of local folklore to the labyrinth-style design on the old family crest. Michelle's long diatribe about the research, likewise, passed straight over my head. I took in two facts: firstly that the room we were in was called the great hall, and then that Aleks was going to give us a tour of the castle the next morning. That would be nice, assuming he didn't conduct it hand-in-hand with Simone.

"You all right, Treadwell?"

"Sleepy," I told Will, and then listened to Aleks talk about our timetable and the other teachers who were not there that evening. I didn't look at him, but instead stared into the fire. Flames danced, causing logs to disintegrate to flickering reds and oranges, black at their core.

"Aye well, abodees looking affa tiret." I somehow understood from this that Holly knew we were tired. "Come on!" She clapped her hands. "Off to bed with ye."

Aleks and Simone remained deep in conversation on the sofa as the rest of us got up to go.

The stairs felt harder to climb this second time, and my bedroom seemed less beautiful. The complimentary toiletries in the ensuite bathroom smelled alien and cold. The bed felt that way too, and it was a long time before the door opened. Aware that my attitude was childish, I lay motionless as if asleep, though uncurled my legs a little to accommodate his.

"Stay sleeping," he whispered.

Aleks's breathing evened out after a short while, but an age elapsed before I relaxed under the starless black sky.

Chapter 12

THE CEILING WINDOW SHOWED bright blue. A silver star twinkled in a corner, a remnant of the night before. A smile passed fleetingly across Aleks's dreaming face. I got out of bed with care, so as not to wake him.

The worn pink granite of the window surrounds felt pleasingly uneven and rough under my fingers. Expansive woodland was visible through the three narrow panes of glass. I stood up on a soft chair to get a better view and gasped at the fairy-tale roofscape that lay below and to the left of the tower. The gable of the great hall rose high to the front, a huge chimney boasted diminutive battlements, and other lower layers of pink castle sprawled out haphazardly in front of me. There were three small turrets, upended cones that had been meticulously finished round and round with ever smaller and smaller lichen-dotted tiles. Tiny mismatched windows blinked in the sun: circles, squares, and one narrow bent rectangle. Sections of roof ended randomly, some with mossy little steps to nowhere; one jutting brick triangle had been shaped to fit the side of a sloping turret. The higgledy-piggledy nature of the scene reminded me of a drawing one of my smaller pupils had given me on my last day of teaching in London.

Enchanting as the rooftop was, my eye was drawn back to the woods. A footpath between trees suggested walks and fresh air and solitary adventure. I wanted to run up the path and started pulling on clothes with that intention.

"What are you doing?" Newly woken and seemingly exasperated, Aleks held up the alarm clock. My explanation didn't change his expression. "Ah, it will be cold," he said. "There is mud, rocks, trees, nothing else. Here..." He patted the bed beside him. "Is warm and nice."

The forest pathway forgotten in an instant, I skipped straight over to him. Delighted to find him naked, I began kissing down the Aleks pathway instead. I loved the feel of the hairs below his belly button and rubbed my cheek against them as I waited for him to stop me, because he always stopped me. Feeling as if my bluff had been called, I smiled back round at him but found his face serious.

"You really want this?" he asked.

"Yes," I answered at once, for it was never actually a bluff, though... I looked down, unsure of where to begin or exactly what to do. Kissing. Kissing was always good.

He kept his eyes shut as I continued my exploration, negating any concerns about the position being unflattering. I revelled in the chance to experiment, and the deeper level of intimacy this development surely indicated. The process that had started with a kiss on a train was ongoing. Being with Aleks was stretching me, propelling me into new and deeply sexual ways of being.

The realisation was profound and a little overwhelming, and then Aleks pulled away and put a stop to everything. For a fleeting second I thought we were moving on to our more usual ways of being together, but he sprang back from me and into unexpected action. A thorough search of trouser pockets took place, and he got back into bed with his phone.

"There is hour before breakfast if you still want to go on your walk," he said, gesturing in the direction of the windows but not raising his eyes from the small glowing screen.

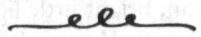

I stood outside the room feeling the chill of the stone step, despite my boots and socks. I'd pulled on yesterday's clothes and exited the room as fast as possible. Neither of us had spoken again. But now many questions circled around me. Had I just been dismissed? From my own room? Or found lacking in some way? Had I done something wrong? I had no desire to open the door and ask, so I decided to avoid further analysis of the situation completely. Running was an altogether preferable option, and I hurtled down the spiralling stairs, the sound of my feet echoing off the curved plaster walls.

An abrupt halt was reached when someone stepped out of their room, and I almost knocked both of us down the rest of the stairway.

"Treadwell, you sounded like a herd of elephants. Oh." Will's words came to an abrupt stop as he looked at me. "You okay, babe?"

"Going for a walk. There's a path. I saw a path from the window."

"I'll come with you."

We crept across the entrance hall and suppressed laughter as our hands fumbled with the various locks on the enormous front door. If there was an alarm, it was silent. The gravel outside was loud and crunchy, the grass beyond soft, and we soon located a path between the trees in front of the castle.

"I don't think this is the one I saw," I said. "But it'll do."

All was quiet among the old knarled trees, an earthy smell adding to the mystical atmosphere of the forest. My fingers brushed soft moss and crispy lichen, and then avoided a wet-looking mushroom. A white owl screeched and flew low over us, causing me to grab Will's hand in fright. It landed on a high branch and swivelled its head to gaze down. "Wow," I mouthed, and we continued along the winding path, which in due course led to a small lake. We stood as still and silent as our surroundings for a moment, the water a black mirror, reflecting the half-naked grey trees of autumn. Here and there smatterings of yellow leaves clung on, bright little lights in the gloom, the contrast even more dramatic when replicated in the dark pool.

I crouched to touch the surface of the lake, scooped a handful of cold water up and discovered it to be quite clear. Something moved in my fingers and I shrieked. "An eel or a fish! I think it had legs."

"Wasn't an eel or a fish then, was it?" Will hunkered down too, and we stared into the dark depths. "Never seen you with your hair down before," he said, taking some of it in his fingers. "Soft."

I reached out and stroked backwards across the top of his head. The short hair sprang back under my hand. "Yours feels just how I always thought it would." I looked back into the rippled water and saw us sitting, hands out, leaning towards each other—

"Aye."

We both jumped at the voice that sounded so close but originated from the other side of the water, a little distance away. The old man continued to speak and then smiled. Not one word did we understand.

"We're staying at the castle," I volunteered, not wanting to seem unfriendly in incomprehension.

"Aye," the man said again. "Ye winna aways be sae glaiket." He turned and walked away into the wood at his side of the lake.

It all became terribly funny. Will stumbled over and almost fell into the pool which only increased the hilarity. We ran back through the wood, startling the moon-faced owl, but had to stop, breathless and bent over with laughter.

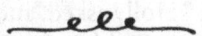

Breakfast was well underway when we walked into the large dining hall. One of the long tables was obviously for staff, but Aleks wasn't at it. He sat with Simone at the students table. She chatted happily. He listened intently. They didn't glance our way.

"Far have you twa bin?" Holly got up from a table, and we followed her to the canteen.

"We went for a walk," I told her. "Found a lake."

"At's a loch up here, ye ken." As she offered me a green smoothie and disgusted Will with the same, the language clarified a little. Some of it was English with a twist.

We found places on the bench by Justin and Sun at the far end of the student table.

"So, wis the water all black like?" asked Holly, sitting beside us.

I nodded.

"That's the Deil's Pool you found. De-vil's Pool," she translated. "There's lots of devil's places nearby. There's the Deil's Lum at the beach, an affa dangerous cave, spouts sea spray like smoke. Aye, he's bin busy roon aboot here. But yon pool, it's supposed to be haunted by three witches who take the form of mermaids to enchant ye. One of them is an ancestor of mine, so watch yersels!"

"There was this little dude showed up." Will laughed as he spoke.

"You met another human being, out here, in the sticks?" Justin enquired.

"Like a little elf," I said. "He popped up on the other side of the lake... loch... devil's pool."

Justin's face showed delight. "An elf? Tall, thin, blond, sexy?"

"More like a gnome," said Will.

"A little old man," I explained. "He wore a purple bobble hat and he spoke to us."

"Do tell." Justin's tone was rich with disappointment.

"Affa short manny?" Holly asked, and I decided 'affa' must mean very. "That'll've bin auld Jackie Buchan. Nobody ever sees him. You were right honoured. Fit did he say?"

"Hang on, I've got it..." Just like Simone had Aleks's full attention. "He said: 'You won't always be so... glaiket.'"

The last word had Holly in stitches.

"Is it bad?" I asked. "What does it mean?"

"Oh aye. It's Doric. The language we spik up here," she explained. "Glaiket means stupid, canna see what's right in front of your face."

"Bloody cheek," said Will.

"That pool's possibly an ancient Pagan site with a name and story like that," Sun informed us. "Knock me up next time you go out."

"Darling," said Justin. "You overestimate Phi's virility if you think she can knock you up. Mind you, a turkey baster from the kitchen, and one of Hearst's used condoms, and we could get a big happy family going here."

The shocked silence that followed this was broken by Simone. "This is the uncivilised end of the table then," she said with a sneer, standing by Aleks's side. It was time for the tour of the castle.

"To the dungeon!" announced Aleks in a dramatic voice, then leading the way out of the hall and into the foyer.

Michelle joined us, and we all crammed into the small elevator which was the only way down. The rest of the building had felt cold. Entering the dungeon was like being immersed in far icier water than Will and I had encountered earlier. Heavy metal doors led to an enormous underground cavern. Six square pillars held up the ceiling. Aleks said something about it being the biggest dance studio in the UK. Michelle said things about the space having been an old storage area. Apparently it had also been used as emergency sleeping quarters in times of disaster, and a hospital ward during the Second World War.

All I could see was the back wall. Historical implements of war hung against the large uneven stones: swords, shields, a pickaxe, chains with thick handcuff ends, and a rusty spear. A blue-and-black tartan wrap was draped innocuously among the rest.

I walked round, the voices of the others a distant hum, and touched a spiked ball of dark metal. The smell of iron merged with a scent of woodland, like blood mixed with earth. The wall displayed sharp things, impossible-to-escape-from things, and those designed to maim or kill. They were not replicas, I was sure of it. The horror of their reality gurgled in my stomach, the breakfast smoothie quickly turning to acid.

"Minging down here, isn't it?" said Will.

Justin found the chains and pretended to be captured. "Is this what happens if we're bad? Very, very bad?" It wasn't funny.

Aleks played the grand piano, but its echoey quality only added to the nightmarish atmosphere of the place.

I studied a small stone family crest on the wall, like the one we'd been shown by the fireplace the previous night. A plump mermaid and a rearing bear regarded each other across a labyrinth design, while three thistles sat under them. The cutesy heart that topped it off seemed an ill-fitting motif for a family that decorated their walls with devices of torture.

"They were real people," said Michelle from right behind me, making me jump. "The Mermaid and the Bear. The family crest was redesigned to mark their marriage in the sixteenth century. The angels in the foyer date from that time too. Are you all right, Amalphia?" she asked, studying my face, her expression that of a dark owl, big-eyed and alert to its prey.

"She's tired. We were up really early," answered Will, seemingly my only ally in the dank place, and Michelle backed off.

It was good to squeeze into the sardine tin of an elevator again, and be squashed and warm between Justin and Will. The doors to the right of the foyer took us into the newer extension part of the castle. A long hallway led through to an impressively large swimming pool. I imagined Simone falling in and looking like a drowned rat. We were shown round a small and modern theatre, all black and square and minimalist, and then Aleks marched us up the stairs, and we took the corridor to the left before the bedrooms.

There were three normal-sized studios on the first floor. They were light and airy and nice. I hoped one of these would be where morning class took place, but somehow doubted it. Next came a room filled with weights and other gym equipment.

"That's more like it," whispered Will.

Justin's delight appeared in the meditation room with all the touchy-feely glitz. Colour-changing lights, spherical chairs and a fish tank in the wall made the world feel surreal again, though less scary than the dungeon. Michelle put on wafty music and talked about the musical notes it contained. We would focus on a different tone each week but always return to the first one, the one used in Amalgamation C.

"Did she say UT?" asked Will.

"UT," nodded Justin.

Michelle believed the ancient tone of UT could help us manifest our deepest desires through the banishment of guilt and fear.

"Ooh, err," said Justin.

"You may also find answers coming to you, questions being answered," continued Michelle. "There are early indications that this specific combination of sound and movement stimulates an area of the brain used for collating information, or maybe it just allows you to access your own innate wisdom."

"Place gets weirder," murmured Will.

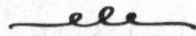

Class was short for our first day, which was just as well as it meant a return to the dungeon.

"You like it, Amalphia?" asked Aleks at the end of the lesson.

"Not down here, I don't, no."

"It is strange without windows," he replied. "And we have to dodge the pillars."

Michelle's research, also taking place in the dungeon studio, came next. We were handed little metal-filled stickers and shown how to affix them to our scalps. Paul sat in keen anticipation at the front of the gargantuan studio, three laptops in front of him on a table. It was better away from the barre, further from the wall of artifacts. The best aspect of the research was that it all took place in the centre of the room. There were several amalgamations to learn, all as odd as the first, but none producing any strange effects.

Aleks took part in the class and the research too. "I am student also now," he told us with a smile. "In some classes."

"Hopefully it'll keep you out of mischief this term," Michelle said to him.

I sat by Justin at lunch in the great hall and watched Simone put her hand on Aleks's arm. "Is it just me?" I asked my friend. "Am I being paranoid and jealous?"

"No, sweetheart. He's doing nothing to discourage her. I fear we may be witnessing what the internet warned us of in the beginning. That blog woman said he was an awful flirt."

It was true. Aleks appeared to be not so much 'putting up with' as 'lapping up' Simone's attention. He was smiling, laughing and talking animatedly.

"Some men work like that," said Justin. "Grand passion for a few weeks, and then they just drift off to someone else. Isn't that right, Hearst? Love 'em and leave 'em. That's your motto, isn't it?"

"No," said Will, laying his tray beside us and sitting down.

"Oh, come on. However, you could come in handy. What's that old saying? The best way to get over one idiot is to get under another."

I stared down at my lunch, unable to eat, or think, or feel.

"Is your bloke being a prick, or something?" asked Will.

Justin nodded. "An astute assessment, young William. Look at her. What's she left with? A handful of magic beans and a head full of confusion. At least they were good beans; no throwing them out the window now, Phi. We don't want a beanstalk that grows the latest phones or a tree that sprouts designer watches and T-shirts... Wait! What am I saying?" He waffled on, allowing me to remain silent and stare fixedly at the table for the rest of the meal.

Afternoon pas de deux class introduced us to another teacher. Mr. Timms, who must have been at least eighty, exuded olde-world English charm in a dithering way. He said nice things about my line as we tried out lifts with different partners.

Then came the rehearsed piece with Aleks, the sexy *Sarabande*. The room was collectively gobsmacked as we demonstrated the balletic metaphor of lovemaking. The wonderful music of Bach filled the huge cavernous room, and I concentrated hard to get everything right. As ever, Aleks partnered chivalrously, a charming gentleman, but this time it felt cold like everything else in the castle.

Michelle interfered. She wanted Will with me, and Simone with Aleks.

"This is not your class," Aleks reminded her.

"Funding takes precedence over everything, Aleks. Read your contract. I need to see this piece, these partners."

He threw up his hands. I walked happily over to Will. Our partnership was simpler, easier, or in fact: "Awesome," as Will declared afterwards.

We were sent to have a swim after pas de deux, which would have been a pleasant way to end the day had circumstances been different. Simone glided up as I paused for breath at the edge of the pool, having just done seventeen speedy lengths. "Have you heard, Amalphia?" she said. "I'm going to be having private lessons with Aleks instead of you now. Things are so much better now we're here, aren't they?"

I managed twelve more lengths before Paul called for attention. "We have a surprise for you all tonight," he said. "Keep your brain monitors on if you can. If they come off, see me at dinner. We maybe didn't think the swimming through." He looked at Michelle who shook her head as if he spoke nonsense.

"Girls, make your way to the first floor," she ordered. "Boys, you head through to the theatre."

Chapter 13

S IMONE RAN AHEAD, AND we soon heard her shriek. "Oh my God, oh my God, oh my God!"

One of the first floor studios was full of clothes. Dresses hung on a portable railing, and shoe boxes were piled against the wall. Holly smiled, as did the two young women with her. "We're having a traditional Scottish Ceilidh tonight, quines," she said, and I got the feeling she was trying to speak very correctly. "Dancing, music, whisky and wine."

Oh no. Oh no. Oh no.

We'd only been here a day. And parties were happening already?

Numb with horror, and hoping events like this weren't going to be a regular occurrence, I chose a black dress with no frills or complicating detail. Simone looked striking in many-seamed red velvet. It accentuated her pale blonde hair which she wore loose, as if she weren't beautiful enough already. The two women, introduced as hair and make-up artistes, did my hair up with clips and hairspray. I watched them put red lipstick on Simone.

"Dinna worry. We'll do subtle and sultry for you," one of them told me, and I closed my eyes to endure.

Sun, Sadie, Simone and I walked down the stairs arm in arm, followed by the hairdressers and Holly who were all attending the party too. "Everybody is," Holly told us. "Aye, you'll hae some bonny loons to dance with tonight."

The boys (bonny loons?) waited in the entrance hall, the quick upturn of their faces giving the impression they'd been there a while. They were likewise transformed, all in smart suits except for Ruaridh who was resplendent in a green-and-grey kilt. Aleks surveyed us. He looked so handsome, and so at home in formal wear, it felt somehow shocking.

"Well?" said Simone, assuming a hip-tilting pose.

"Beautiful," he replied.

"We're to escort you in to dinner," said Justin. "I'm starving. What took you so long?" He held out his arm, and I grabbed hold.

Aleks was already paired with Simone, and he looked at home there too.

"Phi, you look like a proper girl," said Justin, inspecting me. "Did they give you some tit-pushing-up bra, or something?"

Simone released her vice-like grip on Aleks's arm and marched over to us. "For just one night, Justin Bevan, could you stop with all the crassness?"

Justin was open-mouthed in his offence and whispered, "What a bitch," as Simone walked back to Aleks, and we all headed into the great hall.

The huge room was painfully busy with people. When had they arrived? Presumably while we were swimming, or changing. It was all very unnerving.

Justin expressed loud delight at the presence of so many men in kilts and rushed off to mingle among them.

"You are breathtaking." Aleks's voice was quiet behind me.

I turned to make sure he was actually speaking to me. "Really," I said, doubting his sincerity.

"Of course, really."

I studied his face. He frowned.

Paul announced dinner and beckoned everyone over to the tables which were looking much fancier than they had earlier, with high-backed chairs and beautiful white tablecloths. My mood sank lower as I saw that the seating was pre-designated. Being stuck between two kilted strangers could be a nightmare, but luck was mine in this one thing.

"Malph, you're by me," called Will. "Looking super-hot by the way."

"You look nice too," I told him, sitting down in the chair next to him.

He grimaced as I straightened his bow tie.

"Feel a right idiot in this get up," he said. "Tried to get out of it, but it's in our contract. Can you believe that? The wearing of formal attire at events is mandatory."

"Hi, A-malp..." The kilted man on my left struggled to read the name on the place card.

"Phi is easier," I advised.

His name was Ross, and he was young with dark hair, thick eyebrows and smiling eyes that frequently slid down to my chest as we spoke. His accent was strongly Scottish but much easier to understand than Holly's. I liked his black lace-up shirt, finding it evocative of ancient Highlanders and clansmen. It was much less formal than Ruaridh's gold-but-toned jacket, though I liked that too.

"So, you're a ballerina?" Ross asked.

"Not quite."

"She will be," said Aleks from across the table where he sat between Simone and Holly.

"I'll get to see you dance later," said Ross. "I'm a fiddler."

"What?"

"I play the fiddle in a folk band. We're doing the music tonight."

Paul tapped his wine glass for attention. "Before the cel-ebratory meal of haggis, neeps and tatties, please fill your glasses! There's a range of single malts and blended whiskies on the table. Help yourselves and enjoy."

"Which would you like?" Ross asked me.

"I don't drink." It made me chatty which was misleading, and then people were disappointed when they met me sober.

"You have to," stated Michelle from further up the table, wearing some sort of sparkly red ball gown. "You're under contract. We have your standard brain patterns now, and we're interested to see the inebriated ones. It'll just be this once," she added less harshly.

"We're being paid to get pissed?" said Will. "Bring it on." And he proceeded to help himself from the nearest bottle, and offered to fill my glass too.

"Ah, no," intervened Ross from the left, pushing the proffered whisky away with a fingertip. "Try this one. It's smooth and smokey, made just up the road with grain from my farm."

Determining that I would try not to talk too much, I lifted the dark golden drink, took a sip and spluttered.

"Put cola in it, babe," advised Will. "It's better." Liquid was poured from the right. At least it was sweet.

"Is there diet cola?" asked Simone, causing me to splutter in a different way.

"This is how it's done," announced Ross, knocking back a glass of neat whisky in one go. "Such skill only comes with years of practice," he informed me. "Much like your dancing, I would imagine."

I smiled over at Aleks, thinking he would find the comment funny, but he was busy refilling his own glass. Drinking standard set, male competition was in the air. Even Justin was sucked in. I heard him telling Ruaridh the whisky tasted like spicy juice.

Three large haggises, or haggii as Ross said the plural was, were placed on the table along with dishes of mashed potatoes and turnips.

"Isn't that, like, a sheep's testicle?" asked Justin in a queasy voice.

"Actually the stomach," said Paul, then listing the other intestinal ingredients of haggis.

"That's the veggie een for us," said Holly to me. "Beans and oats and pepper."

Some of the others raided our vegetarian haggis but not Will, Aleks, or Ross, the farmer, who kept topping up my whisky. Head buzzing, I sat in the middle of a male triangle that pushed and pulled in different ways: Aleks looked at me but spoke to Simone, Will asked if I was okay, and Ross had a very interesting conversation about the local area with my cleavage.

The meal concluded with cranachan for pudding which consisted of raspberries, cream and yet more whisky. The band assembled, but Ross stayed with us to teach the dances. "My charming dinner companion will partner me for the Gay Gordons," he said, taking my hand.

"What's that now?" asked Justin. "Did I hear that wrong?"

Once it was confirmed that he had heard right, he cajoled Ruaridh into dancing with him. "Phi gets a man in a kilt; so do I; it's only fair."

Off we went round the room. The constant changes of direction were perplexing and arm tangling. A range of reels had us spinning in circles, forming lines and skipping up and down with our partners. I liked dancing with Ross. He was very non-ballet and rough round the edges, but patient and humorous in his teaching manner. I did not like the behaviour of Aleks and Simone who kept laughing at the Scottish dances.

Ross eventually took his place with the band. The lights dimmed as the whisky and music flowed on.

Justin and I sat down on chairs at the side of the hall and agreed that we liked the bum-emphasising look of kilts, and the way the garments swung about during dancing.

Simone and Aleks stayed up on the dance floor. She whispered something that made him smile.

"Really hating her now," said Justin.

"She thinks he's single, remember."

"Pish. She was exceptionally rude to me. Did you not hear her?" He assumed a high-pitched voice. "'Just for one night, Justin, don't be a wanker.' I mean to say, look at her."

I looked over at Simone and Aleks as they moved to the music together. She reached up and placed her hands on either side of his face, and then, with a pounce-like movement, she kissed him. Right on the mouth. Kissed him. And then they were gone, hidden by the rest of the dancing crowd.

I stared at the floor, feeling woozy and blank.

Justin rubbed my arm. "Don't cry here, Phi. You've got clarification now and can move on. Find your tartan tit-gazer and have a good snog."

I shook my head at that awful idea as Will appeared and held out his hand. Will was my dear friend, and he would take my mind and eyes off bad things. We swayed to the music, and he hooked my hands round his neck. I leant my head against his shoulder, sad and tired.

"Something to show you," he whispered, pulling me to the side of the hall and up the corridor to the kitchen area. We ran through a disorienting labyrinth of turns and alleyways.

"I found this cupboard thing last night, when I was looking for food," he said, leading us into a small room.

A sturdy Gothic door swung shut behind us with a loud click. Will flicked a switch, and green lights illuminated the floor from below. We walked down four uneven steps and stood at the edge of a glowing glass surface.

"It's safe to stand on," he told me, and we did so. Various sizes of barrels and a big cauldron were artistically arranged in a small underground chamber beneath the glass. Domed alcoves housed dusty green and brown bottles, and there was a box of clay containers with corks that I had a feeling were antique bed warmers.

"Cool, isn't it?" Will said.

"It's a bit creepy and contrived. What's a feature like this doing way back here?" I looked around. A big dresser held pots and bowls, while a pair of flat stone angels decorated the wall above. The angels held a heart that was being pierced by thorns, and one of them pointed a finger towards the floor.

"So, what's up with you, Malph? From where I was standing, it kind of looked like you were looping in a bad way."

I leant back against the table. "My boyfriend's gone off with someone else." I started to cry and wished I could pick the thorns out of my own heart.

"No way," he said, holding me. "Well he's an idiot then, isn't he? Who's more gorgeous than you?"

"Don't say that. You don't mean it." I pushed him away.

"Malph—"

"Don't!" I ran back up the steps only to find the door handle-less and ungiving.

"Oh yeah, I forgot that," he slurred. "That Holly woman let me out before."

"You mean we're locked in here?" Despair turned to plain anger. My high heels clopped down the steps. "We are locked in here?" I repeated.

"Babe, I'm sorry."

"You are not sorry. You're drunk, and you're stupid, and you're a man, just made to hurt women with your handsome faces and nice words. But it's all lies in the end, isn't it?"

I pushed him, and in his drunken state he fell heavily against the dresser causing all sorts of kitchenware to thunder down over him.

The door flew open. Holly and Justin took in the unfortunate scene. I ran up the steps to them and was soon drying my face on a tea towel in a big medieval-looking kitchen. I stared at the blackened stones of a huge fireplace archway as Justin made strong tea and Holly patted my hand.

"Tell us fit happened. You're affa upset aboot something."

"Yes." The image of that kiss seemed to have been branded onto my retinas.

"Tell me," encouraged Holly.

"I just want to go to bed. Where's Will?" His absence was disturbing.

"Dinna you worry aboot him. He'll stew far he is for a bit. He canna get oot."

"He's still shut in the cupboard thing?"

"Aye."

"But I pushed him, and stuff fell on him. He might be hurt."

"And why did ye de that?"

"I was angry about being shut in the room."

The hot tea singed my mouth. What a night of burning liquids and sights.

"I hope you're nae covering up for him."

"Hearst's not the raping kind," said Justin. "An idiot, who got her locked in a cupboard, probably with the idea of getting a snog. But anything else? Can't see it."

"Oh, no," I said, alarmed. "Is that what you're thinking? No snogging, nothing. I was upset, and he showed me the weird floor. Will's my friend, and I was horrible to him." I felt vaguely sick, and the room seemed to shift a bit to the left.

"Aye," said Holly. "You two should get off to bed. Getting you all bleazin' like this wis never a good idea in my book. Come on, there's a back way. Ye dinna have to go through the throng."

The back passage wound round in an arc and came out near the elevator. Justin darted into the great hall, darted back out and got into the lift with me.

"Good idea, yeah?" he asked, holding up a full whisky bottle.

My stomach clenched as I looked from the bottle to the foyer where Aleks and Simone had just appeared. Was another kissing display about to take place? They saw us just as the doors slid shut.

"He might give chase," mused Justin.

"I doubt it."

The doors jerked open at the top of the stairs. "Let's sprint," suggested Justin.

Miraculously, the downward stumble did not result in a limb-snapping tumble, and we made it safely to Justin's very red room.

I had just finished cleansing my face of the itchy make-up when three sharp raps sounded on the door. Justin put his finger to his lips. We sat very still.

"Amalphia? Justin?" Aleks sounded cross.

"Leave him," whispered my friend. "He's another one that could do with stewing."

Ignoring Justin's advice, I walked unsteadily to the door and opened it, interested to see what would happen, and wanting to get it over with rather than lying in bed worrying about it.

"What is this that is happening?" asked a slightly dishevelled Aleks, leaning on the door frame. "Where have you been all night?"

I leant against the wall for support and stared at him, also trying to understand what was happening.

Justin stepped in. "Drop the concerned act, Zolotov. We witnessed the face-sucking."

Aleks shrugged and held his hands up as if in confusion. "She kissed me. I pulled back. It is nothing. A confused moment. You cannot think there is anything else to this? Malphia?" His tone softened as he looked at me from the doorway. "You are so young. Sophisticated people, they laugh and have fun in social situations like tonight. None of it means anything."

Justin was apoplectic. "That's not sophistication, chum. Sticking your tongue down the throat of that cow was sleaze, whatever you're dressing it up as. Now leave us alone, you patronising prick."

"I didn't—" said Aleks, but then Justin slammed the door in his face and locked it too.

My legs gave way and I slid down the wall to sit on the floor. "Is Simone sophisticated?" I asked doubtfully.

"She's a scrawny bitch. Look, we're all pissed. He is too. Let him stew. Good word that. I like that Holly wench. There's a distinct lack of sorry in the Zolotov tonight. Maybe it'll be different tomorrow. And if not? A quick shag with Hearst will make you feel better."

"Justin, please..."

"I'm telling you, it'll be easy. Listen." He took a drag on the whisky bottle and passed the fiery oblivion to me. "You go to his room and ask if you can have a condom. Say it's an emergency."

I choked on the burning drink.

"Watch it, Treadwell. Anyway, then you ask, very politely, if you can stay there and use it. I swear, you won't have to say anything more."

I stood up, with a little difficulty, and smiled at him. "There's only one man's bed I'm headed to tonight." And I walked across the room, got into it and fell asleep almost at once.

Chapter 14

M Y HEAD THROBBED AS if someone were hammering inside it. A memory, something bad, lay just out of reach.
Justin slept peacefully beside me. I padded to his bathroom
to get water, and the hammering sound came again, this time
accompanied by a voice.

"Only me!" called Holly from beyond the door.

The smell of the breakfast tray she carried was unpleasant,
but the orange juice was nice.

"My face is actually melting off my skull," groaned Justin,
sitting up in bed, though he perked up at the sight of toast.

"Aye," said Holly, picking up the empty whisky bottle off the
floor. "You've to do a ballet class. Only a short een," she specified
on seeing our horrified faces. "Bit of dancing with your partners,
I think."

"Well, hopefully that means Will, because..." The sentence
wouldn't complete. The onset of recall was vivid and raw.

"Oh, it winna be him," she said. "I'll let him oot in a bit and
send him to bed."

"He's still in the cupboard? Holly, he didn't touch me. It was
me who hurt him. You've got to let him out. Or I can go and do
it."

She put her hand on my arm. "Dinna upset yersel, quine. I'll
de it. You get ready for your class."

Back in my own room, relieved not to have met anyone on
the stairs, frailty and reluctance contributed to the slowness of
dressing. Justin arrived, and we lumbered down and round together, lamenting that we had not thought to take the elevator.

Class had already begun in the dungeon. Michelle barked at us to take our places behind everyone else at the barre. Aleks ignored us. I tried to focus on technique, but we'd missed the slower warm-up and it was all impossible. Justin and I leant on each other in the centre as Paul gave a diffi-cult-to-follow lecture about alcohol and neurotransmitters and cerebral activity. The gist was that our brains had de-teriorated the more we drank, which hardly seemed like a ground-breaking discovery.

"The only exceptions were Miss Treadwell and Mr. Hearst, who shared a joint clear peak quite late on in the evening," Paul said, fascinated by on-screen squiggles.

"Where is he, anyway?" asked Michelle. "I assumed he was just late like you two." She was painfully loud.

"Oh, um, no," I stuttered. "He's just going to bed now, I think."

"What?" Michelle looked outraged.

"He got shut in a cupboard," I explained. "If you get us all drunk, all sorts is going to happen, isn't it?"

My anger met hers head on, and my eyes met Aleks's in the mirror. He smiled, seemingly taking my words to mean that I was fine with everything now. My brain may have been curdled by alcohol, but he was very wrong about that.

"Well, fine," said Michelle. "You can walk the *Sarabande* through by yourself."

It wasn't feasible. Even if I'd been on peak form, the piece did not work as a solo.

"Maybe we take turns, and swap round partners?" sug-gested Aleks from his place by Simone.

Michelle rejected the idea, and the deep tones of the Bach cello suite filled the huge room. I stood still and watched Justin try to lift Sadie.

"Right, Miss Treadwell," snapped Michelle. "If you're not going to take part, you may as well leave."

That, I was fine about. I exited the room and considered phoning for a taxi and really leaving. But Justin. And Will.

Holly was struggling to lift a large box in the entrance hall. I took one end.

"Kitchen?" I asked and soon found myself back in the scene of the previous night's tea drinking. A long battered table occupied the middle of the room, and an old-fashioned stove sat at the side under the high fireplace archway. Two huge fridges and two big sinks announced that nothing was done by halves in the castle. I could see why Aleks felt so at home in the place.

I told Holly about being ejected from class, and then everything else too, even Aleks, over a mug of tea and a slice of chocolate cake.

"But..." She was astonished. "How auld is he?"

"Auld... that means old, right? Thirty-eight. But he was so different before we came here. I thought he loved me."

"Aye, well. They all say that, don't they?"

A great deal of tea was consumed that day. Holly told me about her ex-husband. He'd been fourteen years older than her and a controlling bully. "Better off without him, quiney, I'm telling ye."

I made cupcakes and lost myself in the sifting and stirring, pausing only when thoughts of Aleks encroached. At lunchtime, his deep voice carried into the haven of the kitchen, though I couldn't make out the words.

"He's wanting to ken where you are," Holly told me. "I telt him: 'That's a quiney needing peace and quiet. You leave well alone.' Didna like that. You bide with me today. I've telt Justin yer here."

At dinnertime I took the back passageway and snuck back to the top of the tower. My evening plans consisted of a bath, a cupcake, pyjamas and bed.

The knocking was quiet, hesitant even, letting me know before I opened the door that it wasn't Aleks.

"Oh, Will, I'm so sorry. I was upset with someone else and took it out on you, and I hope you're not hurt."

Our apologies mingled as we both spoke at once.

"Malph. Did you think—? I mean, I would never— She was talking like—"

"I know. It's been put right. Come in. Share a cupcake?"

"Better not. If I'm caught in your room, I'll end up chained to those things in the dungeon. How is the prick, anyway, the tosser that dumped you? Have you spoken to him today?"

"No."

That was yet to come, which wasn't a good thought. What a difference a train journey had made. We hugged and Will left.

Louder knocking soon preceded an altogether different encounter.

"Malphia," he said at once, sounding quite stern and coming into the room. "There is exist a big misunderstanding here, I think. I am friendly in social situations. Simone matches me this way. This is all."

I stared at him. Speaking was not a possibility. He was completely unapologetic.

"You are jealous?" he asked in response to my silence. "So watch, and see the truth." His voice softened. "It is all just nonsense, my love. But I will leave you to your sulking, if this is what you wish."

My hands shook a little as they shut the door behind him. I wanted to shout after him, 'No, you're just nonsense!' But that wouldn't have made sense. So I stayed quiet. All desire to eat cake had gone. A small sad cupcake sat forlornly on a plate, anti-social and alone.

Aleks's speech replayed. Words whirled, evil dervishes in my head, making less and less sense with repetition. Exhausted but unable to sleep, I wondered if he was passing the night in a friendly and social way, and cried.

The next two days were, indeed, full of nonsense, if that's what it was. Simone and Aleks were delighted with each other. They laughed and chatted their way through mealtimes.

He was professional when teaching, though, even there, changed. "Eyes up, Amalphia," he said, lifting my chin. "Whatever is go on around you, never be let it interfere with your dancing. Learn this, and you will be a stronger artiste."

I looked directly into his eyes, incredulous that he was presenting his bad behaviour as a teaching device. It was almost as if Aleks had become someone else. His face was alive with wicked humour, his cheekbones more angular. Even his eyes had lost their poetic dark hue. He swaggered and strutted and flirted it up in the great hall.

"Read," said Justin at dinner, handing me his phone and a story of nonsense-filled Aleks.

The blog author looked like an older version of Simone. She wrote about how he would do things to deliberately annoy her, and described the way he would look over to check she had noticed.

I glanced up to find him looking at me. He quickly turned back to his conversation with Simone. I kept my face blank, empty of all emotion, and tried to do the same with my heart.

"I can't help feeling this is still all about you," said Justin.

I shook my head. "I don't match him in social ways. Simone does. Why he didn't start a relationship with her to begin with is the only mystery."

"Bastard deserves her, of course. But, see, when you go out of the room, he calms right down and leaves her alone. He does boring things: has a cup of tea at the staff table, talks to Michelle."

"Yes, well. She's his type too."

"Maybe he's used that UT music-note thing so much that he is actually entirely without shame now," mused Justin, as we watched Aleks pour a cup of tea for Simone and smile over at me. He accidentally spilled tea on his own hand. Justin laughed. I did not.

I left the hall in search of my new evening solace: sitting in the small television room with Will. He watched football. I read books from the old bookcase in there. Mysteries. Thrillers. Not romances. Those, I avoided. The others went swimming, the pool still a much-loved novelty. What Aleks did in the evenings, I tried not to imagine.

Chapter 15

Saturday morning felt bright and happy, and I reached for Aleks, wanting him, needing him, and was momentarily confused by his absence. Betrayed by body and mind yet again, I walked into the bathroom for a splash of cold reality.

Someone entered the bedroom without knocking. There was only one person who would assume he was welcome to do that.

"Ah, my angry little sprite. It has gone on long enough now, no?" Of course it was Aleks.

"What?"

"The game," he said from the ensuite doorway. "Is being over. I think is better."

"Game," I repeated slowly. "You're playing a game with me."

He smiled in response, rueful, a naughty little boy awaiting forgiveness.

"I said those words after the amalgamation," I remembered. "That first time we did it back in college. So it was true." Dreadful comprehension dawned, and the pent up emotions of the week released in a fury as the air reddened all about me. "It was a game from the start. But, why?" I asked, looking directly at him, right into his eyes. "Why would you bother to spend all that time with me, tell all those lies about love, and keep up the act for so long? For some final act of cruelty? Is that it? Or was it just fun to mess with the autistic girl? What sort of monster are you, Aleks?"

"Malphia, no! You have this all wrong."

I pushed past him and paced into the bedroom. "Well, maybe that's just my lack of sophistication showing."

He shook his head. "You are just not used to... Your last boyfriend, he is like brute, no?"

I stared at him.

"He is never being friendly with anyone," he continued. "I'm sorry. This I should not say. I am just—"

"Wrong. You're the one that's got it all wrong. Gavin could turn it on for anyone he thought would advance his career. But I would like you to leave now. Go on. Get out."

"If this is what you want. But I think I should stay, and we should talk properly."

"No. You have no right to be here in my room like this. You're my teacher, nothing else now. So, fuck off."

There followed a shocked silence, as if neither of us could quite believe what I'd just said. I never used the f-word. But it felt like the right term for this moment of finality, and for this man.

Loud footsteps sounded on the steps outside, and knocking cut through the volatile atmosphere of the room.

"Malph!" Will called through the door. "It's only gone and snowed!"

I looked up. The ceiling window was topped with crystalline folds of ice.

"We've gotta go out in it, babe."

"Yeah, we do," I agreed, as he turned the handle. "Don't come in here, Hearse."

"You naked, or something?"

"Umm..." I said, not sure whether to tell that lie. The door opened a crack. "I mean it, Will. Don't come in."

"I'm kidding. Hurry up and get dressed. I'll meet you downstairs."

I pulled clothes on top of pyjamas as Will's feet clattered away.

"You are running off in the snow with your friend?" exclaimed Aleks. "You will not stay to sort this out?"

"You've sorted everything out this week," I told him. "But you'd like that, wouldn't you?" Revelations flowed fast, burning like whisky. "You tried to isolate me from my friends, silencing my phone like that before we came here."

"That was absolutely not my intention."

"It could have been the result, though, couldn't it? But my friends are too good for that. Justin? Still right there for me. Will getting shut in that cupboard overnight was my fault. Does he bear me any grudge?"

I gestured towards the door in answer, and sought boots and jacket. "I'm blessed with true friendship. What do you have, Aleks? A stupid game, and Simone. Makes sense. They all look like her, don't they? Your exes." Jacket zipped up, the facts flowed on. "You've been with her all along, haven't you? That last time, here with me; your eyes were shut because you were thinking about her."

He raised his hand, finger pointed upwards. "Is completely not how—"

"More experienced than me, is she, Aleks? The giver of sophisticated blow-jobs? Check... mate!" I shouted over his protestation and then fled.

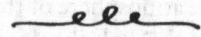

"Finally," said Will as I arrived at the bottom of the stairs and stepped onto the black-and-white chessboard floor of the foyer.

"Don't start," I requested. "I've just had an almighty row with..."

"The prick."

"Yes. When the adrenaline and anger wear off, I may crumble and fall to pieces. So this better be fun and distracting, Hearst."

We opened the door and were half blinded by the low morning sun. The snow was dazzling beneath the orangey light; glittering sparks shone here and there on the fresh and pristine surface. The day had a clean cold smell to it. This was no grey city winter.

We ran out, all negativity banished by the white brilliance. I scooped some snow up and found it joyously easy to squeeze together and lob at the back of Will's head.

"I'll get you for that, Treadwell!"

I ran. He caught up. I tried to push snow down his neck, and we fell, rolling over and over on the ground like children. I sat astride him and laughed, surprised by the happy and carefree turn life had suddenly taken.

A movement to the left had us turn our heads and behold a small deer. We stayed very still so as not to scare her. Another one leapt out of the trees, the larger horned male, majestic and powerful. The doe gave flight, and the stag chased her through a gap in the trees.

We struggled to our feet and sprinted after them. We'd found the path I'd seen that first morning. It took us uphill, through a mature pine plantation. This was a darker and pricklier trail than the other woodland path that led to the pool. The thuds of our feet were muted by layer upon layer of old pine needles, the scent in the air subtle and resinous. Just as I started to fear that we had lost the deer, we stepped out onto a sunny hillside that had several large stones lying around it. They were placed in a circle, some fallen, some pointing up to the sky. A particularly huge boulder was flanked by two flat upright rocks.

As dancers we constantly sought perfect alignment, and that's what was laid out before us that morning. The spacing between the stones, even the ones that had fallen, was faultless and beautiful, as if man and nature had worked together to create an example of exact and impeccable placement. And we were all part of it, the living, breathing beings of the scene: Will and I stood on the outside of the snowy circle while the two deer held corresponding places within.

They gazed at us, then slowly turned and walked away, leapt a barbed-wire fence and were gone across a field, the tips of chocolaty-brown ploughed furrows just visible through the snow and between the trees.

"It's a mini Stonehenge," said Will.

"A stone circle," I agreed. "Really old, aren't they? Prehistoric."

We walked the circle, touching each stone, smiling at the cloven hoof prints. The atmosphere of the place was at once ancient and futuristic. Wisdom and peace were discernible, but so was fun. The castle and everyone it contained were far away in some other time and existence. This was a holiday, a festive occasion, just for us two.

"We need to dance, Treadwell. Can you feel it?"

He was right. We skipped round the inside of the ring, jumping over and onto stones that had tumbled long ago. An unsuccessful, but hilarious, ballet lift took place.

"We should be naked," I said, and then put a hand to my mouth, shocked by my own words.

"We'd die, or something," said Will. "How cold is it?"

He was right again. But the feeling, the fact, wouldn't go away. It was so strong and absolute. Naked was how it had to be. Here. In this moment. With Will. In this circle of stones. "I'm doing it," I told him. "You don't have to watch. Or join in. Or even stay."

He stared at me and then backed away a bit. He stood up on a half-buried rock and took his jacket off. I retreated to the other side of the circle, stepped onto a big flat stone, and mirrored his actions with my jacket. He pulled his top over his head and paused.

"Bit chilly, Hearse?" I asked.

"Turn around," he requested. "Don't look."

Giggling, I obeyed.

"You can turn back now," he told me, moments later.

I roared with laughter at the sight that met my eyes. Trousers round his ankles, Will had formed his hands into a modesty-saving cup.

"What?" he said. "It's freezing, so I'm not looking my best."

Laughter faded as I felt the heat of the sun on my back. It was enticing, pulling at me, commanding me. I closed my eyes and pulled off one layer: my sweater. Yes. The rightness of what we were doing was intense and overwhelming. In a good way. Everything should be natural and free in this ancient setting. It was not a place of sophistication. I threw my pyjama top on the ground, making the top half of my body naked, and gazed over at Will.

He stared back, for once silent. I turned away from him to face the sun, and stretched my arms to the sky in a solar embrace. Golden rays gifted warmth and relaxation and love.

I smiled as he stood in front of me on the ground, his trousers back up.

We hugged, skin against skin, under the fiery orb. His pointy nose and warm breath touched the centre of my chest, and I rubbed hands up through his hair, laughing as it sprang back into place. He was bowed in worship, while I reigned above. And I knew we were going to lie down together on the stone—

A cloud passed across the sun. Everything chilled. And what were we doing?

I sat down on the flat stone and pulled my clothes back on, very glad that I'd not taken my pyjama bottoms off.

He sat too. "Hey, Malph. Don't loop out on me now."

I buried my face in his neck, as if it were possible to hide from confusion and embarrassment.

"This was beautiful," he said. "Don't turn it into something else. Whatever's going on with you and the prick had nothing to do with this, us, here. He doesn't own you."

"It was beautiful, wasn't it?" The stones, the snow, the sun; they were all here creating perfection, and we'd been a part of it for a short moment.

"Something odd, though..." He shivered and got up to seek his own discarded garments. "I was thinking we were going to, you know..."

I nodded. I knew.

T-shirt round his arms, he went on. "But I don't have a condom. That wasn't going to be a part of it."

"It's like we weren't ourselves, Will." Concerns gathered like clouds. "And I don't want things to become awkward between us again."

"They won't, babe. We should promise that." He threaded his fingers through mine and we squeezed a silent vow. "You know what?"

"What?" I reached for my jacket, the cold of our surroundings increasing every second.

"You've got fantastic tits."

"Will!"

"Best I've ever seen. Like a goddess."

"Oh, ha ha. But seriously, I think maybe you have the better idea. Being single, not being owned. Staying all free and easy."

"I didn't mean I would never do the relationship thing. I mean, if..."

"You fell in love." I covered my heart with my hands and smiled a soppy smile. "Take my advice and don't. You give someone the power to rip your heart out and eat it for breakfast."

"Shit, Treadwell. That doesn't sound good."

"I told him to fuck off." It felt like I was describing an event from long ago, one that had become too distant to engender any emotional response.

"Good for you, Malph. Are you going to tell Bevan about this, what happened here?"

"Can you imagine?" And I did, briefly, picture Justin's shocked, but alive-with-gossip, face. "No. This is just ours." Time was passing, ticking along once more without the sun. "Let's go and get breakfast."

We set off, but stopped at the entrance to the trees.

"It seems wrong to leave without, I don't know, saying something," I said. "A thank you, maybe? A révérence like at the end of class?"

I curtseyed to the circle. Will gave an elaborate bow.

We made our way down the path, and it was quite different in the downward direction. Light and magic were left behind as we prepared to return to the ordinary. Snow-dusted turrets appeared over the treetops, a reminder that nothing in our world was particularly ordinary anymore.

Chapter 16

As we walked into the great hall, Justin looked up from his toast and spoke sharply. "Where have you two been?"

"An exciting place," I said, touching my palms to his cheeks.

"Sweetheart," he said, taking my hands in his. "You're frozen. Come and sit down. Zolotov is trying to make conversation with me, and I lack the sophistication to cope."

Aleks, on the other side of the table, was looking at me, and apparently trying to convey some sort of meaning with his eyes, but he was easy to ignore.

"Far have you two been?" Holly echoed Justin in furious approach. She embarked on a long one-sided discourse while escorting us over to the canteen and dishing up our breakfast.

"Did you get any of that?" asked Will as we took our steaming bowls of chocolate-swirled porridge and sat by Justin.

"She scolded us for having gone out insufficiently clad." A giggle erupted, and then another. Poor Holly had no idea quite how inadequate the clothing had been at times.

"It's no laughing matter, Phi," said Justin. "Getting chilled weakens the immune system."

I hugged him. "I love you, Justin."

Simone sat down by Aleks, grapefruit in hand, and eyed us with obvious contempt. "What is that expression again? Oh yes. Fag Hag."

Aleks, Justin and I all spoke at once.

"She's no hag," said Justin.

"Don't call him a fag," I said.

"Simone, enough!" said Aleks, shocked. But it wasn't enough. Not nearly enough. Good as it was that that he had said something, it was too late. And I didn't like hearing him say her name.

Will followed our comments up with: "Is there anything you're not bigoted against, Simone?"

She grimaced at him, and simpered up at Aleks.

"Simone. Darling," Justin said sweetly. "We all know you lack the talent required to, you know, get a job, and will ultimately have to sleep your way into one."

Her mouth dropped open.

"But if you could refrain from practicing at the breakfast table, for just one morning, it would be much appreciated."

Simone touched Aleks's arm, as if for support. "But we all have to watch the 'woman in love with her two gay best friends' act?" she sniped.

"Don't bring Hearst into this," said Justin. "Straight as a Roman road, that one. And just as busy."

"Huh?" asked Will.

"Many have marched down it," I said, glad of the opportunity to laugh, which was as much at Simone suggesting Will was gay as anything else.

"I meant nothing derogatory," assured Justin. "All this sophistication rubbing me up the wrong way, is all."

"Huh?" Will repeated.

I waved a hand in the direction of Aleks and Simone. "While you were shut in that cupboard, Aleks told Justin and me that we lacked sophistication."

"That wasn't very nice, Zolotov," said Will.

"True, though," said Simone, touching Aleks's arm again.

"I had far too much to drink," he said while trying to push her hand away. "I behaved badly."

An electronic downward scale of music from an old retro computer game played in my head. The words 'GAME OVER' flashed red in front of Simone's face. She'd been the game. Not me. Not really. But what difference that made, or what it all meant, I neither knew nor cared at that moment.

Will and I recounted a severely edited version of our sunny exploits to the table.

"I cannot believe you didn't call me," said a disgruntled Sun. "I had no idea we were near such a site. And the deer are straight out of a Pagan fertility tale. So what was the circle like?"

"Snowy," I said, looking to Will for help.

"There were big stones," he said. "Some fallen over."

"Sparkly bits..."

"Sunshine..."

"Hallucinogenic mushrooms, perchance?" enquired Justin. "You seem like you're on something, both of you." His eyes narrowed. "What did you get up to in there?"

"We danced," I told him.

"Ballet?" he asked.

"That didn't go so well," I told him. "It was more like a mad, kind of circular..."

"Tribal," said Will.

"Primal," I agreed.

"I've got to see this place," said Sun. "Is there time before class?" It was established that there was not. "Do you think you had a mystical experience?" she asked us.

We both shrugged.

"Sacrificing virgins and devil worship?" said Simone with a sneer.

Sadie laughed from further up the table.

Sun was informatively cross. "The devil is actually a Christian construct. These sites predate male-dominated society and religion, so it's far more likely to have been created by people who honoured a female deity. There are rites still performed today where a woman can embody the spirit of the Goddess. It's extremely empowering."

"Is it? Phi?" Justin clicked his fingers in front of my face, causing more giggly laughter. "Feeling empowered, are we?"

"Yeah, you know..." I stretched out my arms and observed Simone leaning in towards Aleks. "I feel very Zen. I see how things are, and it's all okay."

"You're definitely in an altered state," said Sun. "How are you feeling, Will?"

"Dunno really."

"Eloquent as ever," noted Justin.

Holly sat down with a large platter of toast for us all and surveyed Simone and Aleks. "Some folks is cosy, anyway," she said.

But that wasn't right, and I actually felt a stab of something empathetic for Simone.

"Phi," continued Holly, turning to me. "I've bin meaning to speak to you aboot Ross."

"Oh?"

"He'd be a right good lad for ye..." So began the sermon on Ross's eligibility. He was a nice boy, only twenty-three, and would inherit the farm which was big and profitable. He could also boast being down-to-earth, had no airs and graces—

"An unsophisticated man of the soil?" interjected Justin. "Now, that does appeal."

"I can just see you as a farmer's wife," said Simone.

"No," I told Holly. "No," I repeated, pointing a stern finger, sensing part two of the Ross parade about to begin.

"Go on, Phi," advised Justin. "You might get a ride in a tractor, a roll in the hay; checked shirts, big boots, a stable..."

"Don't project your fantasies onto me, Bevan," I said. "I'm going for a shower."

Will got up too, but Michelle accosted us before we reached the door.

"Miss Treadwell, I need a word about your timetable. The contemporary teacher starts next week, and two of the lessons coincide with your individual tuition from Aleks."

"I'm no longer having that, the individual tuition." It was hard to concentrate on mundane matters. I wanted to think about sparkling snow and tall stones and the sun.

Aleks whipped round on the bench. "Why you say this?"

"There wasn't any this last week," I noted. "And Simone told me she was having those sessions instead of me now."

"That's not exactly what I said, Amalphia," replied Simone with a light laugh.

"It is exactly what you said. You instead of me, things better now we're here, remember?"

Michelle intervened. "You're still down for them, but you can't do contemporary also as the teacher wants participants to do all of her classes. What's it to be?"

"Contemporary," I said at once to her satisfaction, but not Aleks's.

He followed us into the foyer and demanded to speak with me. Will wandered over to the stairs while Aleks and I went a little way into the kitchen passage.

"Malphia," he said in a low voice. "What you are saying upstairs is very, very wrong. I love you. There is nothing going on with Simone. I was angry to have the door shut in my face on the night of the Ceilidh. I was offended to have it assumed I kissed her, that I would do that. So, I played a game of 'Really? This is what you think I am doing? Look, and see what nonsense that is.' It was sarcastic and stupid, and I am truly sorry. I thought you and I would make up after, and that it would be spectacular."

"Is that what usually happened? With your sophisticated girlfriends? After these games?"

He sighed and closed his eyes for a moment, then looked straight at me. "There is nothing usual happening between you and me."

"I'll take that as a yes, then."

He shook his head. "And now, you are to teach me a lesson by not taking my class?"

"No." I peered at him in the half-light of the corridor. "I love contemporary. I don't want to do only ballet here."

"I want you to—"

"You say that a lot: 'I want.' You're like a spoiled boy who thinks he can do anything and still have everything just how he likes it." I leant back against the cold wall, feeling sort of hot and dreamy. "Your behaviour demeans you, Aleks. Old ways won't work in new times."

The words echoed along the narrow passageway sounding strange and like they weren't really mine. I looked at Aleks and saw him so clearly. He was good, so good at heart, so strong, and open to all that life could be. But something was wrong. He stood small and closed and frightened because...

"You saw me," I said, cringing in the onslaught of emotion I felt from him and pressing myself back against the wall. Maybe that way no one would see, no one would know... "You were embarrassed. Ashamed." I felt disoriented and sick. "You saw me arrive, and you couldn't bear it."

"No, angel," he answered too quickly. "But I was very aware that you were my student. I have started this new career in so unprofessional a manner. Irresponsible and negligent. I was worried I was doing wrong by you."

"So you thought you'd just go with that? Do as wrong as you could?" Giggly feelings appeared momentarily.

Aleks seemed to shrink further as I regarded him.

"This," he said. "In here, today at breakfast. The flirting is all Simone. Is not my fault."

Fact: "It is all your fault. You've led her to believe that you want to have sex with her."

He flinched. "No."

"That's what flirting is, isn't it?"

"No," he said again. "Is just a funny, light thing."

"I didn't see it like that, and I don't think Simone did either. And you can't expect her to suddenly adjust her behaviour because you've bored of your game."

Poor Simone. Looked at from this side of the charade, she seemed such a silly, deluded creature. But then, what had I been? Aleks took my hand and said my name, and I was back in the passage, feet firmly on the ground, and clearer than ever.

"You have to pull yourself together," I told him. "Much could be ruined because of you. Threads crossing at the wrong time cause shifts in the pattern." Everything was fading and making less sense. I felt feverish and sweaty. Was I actually just burbling about the ancient-looking tapestry that hung on the wall beside us? The unicorns it depicted were made up of many threads. I touched a feathery thistle and blurted out: "You have to own the responsibility. And be who you really are."

A shadow crossed us. "Treadwell, you coming or what? We're gonna be well late; we're not even changed."

"Will." I turned in delight, for there was much of great import to be said to him too. "You…" But as I walked towards him, it was gone.

"Looping, babe?"

"Yes." It was cooler in the foyer and I shivered. "Maybe I did get chilled. I don't know what I'm saying."

"It's not her fault the timetable's messed up," he told Aleks.

"It's fine, Will," I said. "Everything's good." And those words became the philosophy of the morning, carried into class, beautiful class.

Moving to the music was sublime, stretching to the full, a body expressing life. Ah, the wonder of life. Aleks didn't understand. And oddly, wonderfully, Michelle did. She was happy like me, and with me, and we smiled at each other in her lesson with the strange little brain monitors. She wanted to see some pas de deux, and that was beautiful too, as dancing with Will always was. We were so in tune, instinctively sensing the slightest change or movement in the other.

Aleks asked Simone to stay back and speak to him, calling to mind the day he'd asked me to dinner. In London. At college. A chink appeared in the loveliness, accompanied by a disturbing recollection of things said in the passageway. I had likened him to a spoilt child and waffled nonsensical rubbish. I'd sensed that something about me embarrassed him. And I was sure that I had intuited that correctly.

"You can't speak to her now," Michelle told Aleks. "It's lunchtime. And I have something to show Miss Treadwell and Mr. Hearst."

Aleks and the other students left. Will and I looked at graphs of brain activity on a screen.

"So, I gather you found the Moon Stones?" said Michelle, as she searched through files on one of the computers. "Did you like them?"

"Yes," I said stupidly, not knowing what else to say.

She gave me a sharp look that suggested she would have liked to scroll through the memory files in my brain. "You two have shown the best action from the beginning, but this morning… Look." She clicked to a different window that was alive with brightly coloured squiggles. "You'd think that was one pattern, but it's actually both of you, in perfect tandem."

Patterns, I'd been bleating something about them during my fit of hysteria in the passageway.

Michelle was still speaking. "See, here are Simone and Aleks." She pointed to an almost empty chart.

"They're flat-lining," said Will, with a small laugh.

"Not quite," said Michelle. "But you see the difference. I don't know what you two have been doing, but whatever it is..." She smiled. "Keep it up."

She kept up the excited chat in the elevator, feverishly fingering a gold chain at her neck, as we all headed to lunch. "The research was not presented properly to you at the very start. That was a mistake. I should have spoken to you all back then, instead of just leaving Aleks to take over."

Sitting down with our classmates in the great hall, Will announced: "We're geniuses. You lot are dim as sheep."

"Maybe she got the graph upside down?" suggested Justin.

Will bent close and whispered, so the others couldn't hear. "That was quite a thing in the stones this morning."

"It was." I paused to think, and recalled the irresistible desire to remove all my clothes. "Oh no," I said, also keeping my voice low. "Do you think it's some sort of mental compulsion I've developed because of the stress of coming here? Am I going to be stripping off everywhere now?" Panic started to rise.

"No," said Will. "I felt it too, remember? The need to dance, and then, once you said it, the need to feel the sun..."

"On your skin."

He nodded. "D'you think that's what's caused the brain thing? What happened up there?"

I glanced over at Michelle who was talking animatedly to Aleks and Paul at the staff table.

"I honestly don't know."

The come-down from the brightness of the morning was deep. Life was flat, and the sun had gone in. Sun, the person, was determined that we were all going up to the circle after lunch, Saturday afternoons being free and all our own. Will, I, Justin and Ruaridh accompanied her. Holly came too, having made sure we were all scarved and gloved to within an inch of being able to breath, Justin having told her that with a Southern English mother and a Mauritian father, he was not made for the cold.

Sun talked on and on: the circle was brimming with feminine energy, and we had obviously been meant to find it. She proclaimed the flat stone to be a power centre and pointed out faint carvings, a twisted knot of circles and lines. It was interesting, but the reverential magic of the morning had gone. The sky beyond the field darkened, suggestive of more snow on the way.

Will and I sat back to back on the flat stone – it felt like our stone – and Justin took a photo of us with his phone.

"Nice one, Bevan," said Will. "Take one with mine too, would you? Could do with a new profile pic."

I wondered where Aleks was, and what he was doing, as many picture-taking clicks took place around us. Ruaridh had an impressive camera, and everyone's online profiles became prehistoric as large soft flakes started to fall.

The rest of the day crawled.

Aleks didn't look our way at dinner. He sat at the staff table and said the odd word to Paul. Simone chatted with Sadie at the student table.

Will and I sat in front of the television in the evening; Justin joined us, moaning about Saturday nights in the country.

We took the stairs to bed. Will went into his room, then Justin into his. I was left alone to climb the echoey stairway to the top of the tower.

Aleks's door was open, and he smiled his golden smile. Simone had her back to me, hand on hip, but I could tell that she was smiling too. I saw the swell of her cheek and heard her tinkling laugh.

Aleks caught sight of me, and I fled back down the stairs.

Justin opened his door, his arms and his pyjama drawer to me, and I held his hand in the dark.

Chapter 17

RAIN PELTED THE CASTLE on Sunday morning, spoiling the appearance of the snow. Aleks wasn't at breakfast. Swimming with Justin and Will provided a brief diversion, but the itchy wrongness of the day wouldn't shift. I felt out of place and like I needed to be somewhere else. Aleks still wasn't around at lunchtime, and I asked Holly about it.

"He's ill," she said. "I would've took some dinner up to him. But seeing the merry dance he's led you with that een..." She jerked her head in Simone's direction. "Well."

All I could see in my mind's eye was Aleks. Aleks in pain.

"I packed his medication," I remembered. "It's in my bag."

"Aye? Give it to me. I'll take it up."

"I'll do it." He wouldn't want to see people when he was ill. I knew that.

"Quiney, I ken ye've got it bad, but you shouldna—"

"I'm taking it Holly, and some food. Is there a flask? He might not feel like eating right now, but soup would be good for him."

She shook her head in disapproval but helped me to get a tray together.

Having ascertained that Simone was going swimming with Sadie, I located the three packets of drugs in the bag in my room. Maybe he already had some with him? This could be an unwelcome and needy-looking visit. Not able to take the risk that he might be suffering, I walked down to his room, gave a gentle tap on the door and went in.

He was sitting up in bed, leaning back against the headboard. "Malphia," he said, voice husky and surprised.

"I packed them." I showed him the boxes. "I didn't know if you had more."

"I was just going to ride it out this time."

"Precious as ever then." I popped four of the large oval pills out of their foil and handed them to him along with the bottle of water from the tray. Only then did I fully take in his appearance. He was sweaty and hot. His eyes looked sunken with dark circles underneath, and his skin was horribly pale.

"You're worse than last time. Shouldn't you see a doctor?"

"This is how it is."

"Come on then, lie down, sleep and let the drug work." I arranged the pillows with the top one pushed back, how he liked them. He lay stiffly, trying to hide the pain. I wanted to say: 'It's me, you don't have to pretend.' But things were not as they once had been.

He took my hand. "I am so sorry."

What could I say? She's beautiful and socially adept; I understand? Because really, I did. This man had never been mine to keep. But his face was bereft, and it was important that he rest. "It's okay. Everything's okay," I told him. The words became a mantra as I stroked his hair, and he soon slept. I kissed his cheek, breathed him in one last time and walked the many steps down to the television room.

"Prick upsetting you again, Malph?"

"He didn't mean to. Not this time. It's just, you know, very, very over now."

It was easy sitting with Will in the little room. He didn't expect me to speak or be social in any way. He went to the kitchen and came back with excessively sweet tea, the mocking of which took my mind off Aleks for about half a minute. I wanted to run back upstairs and check he hadn't deteriorated. Instead, I listened to Will shout in goal celebration and yell abuse at the referee.

Dinnertime arrived, and Aleks was still absent. Simone seemed unconcerned, picking disdainfully at her salad and laughing with Sadie. The evening dragged, the rain continued, the cold grew.

ele

My attempt to walk past Aleks's door failed. A soft tap wouldn't wake him if he were sleeping, and I really wanted to know how he was. I paused, fist raised, because: what if Simone was in there? My hand recoiled.

"You are never needing to knock."

I almost stumbled down a step in shock. Aleks had come up the stairs so silently behind me.

"You're better." His forehead felt warmly cool under my hand, and the colour of his face was normal. We smiled at each other before the new circumstances dimmed everything once more. "I better go," I said.

"But you were coming to see me?"

"To check you were okay and then, I didn't know..."

"What, angel? Speak to me. Don't run off. Please."

I faced him, angered by being made to explain the obvious.

"Well, what d'you think? I didn't know if Simone was here again. It's awkward, at least for me. I'll swap rooms with Justin tomorrow."

"But, for why?" He appeared genuinely perplexed. "I am listening to you, to all you say, and owning the responsibility. I try to speak to her twice in the day, yesterday. Both times Michelle interrupts, so Simone, she turns up here last night."

I shut my eyes. Surely he wasn't going to give some sort of detailed account?

"I apologised to her for my flirtatious behaviour, making clear is teacher-student relationship only, and then I assured her that I will not be inappropriate again."

My eyes opened.

"She is saying she does not know what I am talk about, that she never think anything, and she go."

His face was sincere. I waited to feel better.

"So, we are okay now?" He smiled and moved as if to kiss me.

I jerked back. "No." A plain truth was spoken. "I can't do this."

"Malphia, you will let me explain further?"

My legs felt weak, and they bent easily to sit on a cold stone step as I listened to him.

"You were right," he said. "When I see you arrive with your friends, I am thinking, 'She is so young, what is this we are doing?' Some distance is seem a good idea. Then I played a stupid game, trying to show that what you thought of me was wrong. I am not excusing," he added. "My actions were immature and ridiculous and will never be repeated."

"What about next time you get embarrassed?"

"No, this, it will not be."

"Of course it will. The difference in our ages is a huge issue for you. Don't deny it, because you mention it a lot. Sometimes just to tell me it doesn't matter, but why would you need to do that? It never bothered me."

"Because you are the younger one. So many things have contributed to my actions. I felt panicked that I would lose you, desperate even. Part of me is think, maybe, I would have more chance of holding on to you, if you see other women also find me attractive."

"What?" I stood. I stepped away from him. I tried to think. A huge Gavin shaped hole had just materialised between us. "You're saying it was my fault? I didn't make you feel attractive, so you had to flirt with Simone?"

"No! Angel, no. My idiocy is all my own. I don't deserve you. I know that. I don't deserve a second chance. But my feelings for you? They are so new, and so powerful. What we have is too special to be thrown aside. You are dearer to me than anyone, anyone ever."

I shook my head, more confused than ever, anyone ever. "I know you're good with the pretty words, Aleks, but they're not helping." Memories from the week squared my shoulders. "And they're not true. This wasn't some 'special, just for me' routine. Older women than I have been unhappy to be treated this way too. There's a blog."

His face hardened. "Lilian is not writing all the truth of things."

"Seemed pretty accurate. She wrote about how you would look over at her, to make sure she saw what you were up to. You did that to me."

I headed upstairs. He followed.

"You are right, is unforgivable."

"You're forgiven." My heart hurt and breathing was becoming increasingly difficult. "But I can't be with you. It's like being destroyed." I pressed my fist into my chest, into the pain.

"Please don't. Don't be saying this. I love you."

"You hurt me. You knew it, and you carried on. That's not love. I don't think I'd even do that to someone I didn't like."

"I do love you." His beautiful face was distorted as if in grief. "So much. Never have I felt before. Show me what I must do to prove. I do anything."

"You'll get over it quickly, Aleks."

He looked askance.

"You will. Of course you will. You'll find someone like you: sophisticated, social and beautiful." A silent sob gasped for air between my words. "We're wrong for each other. That's what it's all been about. You just saw it first."

"No. I am begging you, please do not be doing this. We cannot be finished."

The conversation had to be finished. Everything else already was. I put my hand on his chest, a gentle mark of distance.

"I'm going now."

Without looking back, I walked the last few steps up to my room, went in and shut the door. I wanted to turn the key, but it felt cruel, and I knew he wouldn't come in. Not again. Not anymore.

Chapter 18

IT WAS SO VERY cold. The startling temperature offered mild distraction from the constriction in my chest, and the fact that I had apparently packed for summer provided a challenge. I left the Matryoshka doll set in the case and turned it face down. The fat mother looked disapproving, and I didn't want to see her. It wasn't easy to select an outfit that didn't include clothes Aleks had given me, but I did my best with knitted ballet warm-ups and then sought cosier refuge.

Holly was in the kitchen. "What's a do with ye, quiney?"

I told her.

"Oh man," she said and proceeded to speak in clichés: he had it coming; better to do it now, not draw it out; there's plenty of fish in the sea, a bonny quine like you...

Sometime later, still cold and shivering despite having sat on the old metal stove for an hour, I joined my friends for breakfast.

"You all right, Malph?"

"Hearst has a point," said Justin. "What are you wearing? Where did you just come from?" He lowered his voice. "And what's happened?"

It was difficult to look over at my friend, because Aleks stared from the staff table beyond, and I wanted to cry. "Well, you know..."

"The prick?" asked Will.

"Don't call him that."

"You dumped him." Justin was thankfully still talking quietly. He leant forward and took my hand. "Good. He deserved kicking to the wall."

"It's not good. It was terrible."

"Really? Did he cry?" He took my blankness as affirmation of the fact. "I knew he was a weeper. But it is good. You got out with your dignity intact, until this morning that is. Sweetheart, the leg warmers on the arms?"

"It's so much colder today, and I hardly packed anything warm. All I have is knitted dance warm-up clothes. Holly says there's this one shop that does next-day delivery for here. I've been looking at things on my phone."

"Let's see," Justin requested, and then all but shrieked as he looked at the screen. Gone was all thought of sparing the room any detail from our conversation. "No, darling. Give it to me, give it, give." He won the tussle for my phone, the phone given by— "You'll thank me later. Now, let's see how bad things are." He clicked to the online basket.

"Don't be cold, Treadwell." Will pulled off his black zipped hoodie and put it over my head, and then his grey beanie hat too.

"Oh, preheated," I said, pulling the sleeves down over my hands and sinking my face into the fleecy neck that smelled of comfort and crisps. "But you'll be cold now."

"I'm tough. Got another one anyway, and about six hats."

Justin glanced up and gasped in horror. "You're enabling her," he accused Will. "You'll think twice when you see how deep this goes. Look," he said to the whole table, holding my phone out for them to see. "Thermal underwear with long sleeves and long legs, and the granny-style knitwear? We simply can't allow it. As a group, we have to intervene when one of our number loses her grip on reality."

"God no, how ghastly," remarked Simone, making me want to buy the clothes even more. "They'll make you look fat. Well, fatter."

"Bitch," Will muttered quietly.

Simone looked at him sharply, suspecting she'd missed something. It should have been funny, but life had become a plain and humourless process just to be got through. I had no willpower to fight Justin's declaration that he would guide the online shopping later.

It took great resolve not to look at Aleks, especially in the lift as we sank below the ground on the way to class. He was so close. It was amazing how much the corner of my eye could see. He looked tired and unshaven and in need of a hug. My senses were still attuned and alert to him. I wanted to lift up his jumper and press my face to his skin.

His class was awful. He stood vacantly between exercises and didn't correct anyone. With no pianist present, he kept choosing completely unsuitable music from his phone and blasting it through the studio speaker system at full volume.

"For heaven's sake, Aleks," said Michelle during her research class, where he seemed unable to pay attention. "Are you sure you're well enough to be down here?"

Lunchtime in the great hall was cold, the novelty of Will's clothes having worn off. I made the mistake of meeting Aleks's stare and then it was hard to break away, but Will's chatter had become disturbing.

"I think Simone must've given him the boot. He's not quite right. Have you noticed? Didn't think it would bother him that much. Hope he's all right for this afternoon. I'm getting a weekly private lesson with him. You should come too, Malph. We could get him to show us high lifts. You won't have a partner in pas de deux anyway with me gone."

"No, I don't want to," I said, getting up and heading underground with the others.

Simone was also missing her partner, and Mr. Timms suggested we 'gals' partnered each other. But how would it work? Who would play which part? We eyed each other uncertainly, and then Will barged into the dungeon.

"It's sorted," he said to me. "Told him you were feeling down and would be better upstairs with us. He said it was a good idea."

Will was so annoying. Aleks was so annoying. I could have done without this. For once, the dank dungeon had been a welcome retreat from difficult things. However, I left Simone to partner Mr. Timms himself, and headed up in the lift.

Aleks was more together for Will's lesson, though still far from all right. After demonstrating a better hold in a lift, he carried on talking about holding on tight and continued to literally do so. To my waist. "So she knows she is always to be safe with you."

"Malph knows that," said Will, holding out his hand for me. "Yes. She know you for a long time. But one mistake can ruin everything." He still didn't loosen his hold. "Is a betrayal of trust. I understand this."

We stared at each other through the mirror.

"Are we doing this, then?" said Will, impatient, and we finally moved on.

"Is good. You do well," Aleks told us on the way back down the stairs after the class. "Is scary be so high in vulnerable place, so open to hurt."

I shook my head. "I knew neither of you would drop me."

"Ah, but you are unusually brave."

"Better get over there," said Will, as we entered the hall. "Bevan's ordering you stuff on your phone."

I sat down by Justin, glad for Will's interruption, Aleks seeming to have lost any ability for discretion.

"I know what it is you remind me of, in this get up, Phi," said Justin. "A kid from a special-needs documentary."

"Stop being bigoted," I told him.

"You're right. They have stylists and would never look this bad. You, however, have me."

"Aye, and me," said Holly, approaching. She deposited a large mug of something red on the table in front of me. "If ye can drink chocolate, ye can drink that too. Tomato soup. Best thing for upset," she said.

I looked across at the staff table, to see if Aleks was eating. He should eat.

"My room, now," said Justin. "You can bring your sad soup. Hearst may try to enable bad choices. We'll be better off alone."

So I sipped soup, sat under Justin's blankets and let him tell me what to buy. Then I trudged the long stone trail to bed.

"I didn't want to hurt you." The voice from above made me jump. Aleks was sitting on the stairs, outside his room, waiting.

"You have to believe me, Malphia. It was not in my mind that you were hurting." He looked manic. I suspected that no dinner had been eaten. "You have to believe me," he repeated, standing up. "Is not to justify, but you say I see and keep doing. Is not this." He ran his fingers through his hair, causing tufts to stick out, increasing the general air of mania.

"I believe you." I circled around him and stood a couple of steps higher.

He took a step closer. "Stay with me tonight."

His hands cupped my face. I shut my eyes, desperate to remain calm and controlled.

"Let me make love to you, so you remember how good we are together."

"Don't do this to me, Aleks."

He dropped his hands at once, but carried on speaking. "That last time, here, between us. The first morning. This cannot be the thing you remember. I was try to turn everything back to just sex. Is not working; I was overwhelmed by your touch and your sweetness. And horrified at myself for making you—"

"You didn't make me do anything."

I lowered to a crouch on the stairs and he followed suit. We sat closely together, hands clasped round our knees like small children.

"I wanted to do that," I told him, reaching out to take his hand. "You never let me before."

"I didn't want you to do something you might not like, just to please me."

"It was with you, so of course I liked it." The rest of the truth of that moment blurted out too. "In fact, I would have liked rather more of the experience than you were willing to give me."

He met my direct gaze.

"I'm not the sweet little girl you seem to be painting me as," I told him. "And you're not an evil seducer." I kept hold of his hand as it seemed to be calming him. His eyes had lost some of the manic look of earlier. "But I did stand out here afterwards feeling discarded and inadequate."

"All inadequacies are mine," he said. "You are perfect, in all things."

"No," I replied, cross, dropping his hand. "I'm not perfect. But this week, here. This isn't what I'll keep from our relationship. It won't be. That wasn't us. We were over when I got off that bus, maybe before."

"No."

"You gave me so much, Aleks. I didn't know it could be like that: sex, love, relationships. It was the best five weeks of my life."

"No," he said again. "This time we had, I didn't treat you right even then. I should have been taking you out. I know so many places you would love. I realise this when I see you all dressed up for the Ceilidh. You are exquisite, so striking in formal dress. And why am I never see before? Because all I wanted, like the spoilt, selfish creature of me, is to be home in bed with you. I am so shamed."

"That's all I wanted too."

"Tell me what to do."

His face was full of hope, but what he meant couldn't be. My heart couldn't go through this again.

"Do what you came here to do," I advised. "Make us the best dancers we can be. You're really good at that. We're already so much better than we were before you taught us. But, right now? Go downstairs and get something to eat. Then go to bed and sleep."

"This, I can do," he said, at once brightening, and standing, and then he was gone. Only the echoes of his departing feet remained with me on the hard stone stairs.

Chapter 19

B Y MORNING I KNEW my resolve to be gone. I could remember what it was like to be warm, to lie next to him, to hear his heart pound after love and his breathing slow in slumber. I loved him too much to resist another heartfelt entreaty. His pain pulsed within the aching space of my own chest, so real, so wrong, and so easily fixable.

And there he was, waiting, yet again, on the stairs.

"Amalphia," he said. "Do not worry. I am not to be bothering you anymore, only to say this." He'd shaved and smelled all soapy and fresh. "I respect your wishes. My door, it is always open to you. If you want to talk, or sit, anything. Never knock. You understand?"

He was offering friendship. We walked down and round, his hand hovering over the base of my spine, but not touching, not now.

We parted ways in the great hall.

Justin eyed me beadily. "Hearst has a theory that Zolotov got dumped by snotty-tights Simone over there. And now you and he waltz in here together. Anything you want to tell us, Phi?"

"I met him on the stairs. He was nice. Told me I could talk to him anytime."

"That'll be because I told him you'd dumped the prick," said Will.

"Will!" I said, horrified. "Please don't tell people... stuff like that."

If Aleks had heard himself referred to as a prick, it was causing him no distress. At the beginning of class in the dungeon, he walked over to me and smiled. "As you are no longer to have individual lessons, Amalphia, I will push you harder here. Do not think it is me picking on you."

The professional teacher side of Aleks had returned, and while it was a relief that he hadn't become ill again, it was also a shock to realise just how quickly he'd got over me. I pushed the selfish thought aside and concentrated. I had to. Where double or triple versions of any exercise or step were possible, he demanded them. He made me hold my legs up in extension long after the others had lowered theirs. Class was over in a flash of struggle and sweat and sore limbs. For an hour and a half, everything had been okay.

But as I stood with Will and Justin, waiting for the elevator, my whole body stiffened in pain, and I gasped.

"Sounds like trauma," said Will, when I explained what I was feeling. "Any other symptoms?"

"In the night my heart was beating really fast, and it was hard to breathe."

"Panic attack," he said. "You should tell that new teacher. We've got her for Pilates this afternoon. She does other things too, though, like meditation and massage."

The new teacher, Teresa, proved to be happy and bubbly, and somehow shiny seeming. Her cherry-red frizzy hair parted now and again to reveal dangling parrot earrings. Everyone was welcome to take her classes, even the other teachers.

We did therapeutic massage at the end of a relaxing stretchy session in which no strenuous Pilates took place. Will and I worked together and got a lot of attention and guidance. Justin was annoyed at being placed with Sadie again, while Simone delighted in running her hands all over Aleks's back.

The sight of them touching caused a hard rock to form in my stomach. Thin tomato soup ran round it at dinner.

"Did you say something about me to Teresa?" I asked Will, having noticed how she'd gone out of her way to be kind to me.

His nod was reluctant.

"You've got to stop blabbing to teachers. I won't be able to tell you anything."

He looked uncomfortable.

"What else have you done?" I asked.

"Zolotov asked me how you were today."

"And you told him everything. No more telling things, or there'll be no birthday cake."

"I'm getting a cake?"

He was so delighted, my anger melted away. I would enjoy making him a cake and putting candles on it. I would enjoy getting a card and present sorted. These felt like normal and nice things. Living in the castle was neither nice nor normal. The thought that we were going to stay for months was too much to contemplate, and small ideas of departure had begun to form in my mind. The contemporary teacher was very taken with Will and me, to the point where she felt we should transfer somewhere else to specialise. Did I want that? I loved contemporary. I loved ballet. But I loved Aleks too.

It was comforting to see him chatting and eating across the room, but that might change with time. Not being with him hurt so much. I wanted to be like Will, and apparently Aleks: love them and leave them with barely a backward glance.

His door stood open, seven inches open, that evening. All seemed quiet and calm within, but I walked valiantly past.

The week wore on. My body hurt at random moments. I cried in the toilets and the meditation room.

Michelle was absent on Wednesday afternoon, and as we descended in the elevator, Mr. Timms seemed rather excited by the fact.

"Without Miss M. and her computers, we will do something different," he said. "*Romeo and Juliet*. Balcony scene, four sets of lovers. The studio is big enough for everyone to work at once. We will love it up."

"Not feeling the love," moaned Justin as we wandered into the huge cold dungeon.

"Is good," said Aleks. "A small performance reminds us of what it is all about. I suggest we make it interesting, and have a competition to see which is best partnership."

Simone looked smugly confident beside him.

"It's entirely unfair," I said to Aleks, surprised to find I could speak quite normally to him. "You must know the choreography already."

"Not all versions, Zolotov?" asked Mr. Timms. "I suspect you know Cranko, and Ashton, but what about Macmillan?"

Aleks admitted he was not familiar with it.

"Ha!" I said. "Will knows it. We saw it once years ago." Befuddled looks met the statement. "It's his amazing brain, you see," I said, placing my hands on either side of Will's head. "He remembers everything. We're gonna win."

"Yeah, we are," said Will with great confidence, then lowering his voice so only I could hear. "You could act. I mean, really act. Do your thing."

"I don't know." I considered it, then asked Mr. Timms: "Are we being judged on every aspect of the performance?"

"Of course, my dear, of course," our ancient teacher confirmed.

It was possibly the greatest level of concentration I had ever put into learning choreography, for that would be my weakness, and it had somehow become imperative to beat Simone and Aleks. Will had retained a good background knowledge of the piece, and half an hour of rehearsal later, we were ready, relatively speaking, for the purpose of the day. The lift practice from the other afternoon proved helpful too. Mr. Timms talked round the kiss, but did not get us to rehearse it.

Justin and Sadie went first. They muddled through, Justin avoiding the kiss with elaborate side-to-side head movements. Sadie looked a little offended. We all bit back laughter and applauded. Ruaridh and Sun were much better. Aleks and Simone were threateningly good, all because of him, though I had the feeling he was holding back somehow. Their kiss was brief and unconvincing but still reminiscent of the Ceilidh, for me anyway.

"I need a minute," I said, before Will and I began.

"I know what you're gonna do," Justin sang. "They've won. It's over."

It was a scary thought to lose myself, as acting would cause me to do, in front of everybody, and with Will. A muttered discussion took place at the back of the room, the improvised balcony.

"Maybe I shouldn't do it," I said to Will. "You'll have to guide me in the choreography. I don't know it well enough for this."

"It'll stop you being nervous, Malph," he reminded me. "You're always better if you're in character." That was true. Even though the audience was so small, I still found the thought of performing in front of them daunting.

"Just do it already!" Justin was getting impatient.

"Yes," said Aleks. "Is too much... what is word? Conferring."

We began. And I knew I had to act, properly act. This was what I had planned to do: make the most of all opportunities of this sort that happened at the castle.

I was fourteen and in love with Will, for he stayed Will, though I became Juliet. Little vestiges of Amalphia remained to dance and stage direct, and the two girls merged in places. Eventually there was clapping, balcony became floor, and Capulet gave way to Treadwell.

"See, I told you it would be fantastic," said Justin. "We just needed popcorn."

Mr. Timms was effusive. "The girl with the perfect line is an actress also."

Will and I were surrounded, Justin excitedly telling everyone that I could sing too, so was, in fact, a 'triple threat.'

"Have we won, then?" Will demanded.

"I think so," mused Mr. Timms. "Though Zolotov and Miss Treadwell both invented some of their own choreography."

I glanced over at Aleks, but he wasn't looking our way. In fact, Simone and he appeared to be dramatically bad losers.

"Mr. Hearst had it down better than anyone," continued Mr. Timms. "And the acting, my dear – I was transfixed – even if the kiss took up rather more of the score than it should have."

"She's a creature possessed in the moment, no control whatsoever," Justin explained. "I once had dinner with Lady Macbeth. Had to wrestle a knife from her hand. The waiter was genuinely frightened."

"But we won?" Will asked again.

"Hearst," said Justin. "It's the taking part that counts remember; the winning is just all that actually matters." At least he bore no grudge in defeat.

Crammed into the elevator, the doors refused to close as sometimes happened.

Mr. Timms waffled on about 'the craft.' "So is it method acting you employ, my dear? Was the embrace based upon your own first kiss?"

"No. I always hated that type of exercise in drama classes. I just inhabit the character. Or she inhabits me. I don't know."

"But your understanding of Juliet?" he went on. "What would make her behave in so brazen a manner? A girl with no experience of love?"

"I don't know." I jabbed repeatedly at the ground-floor button. "There's no thinking in the process. I don't even remember it all that clearly."

"Treadwell, I'm hurt," said Will. "How can you not remember a snog like that? It was awesome."

"Sorry."

"At least we won."

"Like a dog with a bone, isn't he?" observed Justin. "Kid yourself not, Hearst. If she didn't know it already, she wouldn't even remember your name."

"I'm sure there are no complaints," chuckled Mr. Timms. "Boys sometimes go into acting to kiss the pretty girls."

Justin suggested sharing first-kiss stories: Will's had been behind the bike sheds at school, Sun's with a girl at age thirteen and then his own, also with a girl who cut his lip with her dental braces.

"And what about you, PhiPhiPot?" asked Justin. "You can press that button all you like. It's not going to save you. How was your first kiss?"

I recalled the unfortunate event from childhood. "I was acutely aware that he'd been eating both sand and earthworms."

Justin grinned and looked at Will. "Is this the other side of a story we've already heard? Did the same bike sheds feature?"

"No," I said.

"Hey, Bevan," said Will.

"I could believe you eat worms," Justin told him.

The doors slid shut and we finally jolted upwards.

"Oh, before we'd got to the teachers," complained Justin. "Or was it so long ago they don't remember? Zolotov, squeeze a quick one in before we land?"

I squinted back, not wanting to look at Aleks fully if he was going to say terrible things that would make me feel jealous.

"First kiss that is mattering is on a train," he said. "Is scary. I am shy, thinking she might not like me so much."

"Changed days then, judging from the Ceilidh," said Justin. He covered his mouth momentarily. "Sorry. Involuntary bitch. Just twitched out."

I twitched out of the elevator and into the hall, welcoming smells of food ahead, Justin's ponderings on whether he had Tourette's Syndrome behind.

"Will and Phi snogged!" my loquacious friend announced to Michelle, who had returned and was at the staff table. Justin paused, and raised the back of his hand to his forehead. "I am afflicted, struck down in my prime. What a day of tragedy, Shakespearean and Justinean. Is that a word? It should be. One day it will be."

Chapter 20

THE POST-COMPETITION HIGH THAT had run through dinner was gone, and an anti-climactic depression sat with Will and me in the television room.

"We need chocolate," I said and set off for the kitchen.

Returning a short while later, a mug in each hand and a packet of chocolate biscuits wedged under an arm, I nearly collided with Aleks in the dark corridor.

"This is an amazing thing you do, Amalphia," he said. "I see you change, become another person. Is wondrous, a gift. You did mention your acting before, but I had no knowing you were so talented in this."

"Well, we haven't actually known each other very long," seemed a ludicrous and impossible declaration. Yet, it was true.

"Fifty-eight days since we first meet, in corridor like this." He mimed his hands banging together. "Then forty-nine since..." He reached forward and touched my hair.

I tensed. "I'd better go." I indicated the mugs.

"Yes – I also – am go room and read."

We went our own ways in the foyer, the reason he'd been heading towards the kitchen perhaps forgotten in the awkwardness of the meeting.

My chest hurt as I sat down by Will and looked at the television.

It hurt more as I walked past the seven inches of open door later, and then I gasped in my own room on seeing my bed. Thermal garments like the ones I'd wanted to order, but had not, were piled neatly beside a pink cable-knit cardigan and matching socks. I held the soft clothes to my face before putting them on, and the cold became a little less keen.

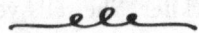

On Saturday morning Justin took one look at me and declared: "No. It is a wet weekend. You can't be one too."

"I've been up half the night working on cheering you up," said Will. "To thank you for the cake, and the football, and the card."

"She doesn't need thanks for any of that," snapped Justin. "She got to go out. She saw burly men in the village shop. It was me that ran up and down the stairs getting people to sign the fuckity thing."

"Justin," I said. "You do not have Tourette's Syndrome. The constant swearing to pretend that you do makes light of genuine cases." It had been happening a lot over the last few days.

"Oh, keep your politically correct hair on. What's Hearst been doing to cheer you up? Hasn't worked, has it? Darling. Was he really, really bad?"

"Quit being so mean to her, Bevan." Will placed earphones in my ears. "Made you a playlist."

It was such a sweet thing to have done that I immediately burst into tears.

Justin shook his head. "See, Hearst, you think I'm being cruel, but you just don't get the Treadwell psychology. Times like this, she needs to be insulted."

"I do not." I sniffed, hoping it came off as haughty rather than pathetic, and turned my attention to the music. "Oh, I know this one, it's..." A song about outdoor nudity. I laughed at his audacity.

"Are they all of this ilk?" I asked.

"Keep listening."

Next came a love song of lots of girls' names: Will's many girlfriends. I laughed again but removed one earbud to listen to Justin's "Dissertation on Phi's psychological make-up: the breakthrough that will change her life."

"I already know what my mother's like, thank you, Just."

"Yes, the daily putdowns. You're never good enough. Everything you do? Worthless. There's always someone done it better, bigger, sparklier. She tells you you're fat, you're ugly—"

"Is this going somewhere?" I asked.

"It's why you can't cope with people being nice to you, and here's the life-changing clincher: once you see the reasons behind the dysfunction, you can start to heal and make better choices." He paused for effect, fully aware that he had the attention of the whole room. "It's why you're attracted to men who treat you like shit. That feels normal to you."

I kept my eyes on his face, careful not to even corner-peek at anyone else, and said: "Rubbish."

"It's subconscious. I know you don't actually think, 'Ooh goody, a total bastard.' But it's true. Let's examine your track record."

I gave him a hard, and hopefully meaningful, look. "Or, let's not."

He ignored me. "Face it. If they don't push you around, eat worms, or flirt with every available bimbo, you don't want to know. But there's been an improvement lately. I've seen both anger and power in you, and we need to go with that and build upon good habits as they form."

I took a bite of toast and chewed, hoping Justin would cease the annoying discourse if not responded to. He was right about things being different this time, though. I had been able to express my feelings to Aleks. I'd felt in a safe enough space with him to do that, but what difference had it really made in the end?

Simone interrupted my contemplation. "Maybe..." she said. "Amalphia would hold on to her boyfriends better if she ate less." She laughed as if she'd said something hugely witty.

I smiled and added more butter to my toast.

"Go fuck yourself," muttered Will, not quietly enough.

"What did you say, Will Hearst?" Simone spat his name like it was a bad word. "I know you lot speak about me behind my back."

Will looked at her. "I said: why don't you go fuck yourself, Simone."

Justin's mouth fell open, and I almost choked on my toast.

Simone stood, furious, and addressed the staff table. "Is he going to get away with speaking to me like that?"

Will gave the staff no chance to answer, on his feet as fast as her. "You can't take it, can you? But we all have to listen to you. Every day you've got some snidey comment for her, and I know why."

I gazed up at angry Will in amazement.

He hadn't finished. "You're jealous. She's a way better dancer than you, and she's completely gorgeous. So yeah, go fuck yourself, Simone. No one else wants to. Be like banging a bag of bones." A tremor ran through him as he sat back down.

It was Michelle who, somewhat unexpectedly, smoothed things over. She stood behind Simone and put her hands on the offended girl's shoulders.

"We all need to calm down," she said. "You've been used to doing the odd lesson together. Now you see each other every minute of every day. Obviously there's going to be personality clashes. Let's do morning classes, then see if we can't find some way to relax and let off steam in the afternoon. Oh, and Amalphia? Being single is absolutely the best way for a woman to be in my experience. You'll be fine."

The tables emptied. Will remained seated. "Sorry, babe, but I had to say something. She's such a bitch."

I nodded, and then fought the urge to cry again as Will and I joined the others in the elevator.

"Is it very wrong that I find Hearst intensely alluring this morning?" asked Justin.

Ruaridh, usually so quiet, said, "I think we all do."

"Leave him alone," I threatened, placing my palm protectively over Will's abdomen.

"Speaking of attraction, Phi," said Sun with a smile. "If you ever tire of the bastard men, you will let me know, won't you?"

"What is this?" asked Justin. "Predatory Gay Day? Nobody told me! Zolotov, you're looking particularly fetching today."

He was. He always did.

Aleks smiled. "Alas, Justin, my heart is not my own."

Mine sank. He'd found someone else already? Here? Who? One of the other teachers? Simone? She still looked very annoyed and did not respond to his words. It couldn't be Michelle again, surely? Whatever, whomever, he'd got over me in one day. 'One day' was my current nighttime crying mantra. I loved him, so I should be happy for him. I didn't want him to be sad. But, one day...

Justin backed out of the elevator, held his hands wide and looked up at the ceiling as if in worship. "It's going to be a good day," he said. "I can feel it. About time too. We were due."

The energy of the weapon-bedecked dungeon did feel more alive and dynamic, and less like the set of a horror film. Aleks tuned into the feeling too. His class was spontaneous and exciting and ended in the most wonderful combination across the room involving a variety of large jumps with our own improvisation at the end. I slid across the floor on my knees and banged into one of the pillars.

Aleks held out his hand to help me up and I hugged him, caught up in the moment, as if in early morning forgetfulness.

"Thank you," I said to him. "This was such a great class."

He didn't hug me back, but stammered, "Oh, yes, thank you."

The good mood broke. For me, anyway.

Michelle, who'd been watching from the front of the studio, declared that Will and I just got better and better. I didn't care. I didn't want her comments about my brain patterns or my personal life.

Then came lunch, and the anticipation of a dreary and sad weekend.

"No, no, no," said Justin. "And did I say, no? We should do something. Taxi. City. Shopping. Dinner."

"Clubbing," said Will with conviction, looking at me. "We could just lose it on the dance floor."

"Yes," I replied, drawn to the idea of nihilistic dancing in the dark. There would be no barbed comments from Simone, no unwanted advice from Michelle, and no Aleks to avoid looking at. And we'd be far away from the cold stone walls of the castle.

"I'm afraid you can't do any of that," Michelle called over. "It's stipulated in your contract."

"We can't go out?" Justin had gone high-pitched.

"You can, if pre-arranged and organised, and everyone is going. The research requires proper controls to be in place. We can't have some of you being stimulated in ways that the others are not."

"But we all do different things here anyway," I said. "In the evenings, at least."

"Within certain parameters," she stated. "God knows what you might get up to if you went to a nightclub. No. You'll have to find something to do here."

A dampening mist settled over the table again, not helped by the frosty atmosphere from Simone and Sadie's end.

Justin sparked, aflame with another idea. "We will use the dramatic talents of the Treadwell, Hearst's ability to cope with said talents, and my knowledge of musical theatre. All may attend my afternoon workshop, even the teachers. In fact, that would be wonderful; we would be so honoured." He dropped his voice for just Will and me to hear. "Let's see how Zolotov likes being paired with the heavy girl. Think Holly would be game?"

Chapter 21

W E ALL GATHERED UNDER the high roof of the great hall for the Musical Theatre Workshop. Aleks and Michelle did not take part, but sat at a table, ostensibly to write notes on the week's classes. Mr. Timms sat there too, openly admitting it was to watch.

Holly was the only staff member to join in with us. "I've never seen you lot do yer stuff," she said. "I'm thinking this'll be fun."

"We'll have you up and dancing too, my lovely," Justin told her. "Right. Treadwell. Hearst. Watch this video and learn it." He handed me his phone.

"Glam rock?" I noted as the song started. "There isn't a proper character to become in this."

"We'll do something dramatic and arty next time," he promised. "But think of Holly. She'll know this music. We can't throw her straight into the hardcore stuff."

I watched through the song with Will, but did not share his enthusiasm.

"Don't get too excited, Hearst," said Justin. "You're not getting a snog this time."

"It's good, though," said Will. "Malph and me have never sung together before."

Disenchanted with the whole thing, I looked round our small group. One person was, notably, missing. "Have you thought about Simone?" I asked Justin. "We're all here." Even Sadie had stayed. "But she's off somewhere on her own, excluded from the group, imagining us having great fun. That's been me so many times in my life, I wouldn't wish it on anyone."

"I said everyone was welcome," Justin huffed.

"I'm not saying sorry," said Will. "Someone needed to tell her off."

"Okay," I said. "But at some point, we're going to have to try and bring her back into the fold. There's only seven of us. It's not like there's a hundred other people for her to mix with."

Michelle stepped in again, speaking from the staff table. "Don't worry about Simone. I'll talk to her. Have your fun this afternoon."

"Yes, let's," said Justin, exasperated. "Now, you two, I want a good clear demonstration of the song and the moves for everyone to get the idea. Okay? Places... and... action!"

It was another small break from being Amalphia, even though I only became a vague, sort-of-cheery character. I liked singing with Will, who remained very firmly Will. And the leg-kicking action of the song was quite fun and silly.

Holly clapped maniacally once we were finished, Mr. Timms, more sedately. I avoided looking at Aleks, and it wasn't clear what Michelle thought.

Justin was, very obviously, annoyed. "Remember how you told us you'd never sung with Phi?" he said to Will. "Well, you still haven't. You could have mentioned the fact that you can't actually sing."

"Hey," I said. "He was good."

"Still got a blind spot when it comes to him, don't you, my sweet? Or some sort of selective deafness. Anyway, that's your time in the limelight over. Go and sit over there. Go! Now, who fancies dressing up?"

A collection of sparkly scarves and other clothing had been found in the back of the theatre, and the others all dived into the box excitedly and were soon looking very much the part. Ruaridh's pink top hat was particularly impressive.

Will and I sat a little further up the table from Aleks and Michelle while Holly, Sadie, Sun and Ruaridh got their glam on. And it just kept going. Justin had their every inflection studied and perfected. And they all took turns to sing the parts.

"Bit boring now," Will whispered. "We could mess around to music in a studio upstairs. Not as good as clubbing, but it would be something."

I nodded. "Wait till he's engrossed with somebody, and we'll sneak away."

Justin faced Holly in flamboyant encouragement, and we sidled out of the room and ran up the stairs, giggling like naughty children. Music on shuffle, we danced around randomly for a while before becoming more focused. One song had Will drop to the floor and roll, then try it out again, and soon we were immersed in choreography and had succeeded in losing ourselves on a dance floor, after all.

"A-ha! The truants!" shouted Justin as he opened the door. "There was some confusion about exactly where you had gone. So this is what you're up to. Let's see, then."

"It's not finished," I said, perturbed to see Aleks accompany Justin into the room. All at once the song lyrics seemed to be about him: games, losing someone, a tender kiss. It was somewhat mortifying. Justin, however, was not to be deterred, insisting we show them our work.

"Okay, but the big lift?" I said to Will. "Just lower me down after it."

"All right," he said. "We can practise the drop next door on those mats later."

Music on, we went through what we had so far.

"It's good," said Justin with an offensive level of astonishment. "Not worth-missing-the-workshop good, but it's promising."

"I am very impressed," agreed Aleks.

"You only like ballet," I said, our choreography being contemporary with a balletic edge.

"I like very much," he insisted. "You have wrought great change in me. In many ways."

"Yes, yes, it's all very impressive," said Justin. "But I'm not missing dinner for it." And, with a slightly odd grin, he was gone.

"Is it dinnertime already?" I asked, astonished. The afternoon had flown by.

"But I want to practice the next bit," moaned Will.

"Is problem with a lift?" asked Aleks. "Can I help?"

Will said yes, and I said no.

"It's not the lift itself," I explained. "It's the fall and catch part that's less appealing."

"It's perfect with the music, and I will catch you," assured Will.

"Show me," said Aleks. "And between us we won't let you fall."

Will caught me round the waist as I twisted towards the ground, but Aleks's hands were there too, a guarantee of safety. We practised a few times, then walked down to dinner together and everything felt a little better.

All was quiet in the great hall. All was calm. Pieces of glitzy costumes were still scattered about, and they added some colour to the huge room. I had my friends and my lasagne, and I felt I could relax a bit at last.

"Amalphia, can I have a word?"

Sun's request was not welcome. I wanted to eat my dinner in peace.

"We're going up to the stone circle tonight," she said. "Much later, once people are in bed. Just you, me and Holly. Female-empowerment ritual."

"Umm," I said, careful not to commit to anything. Rain ran down the long dark windows of the great hall in silvery streams.

"You have some sort of affinity with the place," she said. "You have to come."

I nodded. It might be better than spending the evening crying into my pillow.

"Can I come?" asked Will.

"I didn't realise you identified as a woman," said Sun.

"I don't," said Will, looking confused.

"Well, you have no place in a female-empowerment exercise then, do you? Dress warmly, Phi, and bring some old knickers."

"Slightly worried now," I said to the boys once she'd gone.

"You should be," said Justin. "God knows what all that's about. But listen, you and me, we have to convene up the back passage after dinner, before I go swimming." He very much enjoyed referring to the kitchen corridor as the back passage.

"See, this is the place for dark secrets," he said later as we stood in the half-light of the passageway beside the unicorn tapestry. "I was dragged in here earlier by a desperate man."

"Who?"

"Your erstwhile lover, darling, and he was in a right state."

"Aleks? Is something wrong?"

"He thought you were off boffing Hearst."

"What?"

"Well, 'making love with each other' was what he actually said. Making love? I mean, who says that? Gets away with it, though, doesn't he? Sorry, look, I'll start at the beginning. Dragged in here, all excited, thinking the Zolotov had turned. He's all, 'You must be very honest with me, Justin. She is with William now?' And I'm like, 'Ugh, no, what gave you that idea?' Many things apparently."

"But, why would he care anyway? He got over me in one day."

"Hello! Are you blind? He watches you all the time. His face during the *Romeo and Juliet* snogathon? It was a toss-up which was more interesting to watch, you or him. That's why I said all that stuff about Lady Macbeth. To explain about your acting, you see. He was in pieces. But it was nothing to this afternoon's fandango. I said, 'I don't think that's what's happening, but let's go see.' And he's like, 'No, we can't do that.' So I'm like, 'Yes, we can—'"

"Justin."

"Sorry, it went on a bit, was still going on in fact, when I flung open Hearst's door and screamed. The mess! Dirty clothes everywhere, dishes with dried-up stuff on them. There should be police tape over that door to warn people away. Anyway, he thought the worst. But I heard music, and there you were, skiving off my class, but I'll let that pass for now."

"Maybe it's a male-ego thing," I wondered. "He doesn't want me, but nobody else should either?"

"He's very, very sorry about all that rubbish with Simone. I don't think he'll ever flirt with anyone again."

"What?"

"We both agreed it was inexcusable. I asked him, if he was so bothered about you, what was that all about, and he said that he loves you so much. In fact he said, 'I love her with great force.' I felt quite weak. Go and find him, Phi. Talk it out, go to bed. It'll be better than whatever lesbo romp Sun's got planned."

"I don't believe this, Justin. He's charmed you. Remember what he did, and how he behaved," I said, to remind myself as much as my friend after what I'd just been told.

"Yes," he replied, momentary confusion visible on his face. "But you were so sweet together before we came here."

"Yes. Before. Not now. Not again. I'm going to watch telly with Will."

How dare Aleks use Justin to do this? Or was Justin exaggerating or misinterpreting passing comments? He always forgave Edward, whatever he'd done. Was there some sort of transference going on here? I tried not to dwell, or surmise, or even think about it too much.

ele

I climbed the stairs to prepare for the excursion to the circle, feeling deeply sad about everything. Passing Aleks's room with its ever-open door, I realised what he might think when he heard footsteps on the stairs in the night.

I knocked and put my head round the edge of the door. He was sitting on his bed reading and almost fell over himself to get to me.

"Malphia."

Justin was right. He did seem in a state. He stopped short of touching me and appeared both pleased and worried to see me.

"Hi," I said. "I just wanted to let you know that some of us are going out later, and it might disturb you. It's difficult to be quiet on the stairs."

"You are sneaking out to the nightclub? Michelle is gone for two days to get more equipment so she will not know, and I will not tell." He laid his hand across his heart.

"No." I smiled at his gesture. "We're going up to the stone circle for some sort of female-empowerment... thing."

"Outside? At night? Is been rain, now is frost, will be ice everywhere. Is dangerous for slip, will be dark and so, so cold. Already you are cold. I know this." He took my hands and attempted to rub warmth into them.

"I don't want to go," I told him. "But I've said I will now. Holly's really looking forward to it. She's doing food and looking out coats and boots and things."

"Who else is going?"

"Just Sun and me. Will wanted to come, but Sun said no men, and she didn't ask Sadie or anyone else, so it's just us."

I stopped. I was babbling. For a short time, everything had felt easy and natural like before.

The hug was spontaneous, and it was like coming home after a long and perilous journey.

"I miss you so much," he said.

"I miss you too."

After a while, he wiped my face with his sleeve and I tried to do the same for him with my fingers. Touching his face made me cry more, but I didn't try to hide it. Crying in front of each other felt like lancing the hurt that had grown between us. His bad behaviour had sprung from fear and repressed emotion, so it was surely better to tell these things, to show—

"I cannot bear to see you cry. This morning, at breakfast, I want to gather you up, make everything right for you. But there is this terrible truth. It was I that had made everything wrong. Then Will, he is being the hero, no? Much this week, I have seen. You have a great compassion, even for those is not deserving. I think is like your acting. You can be another person, also feel exactly what they are feeling, understand."

"You've been reading about autism and empathy," I said, glancing at the book on his bed. "How it can seem almost psychic?"

"Ah," he said as if caught in a crime. "Usually I am dismiss labels as we are all unique, but you are using this word yourself, and I wanted to see if there is any way I can be better for you."

"Okay." As a teacher, I assumed.

"I realise springing a surprise, like was done with the Ceilidh, was not good at all, and will endeavor to make sure such a thing does not happen again." As a teacher. "And the choreography this afternoon," he said, moving the conversation on. "It is superb. Truly."

"That was mainly Will."

"The music, the words? They are speaking to me."

"I think you take whatever meaning there is to you in music, a song, especially if, when, well…"

"When you are in love."

Not quite so teacherly then, but nervousness appeared at the thought of enlarging upon the subject.

"I better go and get ready."

"Wait." He pulled off his sweater. "This you wear, and together, your friends and those who love you, we will keep you warm."

I pulled it on, his determination to tell me he loved me making both my eyes and chest ache.

"You look beautiful," he said.

"I've been crying. I now have two bulky jumpers on. I look hideous."

"You don't. But you will let me know when you are back? Just put head round door if you like, or come in, we speak, whatever you want."

"It could be very late."

"I will not sleep until I know you are safe back in the castle, angel."

Chapter 22

A LONG WAIT TOOK place in the top room of the tower. The more time went by, the less I wanted to go on the excursion. Prancing off into the cold night held no attraction, even if it did look a bit moonlit and sparkly out there. It would be preferable, by far, to go and sit with Aleks. Just talk with him a bit, maybe.

Sun finally arrived, having been lighting a fire in the stone circle, and we clopped down the stairs. Every step echoed as we wound our way downwards.

A door opened ahead. Will looked as surprised and horrified to see us as I felt to see him emerging from Sadie's room.

"Evening, Will," said Sun with a smile.

I turned my head and looked down the winding staircase, so upset I could have screamed. A red cloud formed around me.

"I thought you were off at your thing," said Will. "In the circle."

"We're just going now," said Sun.

We left him behind, without another word or look, and met Holly in the entrance hall.

"Are you all right, Phi?" Sun asked as we put coats on.

"Yes."

"You're not, but don't worry. That's what tonight's all about: unburdening, sharing. Women together, secure in our own company."

It sounded like something that would have made Justin stick his fingers down his throat, and I had to concur, though by the end of the experience I was more irritated than bilious. I stormed back up the stairs a couple of hours later. Sun and Holly had urged me to go to bed. They would put away all the food things and clean up the kitchen. Talk about me, more like.

Outside Will's door, annoyance intensified into something positively visceral. I wanted to shout at him, to throw things around, to shock him how he'd shocked me. To be, in short, totally obnoxious. My hand turned the handle, but... I had no right. He hadn't actually done anything wrong. I didn't own Will.

Shutting my eyes summoned an image of a square black crossroads. I could either go through this door, or go upstairs and talk to Aleks. Both wouldn't happen. I didn't see why not. But my anger was senseless. I was being stupid.

I took the stone steps two at a time.

His door was open, and he smiled. "Look at you," he said, touching my hair as I stood in his glow. There was a slightly bemused look on his face, and a quick glance in the wall mirror showed why.

The glass itself was struck dumb by the sight. My hair was bedraggled and wild, my face darkened by smoke. Tears had cut little trails of cleaner skin down my dirty cheeks. "I'm going to have a shower," I said, making for the door.

"No." He held me back, gently as if I might break or scare. "Stay. I will make you a bath. You are cold. Come, you will like; there are bubbles," he said as if this sealed the deal. "While you bathe, I will go downstairs and make hot chocolate. You like this also."

It was comforting to be cajoled by Aleks. I sat on the side of the bath as he prepared it. He then left on his chocolate-making mission, and I deposited my clothes on the floor and sank into the almost unbearable heat of the water.

I used his face cloth and his shampoo and then borrowed a T-shirt and a pair of trunk-style underpants.

"Everything else smells of smoke," I explained, when he returned. "It was either this or go up to my room and get—"

"No, you did completely the right thing, but you still need socks. Come sit."

Bossed around again, I let him put thick warm-up socks on my feet as I sat on the bed. He tucked the blankets round me and handed me a mug, all with a terribly serious expression. He got into his side of the bed. We sat about a foot apart, hands firmly on the hot mugs of chocolate.

"It's good," I said. "You make it so much better than I do."

"Is very difficult. The kitchen was full of bad-tempered people."

"Holly and Sun?"

"Yes. Holly she say, 'Two cups?' So, I explain you are cold. 'And you've taken it upon yourself to warm her up,' she says. Tone is very judging."

"Welcome to my evening."

"This is how they were? They are knowing of our relationship?"

"Holly did. Then they compared notes."

It had been excruciating. Sun had encouraged me to speak about the snowy morning in the circle with Will. I'd described how we had both wanted to feel the sun on our skin, and that we'd hugged in a half-naked state. Holly had been askance, and all, 'I thought you were still smitten with Aleks?' Cue Sun's turn to be agog.

My chocolate was finished. Only a thick dark cream remained. The white china touched the polished wood of the bedside cabinet with a muffled clink. I heard him carry out the same action at the other side of the bed. I held on to the handle of the cup for a second, giving myself time to note my senses enliven like they had that day on the train. I was aware of the cold hard china, the soft warm blankets, his scent, the warmth of his body so near mine... I turned.

Our teeth clashed in the force of the kiss. I climbed onto him, hands feverish under his clothes.

"Angel, we can take it slow. We hold each other and sleep only, tonight. I have miss this so. Our closeness. Our love."

A negative sound hummed in the back of my throat as I shook my head in desperation. "I need you, Aleks. I need you so much. I physically ache for you, every morning. I never remember what's happened at first." A thought, a realisation, and I was angry. "I was never like this before. You did this to me, you made me need you, need sex."

"No," he said, taking hold of my hands. "I think, with one another, we have found our true natures. I have walked around my whole life not knowing who I am, who I could be." He linked his fingers through mine. "And you could have come to me at any time. For anything. You must know this."

I kissed his mouth, and his neck, and then down a shoulder, having succeeded in removing his T-shirt, but he was still determined to talk.

"You are getting the clothes? The thermals?"

"I knew they were from you."

He murmured in Ukrainian while I kissed and bit at him. I wanted to open my pores and absorb Aleks directly in through my skin, so as to never lose him again. Yet somehow everything was different now. And not quite right. Sex felt like a fight. I didn't like him letting me take the lead. That wasn't what I wanted. He'd said he loved me with great force. I needed that.

I got my way, sort of, but something was still wrong. Wary defences remained in me. But every movement weakened them. They crumbled under the tenderest of kisses. He spoke words unknown, in his own language. He sounded gentle and rough and true. It was his words that finally ended the battle, and I let go, torn into little pieces of self, loudly scattered around the bed.

My fragmented form lay helplessly under him, then beside him. He was wet with sweat. I kissed it, and tasted the salt of him. I could hear his heart. I could smell his skin. I was warm.

"I am so very deeply in love with you, Malphia."

I wanted to say it back, but some splinter of armour caught on the words and unravelled them. I almost found myself saying, 'yeah, right,' in some sort of defiance or defence, but what actually came out was: "I love the way you make hot chocolate."

He laughed. "It is impossible for us to be apart, angel. I think—"

My finger stilled his lips. "Not tonight. Can't we be, just us? Here in this moment?"

"Of course," he whispered.

Lamplight was replaced with bright moonlight, but I was too sleepy to stay awake and appreciate its silver beauty. There had been no moon visible in the circle. The great orb seemed to shine for us alone, casting three long window shapes across the bed, across our bodies, and over our love.

My eyes stared directly into his.

"I am so happy you are here," he said.

Grey and silver predominated in the colour scheme of Aleks's room, like the moonlight of the night before. I backed away, off the bed and onto the floor. Random clothes were pulled on.

"Is Sunday," he said. "We can stay in bed as long as we like."

My arms began to shake. "I can't be here. Can't do this again."

"Then, what is this last night?" he asked, the happy, sleepy look fading from his face.

I stayed silent and still, too confused by the mix of emotions I was feeling to understand them myself, let alone explain them to him. I wanted to be with him. Of course I did. But I also didn't. Because it was scary and intense and overwhelming.

"You said you needed me," he said. "So you meant only for sex. You are making us into 'friends with benefits?'" He got out of bed.

"No. I didn't plan any of this."

"Your ache is cured, so you go. You have made your use of me."

I shook my head but said nothing.

"A fuck buddy? This is what I am now?" Aleks saying the word 'fuck' felt jarring and wrong. And how dare he?

"You were the one with the bath and the chocolate," I reminded him. "You were the one telling me to stay." His face was furious, but I was the one to shout. "I certainly don't need you swearing at me! So don't worry, Aleks, it'll never happen again."

I ran for the door, but he followed, and I somehow ended up crying against his chest while he held my head and pressed his mouth into my hair.

"I'm sorry, angel. I am so sorry. Feel my heart." It drummed fast against my palm. "I am panic, thinking we are together, and then we are not. You are afraid to resume our relationship, and how could you not be after the way I have behaved?"

Was I just going to let him carry me back to bed? Apparently so.

He went on. "Maybe this is the best idea? I will still be the man who makes love to you. You come to me whenever you like. Or tell me, and I come upstairs to you. In time, maybe, I can earn your trust again, and we develop into more. If this is what you want."

"No. Aleks. This is a weird thing you're suggesting." I lay back on the bed and folded my arms over my face. I felt him shift to lie close and resisted the inclination to turn and snuggle.

"So," he said. "We tell everyone we are together. No more secrets."

"Would you really want that?" I asked, facing him, and then noticing he had a cut lip. "Was that me?" I touched the hurt place gently and remembered biting him.

"Oof." He waved a dismissive hand. "Always we are responding to each other with great passion. I want anything that will make you feel sure of me again, secure with me. To be secret was always your choice."

I placed a gentle kiss on the puffy lip. "But won't coming out with this affect your job and my place here? What are the rules about relationships between teachers and students? Are they forbidden like at college?"

"No. We are not as organised with our rules yet. But my career is over. Yours is yet to begin. We are meet in the space between. Tell me how it is to be better for you."

I thought about it. "I don't think it's the time for disclosure. Simone's pride has already taken a big knock, and Will might not understand. He likes you, and you work well together. I don't want to spoil that. He knows some of what went on, but—"

"Not that I am 'the prick.'"

"No," I said, because it was true. I thought for a moment. "I need you to promise me something, Aleks."

"Anything."

"When it's over for you – this, us – you must say so plainly, so there can be no misunderstanding."

"This is what you think is to happen?"

"It's inevitable. And I don't want to feel uncertain, or wonder what's going on."

He shook his head. "One morning you will wake and realise you are in bed with an old man."

"Don't turn it around on me. And you're not an old man— Oi!"

The manner in which he had pinned me down on my back afforded a stunning view of his body: taut muscles, smooth skin, male strength...

"Stop trying to distract me with your sexiness," I said.

"Is working?"

"No," I lied.

He released me and turned away. "Already, it is begin."

I knelt up on the bed and leant against his back. "We could both promise to be clear and honest with each other."

"Your maturity is shame me once again. Of course, complete honesty is what we need."

A sinking feeling formed in my belly, and I moved back a little on the bed. "I have to tell you something. I understand better how a confused moment can happen now. You see, Will and I..."

"I already know, and it is not mattering," he said, turning and taking my hands in his. "I sat on the stairs all night after you see her, Simone, here. I knew this is where you must be."

"We didn't sleep together! I stayed with Justin that night." While Aleks had made himself ill sitting on the stairs. "I'm talking about the morning in the stone circle."

"In the snow?" He gave a short laugh as if this made it all fine. "Ah, Malphia, these things, they happen. When you dance together, a certain closeness forms. And there has been some romance with William in the past, no?"

"No." Why had I suggested total honesty? "I had a crush on him long ago. That's all."

"He is the unrequited love you spoke of? I thought was Justin."

I shook my head at the strange concept. Justin was like my brother.

"I have something for you," he said, changing mood and subject.

"I don't need you to buy me things."

"This is different," he said, getting off the bed and opening a drawer. "I bring this from home. Already, I had decided it was to be yours. If we did not fix ourselves here, I would still give, and hope you remember me, and maybe one day..." He shrugged.

He opened a long black velvet box. Inside was a diamond on a silver chain. Intricate workings of smaller stones and metal encircled it, impressions of flowers and birds.

"How beautiful," I said. "I've never seen anything quite like it."

"It was my Grandmother's."

"Then you mustn't give it to me. I might lose it or break it. It's a family heirloom. I can't take it."

He removed the necklace from the box and fastened it round my neck.

"You can lose or break; is yours. She would like that it is worn again, my Russian Grandmother. She would like you. Several times I have thought this. Is no light thing, as she is not liking many people. She would not have been pleased with me recently. Look, it completely suits you."

I stood and looked into the mirror on the wall. It had nothing to say.

"Malphia." He held his arms out, and I was hugged and home and safe and warm. "This is where it all calms," he said. "This is where we balance our fire."

Chapter 23

WILL WAS TRYING TO light the fire in the huge fireplace of the great hall when I walked in. He continued ineffectually setting light to bits of newspaper as I sat down in the nearest orange armchair.

"How was the ladies' midnight romp?" Ruaridh enquired, after informing me that there had been no breakfast. Holly hadn't shown up.

"It wasn't the most fun," I told him.

"What were the knickers for?"

"Oh, burning. Banishing past badness. The melting elastic smelled bad."

Will still didn't look up.

"You need firelighters," I said, putting my hand on his shoulder and joining him by the enormous slate hearth. A quick rummage in a basket soon located some, and the fire in the cradle flickered to life. I smiled at him in a moment of forgiveness, though there was nothing to forgive. His return expression seemed more a sorry than a smile.

"No food?" Aleks asked, coming into the room behind us. "I will make. Come," he said to me. "We find something."

"I am honoured that you are wearing it," he said, once we were alone in the kitchen.

My hand touched the diamond under my jumper for the umpteenth time. "I can't wear it often. I'm frightened of losing it."

"So, this is a special day," he said, tracing the chain with a finger and making my skin tingle. "I have not coped well with finding myself in love. I have been an idiot. Even this morning, I am panicking and saying so many wrong things."

"Blurting. I know it well. But I know you too, Aleks. And I think I can handle you."

"I think you can too," he said with a smile.

The sound of footsteps ended the kiss. We stepped apart. He opened the two fridges, and I looked in the baking cupboard as the boys came in.

"Eggs," said Aleks.

"Chocolate-chip pancakes," said I.

"I'll make coffee," volunteered Ruaridh, and Will put bread in the toaster. Soon we were a happy little family round the big breakfast table, all cosy and content.

"Look at our little Malphia," said Aleks. "She is eating, and she is smiling. I think she must have reconcile with... what are you calling him, Will? The prick?"

My face warmed, and I studied a burned black circle on the much-marked surface of the table.

"No way," said Will in disbelief.

Further comment was delayed by the arrival of Justin. "You're having a secret breakfast back here? Give us a plate then."

"Did you know about this?" Will asked him. "She's back with the prick."

"Is she?" Justin studied all our faces. "Well, this is all completely delicious." He took a smiling bite of pancake. "I saw it coming, of course."

"Not to be worry, Will," said Aleks. "If he misbehave, we can all rough him up a bit, yes?" His smile faltered as he met my furious glare.

Will didn't smile. "So when was this?" he demanded, his hands forming fists on the table. "Last night?"

I nodded, annoyed by his annoyance, and asked: "And what about Sadie?"

His face flushed.

I quickly added: "And Simone and Sun? They might want breakfast. There's plenty."

It was Justin who answered. "Sunshine was just going to bed when I got up. Simone would have some sort of embolism from merely looking at all this. And let's be honest, Sadie could stand to miss the odd meal."

"Justin," I began, keen to halt the unfortunate criticism of Will's girlfriend.

"You don't have to lift her," he said. "She doesn't even have good balance or technique to make up for it."

The entrance of Holly shifted Justin's attention. He availed her of my changed relationship status. No names were mentioned, but they shared a knowing look.

Aleks smiled. Will glowered. Cosiness was gone.

As the dishes were cleared, Holly asked for my assistance in the laundry room. "I shouldna need to tell you fit a bad idea this is," she said as soon as we were alone.

I shook my head and sighed. "We love each other. And he's not how you think."

"Oh, aye. Misunderstood, is he?"

My hand went protectively to the necklace as if to shelter him. "Yes, actually. People don't see all there is of him."

"They see what's been going on, aricht. For God's sake, lassie. If he's treated you shite once, he'll de it again. There'll be more tears afore long."

I started folding clothes and encountered a black thong. The washing basket bore the label of 'Simone.' I laid the underwear down slowly, turned on my heel and walked back through to the kitchen.

"Gone to lift weights, all of them!" exclaimed Justin as if telling of mass hysteria. "That was Zolotov's suggestion for improving things with Sadie. Me, getting muscled up. But it's a good thing the two of you are back together. All is blissful again in these ancient walls, though I did notice he had a fat lip. Don't be too vicious with him, Phi. He's such a beautiful specimen."

"I dinna believe this," said Holly, having followed me through. "Justin, ye ken as well as I do that he's far too auld, he's full o' himself, he's—"

"He wept in my arms, sweet Holly," said Justin. "He took me into the back passage last night. I would challenge you to remain disaffected by such an experience."

She remained staunchly unconvinced.

He went on. "And how often does a cock like that come along? I mean, really, darling... And look at our little Phi. The 'A to Z of Ecstasy' is getting the job done, all right."

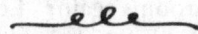

Bright sunshine blasted through gaps in the trees as I walked up the hill. The centre of the path was grey and icy, so my feet favoured the less slippery, crunchy snow at the sides. A faint aroma of pine mingled with the wood smoke from the previous night. The black patch in the centre of the stone circle still smoked and made me think of a charred wound, a glaring human injury in this most perfect of places.

I sat on the big flat stone, and thought of Aleks and all that had happened, and wondered whether I really knew what I was doing. I'd said I could handle him, but was that true? I loved him, but was that enough? What if the strange character-change thing that had come over him when we first came here happened again? Was I excusing him too easily?

I thought about other people too. Will and Justin, even Michelle, Simone and Sadie wafted in and out of my mind. Lying down on the dry stone in the friendly sunlight soon induced drowsiness, and I drifted into a half sleep, aware of the supportive slab below.

A woman smiled, shining with warmth like the sun, wavy golden hair all round her face. She leant forward and touched my necklace, causing little sparks to dance out of it and leap all around. Her hand held a tiny pink stone, a glowing teardrop of rainbows, and she pressed it into my heart. I laughed at the tickly sensation and sat up, eyes open in the sunny circle, surprised not to find a pink jewel embedded in my chest.

My heart drummed with new power. Everything was possible. Everything was wonderful. We were protected and strong, and love was the answer to everything. I floated down the path to the castle and beamed love toward it.

The dark of the place was instantly obvious as I stepped inside, but the sounds of people in the hall led to friends: my lovely, lovely friends.

"Where have you been?" asked Justin as I sat down at the table between him and Will. "You've missed lunch."

I smiled.

"Been on the mushrooms again?" Lovely Justin.

"You've been back in the circle," said Sun.

"We shouldn't have had that fire," I told her. "It's left an ugly scar."

"You're right," she said. "It's not done to leave a sacred site changed in any way. I got a bit carried away but, lesson learned. We won't do anything like that again."

"No, we won't."

"You need food to ground you," she said. "I'll get you something."

"Spit it out," said Justin once she'd gone. "What ritualistic heathenism have you been indulging in this morning? I've already heard about last night from Holly."

I leant my face against Will's shoulder. He was safe. He understood.

"You're all loopy, Malph," he said, rubbing my back. "What happened?"

In a low voice, I told them of the vivid dream I'd had.

"But, but..." butted Justin. "That's like being given a big gift from the universe. I'm going up there. So, it's the flat stone nearest the path?"

Information gleaned, he departed, and Sun sat down in his place with a plate of food. I ate a chip and took my head off Will's shoulder. A sudden and poisonous look from Sadie had grounded me better than any food could.

"Sorry," I said.

"Nah, babe, you're all right."

"We're behaving inappropriately, or I am."

Will's reply was drowned out by the glorious fanfare of Aleks's arrival in the hall. His smile was golden as he made his way over to us.

"How was the strong-man competition?" I asked, feeling intensely tender toward him. "With the weights?"

"Ah, was not competition."

"Men lifting heavy things, and there was no competitive element?" said Sun. "I don't believe that for a minute."

"I am the strongest," admitted Aleks.

"You would be," she said. "So many more women."

I looked at her in shock.

"Oh, no," stuttered Sun. "I meant, pas de deux, ballet lifting." She mimed a lift with her hands.

Aleks held out his hand to me. "I have had an idea. Can you come to the first floor and warm up?"

Chapter 24

B Y THE TIME MICHELLE returned on Monday evening, Aleks's idea had become a large theatrical plan and was well in place.

I had demonstrated his choreography two ways for everyone in Monday morning class. Once, concentrating on technique, and once, just being the subject of the piece: love. It took acting to a new level, without a human character to inhabit. Heart full of Aleks, head lost in the music, my body expressed love, pure love and nothing else. It was dizzying. Will took hold of my arm, to stop me falling over as I swayed about in the middle of the floor after I'd finished.

The day before, I had danced the piece for Aleks alone. He had planned that I should release residual anger and hurt through movement, so we could talk through whatever issues arose. It hadn't worked. I only wanted to move forward, only wanted to love. My interpretation of the choreography had led to a crash of a kiss and a race up the stairs into bed, a practice that became so common in the weeks that followed, it was incredible that no one discerned our secret.

"Is important that we remember what the training is all about," Aleks told the class after that first demonstration. "We need to be working towards a performance."

The dramatic differences in my on-screen squiggles, before and after dancing the love choreography, convinced Paul that this was something worth exploring. He agreed to a Christmas show in which dance and research would be showcased together. So the next six weeks were to be spent preparing to perform said show in front of 'very important people.'

The mood in the castle transformed. Aleks's drive and enthusiasm for the project touched everyone, the very walls of the place seeming to vibrate with excitement.

Both Will and Simone were unhappy about Aleks's determination to dance the sexy *Sarabande* with me himself, but they were quickly pacified. Simone was given a beautiful classical solo, and Will was asked to create a contemporary piece which he based, somewhat to my trepidation, on the stone circle. It was primal, sexual and difficult.

"No way, Hearse," I said, as he walked through yet another idea for the finish. Justin joined us in the wild tribal creation entitled *Circle*. The real stone circle lay abandoned by us all. Justin had been disillusioned by his lone experience there. He had lain on the flat stone for hours until he was cold and grumpy, and no visions or sunshine had been forthcoming.

Sadie rushed past me in tears one afternoon. Aleks and Will looked uncomfortable in a nearby studio.

"Were you rehearsing the balcony scene?" I asked, knowing that Will and Sadie were going to be performing it together. "Sadie's really upset."

"She is not manage," Aleks told me. "The ability is just not there."

"And Bevan's right," added Will. "She weighs a tonne."

"Sometimes this is a genuine problem, Amalphia," explained Aleks, seeing my annoyance.

"Are you going after her?" I asked Will.

"No."

Will might be a good friend, but he was clearly a terrible boyfriend.

I found Sadie in her room. "Were they being idiots?"

She lifted her face out of the pillow. "I can't do it. I'm not, you know... you."

"So, we try something else." What would Sadie enjoy doing? "How d'you feel about musical theatre?" I asked, remembering that she had liked Justin's workshop.

Her interest was piqued.

"We should do something with just women," I mused, there being nothing like that in the planned programme. "Let's try some stuff out."

Down on the, now deserted, first floor, we stamped and sang our way through a few different things.

A clipped voice cut through our practice: "What are you girls up to? I thought everybody was down at dinner."

I looked at Michelle in her red suit and shiny shoes and decided to tell her exactly what we were doing, annoying men and all.

She listened. She nodded. She smiled.

"There was a song, years ago," she said. "About men getting their comeuppance. Being murdered, even. I always adored it. Superb music. Great costumes. It had it all." She walked into the room and, with the kick of a red-clad leg and the flick of an arm, sang a small part of the song.

"It is familiar," I said, somewhat taken aback by both her amenability and ability. "Would you be willing to be in it, if we did that one?"

"Oh, I'd love that," she said.

"Then, I think we'll have a showstopper," I said. "And Aleks has to accept it if you're involved. You're like the big boss, aren't you?"

She laughed. "I would love to hear you say that in front of him. But yes, you can do it."

Sadie and I marched down the stairs and over to Justin, who was having dinner in the great hall. "Justin, we need you to help us," I said.

"With?"

"Staging a musical number."

He laid his fork down.

"I don't actually know the name of the song," I admitted. "It's about women murdering men." I hummed a little of the tune.

"My sweet murderous loves," said Justin. "Much as I like the idea, and have always loved the song – though we'll have to check performance rights – we are rather short on ladies for it."

"Michelle's going to do it," Sadie told him, and his mouth dropped open.

"She's good too," I added. "Then there's Sun, Sadie, me." I put grievances aside and added: "Simone?"

The latter looked disdainfully across the table at us.

"I'm sure you'd be beautiful in it," I told her.

"I'll think about it," she said, turning away. Of course she joined us, and Holly completed the lineup magnificently.

The murderous rehearsals stretched us further; legs grew more tired and the nights later. Justin's demands and pernickety criticisms exasperated everyone, but the song was becoming a truly polished and professional part of the show.

At the top of the tower, Aleks and I lay in bed and talked. We discussed everything from the day's rehearsals to our childhoods. He'd broken his nose falling out of a tree when he was seven. I kissed the beloved indentation.

"What is this 'ghastly' thing he keeps saying today?" asked Aleks, Justin's antics often finding their way into our conversations.

"It's what Simone said when she saw our costumes for Will's *Circle* piece," I explained. "She has a point, actually. We're wearing glorified sticky-tape. I can't believe Michelle is allowing it, but she ordered the stuff without question. My mother is going to spontaneously combust when she sees it. The *Sarabande* is bad enough. This will finish her off."

"No, surely she will be proud. Your solo is to be the highlight of the night. You, yourself, will be the star of the whole show."

It had been a bad moment when I discovered, during a horror-laden phone call, that my parents were coming to the performance, Michelle having invited everyone she found in our files. Happily, the constant bustle of practice left very little time to worry about parental dismay, though it also kept me from dealing with another issue, as Justin pointed out the next day.

"Isn't it about time you told Hearst he's not going to be getting his leg over anytime soon?" he asked after a particularly gruelling *Circle* rehearsal.

"I told you. He's got something going on with Sadie. There's nothing like that between me and Will."

"That ample ship sailed long ago. It's you he gets hard for."

"Oh, stop bleetering rubbish." I had seen Will and Sadie in close conversation several times, so knew they were still together.

"Bleetering? Is this some Scottish word you've picked up? You need to tell him you're wintering in Ukraine this year."

"Will and I are friends."

"Yes, and he's very keen to consummate your friendship in carnal fashion. With the frenzied palooza we've just worked through, I'm surprised he hasn't tried to dry hump you against a wall."

"Justin. You know as well as I that Will has had lots of girlfriends, and I was never one of them."

"Do I detect some remaining resentment over that?"

"No."

"So tell him. I know, Sun knows, even jolly Holly knows, but old friend Will? Fumbling around in the dark, isn't he?"

He was right. Will, my friend, should know who my boyfriend was. "I just need to find the right moment," I told Justin. But amid the mad rush of rehearsals, that moment didn't appear.

I loved the continual honing of choreography and technique, the discovery of small nuances that made huge changes, and the ongoing pursuit of perfection. The hurtle towards Christmas was too fast to think much about the goal, the show, the fear. Then Aleks had a meeting with Michelle late one evening from which he returned distraught.

We sat on the bed, and he told me what 'she,' a word hatefully said, had planned. The monitoring of our brain activity was to be displayed on a giant screen behind *Circle*.

"Will won't want that," I said at once. "The choreography is all very primitive. Justin's been winding him up by putting in modern moves, and it's not gone down well at all."

"This, he will have to learn," said Aleks. "Dancers, choreographers, we all take second place to whoever controls the money. She is to give a talk at the start about the research. I am her test subject for the therapeutic side of things."

"What does she want you to do?"

"Ah, nothing. She has film, always is film everything. I don't know what exactly she will show: my operation, recovery using her techniques? She has it all. I just say fine and walk out, not to let her see she has get to me."

I suspected he didn't want me to see this footage of Michelle's. "We'll all be backstage," I reminded him.

"No, this she is specifying: all are to watch to understand. To learn the value of her work, but also, I think, it is you she most wants to see. Is possible she suspects something about us."

The air reddened. How dare Michelle upset him like this? "Aleks." I held his face. "There's nothing she can show me that will change how I feel. You're wonderful and I love you. The fact that you've been through bad things only proves that you're brave and strong."

He didn't look convinced.

"I won't see it anyway," I said, his distress pushing the hitherto-avoided fact to the fore. "I get really bad stage fright. I sometimes try to run away at the last minute. That's not an exaggeration. Ask Will. I've always been this way. You'll have to stay with me in the wings if you want me in the show. Sometimes I'm sick too. So if she forces me into the auditorium, I might vomit on some of the very important people."

"This is true?" His focus shifted at once. "Then it is even more vital that you gain performance experience. In time, with practice, this, it will improve."

It was my turn to be unconvinced, but Aleks was enthused again, full of stories of other dancers who had overcome their fears.

I lay in his arms and hoped we would always be this way, together in love, keeping one another safe from fear and harm under a starry sky.

Chapter 25

ICICLES HUNG FROM THE tops of windows on the morning of the show, as immobile and frozen as me. Aleks's advice was to take the day in small parts, to contemplate one thing at a time. He ran me a bath, and then saw that I was dressed before he departed the room.

My breakfast remained uneaten. Class was an automatic event, much of which I got wrong. At lunch, feeling empty, I accepted a piece of chocolate from Will.

The castle began to fill with new people. Some were staying in guest accommodation on the second floor, others in local hotels. They were all shown where to go by Holly and her extra helpers who had been hired for the weekend.

"Hearst, you could have a Christmas shag-fest," commented Justin after colliding with a giggly young woman in the foyer on our way through to the theatre.

My parents loomed large before us, the sour expression on the wide face of my mother suggesting she had heard Justin's remark. She managed to sound vaguely revolted and completely uninterested as she asked how we were all getting on.

"Fucktastically, Mrs. Treadwell," Justin replied.

She winced.

My father inspected the floor, the ceiling, the stairwell, then peered through to the theatre wing. "How on earth did they get permission for a modern extension like that?" he asked. "The place must be a listed building, surely?"

"They won't know about that, James," snapped my mother. "Dancers' heads are stuffed with ballet-shoe ribbons and diets. Though you appear to be eating well." She looked me up and down, and stared pointedly at the melting chocolate in my hand.

My parents headed to the great hall for welcome drinks, and we continued on our way to the theatre.

"Thing that gets me," said Justin. "She always makes these snide comments about people being bigger than she thinks they should be, but she's probably the biggest person in the building."

"She says she has a glandular condition," I explained. "But, that's not the point. I'm about to wear sticky-tape in front of her. Sticky-tape."

"And you're gonna look super fantastic in it," said Will. "Try getting angry about her 'eating well' comment. That might help."

"What is this?" asked Aleks, catching the tail end of the conversation as we arrived backstage.

"You have yet to meet famille Treadwell," Justin explained.

Through in the dressing rooms, we applied make-up and put on our costumes. Then we warmed up at the portable metal barre backstage.

Bend, stretch, breathe. Quake, dread, freeze.

Simone, Sun and Ruaridh left to listen to Michelle's introduction.

"Do you want me to stay?" asked Will, as we stood in the wings at the side of the stage.

"Is better we have a moment alone," said Aleks. "Before we perform together."

"Don't let her out of your sight," advised Will. "If she says she's going to the bog, she'll actually be hot-footing it into the woods."

"I won't be," I told them. "The window in the toilet down here only opens a couple of inches. I checked."

Will walked back toward the changing rooms as we heard Michelle start her speech on stage.

"I bet she's being really boring," I said. "She might put people to sleep. Which could be a good thing."

We were almost there now. The sexy *Sarabande*. On stage. In front of all these people. How could this be real? Why was I doing this to myself? What had I been thinking? I wanted to run, to be as far away as possible from the theatre, but looked down at my body instead, clothed as it was in what was basically black underwear. Big well-covering underwear, but still. Underwear. In front of everyone. In front of my mother.

"Malphia, look at me." Aleks placed his hands on either side of my face. "Is you and me, here in this moment."

"Just us?"

"Yes. This." He kissed my forehead. "Is time for us to dance together now."

We walked onto the stage and did just that. I looked at just him. I just worked through the familiar choreography to the best of my ability as I always did. Yet, he was different. I experienced a sort of thrill through him. It was rather a heady and delightful feeling, but not mine. We finished to riotous applause which made me jump in shock, though I should have expected clapping.

A man in the front row of the audience shouted, "Way to go, Phi!"

"You have a big fan here," said Aleks, through a stage smile. "Should I be worried?"

He held my hand as I performed a deep curtsey. "We should all be worried," I told him quietly. "Especially if he's going to keep shouting like that."

We joined Will back in the wings, the lovely safe wings, where he was peeking through the side curtains. "Is that him? The guy who shouted. Is that the prick?"

"He can be a prick," I said. "That's Edward."

"This," said Aleks, indicating the smart suited man through the curtain, "is the Edward you have told me of? He is nothing like I imagine."

"He's a solicitor," I told them. "Specialises in theatrical contracts, that sort of thing. Will, can you nip out and tell him to shut up?"

"I don't wanna speak to him."

"Look, it's hard to know how Justin will react. He may be overjoyed, or he may fall apart."

Will appeared befuddled.

"He's Justin's boyfriend," I explained. "Sort of. Sometimes."

"Oh," Will said and laughed. "Bevan's going out with a lawyer?"

"Yes," I said, becoming increasingly annoyed with Will.

Simone ran past to do her solo, all white and frilly in a tutu.

"It'll be your choreography he messes up if he's upset," I pointed out, and Will's face changed.

"But what do I say?" he asked. "'Hi, I've never met you before, but could you shut your gob?'"

I thought a moment. "Say: Amalphia asks if you could be quiet as Justin needs to focus on his performance and not your philandering presence."

"I can't say that."

"Miss out the philandering bit then."

Will was successful in mission. Not a peep was heard from Edward for the rest of the show, not even after the murderous piece which, judging by the audience reaction, was the favourite.

I teared up when I saw Justin in the sparkly purple suit he was wearing to introduce the song. "You're just stunning," I told him.

"I know," he replied, looking a bit teary himself.

Will and Ruaridh made excellent murdered men, and all the girls hugged backstage at the end. The song had passed by quickly and had actually felt fun.

"That was immense fun," said Michelle, echoing my feelings, then kissing me on both cheeks. I fought the urge to wipe away lipstick with my hand. She'd been really friendly and nice with us all through the rehearsals, but this physical contact reminded me of the intimacy she'd once shared with Aleks, and the performance-high dissipated.

"You should make it up to Will for killing him," she said. "I'm sure there'll be opportunity at the party." Her smile felt wide and creepy.

"What did she mean by that?" I asked Will and Ruaridh, once Michelle had gone.

"She means you should snog him, Phi," said Ruaridh with a grin.

"Not the worst idea ever," said Will, his own grin then fading. "Oh, but of course. Bevan's bloke's here. I suppose yours is too? Is he a boring suit as well?"

"I've been meaning to speak to you about that, Will. You know, it's... He's..." Say it, say it. Just his name; it's not that hard. But the man himself was holding up my pink gauzy dress. For my solo.

Aleks spoke of the approaching doom. "Just be love. Love cannot know fear, Malphia."

I sighed, taking the dress, resigned to my fate, and just hoped my feet would move in the correct way once the music began.

It was a lot better than anticipated, and over very fast as if I was in some sort of dream or stupor. Love certainly made time and feet fly, or maybe it was Aleks at the piano that did that. We held on to each other in the wings afterwards and watched Ruaridh and Sun do something amazing and gymnastic that I would have liked to have seen from out front.

Then, sticky-tape applied, I held Will and Justin's hands as Michelle fussed over the monitors. She made sure the little stickers were all affixed to our heads properly. There had been no getting out of it. Digital lines were to light the backdrop of our ancient circle.

And it wasn't just Will that was upset. "I'm the control, aren't I?" said Justin. "The dimwit in the group, for everyone to see."

"Let's ditch them," I said, looking round to make sure Michelle was nowhere near. "There's nothing she can do about it." We plucked the hair-tugging plastic circles from our heads and dropped them on the floor. The small defiance, coupled with the presence of my friends, made me feel braver, and I stood braced and ready to begin.

I performed the deep chassé that started the piece, sliding slowly onto the stage with bent knees to the drumming start of the music, arms stretching above as if I were just waking. One hand invited the sun to rise as I walked the circle, then I summoned my two cohorts with a stamp and fast arm gesture. They knelt, submissive to feminine power, and the sun rose.

We went wild. I launched myself through the air at Will who caught and raised me into a turning lift. We leant together, twisted, turned and rolled.

Will and I pulled Justin into another, totally different, lift where he curled round our heads, foetal, a baby unborn, unmade in time. The light rose higher and shone down white from above, outlining our figures against the rest of the dark stage. We stood side by side, suddenly still. Justin stepped back and out of the light, vanishing from view, as I fell to the ground under Will. My legs circled his waist, we both arched back and the stage went black with a single beat of a drum. There was a stunned silence before the clapping gradually started up.

Aleks arrived backstage as we were embracing and jumping up and down, buzzing with adrenaline. "You have blown me away," he said. "But Michelle, she will be furious."

"We took the monitors off," I admitted.

"You are stepping on something she is fanatical about. Say you don't know what happened, that it must have been a malfunction. She is talking to people, so you are spared for now."

"Talking of people, Phi, you'll never guess who's here?" Justin beamed at me and I assumed he meant Edward. "Your babies!"

I gasped in delight.

"You have babies?" asked Aleks, bemused.

"Yes," said Justin. "Three of them. Didn't you know?"

"Justin," I said urgently, needing to tell him before he found out any other way. "Edward's here too."

I knew at once it was okay. His ever-expressive eyebrows showed merely a hint of happy naughtiness.

"That was him falling apart?" enquired a somewhat disappointed Will.

My dress was shiny purple with a splash of stars across one shoulder. Simone was in red again, but the dress wasn't such a nice fit as the last one. She tugged at it in dissatisfaction. Sun was all natural in green while Sadie looked chic in black velvet, accessorised by long gloves and pearls.

"You're like a glamorous heroine out of a film," I told her.

"Thanks," she said. "I love your necklace."

Aleks and Will waited outside the hall doors. I patted their tuxedoed chests. "Both so handsome."

I didn't hear their returning compliments as I was suddenly infused with spine-tingling horror. I'd been so preoccupied by the show, and then the fun of choosing shiny outfits, that I hadn't given the after party any thought whatsoever. But here we were. Standing on the threshold of another Ceilidh-type event, another ordeal to be got through.

Will pushed the big door open a chink, the noise from within revealing the huge number of people in attendance. "A room for you to flirt your way round, Zolotov," he remarked.

"You gonna shag your way round it, Hearst?" asked Justin, arriving behind us, back in his glittery suit from the murderous song. "I personally intend to do both. Alas, sweet Phi, there can be no similar hope for you. Mother Dreadwell awaits."

And the door swung wide open.

Chapter 26

TWO SMALL GUIDED MISSILES parted the crowd and almost knocked me over. I hugged my babies: Ophelia and Freya, the daughters of my old teacher Peter, who followed closely in their wake. I'd missed them. Their guileless compliments on my dress and dancing, and genuine delight and wonder at the castle, brought home what an exclusively adult world we'd been living in.

Benjamin, a little over one year old, eyed me suspiciously. "He doesn't remember me," I realised.

"He does, Phi," said Yvonne, Peter's wife.

"You're looking beautiful, darling girl," said Peter. "I have to hand it to you, Zolotov. I had grave doubts, but they've all come on, even little Justin." Without pausing for breath, he turned straight to Will. "That was very interesting choreography, William."

"Say what you really think, Peter," I suggested.

He smiled. "Your solo was my favourite, my dear. It was ethereal and magical. As for the rest, the *Sarabande* was risqué, but *Circle* broke some boundaries. Your mother may have had a small stroke."

The dour matriarch stood nearby, squat and toad-like beside my father's spindly height. The half-empty gin glass in her hand was not a good sign.

"I'm not facing this alone," I said to Will. "Your shagathon will have to wait." I took him by the arm, and we walked over to my parents.

"Well, Amalphia," said my mother. "I have to say that was not quite what we expected. There were some very nice pieces. That girl in the red dress; beautiful, isn't she? Her solo was excellent."

"Weren't you impressed by Will's choreography?" I asked, hating how she had completely ignored him.

My father brought his property surveyor's attention down from the ceiling, and said, "I liked the scenery for that last bit. It was historically evocative and suited the building."

"Don't be silly, James. That whole thing was obscene."

Absence had not made my mother more bearable. As ever, I recoiled inside and longed to remove myself from her company. Peter introduced Aleks, and she remarked that she'd read about him. Aleks praised me to my parents, saying how proud they must be to have such a beautiful and talented dancer for a daughter.

"He's certainly full of himself," she said, once Paul had whisked Aleks and Will away to do the rounds of people, and Peter had gone to help Yvonne with crying Benjamin.

"He only talked about me," I pointed out.

"Yes, but as if he knew everything. I know the type. Would be quite good looking if he wasn't so 'lived in.'"

"Lived in?"

"Been around a bit, hasn't he? They're not the same as us, Amalphia, these foreigners." She lowered her voice. "They do bizarre things in bed. Not that that need worry you."

I understood the inference at once: someone like him would never look at someone like me. At least, not in a bizarre-bed way.

She brightened, excited about her next subject. "Now dear, have you heard from Gavin at all?"

"No."

"Oh." Her disappointment was that of a petulant child, prize taken away. "I had hoped he might be here."

"I told you he was abusive to me."

She sighed. "You're a difficult girl. You need a firm hand."

No matter how much I expected the worst, it always pulled me up short. I wavered between making a comment about the firm handling of my childhood, or the fact that she had only liked Gavin because he joined in with her disparagement of me with such gusto.

"Possibly all is not lost," she said with a sigh. "I noticed that young man over there admiring you earlier. Some men like bigger girls, you know, and he spoke so nicely to me while we were waiting in here."

I followed the direction of her gaze. "Edward?" My hysterical laughter attracted a few looks.

"Oh, you know him? Very well educated. I could tell."

"He's a solicitor."

"Is he?" The whites of her eyes showed as she regarded Edward with even greater liking. "Of course," she said. "Some of these professional men have a fetish for ballet dancers, don't they?"

I backed away. "I need some air."

The entrance hall was quiet and dim, the back passage even more so, providing a calm intermission for the senses. I let my fingers slide over the cool of the wall tiles, some of them bobbled with patterns, and paused to examine one that was a veritable work of art. It depicted a three-storey house surrounded by trees. I could imagine the wind rushing through the branches, all fresh and wild and free.

"You are finding the party bad?" asked Aleks, appearing at my side.

"Mmm..." But his kiss was good and his body enticingly warm against mine. My hand found a doorknob beside us. The door opened to a large room that was full of boxes. An old armchair cast a long grey shadow in the moonlight. "Ooh, we should definitely go in here," I said.

"No, you have to return to the hall. This is your night." He closed the portal to the silvery kingdom of joy. The passageway felt dark and dismal in comparison.

"Fine." I uncupped my hand from the front of his trousers, where it had somehow found itself, and turned away, the rejection stinging all the more in the aftermath of maternal derision.

"Malphia, don't—"

But I was gone, straight into other arms in the foyer. Actual maternal hands held me back as their owner examined me.

"I saw you speaking to your parents," said Carolyn, Justin's mum, her sparkling green eyes studying my face. "You were beautiful, my darling, completely beautiful. Don't listen to anyone who says anything else."

"Justin was good, wasn't he?"

"Oh yes," she said enthusiastically, then spotting Aleks.

I introduced the two of them, and they shook hands.

"I hope you're looking after my children properly?" she said to him. "I can be quite fierce to anyone who hurts one of my own." She knew about our relationship. Justin was close with his Mum. Not much got left out of their long phone calls. "So, how are you enjoying teaching?" she asked Aleks, reverting to her usual kindness.

As we headed back to the party, he told her how proud he was of us all, how it gave him great joy to see us do well.

"Good," she said and squeezed his arm. "A new direction in life can be daunting. Phi, I'm going to speak to your parents."

Aleks and I joined Justin, Will and Edward at the buffet table. I introduced Aleks to the philandering one who was looking smooth and suave as ever, not a slicked-back ginger hair out of place.

"Is it all right if I keep your phone?" Justin asked, having been keeping it safe in his suit pocket during the show. "To take pictures of the party. It's better than mine, and we need some good shots. You never take pictures, and there's actual famous people here tonight."

I nodded my agreement as Edward held out a red-wrapped box.

"I have a present for you," he said to me.

"Oh, great, thanks," I said, deadpan, and regarded the box with slight unease.

"Go on, open it," urged Edward. "I saw them and thought of you."

Ribbons and paper fell to the ground, and I laughed at the chocolate nutcracker princes. Justin told the others about our trip to a less than brilliant production of *The Nutcracker* one Christmas, where I had expressed the idea that it would be more enjoyable if the dancers were made of chocolate.

"If you date one of these two, it's better if the other one likes you," said Edward, with a glance at Aleks. "So, I keep trying."

"I like you," I said, removing the foil from one of the princes and offering the box round. "Sometimes. A little bit. Thank you for the gift, anyway." I bit the head off a small chocolate man.

"It's good to see you having fun, Amalphia," said Michelle, arriving beside us, and accepting one of the chocolate princes. "And it's just as well you two are my favourites, isn't it?" She pointed at Will and me as she spoke, then narrowed her eyes. "You naughty little things."

Paul, who had arrived with her, was more animated and connected than I had ever seen him. "Yes, yes," he said, actually looking me in the face. "It's time for your round of glory, Miss Treadwell."

I briefly imagined this to be some sort of daring athletic feat, which, in a way, it was.

"All eyes are on you tonight," Paul told me, taking my arm and ferrying me off through a sea of fake smiles.

Madame Genevieve was unusually sweet and cuddly, wearing some sort of sparkly Mrs. Claus dress with matching red-and-white fur-framed glasses. She told me that my potential was finally showing as she had always known it would.

Justin, who had accompanied us, noticed another familiar face. "Look, the Baby Jesus is all grown-up with muscles and everything."

Luke did, indeed, have broad shoulders and a trendy unshaved look, but his shy smile and hug felt the same as they had before. Justin stayed speaking to Luke as Paul and I gloried on.

An older Russian man who knew Aleks actually offered me a job. "You are the latest Zolotov prodigy," he said. "Many ballerinas he has promote, and they never go wrong."

The need to respond was removed by the ongoing speed of the tour.

Paul introduced me to a vaguely recognisable person called Colin McKen, who was to be a guest teacher next term, and then he left me alone with him.

"You seemed very comfortable performing such sexualised choreography," said Colin. His accent was Scottish, and posh, and sounded a bit like Michelle's.

"I was concerned that most of my costumes consisted of only underwear," I told him. "But I forgot about it once dancing."

He roared with laughter, tossing his head back in a possibly rehearsed move to show off his messed-up-bed-hair look. "If you can do that with Zolotov and those boys, I wonder what you can do with me. Can I get you a drink?"

"I have one over there," I lied, waving in Will's direction, glad of the excuse to escape the man and return to my friends.

Michelle looked up as I approached, distracted from her discussion with Aleks by Benjamin's increasingly loud crying. "I didn't think I'd invited any children," she said, as the baby's cry turned into screaming.

"They're Phi's babies," Justin told her, and I turned and walked over to Yvonne and the children.

"I could take them all through to the TV room to watch a DVD," I suggested. "There's some cartoon ones."

"No, Phi," said Yvonne. "I don't want to spoil your night. I'm going to take them up to the room."

"I could do with a quiet break myself," I told her.

"Well, if you're sure..."

I put Benjamin on my hip. He stopped crying at once, and grabbed at my necklace with his chubby hands. The girls chose a selection of treats from the table, and we headed out of the hall, a plate of pretty cakes carried with great reverence by Ophelia.

I sat on the sofa in the TV room and slipped off my shoes, finally able to enjoy the party food and relax. We were singing along to a song from a colourful animated movie when Will stuck his head round the door.

"Hello, girlies."

"We are not girlies," Freya informed him. She had never forgiven Will for making her ballet class play a game involving flesh-eating rats when I had been ill the previous summer, and he had taken over for me.

"We're ladies, Will," I said. "Show us the proper respect."

It wasn't long before Justin arrived wanting to know why we had made off with all the best food. "Now, that's fucktastic," he said, biting into a cake. "And that's the word of the day too."

"Justin is a very rude boy," Freya told Will. "He says bad words."

"Yes, Justin," I said. "Consider your audience before you speak."

"I've profaned the ears of the babies," he said. "What is to become of me? By the way, for a moment there Michelle thought they actually were your offspring. She had a good look at Peter, then Hearst, wondering whose they were. It was a bit weird to be honest. She seemed quite excited, and then disappointed when she was put right."

The boys soon bored of our company and went back to the party. Benjamin fell asleep in my lap, Ophelia walked round the room in my shoes, and Freya and I drew pictures of fairy-tale creatures. That was the scene Aleks walked into.

"Oh," he said, pausing in his stride. "Look at you. But you are missing your party."

"I'm really not," I confessed, but asked him to get Yvonne as the children needed to go to bed.

I carried Benjamin up to their second-floor room and managed to lay him down without waking him, which felt like quite an achievement.

Back on the main stairs, Aleks leant against the wall. "Can it be my turn now?" he asked, pulling me up against him.

"For cakes and a cartoon?" I enquired, blinking up into his face.

"One slow dance. Is darker lighting now, so no one will notice or think anything."

Justin accosted us as soon as we entered the great hall. He had dancing plans too. Terrible ones. "It'll be a glorious finish to the night," he declared.

I disagreed. "It'll be awful."

"I remember that routine," said Will. "I was well jealous."

"Why?" I asked, incredulous.

"You used to hang out with me, and choreograph stuff with me, until Bevan came along. I would love to do that dance with you."

I looked at the two beseeching faces. "Okay. Though my mother may burst into flames."

I wasn't too thrilled at the prospect of Aleks seeing the routine either. What had seemed an enterprising choreographic stunt in our first year of college could be mediocre now or, as Madame had said at the time: lewd, crude and offensive.

We joined the general dance-floor swaying for a minute or two before Justin raised his hands in the air. I blocked all thought, and just let myself go in the crazed manner of the 'sexy dance.' People stopped dead and stared. Will and I did the lifts in spite of my dress; I felt a seam go. Then, amazingly, others joined in.

"We've started something!" shouted Justin over the music. Ruaridh and Sun gyrated beside us. Luke was determined to prove how strong he was. The lifting and swinging and twirling soon became too much, and I ducked under arms to sneak away, only to find myself face to face with Colin Mcken.

"What an intriguing creature you are, Miss Treadwell," said Colin, hands firmly on my back.

Looking round for help or an excuse to extricate myself, I spotted Aleks on the far side of the room talking with a glamorous-looking blonde lady.

Colin chattered on about networking and futures and possibilities. Nothing made any sense. "Where does a ripe beauty such as yourself bed down in this old pile of stones?" he asked as his hands squeezed my bum.

I pushed him back. He laughed, and then Aleks was there saying: "You'll have to forgive me for cut in, but I have danced with all my students tonight, except Amalphia."

Colin bowed in mock politeness and melted away into the crowd.

"Thank you," I said.

"I liked the dance you were doing with Justin."

"No, you didn't. You weren't watching." I rested my head on his shoulder, and a blissful relief from the day descended as we moved slowly to the music.

"Don't think I didn't want you," he said quietly in my ear. "Before, in the passage. All of today is a performance for me. I am trying to be absolutely controlled."

"But you don't have to be when it's just us," I said, standing on tiptoe to put my mouth to his ear. "You can lose control with me, Aleks."

His face turned towards mine. I felt his breath on my cheek.

"I go up now," he said. "Warm the bed for you. Follow soon?"

The hall was emptier, but the buffet was still well stocked. I planned to eat one small cake and then go. A small crowd had gathered to watch Justin and Edward perform a tango. Will lolled against the far wall while Sadie talked excitedly at him. He smiled at her and looked over at me. I gave him a small wave, glad that we were all happy.

It was good to remove my shoes in the foyer, the cold of the black and white tiles soothing to tired feet. The doors of the elevator stood open and waiting. I stepped inside and screamed at the "Boo!" and sudden movement that came from the side.

"What are you doing? You nearly gave me a heart attack." I put my hands on Aleks's chest and laughed at the shock of it.

"I discovered that I couldn't leave you."

"Well, you know what this means?" I said, cross, hands back on my own waist.

He shook his head, face-crinkling smile irresistible as always.

"The bed will be cold."

"Not for long," he replied, smile gone.

The tumultuous feelings of the day found an outlet as we kissed and kissed, and kissed again. He picked me up, and the doors slid shut.

"This is the best time of the day," I said a little later, once speaking was possible again.

"Not for you," he said in disbelief. "Not today."

"It is."

"But this is your day of glory. Everyone is speak of you, ask about."

I made my own noise of disbelief and snuggled closer.

"Okay, so what is second-best part?" he asked.

"Dancing with you."

"Ah yes, we have such a strong connection, knowing every inch of each other's bodies as we do. Though you are a wonderful partner, Malphia, needing far less support than many more experienced dancers I have worked with. I wish I could be twenty years younger for you."

"I meant just now in the hall," I said, laughing before seeing his solemn expression. "And you don't need to be any different. You're perfect. I love you. Now, go to sleep."

Chapter 27

T HE MORNING WAS UNEXPECTEDLY cold. Aleks sat, leaning back against the headboard. My smile was not reciprocated.

"The shining one awakes." The world wavered in the harshness of his voice. "I saw you last night," he said. "Is a different picture, you with all these people. They love you, no?"

I sat up and stared at him, trying to work out what this was.

"And what was I do?" he went on. "Take you away from it all, to keep you here for myself." His gesture encompassed the bed as if there were something inherently wrong about our being there together.

"Do you mean when you took me away from that Colin person?" I asked. "Because he was horrible, Aleks. I was glad you cut in when you did."

"You have seen him dance?"

"No."

"Maybe you should. You will see he is being relevant."

"Aleks." I sat closer and rubbed his literally cold shoulder. "I don't understand."

He got out of bed and retreated to the windows and stood staring out of them. "Last night," he said, still in the harsh voice. "Three men are asking me if you are involved with anyone. No one is imagine you would be here." His laugh was entirely lacking in mirth, the word 'here' again derogatory. "I am overhear Simone and Sadie, backstage," he went on. "They discuss the footage you never saw, that I made sure you didn't see. 'Sounds nightmare,' says Sadie. 'Lucky escape for me,' is Simone's answer, and they are laughing."

"Simone's a cow, Aleks." I pulled on a T-shirt and went over to him. "You have to learn never to listen to anything she says. I have."

He took hold of my hands and pushed them back, rebuffing the attempted embrace. "No," he said "You should listen. She is not the first woman to see how it is. You saw Lilian's blog. You read all these reasons she left me?"

"No." I'd only ever read that one small bit.

"See, always, you are not thinking. 'Your career may be over, but mine isn't.' This is what she say to me. She has not write that part. But you don't look to the future, do you, Malphia?"

"Not generally, no." It was scary and mysterious, like his anger. I looked out the window too, and saw the path to the stone circle, all green and quiet and still.

"A dancer needs to think of herself," he went on. "What contacts could be useful. But you are all about your friends..." They received the same dismissive gesture as the bed. "Me, your babies..." He flung his hands up and recommenced the window stare.

My babies. He'd seen me behave all mumsy, preferring to sit with children than attend a societal event, and it had shocked him. Repelled him, even.

My shoulders grew cold too, and I knew the right words for the moment. They were ones I'd used before, in another dark and confusing time. "I get it. You saw me. So, fuck off."

He turned away from the window fast. "I am saying to you that there was a room full of options—"

"You saw me," I repeated. "And you saw a room full of better options. So go look for them. They're probably still in the castle."

"You want that I go?"

"Yes. I think I'm being clear about that. This conversation is not what you promised me, Aleks."

"Fine," he said and walked out.

The fact that he was naked did nothing to diminish the cold finality of the moment. The bang of the door reverberated as

I stood on the soft carpet waiting for the redness of the air to calm, for badness to be over, for life to be right again.

His trousers lay at my feet. I placed them gently on the chair. His socks followed. Then there was the shirt. I held it to my face and breathed it in, but that didn't help. Something dreadful had happened, and I couldn't bear to think about it. But some facts had to be dealt with. The castle was full of women who had been, or might soon be, girlfriends of Aleks. I couldn't be here too. I would go home with Justin for Christmas, and after that? No. It was too soon to think about that too.

My original plan to stay at the castle for the holiday meant I hadn't packed. The bus for the train station left in an hour, and it would be good to be busy. The suitcase and drawers were not kind, containing clothes Aleks had given me, along with the necklace. Carefully laid in its box last night, I knew it was time to give it back. The beautiful heirloom was not for me. He would agree that now. Maybe wearing it in front of everybody last night had contributed to his outrage? I placed it on top of his clothes.

Packing abandoned, washing and dressing were easier options, but over too quickly. Options. I stood in the bathroom, somehow holding his shirt again, and tried to understand what exactly he'd meant by that. I had jumped very quickly to an assumption—

He swept back into the bedroom, dressed in black jeans and a long-sleeved T-shirt just like when I'd first seen him, which was a stupid thought because it was his usual attire. My eyesight misted, and that was good because I didn't want to see him.

"There is another person you have learn never to listen to," he said. "A very stupid man."

"You forgot your shirt." I thrust it in his general direction on my way back through to the bedroom. "Your other clothes are there." Packing simplified into a fast chucking in of everything.

"Why is this you are doing? You are staying here for Christmas."

"No, I'm not. I do have other options, you know."

"Who is this being?" he asked loudly. "You are to be telling me now. Some man is asking you to go away with him? Is William?

The Jesus boy? Colin? The farmer?" His voice rose in volume with each odd and fast suggestion.

"I'm going home with Justin. I'm sure his mum won't mind."

He sat down on the bed, looking deflated and sad and strange.

I sat too. "This reaction doesn't make any sense, Aleks. You just dumped me."

"No. How can you be saying this? I am being jealous. So very jealous. And I am sorry."

"No. You said you saw me. Bad things about me. You said I don't think properly, and that I should be more like Simone. You said we shouldn't be here together. Here..." The gesture he'd made was easy to imitate.

He took my hands in his. "Sometimes I am feeling one negative thing, and making many steps and imaginings, and growing it all into a big disaster. This is what you have to not listen to. Come, we go back to bed and start the day again?"

"I can't," I said, not quite sure how large the statement was. It sounded like something from another bleak time. "If I don't show up downstairs soon, my mother may come up here."

"But you will stay for Christmas?"

I said nothing, not sure what to do about that now.

"Malphia." He pulled me into a hug. "Here. Remember. This is us."

So, I was staying. Probably. Maybe. Perhaps.

We walked down the stairs hand in hand.

"I will take you to Glasgow tomorrow," he told me. "Holly says is best place for shopping and vegetarian restaurants. Will be a nice drive too. We will see some of Scotland, other than these walls."

We released hands in the foyer, sounds of bustle and breakfast coming from the great hall.

"It will be easier for me when our secret is ended," he said. "I am hope, soon?"

"I don't think that's a good idea at all."

"Why not?" His voice regained some of the cool air of earlier.

"Aleks," I said in frustration, flummoxed by his up-and-down, hot-and-cold behaviour. "Remember last night? And how you felt about it this morning? Look how I embarrassed you in a room full of people who didn't know about us. Can you imagine if they had?"

"Malphia, no, don't—"

"Don't what? Be realistic? One of us has to be. You're going in there to schmooze with your sophisticated friends. I'm going to be told how crap I am by my mother, when the truth is neither you nor her have to bother. I already know."

I stormed across the room and chose a smoothie for breakfast, surely the least likely food to garner criticism. Turning to locate my parents, I discovered that Aleks had sat down by them. I walked over to the table, the dread of what he might be about to hear, acute and painful. The words 'lumpy-bumpy' would make me appear more unfortunate than ever. He smiled as I sat down beside him, across from my parents at the table.

My mother paused in her eating of a 'full Scottish breakfast' that included black pudding and haggis fritters, to dive straight into one of her favourite subjects. "I know you think these smoothie things are healthy, dear, but they can be as calorific as a fried breakfast."

Aleks looked steadily at her and said, "Amalphia doesn't need to be worried about that."

"It's not the same for male dancers," she stated as if she, who had never done so much as a simple tendu, knew more about ballet than him. "Girls have to be careful not to be too curvaceous. They need to watch their weight."

"And some become ill doing so," he replied.

"This attitude explains a lot," she said to him, then directed her contempt back in my direction. "I noticed last night that you're beginning to look a bit lum—"

"I think what your mum's trying to say is that your tits are too big," interjected Justin from his place a little further up the table. His words earned him a subzero glare from my mother and much heartfelt gratitude from me. He knew what she'd been going to say, and he'd stopped her.

Carolyn smiled at her son. "I agree with Aleks. You have a beautiful figure, Phi. Don't start getting paranoid and going on strange diets."

Justin nodded. "God no, you wouldn't want to end up with none at all like Simone."

Simone spun round on hearing her name to find everyone staring at her. She looked exhausted, with big bags under her eyes. Maybe she'd partied too hard the previous evening? With a toss of her hair, she turned away from us again.

"Been there, done that, the extreme-diet thing," I said, meaning to be light and funny, forgetting who was there.

"That doctor didn't know what he was talking about," snapped my mother. "How could you be anorexic at that weight?"

"You were this way?" asked Aleks, looking intently into my face.

Ignoring my parent's protest to the contrary, I told him the truth. "Yes. It was better once I was at college. They were very right-on about everything: healthy eating, healthy weights."

"And then I introduced her to the best cake in the world, and she hasn't looked back," added Justin.

"You know, that place in Covent Garden," I said, before realising that the fact Aleks and I had eaten cake together would come as a revelation to some.

Justin distracted everyone again. "Speaking of introductions, Mrs. Treadwell, have you met the Cockheads?"

The man and woman sitting with Simone looked embarrassed but resigned.

"Who knew?" Justin went on. "Simone's real surname is not Conner at all!"

I glanced at Aleks. "You don't have to do this," I murmured quietly to him. "You know, talk to my parents like this."

"I want to be next to you. I want to support you."

We were suddenly surrounded by small excited people.

Peter's family squashed me with cuddles. Benjamin grabbed my hair and proceeded to rid his fingers of whatever breakfast stuff he had been eating. I stood up from the table and lifted the baby high up into the air, making him giggle and forget my hair.

I could hear my mother's oft-told lecture on healthy-weight charts and how the numbers had been made up by fat people. Aleks's eyes met mine in an intense gaze.

"My, he's all brooding and smouldery, isn't he?" whispered Yvonne in my ear. "The sex must be amazing."

My mouth dropped open.

"Write and tell me everything," she called back as they took their leave.

With barely time to put my jaw back in place, my parents insisted I see them off. "We've hardly seen you," said my mother. "And you not coming home for Christmas. It's just awful. What will people think?"

"That I'm working really hard? Totally devoted to ballet?"

She looked, rightfully for once, highly sceptical. "It's terribly anti-social, even that Justin is going home."

My father muttered some parting disapproval about the outside of the castle having been harled with small stones and painted pink, and then they left.

I waved them off in their taxi and stood motionless on the drive, a quiet pause in a mad morning. The nearby trees rustled as if in invitation. A large bus rolled across the gravel and slowed to noisy stop in front of the castle.

"I've never seen a pair of jeans look that enticing." Colin Mcken grinned at my side. "I'm lengthening just looking at you."

I stared. Did he mean what I thought he meant?

"My taxi's here," he said. "Let's find a hotel, and get to know each other properly. You'll be my favourite little dancer before the new term even begins."

I backed away three steps and then turned and ran into the castle, hoping I had somehow misconstrued the unfortunate speech.

Chapter 28

"T HE BUS FOR THE station and airport is here!" Holly hollered in careful English as I entered the foyer. Justin stopped for a hug on his way to the bus.

"Zolotov all right this morning?" he asked as he returned my phone to me.

"More or less," I said.

"Of course, you didn't see it. Michelle played a film of him falling on stage at the start of his arthritis, then footage from when she first worked with him. Did you know it used to take him an hour just to stand upright in the morning? Quite a thing to have everyone see. And they were all speaking about it last night. In front of him too, Phi. He pokerfaced his way through it, but it must have stung a bit."

"Ah." I had to find him. And talk to him. I had misinterpreted the 'options' thing very badly.

"Anyway, have a sexy Christmas, darling!" And Justin was gone.

I took two steps towards the great hall, and then my way across the foyer was barred. A brightly smiling Michelle was suddenly very close and in my face, holding up her sparkly red phone for me to see. "Can I show you this, Amalphia? Just quickly before we all leave? You missed it last night." I saw Aleks on the phone screen. A thinner, sort of grey-looking Aleks.

"I don't have time," I told her. It was true. I had to find present-day Aleks.

"No problem," she said, still smiling. "I'll email it to you."

And, after inflicting a perfumey hug on me, she headed over to Holly to ask if her taxi had arrived.

I set off in the direction of the great hall again, but Will shoved past me looking all dishevelled and hungover and cross.

"Are you okay?" I asked.

He grunted something and continued walking.

"You off home, or going to Sadie's?" I asked, hoping for a goodbye at least.

He spun round. "What the fuck would I be going to Sadie's for?"

For the second time that morning, I just stared at a man, silenced by both his face and words. Will actually looked like he was trembling with rage.

"Fucking Zolotov?" he said.

"What?"

"That's what you've been doing, isn't it? Heats the bed up for you, does he?"

I stood with my mouth open, unprepared for the conversation, wanting to run away from it, yet frozen to the spot in shock.

"Were you ever going to tell me?" he demanded.

"Yes. I tried to. It was difficult."

"How old is he anyway? You after his money, or something?"

"You bastard," came out in a hoarse whisper, and I unfroze and ran for the stairs.

He caught my arm at the foot of them. "And what's he doing? Have you thought about that, Malph? Screwing his way round the castle? First Simone, now you. It'll be someone else soon."

"No, Will," I snapped, snatching my arm away from his grasp. "Don't tar him with your own habits. You're the one who screws around. With everyone except me, of course. Is that what this is about? You never loved me, so you don't think anyone else could either?"

He shook his head in a stunned manner.

"Well, fuck you, Will Hearst. Stop judging my life and look at your own!"

I ran all the way up to my room and kicked the door, decided that Will's shin would be the better recipient of such violence, and reversed the run.

The foyer was empty. I ran to the door and saw the bus just disappearing into the trees. I jumped in rage a couple of times on the outside step before sprinting up to Will's room. It felt good to pummel the pillows, but they released an aura of crisps and a musky something that soon had me flop down upon them, defeated.

I should have told him. Of course I should have. How had he found out? Simone and Sadie had been being bitchy last night. Did they know? Had they said something? I was suddenly struck by the fact that Will had never actually told me about his relationship with Sadie. For a moment the realisation was enraging, but I recalled how it had felt to learn about it in an accidental manner.

I sighed and sat up, and took in the horrendous mess of the room. Will. I made his bed, removing all traces of my pillow abuse, and then moved on to the floor. How many socks could one person own? The laundry basket was soon full, and I sat on the bathroom chair and blew my nose on one of the socks, tidying having somehow made me cry.

What if Will's anger didn't pass? He had looked at me like he hated me. What if he didn't come back? I wanted to chase after the bus. Communication was needed: calm, grown-up communication.

Composing the text took some time. I was a bit incoherent, but desperate in my attempt to make him understand that I had wanted to tell him. Sorry was said in a variety of ways, both for the secret and for the things shouted in rage. I finished with: *Will, I love you, I need you, please don't leave me.*

Oh no. I'd just sent a confused babble of momentous length to a profoundly dyslexic person. The bathroom got an adrenaline-fueled clean, and finally the phone beeped.

Ignore me, Treadwell – I'm a wanker.

Relief laughed out as I walked back into the bedroom, got under the duvet, and typed: *You're not a wanker, Will.*

Him: *I am - hungover as well - sorry.*

Me: *Should this wanking issue be a worry then, seeing as I'm lying in your bed?*

Him: *WTF?*

The phone rang before an explanation could be written.

"What the fuck you at now, Treadwell?"

"Following the example of those around me and sleeping my way round the castle."

"Malph, you gotta forget that. I didn't mean it. It was just a shock. I saw you last night." I'd clearly been altogether too visible the previous evening. "In the elevator," he clarified.

"Oh." I cringed.

"But you'll forget the crap I spouted?"

"What was that about money?" I said. "Do you really think that of me?"

"No. Sorry."

"I'm not even comfortable with him buying me presents, and now that's going to happen again. We're going to Glasgow tomorrow, and what do I get him?"

"He's got you. What the fuck else does he want?"

"Overkill, Hearst. I'm very much aware of my shortcomings compared to the other women he's been out with. Michelle's one of them. Did you know that?"

"No way. I don't see that."

"And what a morning. It's nice to be in here alone for a bit. But, we're okay?" I asked. "And please forget what I said too. I actually admire the way you are. It sounds appealingly honest and simple."

"I'm a bit of an idiot, but never as bad as Bevan makes out. He's trying to get everyone on the bus singing right now. I'll hold the phone up so you can hear."

I was still humming *She'll be Coming Round the Mountain* as I walked down the stairs a few minutes later, on my way to find Aleks.

He burst out of the small office by the television room as I arrived in the foyer.

"I find this upstairs on my clothes," he said, holding out the necklace box. "And I think you have gone. And this was always to be yours, always. So I am look up Justin's details to follow and explain. And then I think: no, this is like stalking, and I should not do... But you have been crying. I see this. Malphia, there is being a huge misunderstanding. Never am I embarrassed. Not by you. By myself, yes. But never you."

I put my hand on his arm. "It's okay," I told him, then hesitated, knowing he would abhor pity, and that in his highly reactive state any form of empathy might be construed as such. "I wasn't crying about our disagreement. I just had a row with Will."

"He is not gone?" he asked, carefully placing the necklace round my neck and fastening the catch.

"Oh, he is. Some of our talk was by text and phone."

"Come, sit by the fire and tell me."

Through in the great hall, the flames beamed their heat and comfort into the cavernous room, and all around us, as we sat down on the sofa.

"He saw us in the elevator last night," I said.

"Ah." He nodded. "I knew it would be bad for that boy once he knew."

"He was cross that I hadn't told him." I lay down on the sofa and rested my head on his thigh, sensing that both of us were feeling drained by recent events. "He never actually told me about him and Sadie either, though, so it was all very annoying."

"Will and Sadie?" said Aleks. "I don't see that."

We both gazed into the fire for a while, and I started to feel my body relax. And his. There was a sense of relief in us both.

"I'm glad it's all over," I said. "Yesterday. This week. This term."

"I am too."

I turned my head to look up at him in doubt, and was about to say how I had felt that thrill from him, during the show. But then I didn't. Wouldn't that just be reminding him of all he had lost? I was coming to believe that I would never have it, never feel anything like that about performance. But I didn't say that either. He seemed like he was going to speak, but he stopped himself too.

I closed my eyes and relaxed further.

"Is so quiet," said Aleks. "Listen."

The absence of footfalls, voices, doors and distant piano music was actually quite eerie. The only discernible sounds were the crackle of the fire and our breathing. The ceiling twinkled with something bright.

"Who put those decorations up there?" I asked. High above us were holly, fir branches and ivy, entwined with sparkling silver ribbons.

"Your friend, the farmer. He brought big ladder."

The whole room was a glittering wonderland, bedecked with a perfect blend of fresh greenery and sparkle. The huge tree by the windows was exquisitely hung with white lights and old-fashioned baubles. "How did I not see any of this before?" I wondered.

"You are lost in anticipation, excitement, performance, party. Now is calm, beauty, perfection. This is our Christmas."

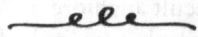

The Yuletide atmosphere of the castle, and the fact that we were alone together, quickly shifted us to a joyful and tranquil way of being.

Eating in front of the fire became a delightful festive pastime. Making love in front of it was even better. The flickering orange light picked out every detail of Aleks's beautiful body and cast long erotic shadows across the room.

We laughed at the echoing nature of the high ceiling. "I love you!" he shouted, causing aftershocks to leap from the roof and walls, and cookware to rattle in the kitchen.

We parted ways for a short while during our trip to Glasgow, to do our festive shopping. I stopped in wonder on approaching the designated meeting place. Aleks stood waiting, darting suspicious looks at passersby, his demeanour entirely defensive and ill at ease. To see him like this was new, and I wanted to learn every facet of the complex man who waited for me. His face lit up as I ran over, and he transformed back into my lovely Aleks once again.

It was novel to walk hand in hand through the crowds and eat out together, a couple in front of others. We kissed on the big Ferris wheel in George Square, and laughed on the carousel.

Midnight Mass at the small local church on Christmas Eve was enchanting, the high-spired building sparkling with frost and magic; the interior was brightly decorated in red and gold, and the congregation were friendly and welcoming.

Aleks smiled as we walked away after the service, through the cold night air. "I take you home and lock you in the tower now, for me alone."

"Sounds good."

It was. We luxuriated in bed and swam naked in the pool. We played a film on a big screen in the theatre, but kissed more than we watched it. "We are like teenagers," he said. I didn't remind him that I actually was a teenager. I would be twenty soon, and maybe that would make things easier. Not that anything was difficult anymore.

Doing everything together, as in the beginning, our beginning, was heavenly. We washed each other's hair in the bath, snuggled by the fire, and I kissed his flat fingertips. This was the way life should be all the time, one long, extended lovemaking. We decided to be open about our relationship once everyone returned in January, and happiness felt complete.

Then, in an instant, everything changed.

I was making my way across the foyer towards the great hall to build up the fire, having left Aleks getting dressed in the pool changing room, when the big front door of the castle opened and a cold breeze blew in. With the breeze, came a person. The woman was bundled up in a plush red jacket with a fur-lined hood. She wore jeans and big biker boots, and it wasn't until she pulled back the white fur of the hood that I realised it was Michelle. She smiled in surprise, looking slightly amused as she took in my attire of T-shirt, underwear and socks.

"Amalphia," she said warmly. "How lovely. You've come back early too."

"No, she hasn't," said Aleks from behind me, pulling his shirt on as he walked into the foyer. "She stayed here."

As he put his arm round my waist, Michelle's face changed. She didn't exactly look angry. Or even surprised. Her expression was strangely blank. Cold and stony. She smiled a tight smile and took hold of her suitcase by its handle.

"Best get on," she said, heading for the elevator. "Lots of work to do."

Part Three

Circle

Chapter 29

I T WAS WITH EXCEPTIONAL happiness that I observed
Justin and Will coming into the great hall on the day before
the new term began. I actually felt tears well behind my eyes at
the sight of them.

"He's got you doing menial tasks?" Justin asked, askance, as
I placed a vat of sweetcorn in the warming area of the canteen.

I shook my head and explained. "Holly's extra helpers didn't
turn up, so I volunteered. There's new students arriving today,
and there's all sorts of preparations going on. It's been good to
have something to do, to be honest. It's been so boring without
you two here, and also—" I dived behind the counter, whispering, "Don't tell him I'm here."

"Young friends of Amalphia," said Colin McKen, fortunately not having caught sight of me. "Have you seen her?"

"Gone for a walk, I think," said Will. "To the village."

"That doesn't surprise me," said Colin. "A definite tenden-
cy to wander, that one. Been leading me a merry dance this
morning, I can tell you. Lunch is not until later today, boys, to
accommodate the new arrivals, so no point hanging round here.
I think I might venture outside for a bit of fresh air myself."

"He's gone," said Justin. "Famous, isn't he?"

"And totally letchy," I said. "Listen, there's food in the
kitchen if you want something now, though your belated
Christmas presents are on your beds."

"I shall go and inspect, and then return for lunch," declared
Justin, leaving Will and I alone and a little awkward with each
other.

"Come through," I said, hurrying back to the kitchen. I took leftovers out of the fridge and laid them on the table, beside the triangular notch that was missing from one end of the battered piece of furniture. I touched its roughness, uncertain what to do next.

"Treadwell." Will held his arms out. It was a hug of warmth, crisps and forgiveness. "I got you something," he said. "Well, found you something." He took a small tissue-paper-wrapped object out of his pocket and handed it to me.

I gasped as the paper fell to the floor. "This is the stone I saw in that dream!" The pinkish purple stone was the same size, shape and colour as the one envisioned in the circle, the one that got placed in my heart by the golden lady. "Where did you find it?"

"Stone circle," he said. "I went up there to see if I could get some choreographic inspiration, last term, you know. I saw a movement out of the side of my eye. It was a molehill, I think, beside the flat stone, earth all freshly pushed up. This was sitting on top of it, and I just knew it was for you."

"How magical," I said, gazing into the sparkly depths of the stone. "This is like the best present in the world. Thank you, Will."

Justin returned with his present, which he also found to be quite meaningful. He pointed it at people and things now and then to emphasise words.

"I will put it in a pot and melt it down," I warned, the fourth time the phallic chocolate was brandished in my direction.

"You're not touching my beautiful penis," he said, holding it protectively to his chest. "I'm going to use it to test the newbies' responses. We'll soon weed out the Justins from the Simones. So, how was Christmas at the castle?"

"Boring, latterly anyway."

"What, precisely, has become boring?" asked Justin. "Is it bedroom related? Do you want me to speak to him, man to man, give him some pointers?"

My hand quelled the eagerly upturned confection, and I explained about Michelle and 'the great work.' It was a continuation of something Aleks and her had done in the past, which was an uncomfortable notion. "They had me doing the exercises to begin with in an attempt to involve me, but it was mind-numbing. She names injuries, then Aleks works out what exercise will help, which muscle groups need strengthening. They write it all down; they try it out; they do it again. So, I've explored everywhere outside, been up to the circle, and been swimming. I did all your washing," I told Will. "Even ironed it. And today, I've been making beds and cooking."

"What a good wife you'll make me," said Justin, "when the time comes."

"What?"

He smiled. "I thought we could do that, if no one wants to have kids with us by the time we're forty. I don't know what age your eggs run out." He waved a hand in the direction of my abdomen. "Don't be frightened, Phi. We wouldn't have to shag. There's a lovely room with gay porn for me, and a syringe-wielding doctor for you. Don't laugh; it's a good plan."

"It's hugely flawed," I said. "Even if I were ever to agree, my bits don't work right, remember? I'm medicated to control them."

"You would come off the pill obviously, duh."

"Women with polycystic ovaries often have fertility problems. Some of them never manage to get pregnant. Given how badly I have it, that's gonna be me."

"I didn't know that," said Justin, looking genuinely forlorn. "This messes everything up. Oh, and that's sad. You love your babies."

"I can love other people's babies. It doesn't bother me."

"Well, d'you know what might be fun?" he said with a wicked grin. "I could offer my sperm to Simone. I'll sit her down, let her have a bite of my lovely chocolate penis here. What girl could refuse?"

"Can you wait till I'm there, so I can see that?" I requested. "But I have to go do my kitchen wenching now."

"Get much wenching in yourself over the festive season?" he asked Will.

"No."

"Well, don't worry. There may be some comely maidens among the new crew."

"I think they're all only sixteen," I said.

Justin nodded. "A three-year age difference. You're right. That's positively indecent."

"She is right," said Will. "But what you were saying about having kids? Who'd want to, anyway? I mean, what if something happened and you weren't there? Anything could go on. Why bring them into the world in the first place?"

"That's bleak," said Justin. "Oh, I see." He patted Will's hand. "Slow swimmers? If you ever have the need, I can step up, or step in. I'm not sure of the correct terminology."

"Justin, has something happened to your hormones over Christmas?" I asked, and then put on my apron.

Helping with lunch was both an interesting and worrying job. A dairy allergy here, excessive slimness and scarring acne there, and a 'really don't give a flying anything about anything' attitude from a Goth girl with artistically impressive make-up and spiky black hair.

Aleks and Michelle came last in the queue. He smiled questioningly at me, took his food and sat down. Michelle was not so restrained. "You have trouble defining your role here, don't you, Treadwell? One minute you're trying to be a dancer, then you're a nanny to babies, now a common dinner lady. Salad, no-fat dressing for me," she ordered.

"Under here, Phi," said Holly, indicating a bowl of salad and then, unseen, pouring a substantial amount of olive oil into it.

"Do you do that often?" I asked, once Michelle had taken her salad and gone.

"Every day. Fit ye needin'? There's chocolate cake."

I sat by Justin and Will among the buzz of people and found that all the extra company felt good. I had downplayed the misery of the preceding week to my friends. Michelle had been cool and polite in front of Aleks, calmly observing his affectionate behaviour towards me, but when encountered alone, she was sharp and unpleasant. Gone was the friendliness of last term. I was no longer Amalphia, her favourite, but Miss Treadwell, a name always said in derision. She sneered at my ironing and cooking, but it was an overheard conversation that had been the most upsetting.

"You will be discreet about it, won't you, Aleks?" I'd heard her say. "It would look highly unprofessional in front of the new students. She's little more than a child herself..." I hadn't heard his reply, but her tone inferred he was indulging in a whimsical activity or passing fancy. I sat in the stone circle a long time that day, missing a meal to avoid the two of them.

Back in the dining room, with my newly returned friends, I looked over at the staff table. Aleks and Michelle were deep in discussion. I directed my attention to Goth Girl who was laughing at something Justin had said.

"So you're a dancer here," she said to me. "Do we all have to do chores?"

"No, I was just giving Holly a hand today."

Questions shot back and forth across the table, about the place, its facilities and staff. I told the new students that their cottages were nice, having been hired out as holiday lets in the past.

"Better rooms than us?" asked Justin.

"They're cosy, more homely than ours. Four students to a cottage, I think."

"What's our teacher, Mr. Zolotov, like?" asked Bekah, as I had gathered Goth Girl was called.

"What would you say, Phi?" asked Justin. "Sum him up in a few words for us."

"He's a good teacher," I told her. "You're lucky. We've got Colin for morning class every day, and not a single lesson with Aleks."

That news had been distressing. But my friends were back, classes didn't start till the next day, and I suggested a swim.

"There's a pool?" was excitedly asked by a few people, and everyone wanted to join us.

"But we've got a tour with Mr. Zolotov this afternoon," said Bekah, perhaps not quite as rebellious as her outward appearance suggested.

"Let's ask him if it's all right, shall we?" said Justin, then calling across the hall: "Oh, Mr. Zolotov, will you allow your class to come swimming with us? Or are you going to be very strict and boring, and forbid it?"

Aleks came over. "Of course you can all go swimming. I will come through in a while. You are getting to know each other?"

"Oh we are, Mr. Zolotov, we are," beamed Justin.

Swimming with the younger students was fun. Their arrival changed the energy of the place, making it seem somehow brighter and new. Will grabbed my waist from under the water as I bobbed at the edge, and thanked me for his present, confirming that he did not already have the latest Arsenal strip. "It's going to be different this term, isn't it?" he said.

"Not better different."

He glanced towards the door as Aleks walked in. "Remember, Malph, I'll always be here for you." He kissed me on the cheek and darted away under the water.

Aleks called out to his class to get changed, and they all clambered out of the pool and disappeared into the changing rooms.

"Is good to have your friends back?" he asked, dance trainers squeaking on the damp tiles as he crouched by the side of the pool to speak to me.

"So good. And your new little ones. They're all calling you Mr. Zolotov. Is that a thing now?"

"Ah. Michelle, she feels we should..." He cleared his throat. "We should develop a more professional relationship with these, our first-year students. Is not the right time for you and I to be open, after all."

"Yes, I caught some of that conversation."

"Later. We talk later," he said, and moved away from me to await his pupils.

I knew it wasn't true. We wouldn't talk later. We never did.

Throughout the latter part of the Christmas holidays, the great work with Michelle had continued late on into the night, every night. I had stayed awake and waited for his dramatic rush across my room that always ended in a fervent kiss and a hurried scramble out of clothes. To be so wanted was wonderful, and I met him in that desire, our usual gentleness exchanged for a kind of frantic desperation. It was sexy and exciting, but also unsettling, for what had wrought this change?

I, who had been used to crying and screaming in love, now wiped his tears and sought to reassure. He spoke impassioned words in his own language, and sometimes fell asleep on top of me. I cradled his head and gazed through the ceiling window at the stars and the dark sky, at the frost and the rain.

Thoughts and questions intensified when I had lain in bed for three days of period badness at New Year. I looked at pictures and videos of Aleks on the internet and wondered many things: had he been in relationships with all the dancers he'd partnered? Had he known every inch of their bodies too? Were they the ones he'd promoted, the ones the man at the Christmas party had mentioned? Aleks's career had ended nine years ago. What had he done in all that time? How long had he been with Michelle? Was she the reason he arrived at the top of the tower in such a state? And why did she hate me so much? She appeared to regard Aleks with some disdain, so it seemed unlikely that she was jealous or wanting him for herself. Unless they'd had some sort of enemies-lovers thing going on.

The largest of the Matryoshka dolls looked back at me from her place on the bedside table, appearing similarly perplexed. The smaller ones smiled on, happy and naïve, protected by their rotund mother.

The rest of that first day back passed quickly. We joined the younger class in the theatre to watch a film of the Christmas show and had fun clapping ourselves. 'Blown away' had been a good description for the effect of the *Circle* piece. Will, Justin and I looked at each other in shock after seeing it.

"I'd no idea it looked so..." I searched for words.

Justin found some. "Like you were about to be inseminated by a faulty donor."

"I could get the job done, Bevan," countered Will.

Justin shook his head. "Your boys would reflect your dismal attitude, Hearst. Totally unenthused sperm."

It was unfortunate that Aleks chose that moment to cut the film and the sound of applause. Justin's last three words echoed round the quiet auditorium and heads turned. We were soon surrounded by fans, *Circle* having impressed our younger counterparts greatly.

A little more talking than usual took place that night at the top of the tower. "I love you so much, is drive me mad," said Aleks, words that sounded hollow and disingenuous when replayed in my head later. He didn't like that I'd learned to say 'I love you' in Ukrainian, telling me I had far better things to be doing with my time than learning a language I would never need. "And I will have no secrets left," he said, attempting to add humour to the strained moment.

"I miss talking with you, Aleks," I told him as he sped away the next morning.

He stuck his head back round the side of the door. "Is only for a short while, this... this madness." His smile looked forced. "You will have your new teacher today. Already there is change."

"I doubt it's for the better," I called after his retreating form, grieving the lack of a goodbye kiss.

Chapter 30

D OWN IN THE DUNGEON, for that's where every class on our new timetable was to take place, Colin McKen rubbed his hands together. A strip light buzzed and flashed above him, giving the impression of lightning and horror, as if the place needed extra dramatising. It soon became clear that Colin had an unusual method of teaching.

"Little Miss Double Ds," he said to me. "Your arms are either too high or too low. I will show you the clearest marker you have. Everybody watch and learn." He took my hands and placed them over my breasts, leaving his sweaty fingers there just a little too long. "See?" he continued. "That is the perfect level, out to first position with them at that height, and then to second. Tit level. That's all you need to know about arm positions, not called port de bras for nothing, are they? Bra? Get it? Ha ha."

We got it. But nobody else laughed.

Colin walked round the class. He flicked Sun's tricep and called out, 'Bingo Wings!"

Sadie was repeatedly referred to as the 'Mayor of Cankle Town.' Colin then got down on his knees to apologise and correct the wording to 'Mayoress.'

But the real jewel of the morning was saved for Justin.

"Mr. Bevan," said Colin. "You are not pulling up correctly. There is a secret here too." He turned his head to check that we were all listening. "Shut your eyes," he told Justin, who, warily, did so. Colin went on. "Now, you spend a lot of time with the luscious Treadwell, so this should give you no trouble at all.

Imagine her on her knees before you." My friend's eyes shot open. "That's it, perfect," declared Colin.

After what seemed a very long lesson, with much reference to tit level and encouragement to feel various sexual sensations, there was Michelle's research. It hadn't changed at all, except for the presence of Colin who stood uncomfortably close to me for the duration.

"Just your type, Treadwell," said Michelle in a low voice as we headed up in the elevator to lunch. "I see you've worked your wiles on him already."

We made our collectively affronted way to the great hall. Simone did not seem to have heard anything Colin had said, and accused the rest of us of starting a vendetta against the 'poor man.'

"Did you hear what he said to me?" Justin was still very upset. "It was very offensive towards you too, Phi, suggesting you're some kind of slut. Or maybe, hoping."

"Don't," I said in disgust. "I can kind of see tit level." I pointed my hands in towards my chest and then out to first position. "But wouldn't it vary hugely person to person?"

That perked Justin up a bit. "Yes. Saggy ones, and you'd be down here. Wonky boob job: one up, one down, and... Oh bless. Simone didn't understand any of it, did she?"

The younger students filtered into the room with Aleks who approached the table. "How was your new teacher?" he asked us all.

"Litigiously obscene," stated Sun.

"I feel violated," replied Justin.

"I thought he was quite charming," said Simone.

"Amalphia," said Aleks. "How did you find the class?"

"Bad. Though not quite as bad as I had feared."

Justin snorted. "What did you think he was going to do? Turn a machine gun on us? Oh, here he comes..."

We all fell silent as Colin strolled over. "My young protégés. Girls, see that you don't eat too much. Pas de deux this afternoon, remember." He wandered off to get food, and Aleks followed him.

"There's cake in the fridge," I informed the table.

"Sounds good," said Sadie.

Sadie and I dodged round Colin and Aleks on our way into the kitchen and returned resplendent with plates of chocolate-mousse cake and a jug of cream. I smiled over at Colin but immediately regretted it when he smiled back, not seeming to notice the rebellious cake.

Pas de deux wasn't too bad, or, again, not as bad as expected. Colin partnered expertly without any obscenity or inappropriate touching, though his hands were unpleasantly sweaty and hot. We practiced lifts from a piece we were studying, and then our ever-enthused contemporary teacher arrived for her lesson. She got Will and me to teach the running leap from *Circle* to everyone else. Even our Pilates class took place in the dank dungeon now and so felt less nurturing, the dark not suiting Teresa and her dangling parrots at all.

We were all quiet in the elevator as we headed to dinner. The lights of the great hall felt rather dazzling after four hours straight underground.

"We're turning into mole people," said Justin. "What is to become of us? Destined to play myopic scuttling vermin in horror films. That's all we'll be fit for. Have a word with management, will you, Phi? This can't go on."

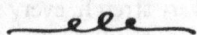

Aleks actually initiated a conversation about the training that night in my room. "I spoke to Colin, gave him my notes on you all. It should be better. Michelle says you get on well with him."

"She's lying."

"Malphia," he chided. "Why would she do this?"

"You tell me. But she is. It's just a fact. She also told me he was 'just my type' and that I had 'worked my wiles' on him."

"Maybe you misunderstand her."

"I understood her, Aleks." Questions blurted out. "Does she still have feelings for you? Is that why she hates me now?"

He laughed. "Believe me, no. And I'm sure she does not hate you."

"Then why the change in attitude?"

He frowned, as if thinking about it. "I don't know. But I do know that sometimes you can be..." He paused, choosing his next word carefully. "Provocative. Like with the cake today."

"That wasn't provocation. It was defiance. I defy Colin and all his works."

"And me? You defy me?"

"Well, start telling me not to eat cake..."

"Ah, what would you deny me then?" he asked softly, mouth warm against my ear.

Humour evaporated. "I don't think I would ever want to deny you anything."

"I am wishing this would be true," he said, serious and thoughtful for a moment before butting my face with his nose and ending the discussion.

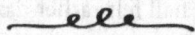

Aleks's notes did not have the desired effect. Colin kissed my hand and announced that he had a special treat in store. I was to do everything en pointe, to push, stretch and develop me. He really meant everything, even where it removed all benefit of the exercise: every bend, every stretch, every single jump, and there were so many dramatic and difficult jumps.

Colin's class consisted of a barre so short it didn't provide a proper warm-up, followed by repertoire that he'd previously performed to great – self-professed – acclaim. He taught us a male solo made up of huge leaps and turns that I would have struggled with in soft shoes. My feet were buzzing and hot by the end of class when Michelle entered the arena.

The word 'splendid' was knocked back and forth between the two teachers like a tennis ball. She asked to examine my feet and shoes. The toe protectors were batted aside. "We never used these when I was training," she said. "You'll find your own strength and toughness without them."

Despite the fact it was clearly unwise and against current thinking, I went along with it, mainly to show her she couldn't get to me. Suddenly her class was all en pointe too, for me anyway.

"In pain, Treadwell?" she asked.

"Yes."

She shared a waffling conversation with Paul about the wonders of negative stimuli. My on-screen results were apparently 'impressive beyond anything seen before.'

"The Nazis studied the autistic mind, of course," said Michelle.

Paul nodded. "They sent the less able to the gas chambers."

"They did, didn't they?" said Michelle with a wide smile in my direction.

"Refuse to do it anymore, Malph," advised a horrified Will. "They're a pair of fascist gits."

Maybe he was right. Maybe I should stop. But what would that mean for my place here? My head felt muddled. It was difficult to think clearly with the excruciating soreness of my toes.

Will's hands were soothing on my feet later, the cake was sweet, and the week continued painfully on.

I mentioned the situation to Aleks the following night, feet throbbing. He saw it as good that I was being upheld over the others, and pushed, but he wasn't in my bed to discuss pointe work. And really, neither was I.

Thursday was difficult. I avoided looking at my feet and worked on ignoring the pain. At lunch I begged a bucket of ice from Holly and sat with her in the kitchen, feet pleasantly numbed before the wobbly disaster of pas de deux. Not even attempting contemporary, I stumbled up the stairs, hot and dizzy, regretting not having taken the elevator.

My fuzzy mind listed essential tasks.

1) Lock door against Colin's possible arrival which had been hinted at in class.

2) Collapse on bed.

That was as far as I got. Collapsing was good. Sleep was better.

ell

"Time to get up, Phi! Quite a while ago, actually. Come on, open up; bashing down doors is really not my thing."

The room moved slowly to the right. I realised I was very cold. Yesterday's leotard stuck to my skin, and my feet didn't feel like my feet. They were swollen up in pointe shoes that I had obviously slept in.

"Phi? You in there?"

"Yeah. Gimme minute, Justin."

What to do first? Shoes or door? Door. He might help with shoes. I made it there and laughed. Unlocking was difficult as my fingers were slimy and weak.

"Oh my, look at you," said Justin. "What's so funny?"

"I'm lilting to the side. Or is it tilting?" I'd bounced off the wall on my way across the room. "Help me get my shoes off." I slithered down against the door post and sat on the floor.

"You're roasting," he said, feeling my forehead.

Shoes undone and gingerly removed, much dried blood was evident, and other stickier stuff.

"Well, there it is," said Justin. "Those psychopaths have ridden you raw. The school doctor is here to see the little ones. They came pre-injured for the research. It's quite creepy really. But you should go down there too."

Getting there would be a daunting task.

"The doc's a sexy bit, Phi. You'll like him. Tall, possibly ripped under the shirt, a caring look, bet he's got a bedside manner to die for... But you're not walking, are you? Stronger arms than mine are needed. Stay there."

He'd gone to get Aleks. Everything would be all right now.

It wasn't Aleks that came back up the stairs with Justin, but Will, who folded back the tights from my feet and revealed yukkiness I didn't want to see. 'Fuck' was said a lot, and 'bastards' which I found exceptionally amusing.

"She's looping, Hearst," said Justin. "I think she needs drugs."

"Where's Zolotov?" Will asked as he lifted me, the gentleness of his hands contrasting oddly with the angry way he spoke.

"Wasn't here," I sighed, leaning against him, smelling the Will smell. It was comforting to be carried by him. He was just right. Not too rough, not too soft, just perfectly warm like a bowl of porridge in a fairy story.

The doctor's small white room on the first floor was cold and deserted. The sound of piano wafted through from Aleks's class. Will placed me on the high bed, and a horrible teeth-chattering shivering started. He took off his top and dressed me in it like a child, lifting my arms through the sleeves. I observed all this as if from far away, and then lolled against him.

The doctor arrived, all smiles and concern, and asked the boys to wait outside. "How did this happen, Amalphia?" he asked.

I gave a garbled account of the last few days as he put a thermometer in my ear and then cleaned my feet, a process that stung. He handed me a tissue, my eyes having become very wet.

"You've a serious infection," said the doctor. "Your temperature's very high, and you're clearly in a lot of pain." He scribbled a prescription for antibiotics and painkillers. "I'll get your boyfriend to run down to the housekeeper with these, and you should start taking them pronto."

"Not my boyfriend," I said, as a sensible thought occurred. The pill. I would need more of it soon.

Dr. Duthie prescribed it, and I chatted with him while he dressed my disfigured toes. I was ordered to rest and take no classes until better. He would come and see me before he left the castle in the afternoon.

Back upstairs, Will and Justin stayed with me, slagging off Colin and Michelle, missing their 'crap anyway' classes and generally being nice company.

Holly arrived with soup and drugs at lunchtime and sent the boys away. "Has dancing boy bin up to see ye?" she asked, giving me no time to reply, already knowing the answer herself. "Ye need to open yer eyes, lassie. He's got his toast buttered on both sides, hasn't he? Sitting doon there with her, and you being affa accommodating up here." She patted the paper bag from the chemist.

"It's not like that."

"Aww, dinna take on, quiney. I'll see if I can catch him before he heads back upstairs to his class."

The drugs soon worked their magic, and I woke later to the sound of the door, a darkening room and absolutely no sympathy.

"Malphia, what is happening?" demanded Aleks. "Michelle says you are sulking about the pointe work."

My head wasn't clear enough to be suitably outraged, but I made an attempt. "Oh well, if that's what Michelle says."

As if on cue, there was a knock, and the door opened to admit the doctor. "How are you doing now?" he asked me.

"Better. Sleepy."

"I'm glad to see one teacher taking this seriously," said Dr. Duthie, eyeing Aleks. "The others don't seem to appreciate the gravitas of the situation at all. That's a strong painkiller I gave you. It will make you feel drowsy."

Justin and Will came in and exchanged a glance on seeing Aleks.

"The dashing young men from this morning," said the doctor. "I leave you in good hands. I'll be back to see you tomorrow, Amalphia, after my morning rounds." He gripped Will's shoulder on his way out. "She's in need of some TLC. Look after her."

"We plan to," said Justin, and the doctor left.

"So, you two knew of this." Aleks was angry. It wasn't good. "Why are you not saying something to me?"

"Would you have been interested?" asked Justin.

"What is this meaning?"

Justin's voice was cold. "That if you gave a fuck beyond an actual fuck, you would have known anyway."

I curled up, unable to cope with the confrontation or the implication.

"Stop it, Bevan," said Will. "You're upsetting her. It's all good, Malph." He crouched, bringing his face level with mine. "We're taking you to the cinema. There'll even be popcorn." This all seemed very unlikely. "Paul's letting us use the screen in the theatre to stream any film you want. So, up you get." He made as if to pick me up.

"Wait," said Justin. "She can't go like that. What d'you go putting that on her for? She looks all dancing cuckoo's nest." Justin indicated my top which was Will's from earlier.

"She was cold," said Will.

"It's nice." I held the ends of the sleeves up to my face. "Warm and soft, and smells of Will."

Justin made a gagging noise. "We all know Hearst smells, Phi. It's not a good thing. What are these drugs you're on? They're obviously fabulous." He tweaked the offending knitwear. "But I suppose this will have to be tomorrow's problem."

Will lifted me up, and Aleks left abruptly.

"Know how to pick 'em, don't you, love?" commented Justin in the elevator. "I mean, he's better than the last nightmare, but... Sorry. I'm lowering the tone of the evening."

It lowered further a few moments later when, crossing the entrance hall, we met Michelle.

"Still sucking up all the male attention in the building, I see," she said as she passed us.

"Do you actually want to be sued?" Justin asked her.

Her heels didn't miss a click on the black and white squares of the floor as she walked on.

"There's no doubt about what we have to watch," said Justin, through in the theatre. "A documentary about her."

"Such a thing exists?" I asked, smiling at Holly as she arrived with popcorn and then laughing at the name of the horror film that Justin had brought up on the huge screen.

"Fanatical foot-crippling harpies: let this be a warning to us all," Justin urged everyone, the majority of the students having joined us for the cinematic evening.

Tales of my affliction had buzzed round the castle. Everyone was so nice that tears kept threatening. Sadie brought me rubber toe protectors that she said were superior to the ones I usually used. She sat down on the other side of Will, and they shared a whispered conversation.

By the time the mad woman on screen held her sledgehammer aloft, my feet hurt and I felt a bit sick but insisted on walking back upstairs myself. "I'm not a complete invalid."

"Let Will carry you," said Sadie. "Make use of his strong arms."

Justin, Will and I piled through my door, and I went straight for the pain meds.

"Quite the little junkie now, aren't you, sweets?" noted Justin.

"I'm sore. They'll help me sleep. Don't want to have bad dreams after that film."

"D'you want any more help, Malph?" offered Will. "Like getting changed or whatever?"

"From you two? No thanks. I'll manage. But hey..." I held out my arms for a group hug. "Thanks. You know, for today."

"No problem," said Justin. "Though I do expect you to bear my child."

"I think we established there would be no bearing of children?"

"No," he said. "As I recall, the issue was not satisfactorily resolved."

"Consider it to be so now."

"Come on, I found you a sexy doctor. He could fix us up nicely."

"Goodnight," I said firmly, and they went.

I stood by the bed and sighed. What a day.

"Can I help?" Aleks stepped out of the bathroom, causing me to turn too fast and get dizzy.

"You scared me! And no. I'm too tired and sore for sex, so if that's what you're here for, you might as well just go away again." Facts, all.

"I am sorry it has seem this way."

"There's no filter between my brain and mouth just now," I told him.

"There is no need of filter between..." There was a significant pause before he said, "lovers." Lovers were people who had sex. Or were they people who loved each other? What were we?

He deftly undressed me in a non-sexual way, dropping Will's top on the floor, lowering my leotard and putting his own black T-shirt on me. He managed to remove tights and trackies without hurting my feet which he left in the slightly bled-through socks.

I lay down. "I'm fading. Drug's working." It was rather pleasant, like floating away on a puffy cloud of warm blankets.

"What is he thinking giving such strong medication for the blisters of pointe work?" Aleks asked.

"It's not just blisters." There was no energy to explain further.

He held me and I felt safe. My fingers felt the soft hairiness of his arm as he talked about dancers who had become addicted to painkillers. These drugs should only be taken for serious injuries, he told me, not eaten for breakfast.

I listened. Sort of. He said he would hate that to happen to me. I was so young. And so perfect. And then there was just blissful nothing.

Chapter 31

*E*NJOY YOUR DAY OFF.

So said the yellow page of notepaper left on his pillow. No kiss. No love.

The mad scene from the ballet *Giselle* stared from the mirror. My hair was everywhere, and I looked generally unwell and unkempt. So: bath. I put my feet up on the side of the tub to keep them dry and ran the water in around myself. Getting out was rather more awkward. I dried my hair, then pulled on jeans and a pretty lace-up top.

It was sunny. I planned to meditate in the circle with Will's stone after breakfast. The thought of breakfast made my empty tummy gurgle, and I hurried downstairs as fast as tender feet would allow.

Holly beckoned from where she sat with Justin, Will, Bekah and, unusually, Ross, the farmer. Aleks and Michelle didn't glance up from their involved-looking conversation. I sat down by my friends and ate six slices of toast with jam while telling of my ingenious bathing method. They listened and then, en masse, made plans for my day.

"A ride on a motorbike, oot in the sunshine, is jist fit yer needin'," declared Holly.

"I'm going to get a bit for a tractor," said Ross in explanation, looking rather bad-boyish in his worn black leather jacket. "I'll be passing back this way later, and could drop you off."

"Have you ever been on a bike, Phi?" Bekah asked.

"Not a motorised one." That seemed to settle it. Even Justin and Will were in agreement. I eyed them suspiciously. "You two in cahoots with each other is unnerving."

It wasn't until I returned several hours later, just as lunchtime was ending, that all became clear. Justin glanced at the staff table and called out, "That was a bloody long ride. Kept going a long time, did he?"

Will smiled in a slightly shamefaced way.

"You thought he'd be jealous," I realised. "I doubt he even noticed I was gone."

"Did too," said Justin. "Came and asked if you were back, earlier. He was all twitchy."

"I don't know if you deserve these now," I said, removing the gifts I'd bought them – locally brewed beers – from my new bag.

"That's a Goddess symbol," said Sun, eyeing the bag with its circular design.

"Got it in the village pub," I told her. "The Green Womyn. You would love it. There's all sorts of Pagan stuff on the walls and photos of the stone circle. I got you a postcard designed by a local artist." I handed over the artwork entitled *The Womb of the Earth Mother*. It was a black-and-white line drawing of a baby growing in the ground beneath the stones.

"We're all playing football in front of the castle this afternoon," said Justin, interrupting Sun's one-sided discourse on the Divine Feminine. "We can drink this beer and pretend to be burly men. So, where else have you been?"

"A tractor shop," I told them. "It was full of shiny red and green tractors, like giant toys. Then a farm. I took pictures of the horses, look."

I handed Bekah my phone, and she scrolled through the photos with interest.

"It was a bit embarrassing," I told them. "Ross left me in the kitchen with his mother for a while, and I couldn't understand what she was saying. Holly's been speaking toned-down lingo. I drank tea out of a flowery cup and ate homemade millionaire's shortbread, and then I got to feed a lamb with a bottle. It wagged its tail like a puppy."

"This is all very interesting," mused Justin. "These farmers, some of them are actual millionaires, of course, and, oh—" His volume increased. "He took you home to meet his mother, put a baby's bottle in your hand. I feel a song coming on..."

I leant on my elbow and squeezed the space between my eyes to calm myself.

"Ee, aye, the daddio, the farmer wants a wife! All together now!"

Thankfully no one took him up on the offer, and the song faded away as Holly approached with the doctor.

"You look like a different girl today, Amalphia," he said. "Let's check those feet, shall we?"

Aleks joined us as we walked up the stairs towards the doctor's room, but there was no chance to speak with him as Dr. Duthie was eager to know all about The Green Womyn.

"The black bottom pie is amazing," I told him. "And the place is cosy: big log fire, comfy sofas..."

"I think I'll take my wife there tonight," said the doctor. "I've been a neglectful husband of late."

Outside the medical room, he reminded me that I had the right to a private consultation.

"No, that's okay." I smiled at Aleks but didn't get much warmth in return, so just sat up on the high bed and undid my boots.

"How are they feeling?" the doctor asked of my feet.

"Better, though still really sore."

"I was surprised you were well enough to go out. That was a very high temperature you had yesterday. However, the outing has obviously been good for your mental state, something else I was concerned about."

As the doctor continued to quiz me, the choice to let Aleks stay seemed less wise.

"No, I'm not depressed," I said in answer to a question. "At least, I don't think so. I'm in pain. I feel frustrated and annoyed quite often."

"Do you feel like you're being bullied?"

I thought of Michelle and Colin. "Yes."

He wrote something down. Red spots showed through my dressings. He removed them and spoke in unison with Aleks.

One said, "Oh, that's excellent." The other exclaimed in Ukrainian.

"They're much better than they were. See this here..." The doctor pointed to a red line stretching upwards from the large scabby section on my toes and lower foot. "This was what concerned me most, infection spreading fast. However, the antibiotics are working, so keep taking them. And no classes until you feel you're ready."

"You could do my morning class," said Aleks, tone gentle. "It is remedial and adjustable, any pain and you stop." Back in the corridor, he continued. "Malphia, I am truly sorry. I did not know you were so hurt."

"You did know."

We started to walk back down the stairs, me in socks, not wanting to put boots back over stinging feet.

"I thought you were just..."

"What?" I looked at him. "You believed Michelle. That I was sulking." I was horrified into an ironically sulky silence.

"A little attention-seeking is no bad thing," he said. "The diva is surely part of a dancer's make-up?" He smiled and did a shoulder-wiggling dancey move as he spoke, which only made what he was saying all the more offensive. How dare he look all sweet and sexy while being so annoying?

"Attention-seeking? You sound like her. What's the point of telling you anything? I'm going to watch the football."

"So. You just run back to your friends." The tenor of his voice was no longer so gentle.

I whirled round. "And why shouldn't I? Where would I be without them? Lying up there, dead of septicaemia!"

"You are being the actress now, so dramatic."

Fury grew, the space around me turning brilliantly red.

He changed tack. "And the farmer. He is your friend now too?"

"I haven't known him long enough to tell." The words escaped through gritted teeth. The more honest answer would have been 'no.' I had not felt at ease with Ross, and was convinced that he'd been as cajoled into the whole escapade as I had. But Aleks had spoken in a negative way about my friends, so I had other things to say.

"Do you even understand the concept of friendship, Aleks?" I asked. "It's something so strong. It never lets you down, it's always there for you, always listens, trusts, believes. It's beyond price, it's..." I had the perfect example in my pocket, put there for the earlier meditation plans, and took it out now. "True friendship is like a precious stone, unbreakable and beautiful."

The sun shone through the high foyer windows and straight into the small pink stone, sending coloured beams out in several directions, highlighting the carved angels of the ceiling and bedazzling us both.

I looked at Aleks as the light faded. "I love my friends. I'm going to be with them now." I could hear football sounds – a whistle and shouting – from outside, and wanted to be out there too.

The flounce downstairs was painful, lacking in dignity and speed due to my injury, and then Colin blocked the way. "My dear, Miss Treadwell. How are your delectable toes today?"

"Entirely without skin, Colin, like you give a flying—"

"My feisty little temptress. I am a mere mortal man. I understand so little of what I do."

"Yes, there's a lot of you about. And I'm not your little anything."

The heavy castle door slammed satisfyingly behind me and Will approached. "I don't need carrying," I asserted, anticipating his plan.

"You're in socks on the gravel, Malph, so don't be stupid. And you're going to be our ref." It seemed everyone was there, everyone except Simone. "Girls against boys," Will told me as he carried me. "Bevan's playing for the girls to even things up with the numbers."

"I thought you were going to be a burly man, Just?" I said.

"That was never going to happen, darling!"

The afternoon took on a holiday atmosphere, especially after half-time when I shared Will's beer before remembering that my medication wasn't supposed to be mixed with alcohol. The holding up of red and yellow cards became ever more random.

"Can't hold your drink," said Will at dinner, after piggy-backing me into the hall and fetching us food.

"I'm not drunk, Hearse. I'm prescription-drugged, and that's quite different."

"You certainly showed bias in your refereeing," Sun called up the table.

"She always did favour the boys, Sunlight," said Justin. "Hearst kicked my legs out from under me. She watched, laughed, then red-carded me for standing still too long!"

"Look," I said. "The actual rules don't concern me. My decisions were based on how interesting things were to watch. A performance-based system, if you will."

"You're just all sore LOSERS!" Will proclaimed, and then turned quietly to me. "Holly gave Zolotov a right bollocking when you were out. It was awesome, you should have heard her." His impersonation was uncanny: "'When you were nae weel, that quiney was beside herself with worry. But you dinna care a shite, div ye?' There was more, but it was so fast, I didn't get it."

Aleks certainly wasn't having a very good day.

The rest of the evening was spent with Will in front of the television. He held my feet and watched an action-packed and violent film. I read a crime novel lent by Ruaridh.

Aleks came in as I was considering going to bed. "How are you feeling?" he asked.

"Fine." I looked back down at the book.

"You are tired," he went on. "I carry you up?"

"I'm quite capable of walking. And I want to be alone."

"Okay, but you will let me know if you need anything?"

I increased the pretence of reading. He left.

"Wow, Malph. That was cold."

"He believed Michelle that I was just sulking. He basically said I was an attention-seeking diva."

"Has he met you?"

"I know!" Releasing tension about Aleks loosened my usual restraint in other areas. "So how's your relationship with Sadie going? Does she not mind you sitting in here with me?"

"It's not a relationship. She just doesn't hate me like, you know, usually happens."

"Well, that's progress."

We sat in silence for a moment and then began to laugh.

"Who are we kidding?" I giggled. "We're going to end up doing that alternative arrangement of Justin's, aren't we? I can see it now. You and me at home, raising his and Simone's kids."

"So you don't see anything like that happening with Zolotov? No happily ever after? He's not the great love of your life?"

"He's about to break up with me." There. I'd finally voiced it, the very plain fact that I'd been avoiding since the start of term.

"I don't believe that."

"The vibes have been coming off him for a while."

"Prick."

"He's not. He's a good person, Will. Intense. Dramatic. But fundamentally good."

"Where was he yesterday, then?"

"Working. Doing his thing. He has this incredible ability to be completely focused, to exclude everyone and everything else but the task in hand. I think you need that to be successful in ballet. I don't have it, not to that degree anyway, else why would the fear get to me so? He knows it. The more he learns about me, the less he likes me."

"Bollocks. For starters, you're the best at ballet; you can do anything you want. And he's still well into you. You're warm, you're funny, you're cuddly. I bet Michelle was none of those things."

"He would appreciate her single-mindedness about the work. He's called me out on being 'all about my friends.' No, I have to face up to this, Will. He doesn't feel for me what I feel for him. He can't help that. I'm the selfish one."

"No, babe."

"He's not going to finish it now while I'm injured. I could, though, couldn't I? Tell him we could just be friends? Let him off the hook? But I won't, because I'm holding on to every single last moment I can get of him." I disintegrated into a teary mess on Will's shoulder.

"D'you think he'll go back to Michelle?" he asked.

"No, but thanks for that thought. Gonna take a big pain pill and knock myself out."

Aleks was sitting on the stairs below my room. Various sentences suggested themselves to me: I thought you'd still be working; sorry for being so mean; you'll get cold sitting there; sorry for clinging to you like a leech because I love you so much and don't want you to tell me it's over and please don't leave me ever, ever, ever. But he was sad, and I could make it right.

"Aleks. I know that—"

His finger silenced my lips, and he whispered, "Just us."

We were so very gentle, so different from how we had been lately. I cried. He spoke earnestly in Ukrainian between kissing my tears, and my belly, my breasts and my throat. Maybe I had been wrong. So many kisses couldn't lie.

But neither did the soft kiss in the morning. The air was thick with goodbye.

I did his class and found gentle kindness there too. Bekah and her classmates were gratifyingly delighted by my presence in their midst.

Days passed quickly without the dungeon. Nights continued to feel like a tender endgame. Maybe it was Aleksandr Zolotov standard practice to finish things as sweetly, as softly, as possible? I didn't know. I couldn't tell.

Colin approached me on his knees at breakfast, with hands clasped, to give a greatly dramatised apology.

Justin took a photo of the incident. Later at dinner, he told us: "Got a caption competition going on socials. Funniest one wins a photo of me naked. It'll be tasteful, don't worry, though some are asking if it can be of you instead, Phi. I don't suppose...? No? Well, probably better not. Your feet would ruin it. There's lots of entrants. Everyone wants to know what it's like up here. Agog, that's what they all are. I think it could go viral…"

His prattle did little to disperse the mist of sadness, not that he knew anything of it. Bekah had attached herself to Justin, and they laughed and chatted like we used to. It was Will who saw, and squeezed my hand, and I noticed something wrong in him too.

"Michelle hates me too," he told me. "Says I'm a brainless caveman without you. It's a real downer."

It all had to end. I would tell Aleks my feet were better enough to return to normal classes, and he would tell me what he had to tell me.

I ran over for one last hug when he came through my door that night, but revulsion scattered my thoughts and intentions.

"You smell like Michelle," I said. "Her perfume. It's as if she's in the room with us." The scent was cloying as ever, an evil encircling fog. His face, bemused by my reaction, showed red lipstick on both cheek and mouth. "Really?" I asked, astonishment muting heartbreak for a few seconds. This was how he was going to do it? "Well, I suppose you are being quite clear," I said. "Thank you for that. Okay, go on then." I opened the door and looked at the floor.

"You are throw me out?"

"Just go."

Maybe it was better this way. There would be no conversation in which I might cry or behave in a pathetic manner. He held his hands up and walked through the door. I closed it as softly as possible.

Chapter 32

I T WAS A SURPRISE to see the pink and orange sunrise. I looked at the sky in resentment. The stars hadn't shone through the ceiling. The sun ought to know better. However, bright colours might be the way to go. Would a strappy red leotard distract the eye from my puffer-fish face or accentuate it? The many thin straps of the garment crisscrossed my back in a pleasing design. It was different. It was daring. I wore it.

Will linked his fingers through mine at breakfast as my back faced the staff table. I didn't want to see anything of any of them.

"He's a pillock," said Will.

"He actually was," I admitted.

Justin arrived with his toast. "Budge up, Phi, that's my place. Oh. Is something amiss? Has there been a row?"

"Please don't make a big deal, Just," I requested. "Or be loud in any way."

"Moi?"

"They've broken up, Bevan," Will informed him. "Now, chill."

"Are you sure? I mean, this has happened before. It's maybe just how the two of you roll."

I shook my head. "It's different this time."

Justin wasn't convinced. "Okay, sweetheart, we'll see."

I didn't want to see. Seeing him with Michelle would... I didn't want to think either.

The dungeon was warm and muggy, the sense of something dark and bloody augmented in the strange and inexplicable heat. Colin's warm-up routine was slightly more robust than usual. He shot over when I took off my knitwear, faux corrected my port de bras and murmured that I had dressed up for him. The third time his hands 'accidentally' got tangled in my leotard straps, referred to as 'the web of desire' by him, they crept towards the front.

"Get off me!" I yelled, frozen in horror.

"But I am caught, Miss Treadwell, entrapped by your feminine charms."

"She said get off, McKen." Will hauled him back.

Colin found it all very amusing. "Oh, I see. I see, I do."

Whatever he saw didn't improve matters. He said that fairy-tale princesses who lived in tall towers were not meant to be chaste forever. After a long combination that everyone else had learned in my absence, he commended me on picking up the choreography so fast. "I can see your true nature, Miss Treadwell. There's passion, fire, a love of good sex, or maybe just a desperate need for it. Which is it, I wonder?"

"I want to hit him," whispered Will.

"Then you would be in trouble, not him," I whispered back.

The audacious leotard had a different, but equally unfortunate, effect on Michelle in her class. "Quite the little harlot, aren't you, Treadwell?" she said in a low voice, unheard by anyone, except possibly Colin. "I knew you would be back down here today."

Of course she had known.

"Fuck," I enunciated carefully, "off."

"Out," she said equally clearly, virtually spitting the last 't.'

Will came with me as I walked towards the door. "Who wants to stay here and look at someone with a face like a smacked arse, anyway?" he said to Michelle.

Weak with laughter, we hugged each other in the elevator, but sobered on entering the, mainly empty, great hall.

"D'you think we'll be expelled?" I wondered.

"Do we care?"

Aleks was sitting with Paul at the staff table. It had been a huge mistake to look that way. A pain in my chest stabbed and squeezed, suggesting that the time had indeed come to be somewhere else.

The younger students arrived downstairs, and were keen to know why we were above ground so early, and open-mouthed when they heard.

Holly came over with tea and cake. I picked at the icing.

Our own classmates arrived in due course, with much shoulder patting and ruffling of Will's hair. The two of us stared determinedly at each other, expecting retribution as Michelle came in, but she sat down by Aleks without a word.

Justin sighed, hand to chest. "Look at you two, all grown-up and insulting teachers. Phi, hearing you swear like that was a proud moment for me. If they expel you, I'm coming too. I did consider joining in and telling her the eighties wanted its suit back – does the woman own any other clothes? – but the pair of you were a hard act to follow."

"You've got to think," said Ruaridh. "What's to keep us here now? Morning ballet's not worth doing. Michelle's thing is of no benefit to any of us. The other classes are okay, but nothing special. Zolotov was the only spectacular thing this place had going for it, and now that's over? We could be down south, back among it all. Just saying."

The longest speech I'd ever heard Ruaridh give was followed by a contemplative silence. Bekah broke it. "But I don't want you to leave," she cried and flung her arms round Justin in a way that made me wonder if she fully understood that he was gay.

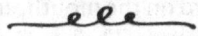

Colin was on his best behaviour for afternoon pas de deux, which was just as well as the pointe work really hurt. Aleks observed the latter part of the lesson. I did my best not to look at him. Mr. Timms kept me behind at the end to go over what I'd missed. He made me walk through the choreography with Aleks, then asked us to practice it another couple of times on our own, and left.

I tried to stay silent once we were alone. Aleks did not.

"Malphia, I did not know I was all..." His hand circled his face and he grimaced. "Michelle, she is excited to be progressing.

Last night a big section of the work is finished, and she hug and kiss me. In friendly way only, you understand. Earlier she is spraying her perfume, and I was near, caught in the cloud of it. This is all." His expression was open and honest, hopeful of reconciliation.

"Oh," I said, feeling a bit blank, response delayed.

"So, is going better down here?" he asked, as if everything were fine again.

"No, Aleks. It's dreadful." Reaction had arrived and it was angry. "Colin's useless and sleazy. Michelle is deliberately cruel. We're isolated here, away from everything. The whole class wants to leave the castle now."

"You? You are wanting to leave?"

"Staying here is no longer making me a better dancer." The words were made small and petulant by the big studio, as if my career was all that mattered, and that wasn't right, but none of what was happening was right.

"So," he said. And then again, more loudly: "So."

"That's about how much you care, isn't it? You're all happy and friendly up there in lipstick land. The rest of us barely exist for you now."

"You think you have me all worked out. But you have no idea." He placed his fist over his heart.

"Tell me then," I demanded.

The corners of his lips twitched downwards for a second before he kissed me hard on the mouth, an action that I reciprocated with biting immediacy. The late-in-the-day unshaven-ness of him made me tremble. I wanted to feel his rough face and mouth against other places, sensitive places. I shoved him back, shocked by the way I'd responded to him in the middle of an argument.

"Tell me," I said again, trying to ignore the sexual nature of my anger. It wasn't red this time; it was purple and sparked through with silver danger.

"I see you," he said.

"Oh, this again. Great. What exactly is it you see this time, Aleks?"

"Look," he said, turning me to face the mirror.

I shivered at his touch.

"Everyone sees it, except you," he said. "Michelle, she is jealous. You are young and beautiful, and all is ahead of you. She trained as a dancer, but injury ended that for her at an early age. She has done many scientific degrees after this – she is triple PhD – but I do not think it has made up for the loss."

I needed him to take his hand off my shoulder, and yet didn't want him to. I glared at my reflection in annoyance.

He went on. "The other one, Colin, he is notice everything. The way you move, smile, look. Always, you will attract attention from men. Is something you will have to get used to."

"You're saying it's my own fault?" I turned, breaking the physical contact.

He shook his head. "They are awkward people. The dance world is full of difficult, unpleasant persons who see nothing past their own agenda. Is good training to learn to work around them."

"Learn to accept abuse as normality. That's your advice? Your sole contribution to my training now?"

"Why?" he said, as furiously as I felt. "Why do you always do this?"

"What do I always do? You know what, don't tell me." I held a hand up to silence him. "I've had enough of this nonsense."

The elevator doors betrayed me, refusing to close and giving him plenty of time to catch up. We leant against opposite sides of the tiny room.

Just breathing. Just glowering. Just us.

By the time the doors opened in the foyer, I was pressed against the wall with my legs wrapped round his waist. His hair was in my grip, and I whined into his mouth. Somewhere, a militant feminist fairy fell down dead.

He pushed the button for the tower, but I wriggled free and staggered out onto the chessboard floor.

Bekah came hurtling down the stairs crying, and ran through the doors to the theatre corridor.

I followed her, hugged her, listened to her terrible tale, and wondered if there was any way that the day could get worse and what should be done about it.

One thing at a time. I located Justin in the big hall. He got up from his dinner at once, and went to see Bekah.

Weak and jittery, I needed food before braving anything else and turned towards the canteen.

Michelle spoke loudly from the staff table. "Amalphia's been having another little strop, has she?"

Had Aleks told her something about our argument? A glance at his impassive face revealed nothing.

Michelle hadn't finished. "You've found another baby, or maybe pet is a more apt word this time, to care for with Mr. Bevan, have you?" she asked with a laugh.

It was actually unbelievable. "You really think you can get away with anything here, don't you?" I said to her.

The red lips smiled.

I spoke on. "You can hang as many medieval torture implements on the walls as you like, Michelle. It doesn't mean we live in those times. Or Nazi Germany. You're not queen of the castle. You're a teacher, and there are certain lines you can't cross." The smile was unnerving. It was like speaking to the Cheshire Cat. Blurting everything out in front of everyone would be unprofessional. I'd been a teacher before I came here. I might be again. Wanting to keep my own conduct as it should be, I tried to use exact and legal language. "You've been exhibiting bullying and threatening behaviour towards the students."

Will stood by my side and held my hand.

"Well, isn't this just precious?" laughed Colin.

"You're not much better," I told him, then just listed facts. "You're foul-mouthed, lecherous and the most ineffectual teacher I've ever encountered. You've indulged in inappropriate touching, and everyone hates you."

He feigned horror but also managed to convey a patronising air, as if letting a charming child off with a misdemeanour.

"Miss Treadwell," said Paul. "I really cannot allow you to talk to members of my staff like that."

"Your staff?" I said. "So you're the most senior person here?"

"Well, we all have our own roles," he said, glancing up the table at Michelle. "But I'm as senior as anyone, yes."

"Then I need a meeting with you about a very urgent matter. Right now." I squeezed Will's hand to steady myself, appreciating the immediate return action.

"Miss Treadwell," Paul said again. "Your reputation for being dramatic is well earned, I see. Tomorrow will be soon enough."

"You want dramatic? I could just call the police."

"Now, Miss—"

"Don't patronise me again, Paul. You're another one who doesn't seem to give a fuck."

He flinched at the word and took his glasses off. I didn't regret saying it, though I did note that the castle was turning me into a frequently f-wording person.

"We don't really register as people to you, do we?" I went on. "We're lab rats to be used for your own ends. Lines on a screen."

I looked along the table. Colin and Michelle both had small smiles, different but similarly aggravating. Aleks met my gaze, but did not smile. It was his turn to hear my truth. "You seem to be the best of them, Aleks, but really you're the worst. You're not a bully – you don't behave like them – but your silence condones and enables their abuses. And I have no intention of getting used to it. Ever."

The word 'ever' reverberated high up in the roof, a sad reminder of a different echo, as a crowd gathered round.

"Well said," praised Sun. She started clapping and the rest joined in. We then, en masse, swept out of the hall to the foot of the stairs.

Will shouted, "To the top of the tower!"

"What is going on?" asked a confused Justin, as he emerged from the theatre corridor with a colourfully made-up Bekah.

"We're revolting," Will informed him.

"Speak for yourself," said Justin.

Numb feelings set in as we all rushed up the stairs and into my room. There was oohing and ahhing from the younger students when they saw the barre and the ceiling window. I sat on the bed with Will and Justin, and listened to the many 'evil Michelle' stories. Our class, minus Simone who hadn't joined us, had many tales of Colin, his useless warm-ups and constantly crass mouth. Aleks wasn't mentioned, of course he wasn't. He hadn't done anything wrong. Edward was phoned for legal advice, and a list of demands was constructed.

My mind could only half follow the discussion. I thought about Aleks's school life. This must all seem very minor in comparison to sticks and beatings. I hadn't even told him the worst parts. The worst. Why had I said that about him? It wasn't true.

Justin dragged me out of my reverie. "Ed doesn't think they'll expel you, sweets. They'll be running scared of litigation now, what with everything. He says they didn't explain the research aspect properly to us, so we could refuse to let them use any data they've gathered. We may have signed our consent on those forms, but it wasn't informed consent. Push them into a corner with that, and get them to give you whatever you want, is his advice." It was clear that everyone expected me to spearhead the rebellion and face the enemy on their behalf.

Holly arrived with biscuits, crisps and cola: rebellious food. "You were awesome, Phi," she said. "It was needin' to be said, all of it. They've telt me to tell ye that they'll meet you in the first upstairs studio at eleven, tomorrow morning, to 'discuss your concerns.' All your classes are cancelled for tomorrow." She deployed this in her best posh voice. "Aye," she then said, expressing much suspicion in the syllable. "Dinna go by yersel, quine. It'll be you against the bunch o' them. Plannin' to make ye feel this small." Her finger and thumb measured the centimetre I was to be made to feel.

Justin and Will would come too. They offered to stay the night with me, but I needed to be alone. To cry, to shower, to cry some more. To put on a big shirt of Aleks's that I found on a chair. We would probably never see each other again after tomorrow.

I found I couldn't stay in my room on my own. I couldn't leave things this way. So, I ran down and round the cold stone stairs to the silvery grey bedroom below mine.

Chapter 33

H IS ROOM WAS EMPTY. The bedside lamp was on, the bed itself rumpled as if he had been in it. Maybe I should get under the blankets and wait for him to return? I didn't care if he was angry. I wanted to feel his wrath and respond, hopefully more appropriately and clearly this time.

He stepped out of the bathroom, naked, his face looking sort of pink round the edges. He'd been crying. I rushed over and held him, moving my hands around different places on his back as if the hurt could be removed that way. If I hugged him everywhere, pressed him to me, covered him with love, everything would be okay.

Defiance of some sort detectable in his face, he pulled my shirt – actually his shirt – up and off, over my head.

We stood before each other, just us, nothing in between. He put his hands on either side of my face and kissed me twice, softly like the first time on the train. I shivered. He made a guttural sound as I slid down his body, dipping my nose into the indented line that marked the middle of Aleks. I took hold of his beautifully hard penis and touched it to my cheek, my lips, my tongue.

Suddenly we were airborne and then on the bed. I shrieked in shock at the flight, and gasped when he pinned my arms back behind my head. His face was grim. I wriggled under him, but there was no give in the grip he had on my wrists.

"You want this?" he asked, voice kinder than face. "You're sure?"

I nodded, deliciously overwhelmed by the male power of Aleks. He lined our bodies up and was, all at once, in me. I yelled in surprise, but also for the total joy of it. All needs met in an instant. All worries gone.

His eyes stared into mine as we moved into a new paradigm, love and power realigning around us. I smiled up at him, and he barked some sort of order.

He released my arms and flipped me over in one move. Gentle hands stroked my back and placed me on my knees. The sensation was different in the new position, animalistic and raw. I fell down on the pillows, jibbering something non-sensical. I was his, completely his, and at the same time more free than I had ever been. Free to be myself, to let go and fly high on waves of boundless beauty, above all worldly concerns. The feelings found a voice and a name: "Aleksandr."

At first I wasn't sure if I wanted his tongue's delicate dance. It was always too intense, and after such a stretching of the senses it might be unbearable. But everything was altered now, met as we were in this wild abandonment. I raised my hips to his mouth and demanded more and more until breathless exhaustion led us back to one another, face to face.

On his elbows, he kissed my mouth as we joined in gentleness. Our eyes locked. I wrapped limbs around him. Little golden lights rained down upon us in celestial celebration, as if from the sky, as if they had fallen through the ceiling window. We lay silent and close and protected in their starry glow.

My hand slid from his chest to his back as he leant away from me on the bed. I felt his buttock, his thigh, his knee, beautiful parts of Aleks all. He fed me cold water, then brushed my lips with his thumb. I leant my head on his shoulder as he drank, my fingers tracing trails through the sweat on his chest.

"Come, not get cold." He'd spoken. Everyday words of reality might call back unpleasant facts. The blankets he was arranging over us wouldn't keep them out. His strong arms might, my head in his neck, nestled and safe and home.

"Is time for me to speak my heart to you," he said.

He sat up. I sat up. He held my hands. I studied his fingertips.

"Is difficult, Malphia, like being in new country, not know language or how to be. At twenty, I would have run miles if someone had said these things to me." He paused. "I love you."

I braced for a 'but.'

"I want to spend my life with you. I know this since the Christmas party."

Emotion wouldn't settle. Happy and astonished quickly morphed into disbelieving and confused. "I thought you were going to break up with me," I told him.

"I know. I am hearing you speak to Will about this."

"Oh." A blank moment preceded realisation. "And you didn't put me right. Because I was right."

His eyes closed as if in pain. "It is for the best."

Oh. No. I couldn't do this again. Couldn't be here. So I just ran. Up the stairs this time.

My own pillow, in my own room, bore the brunt of rage and sorrow until he came in and sat down on the bed. I froze like a trapped wild creature, as if stillness could prevent further hurt.

"I am almost forty years old," he said. "I have a condition that is often degenerative. You know what this means?"

I looked round at him as he went on.

"I could be incapacitated, in a wheelchair, fit for nothing."

"You would hate that," I said. "Though you could never be 'fit for nothing.'" I lifted the blankets, and we both lay under them, facing one another on the battered pillows.

"But you understand?" he asked, touching my cheek.

"That you're being extraordinarily precious, yes."

"Is no life for you."

"I'd be great. I'm practical."

"This is not the point. You have the talent, the passion, to make whatever you want of your life. You should not be a nurse to an old man. I might not even be able to make love to you."

"There are many ways to make love, Aleks. Being disabled, or different, makes life harder in specific ways, but it doesn't mean there's less capacity for joy. Or love."

"You have not heard all," he said, voice heavy and serious. "Last night, I am knowing I should let you believe the lipstick thing. After such a betrayal, we would be truly finished, and would that not be best for you? But then, the selfish part of me told you the truth, and tried to put it right. Because I had this idea, that in years, if I am staying well, I would find you again—"

"That doesn't make any sense."

He raised his eyebrows.

"We'd only be together if you were well? You've said before that we have a strong connection. It's true. I know when you're ill; it's just the most terrible out-of-place feeling, and I have to be with you. This half-baked choice you're making for me wouldn't change that. And what were the other details of the plan?" I demanded. "Were you going to marry some beautiful, sophisticated blonde woman? Because she'll be useless." I sat up, already loathing the imagined person, ignoring his denial of her. "I could train as a nurse and turn up as if expected. Blondie won't care or question. Don't worry, I'd wait for her to go shoe shopping before giving you a blow-job."

"Malphia," he said, wavering between laughter and disapproval.

"This better not be a game, Aleks, or some weird way of letting me down gently. I asked you to be honest."

"And it seems I have no capability to be anything other with you. I was not intend to tell you any of this."

"That you're dumping me over some futuristic scenario that will probably never happen? For my own good? I could fall down the stairs and be left disabled. I could develop a terminal disease. How would you feel if I told you to get lost because of it?"

"I want the best for you," he said. "I want you to have a successful life, to be happy and fulfilled."

"And being with someone who wants those things for me isn't the best? Aleks, I'm at my happiest when we're together. Even when we fight. I'm so alive." My hands ran up and down his body, touching legs, abdomen, chest. "You are the best. Absolutely the—" I stopped, recalling the opposing statement I'd made about him earlier in the great hall, and everything else that had happened. "Oh well. You'll get your wish. I'll be leaving tomorrow."

"No, angel, this is not how it is. Not in any way. It is the thought that I could take from you, or even harm you..." He leant up on an elbow. "But, this thing, here with these ones downstairs? The power is all yours. They need you. They are to offer you more money, behave like they are the great forgiving ones, and hope you settle back down."

"It's not about money."

"I know. Let me think a minute." He got out of bed and walked over to the three small windows. He marched back. "You see, if this was just an affair, something that would fizzle away naturally, it would not matter." He headed to the window again and looked out a moment, hands on either side of the curved stone surround. "We could enjoy our time together with no worries." He approached the bed.

"Aleks, you should put some clothes on. It's so cold."

He stared at me. "It's so unfair. Because it is more, because it is love, nothing is simple."

"Part of it's my age again, isn't it?"

He frowned.

"And that's unfair. It's not like a correction in class. I can't work on what year I was born. But you're prioritising the details. You are. It's like..." I tried to clarify my thoughts. "The people you love, and the things you love to do. They're what really matter. Then there are the details, like where you live and work, your age and your health. It's wrong to base big decisions on the details when they're unknown or imagined circumstances from the future."

He nodded. "Give me some minutes." He stayed by the window so long that I was tempted to force warm-up garments on him but, not wanting to interrupt his thought process, I sat in the bed, breathing, trying to stay calm and centred about everything. Him. Me. This place. The situation here. The situation with us. There was a lot going on. And – he was right about one thing – none of it was simple.

He eventually joined me in the bed again, and I pressed myself to his chilled form.

"I hate this," I said. "It feels like you're deciding everything, and I have no say."

"No decision. Suggestion only. In the end, you have all the power with me too."

I lowered my head and listened to the steady beat of his heart as he spoke.

"Tomorrow, in the meeting, you ask for all that you want. If they do not offer you a good enough deal, I suggest you leave."

My chest constricted.

"I will come with you," he added. "If you are still having me."

I tipped my head back to examine his face and found only straightforward honesty there.

"We could live in the flat in London," he said. "You like it there." He touched my nose with his lips. "I can finish your training. You are wrong in thinking I didn't want this. It has been very bad for me to realise that Colin is an idiot boy. I had hoped he would be a good teacher."

"But, your job here. You love it. You've been spending all your time at it."

"I have been try to use as a distraction, but then I spend all day thinking about you anyway." He kissed me, his excitement about the plan growing. "There are other jobs. We can both work from one base. You dance. I teach." He paused. "There are two spare rooms in the flat; Justin could stay also if you are liking. One we will keep for days when I have been stupid. You can storm off to your own space before returning to our bed later. This is how we are, no?"

I stepped out of bed, out of his reach. "No."

"No?" His brightness vanished.

"You're being unrealistic. It won't last. Something will upset you. You'll find more faults in me or go all quiet and distant. And what about the meeting tomorrow? There's lots I have to say, all sorts of things you don't know."

"All the badness of me?"

"Not you, no."

"If we stay here, we must learn to separate our working lives from our relationship. Is really a teacup storm, this thing today. Nothing that is said will rock us."

"How can you possibly know that?"

"Because from now on, I am to live from here." He stood beside me and placed my palms on his chest. "No secrets, not from you, not from anyone. There is only one question. What do you want?"

Chapter 34

B Y THE TIME JUSTIN arrived in the morning, Will, having turned up minutes earlier, was sitting on my bed eating some leftover pasta that had been cooked by Aleks in the night.

Justin examined the two of us and pointed an accusing finger. "How long have you been here?" he asked Will. "And do you both have something very exciting to tell me?"

"It wasn't me," said Will, about what, I wasn't sure.

"So." Justin's voice was dark. "Betrayal. And by our leader, no less. Oh, she's trying to look innocent."

For the second time in twenty-four hours, a man turned me to face the mirror. I laughed in surprise at the purple love bite on my neck. Aleks's parting words of "Don't hide it," made sense now.

Justin's eyes met mine in the mirror. "He came up here and fucked you into submission."

"No, he didn't. I went down to see him, and then we came up here."

"What?" said Justin. "There's a reason bints get walled up in the top of towers, you know. You clearly can't be trusted for a minute. Even then, you go tossing your hair out the window for any passing Tom, Dick or Aleks. And now it'll be left up to me, your magical Fairy Godfriend, to sort it all out."

"Aleks is on our side, Justin," I told him.

"Oh, pray tell, what did King Aleks have to say?"

I outlined his comments on the situation.

"Leave?" Justin asked sharply.

"S'right enough," said Will. "If it stays shit like this, there's no point in staying."

I nodded in agreement.

"But where is the Treadwell's broken heart?" mused Justin. "The whirlpool of despair that, only yesterday, threatened to pull us all under? What has gone on this night?" He paced over to the bed. "Hearst, you're sitting right in the middle of the crime scene. Doesn't that bother you?"

"Nope," said Will, using his fingers to get the last of the pasta sauce out of the bowl.

Justin spun round to face me. "He asked you to marry him!"

"No, he didn't."

"Something, though," he said, circling me beadily.

"We should be focusing on this morning's meeting," I said, to no avail.

"You're moving in with him. Into the fucking palace. That's it, isn't it?"

I shrugged.

"See, I knew that wasn't them split up," Justin told an open-mouthed Will. "You'll need to wear something with a neck, Phi."

"I'm fine like this," I said, pocketing my pink stone for good luck.

Justin sighed. "The last vestiges of propriety have disappeared overnight, rebellion having paved the way for total anarchy. Well, who am I to fight the turning tide? Let's do this thing, comrades."

"All set for the firing squad," commented Justin on seeing the one chair placed in front of the long table where three people – Colin, Michelle and Paul – already sat. Aleks stood with his back against the barre, but he joined the others at the table as Will dragged two metal-legged seats across the floor for himself and Justin. Michelle shuddered at the scraping sound.

"Firstly," said Paul, straightening his pages of notes as we all sat down. "We want to clear up a little misunderstanding. Colin? I think you were going to say something?"

"Yes," agreed Colin. "Though first, may I just say how absolutely divine you look today, Miss Treadwell. Elegant and alluring as ever."

I stared back expressionlessly.

Paul cleared his throat. "This isn't quite what we..."

"Oh, I know, I know," said Colin. "I am truly sorry. I apologise from the bottom of my heart, the very depths of my soul, if I have caused you to feel anything other than completely respected at all times."

"If?" I asked.

"Yeah, what the fuck, McKen?" blurted Will. "I had to pull you off her. Your hands were, like, everywhere."

"Oh, the day of the red leotard," interjected Michelle. "I can attest to the fact that nothing untoward took place. Treadwell and Hearst were just inviting trouble as usual. What are you doing, Mr. Bevan? If you're going to turn up uninvited to a private meeting, you could at least pay attention."

"Just checking record was on," he said, holding up his phone. "Mustn't miss any of these lovely litigious comments. So, a red leotard in a ballet class is being declared an invitation to grope? Interesting stance you're taking. Do go on."

Michelle was clearly livid, but she stayed quiet. I didn't look at Aleks.

"May I just say that Amalphia has my total support?" said Colin. "The manner in which she was spoken to during the research yesterday was completely unacceptable, and I fully understood her impassioned response."

"It was unacceptable," I agreed. "But so is much of what you say. 'Bingo Wings' and 'Cankles?'" I didn't want to mention the 'Double D' thing in front of Aleks. "Name calling is bullying."

Colin smiled. "Oh, come now, points well made, surely? Amalphia," he said, sounding each syllable slowly. "Even your name is a delicious, orgasmic experience for the tongue." There were uncomfortable or surprised movements from the others at the table, but Colin wasn't finished. "You and I are very alike, both plain-speaking, passionate individuals."

"In that case why do you have so much trouble understanding the words 'no' or 'leave me alone' or the fact that I have literally fled your presence several times?"

"The game of cat and mouse is an old one, pet," he said with a smile.

"I'm not playing a game."

"Then let's be blatantly frank. I want to fuck you sideways."

Aleks had him by the collar. Will cleared the table to join the fray, and I scrambled after.

"No hitting," I said. "There's been enough hitting..." I trailed off as Aleks ordered Colin to leave.

The incorrigible man continued to speak from the doorway. "These young boys don't know how to make it good for you. I would be so much more—"

Aleks shut the door over him. "This is how he has been?"

I leant back against the table. "I can't believe he didn't tone himself down in front of everyone."

"You said something of this," said Aleks. "I didn't listen."

"I didn't tell you properly."

"Yes, yes, we're all very sorry," said Justin. "But do we have an official acknowledgement that McKen's behaviour is inappropriate?"

Michelle shook her head. "Treadwell's always got to be the centre of some little drama, the boys all clustered round."

"Michelle, I think we have to take this seriously," said Paul, putting on his glasses. "If we could all sit down again, could you clarify what you said, Miss Treadwell? Colin hit you?"

"No," I said, as we returned to our chairs. "You didn't tell them?" I looked straight at Michelle.

"What nonsense is this now?" She sighed and rolled her eyes.

"You assaulted a student. She could press charges. You could lose the right to work with young people. You really do think you're above the law, don't you?"

She glared back, eyebrows furrowed as if in non-comprehension.

"Yesterday afternoon," I explained. "Michelle shouted at Bekah about her make-up and clothes—"

Michelle interrupted. "Even you don't turn up to class looking like that, Miss—"

I spoke over her. "She then pulled Bekah across the room by the arm – it left a mark – and slapped her face."

"Photos of both marks already sent to our solicitor," added Justin.

"Well, it's not true," said Michelle, incredulous, looking to her colleagues for support.

"The most talented girl in each class," said Aleks. "I know this kind of spite. You are threatened, so you aim all your anger their way."

"Oh, she's got you expertly sucked in." Michelle looked at me as she spoke. "I'm starting to think you'll do more or less anything to get your own way, Treadwell. You're even training up a demonic little protégé to join you in your endeavours."

"A very serious allegation has been made against you, Michelle," Paul pointed out.

"This is to deal with first," agreed Aleks. "But also will need complete overhaul of timetable, sacking of unsuitable staff, a system of communication so students do not have to take huge problems on themselves. There should be a school counsellor."

"Oh, is pillow talk not good enough?" snapped Michelle. "Perhaps if you didn't spend so much time with your cock in her mouth, you'd be able to think clearly. We all know she's your WHORE!"

Paul cleaned his glasses. Whatever Will and Justin said was drowned out by Aleks. He spun Michelle's chair round and shouted into her face about how a loving relationship was beyond her comprehension. She was a cold creature who found warmth between people to be a shocking thing. His voice thundered and it was terrible.

I ran round the table and touched his arm.

"I will not work with you again," he told Michelle, more calmly. "This is it now, finished."

He took my hand and we walked away from them, out of the studio, down the corridor and onto the stairs. We hugged. He said sorry repeatedly into my hair. I shook my head because it wasn't his fault.

"Well, that was fun," said Justin, arriving beside us with Will. "I told her about the informed consent, said she couldn't use any of the data already gathered. That upset her more than the telling off you two gave her. She kept saying 'what?' really loudly. I think she still is." He cocked his ear towards the corridor, and we all listened. There were raised voices. I hoped they weren't getting nearer.

"We need to go," said Aleks, looking at me. "We can visit the pub you are liking. We get a break; they calm down. Wait here, and I'll get our coats."

I glanced back down the corridor.

"Okay, not here." He pulled keys out of his pocket. "Wait in the car, maybe reverse out?"

He took off up the stairs and Justin, Will and I made our way outside to the outbuilding that acted as a garage.

"Ballet pays some people!" exclaimed Will on seeing Aleks's car.

I pointed the key and pressed the lock button, liking the flash of lights it elicited.

"You gonna back it out?" asked Will.

I looked at him as if he was mad. Why Aleks had suggested such a thing when I didn't know how to drive was beyond me.

"Can I?" asked Will.

I handed the keys over a little hesitantly, not quite sure how Aleks would feel about it, and we all got into the car. Justin screamed as Will backed out at great speed, taking us into a long backward curve over the crunchy gravel. I laughed, having quite enjoyed the experience.

Aleks opened the driver's door with a smile, but also a thumb that indicated 'out.'

"Bet it can shift," Will said as he joined Justin in the back seat.

"On way back, you can have a go," promised Aleks. "But for now..." He wove his fingers through mine over the gear stick. "We all need to just..." His other hand finished the sentence, thrusting forward on an audible out breath, and we tore round the side of the castle and shot off up the track.

It felt so good to be leaving, escaping to brighter places. We paused at the end of the tree-lined road, the old metal gates and the stone mermaid and bear releasing us to the wider world.

The pub was wonderfully warm and welcoming after the cold shouty castle. Old wooden beams, plush rugs and a crackling fire greeted us in the lounge. Aleks and I sat on the sofa by the fireside.

On having his 'many working-booted men must come here for lunch' suspicions confirmed, Justin removed to the public bar, and Will went with him.

The stodgy pub food was comforting and fortifying. The music Aleks put on the old juke box was romantic. The fire glowed redder as we relaxed back on the sofa with hot chocolate after the meal.

"This time tomorrow," he said. "We could be back in London. Drive all night."

"We haven't had any sleep," I reminded him. "It wouldn't be safe."

"So, we take a few days to travel, see the country, be together. Or maybe everything will fix. Not her. She is never coming back from that. But the rest? We will see."

I knew which option sounded better and was already envisioning staying in a range of nice hotels with Aleks, sleeping in a range of comfy beds with Aleks, and trying a wide range of different positions—

"Is your friend." He pointed to a window on the far side of the room. It provided a view of the bar where Justin and Will were talking to Ross. "I don't want you to go out with him again, Malphia. I don't trust him."

The proper reaction was obviously to screech that I could do whatever I liked, with whomever I liked, whenever I liked. But I looked at his twitchy face and just stated a fact. "I don't intend to."

"We can hear that dirge in the bar, you know," Justin complained, coming through and seeking out alternative songs on the music machine. "You need to go persuade Hearst to drink coffee. He's a mean drunk."

"You're drunk?" I asked him.

"I am slightly tipsy. He got into some manly display of testosterone with Farmer Giles, not that it wasn't amusing at the time."

I found Will slouched over the bar, black coffee untouched in front of him.

"You and Ross got drunk?"

"No," he lied. "He said you must have a thing for older guys."

"That wasn't very nice." Not going out anywhere with Ross? No problem.

"Bevan says the last one was old too."

I glared at the speaker of untruths as he came through to see how the sobering up was progressing. "What's this you've been saying, Justin?"

"The other old dude?" Will explained.

"Enlighten me," I requested. "Because I have no recollection of this person."

"Well, he was slightly older," said Justin. "A little poetic licence has to be excused in a bar full of brawny men, Phi. The story was just better that way."

"He was four years older than me. And I can't believe you brought him up."

"Neither can I. Sorry." A moment of serious sincerity took place. It passed quickly. "No, Hearst," said Justin with a wicked look. "It's an unfair conclusion we came to, for the only other great love of our dear Amalphia's life wasn't older at all, was he? What a sad tale of unrequited desire and jealousy that is." He covered his mouth. "It's the drink. I think we all need some fresh air."

"Who was that then, this other bloke?" Will slurred. "Do I know him?"

"I believe you may have a passing acquaintance, sweet William," said Justin, enjoying himself far too much. "I sometimes suspect there's still a little candle burning there. It's eclipsed by the current flame, but who knows what the future will bring?"

There were no warm flames or soft candlelight on the drive back. The day darkened as the castle neared. I stroked Will's hair as his comatose head lay on my legs, Justin having refused to sit beside someone who was a puke risk. Michelle's face appeared in my mind as we drew up beside the high pink walls of the old keep. Hopefully we would soon be driving away from it, off into the night.

Will went to bed. I waited in my room. Aleks and Justin went to seek out Paul, and it wasn't long before they arrived at the top of the tower all fired up with enthusiasm.

Michelle had been stripped of teaching privileges pending an internal investigation, which presumably translated to Paul polishing his glasses while having an awkward chat with Bekah. Aleks had been offered the position of Head of Dance Studies, giving him complete control of the dance school. The research was suspended for now. Paul would be talking to each one of us in the hope of getting the needed 'informed consent' but Michelle's involvement was, most likely, at an end. I was being offered a part-time teaching post: exam work for the younger students. Justin's workshops were to be a regular thing, also paid.

"What do you think, Malphia?"

"I think you could make this into an incredible school."

He was clearly alight with the challenge, ideas already flitting through his head. I pushed my own disappointment aside and kissed him. We were together, and he was going to teach us again. What did the details matter?

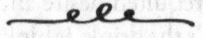

It was with some astonishment that I later found myself interceding on Colin's behalf. "Whoever hired him to teach here has a responsibility to rehabilitate him," I told Aleks. "He's got a very high daft-quotient. He doesn't seem to realise there's anything wrong with the way he behaves. Make him watch competent teachers and attend courses on appropriate methods of speaking to and correcting students. Otherwise he'll go off and do the same things elsewhere." I had already suggested contacting Edward for assistance in drafting proper bullying and harassment policies, and added, "Colin should have to copy the policies out and learn them by heart."

"So," said Aleks at dinner, scrolling through his phone. "Colin is on probation. I have to find another ballet teacher."

I was deeply relieved that Michelle wasn't present in the hall. Relief was written on the faces of the other students too along with excitement about what the coming changes might mean. Bekah was particularly thrilled and quick to drop any idea of pressing charges. She whispered celebratory plans that made me laugh at the time.

"I would much rather stay here with you," I said to Aleks later, at the top of the tower, reluctant to leave him.

"Is good for you," he replied. "Have fun with your friends, release tension. I will just be sort this." He waved the timetable as the phone rang again, and another conversation with a prospective teacher began. Catching my name among the Ukrainian, I got ready and made my way down the stairs to meet the others.

***

Everything was quiet and dark when I tiptoed across my room to the bathroom to give my face and teeth the cleaning of their lives.

"Good time?" Aleks asked from the doorway of the ensuite.

"Not really. I didn't mean to wake you."

"Tell me," he instructed, standing behind me and circling his arms round my waist.

I told him how Will and I had been really tame and boring compared to Bekah and her classmates. We'd avoided the smoke-scented cottage. We'd almost fallen asleep on a sofa watching a DVD. We'd not wanted any alcohol nor had the energy to dance. Then came Justin's truth-or-dare game. "He made up the questions as he went along. They were all embarrassingly apt. Will chose the dare, and it was a game of Spin the Bottle."

"So, you have kissed Will tonight?"

"No. I have never kissed Will. That *Romeo and Juliet* thing doesn't count as I wasn't myself," I added, seeing his doubtful face in the bathroom mirror. "But it should have been Will. The bottle pointed at me. And I wanted to. I've always wondered what it would be like. Sorry, I know it's inappropriate to say, but it's true."

"Your honesty is let me know is nothing for to be worried," he said quietly.

"Justin accused Will of cheating with the bottle, then shoved him out of the way and kissed me himself. I pulled back, he followed me, and it was terrible. Like kissing my brother, or something. I ran back here."

"Justin is still very young. Maybe is confusion in him?"

"More like something from the smokey cottage. I hope he doesn't remember. Don't fancy having that discussion."

"So you have come back to me."

"Of course."

I leant back against him. He lowered his face to my neck. I could feel his breath and the tip of his nose and the movement of his mouth as he spoke.

"I have been thinking about this you say last night: the many ways to make love." My body melted further into him. "Tell me more. How will I love you tonight?"

"I liked it from behind."

He kissed my neck.

I blurted more. "I liked the way you held me down. And that you bit me."

His teeth found my earlobe. "You like to be dominated. Sexually only, I am think."

Our mouths smiled as they met.

"You have stood up for yourself now," he went on. "Been strong and fearless. Maybe this has freed you to discover other aspects of your nature? I am so happy to be the one to explore this with you. Last night was completely instinctual. After all that has gone on, all that has been in my mind, was like claiming you, to say that you are mine."

"I am."

"Hold on tight," he said, placing my hands on the sides of the sink. "Adventure starts here."

Chapter 35

A LEKS SAT DOWN BESIDE me at the breakfast table the next morning. Bekah looked a bit perturbed, but nobody commented on the situation. There was a strong sense of relief in the air as we all ate our toast, as if life at the castle had entered a new, and infinitely better, phase.

"You are sure?" Aleks said quietly to me.

I looked round at him. "About what?"

"The end of our secret?"

"Oh. Yes. If you are."

He smiled. "Shall I show you how happy I am about it?"

I nodded, and he kissed me softly, and then again, not quite so softly.

"I will see you downstairs," he said and left to prepare for class, looking very happy indeed.

Bekah's eyes and mouth were wide. "You and Mr. Zolotov?" she asked. "Since when?"

"Oh, forever," answered Justin.

"But he's so old."

"It isn't news to anyone else," sniped Simone. "You thought it was such a big secret, but we all knew."

I glanced round the table.

"Will told me," said Sadie.

"Justin told me," said Ruaridh.

"It was such a lovely piece of juice, Phi," said Justin. "You can't blame us."

I left the table, and the discussion, to seek Aleks in the dungeon.

Colin sat alone on a bench in the large subterranean space. He brightened when he saw me.

"Miss Treadwell. I owe you a debt of gratitude for saving my reputation. It would not have looked good for me to be ejected so quickly from my first teaching position."

"No problem," I said. "I thought Aleks was down here."

"It seems to be a trend in this castle, not finding the person one expects in any given room at any given time."

"Apparently so." I had been astounded to hear that, while I'd been out at the party, Colin had finally made true his threat of turning up in my bedroom. He had been surprised to find Aleks there, saying 'oh' several times before turning and walking back down the stairs.

"You can't be persuaded to keep some sort of timetable for the men in your room?" he asked now.

"There's only one man," I replied. "And that's the sort of thing you're not supposed to say. You've got to be professional going forward."

"Professional like Aleks?" he said in a dry tone. "He's not holed up in his room alone every night, is he?"

"Why don't you ask Michelle out?" I said, a little surprised by my own spontaneous suggestion. Was I trying to get back at Michelle by sending Colin her way? If I was, it was a failed attempt. Colin's expression was one of horror.

"Oh no," he said, shaking his head. "Far too scary for me, that one."

~elle~

At dinnertime, Bekah was keen to put right her earlier reaction. "You're like the mum and dad of the castle," she said of Aleks and me. "You can't ever split up, or it'll scar me for life."

"Yes," agreed Justin. "There's been enough hoo-ha." There was then a pause in which, though his body didn't actually move, he seemed to wilt, to sink in on himself and depress. "Things are too good to be credible," he said. "Phi's love life's all sorted out. I'm being paid to teach musical theatre. I have a sweet new friend." He laid his head on Bekah's shoulder and went on. "Michelle has been stopped, Colin gagged. Something bad has to happen to balance out the universe."

It was at this point that I became aware of a change in the atmosphere around me. I detected a familiar and cloying scent. I spun round on the bench to discover that Michelle was standing right behind me.

"Amalphia," she said softly. "Can I speak with you?"

She looked small. And sad and lost somehow. I moved closer to Will and indicated that she could sit. Everything was quiet. Everyone was listening.

Michelle sat down as Aleks arrived beside us. He stood behind me and placed his hands on my shoulders.

Michelle ignored him and looked at me. "I need to work with you again," she said.

"What?" said Aleks. "Where is the apology?"

"Yeah, what the fuck?" added Will.

I held up a hand. I could speak for myself. And I did. "I'm surprised you would want to work with a whore."

"I am sorry," she said. "If I could go back in time and undo comments I made in anger, I would. But you are the star that the research has uncovered. The potential for discovery, the potential for good, is immense, Amalphia. Would you give me ten minutes a day?"

"She will not," Aleks replied. "You have no right to ask this. The research is over." It was. Only Simone had still been willing to take part in it, and she wasn't enough. We were to continue out the year as dance students, nothing more.

"You would be employed on a private basis," Michelle continued, never taking her eyes off me. "Some have been helped greatly already, of course. Many more people could be benefitted in the future with this work. If only we can complete it."

It had helped Aleks. I knew that. "What would it involve?" I asked, deliberately looking straight into her eyes. They were blue.

She looked straight back at me. "Brain monitoring with different amalgamations."

"Pointe work?"

"No."

"Negative stimuli?"

"No."

"Ten minutes a day?"

She gave a quick nod.

"Okay," I said. "Ten minutes. Before dinner. After my other classes." That way it wouldn't take anything from them, or drain me for the rest of the day. It shouldn't have been a big deal, but somehow it felt like it was.

"Thank you," she said and touched my hand, her long red nails indenting the skin like blood-stained claws. The instinctive recoil was unavoidable. She twitched slightly as I pulled back my hand.

"I don't believe this," said Will.

"I also am not agreeing that you should do it," said Aleks. "But if it is what you want, I will sit in. Observe."

"That's fine," said Michelle, still only looking at me. "You usually have a private lesson in the dungeon at the end of the day, don't you? I'll come down after that."

I tipped my head back against Aleks's stomach to look up at him, realising I hadn't thought my suggestion through properly. Those lessons had so far ended in various types of hilarity-inducing bossy sex. The computer desks had been put to new use, as had the piano. The earth had literally moved when a piano foot went through the floor. I'd never seen Aleks out of breath with laughter before. And I wanted to see it again.

Michelle got off the bench. I watched her walk away. She stumbled slightly as she reached the doorway, going over her ankle on her high heel, but she carried on walking.

"Is she okay?" I wondered. "She doesn't seem her usual self."

"This is not for you to worry for," said Aleks.

"Maybe not," I agreed. "But is anyone checking on her? This is the first time I've seen her down here since it all."

"You're a more forgiving person than me," said Justin. "Whatever she's going through, she brought it on herself. But I do fear the balancing of the universe may have begun."

The ten-minute research sessions turned out to consist of a few simple arrangements, easily done. They were so basic, I suspected they were being made up on the spot. Aleks expressed exaggerated disinterest as he wrote up his class notes at the piano. Michelle always thanked me politely once we had finished, and the day progressed in its normal sexy way as soon as she departed the dungeon.

—— *ell* ——

The new teacher arrived, Aleks's old friend that he hadn't seen in years.

Pasha was attractive and knew it; I could see that he enjoyed the admiring looks he received on entering the hall at dinnertime. Dark wavy hair matched dark eyes that held more than a hint of naughtiness, while his body was a wide block of muscle. His cheeks had dimples and his chin, a cleft. The old friends hugged with much manly back clapping. There followed a loud exchange in Ukrainian, and I was summoned with a shouted, "Malphia!"

The high level of happiness that Aleks expressed while introducing me to his friend was endearing. The sweeping appraisal my body got from the dimpled one was not.

"She is very beautiful, Zolotov." Pasha kissed my hand with a flourish and a look that immediately downgraded Colin to the rank of badly behaved puppy. Here was a calculating reptile.

Aleks asked if I minded the two of them going out that night. I'd replied that of course I didn't mind, and that had been entirely honest when said there in the great hall.

It no longer felt true when I saw him all handsome and smart in shirt and jacket in the foyer on his way out.

"You look like you're on the pull," Justin said to him in a gloomy tone.

"You are joke, yes?" said Aleks. "Pasha wants to see Aberdeen. We will be home late. Go sleep, Malphia. I will try to creep in." And with a quick kiss he was gone.

"Prepare yourself, Phi," said Justin. "The end of happy-fun-time approaches. Trouble draws near." He gazed into the distance. "By this time next week, you'll all be saying: Justin was right. Now we know our doom."

Evil portents were difficult to disregard at bedtime, solitary and cold as I was. Fleecy bunny pyjamas were no comfort, and after what felt like hours of lying awake in the dark, I sought the refuge of the kitchen. The hot chocolate was lumpy, the stove barely warm in the old fireplace and the clock's message stark: it was after one-thirty in the morning.

A muffled bang carried through from the foyer. I hurried across the hall and there they both were, Aleks just closing the locks on the main door.

"Is your vanilla crème pie, Aleksandr," said Pasha.

"My angel," corrected Aleks, walking carefully over. "Why you not in bed, all cosy warm?" His slight slur was sweet, and his mouth tasted of vodka.

"Couldn't sleep. Made hot chocolate."

Pasha's laugh was not sweet. Aleks went to the bathroom, leaving the two of us eyeing one another uncertainly on the chessboard floor while stony-faced angels looked down from above.

Pasha spoke first. "So, this is the woman who tames the great Aleksandr Zolotov. He was a stallion! Ahh..." He looked round and sat down on the stairs, the effort involved in standing apparently too much for him. "Tonight, all was hopeless," he said. "I see hot women for us." The night grew colder. "But he has no interest. Is look menus. Food. 'Amalphia would like this, must take her here.'"

"Oh." I sat on the far side of the wide stone step from him, feeling a little warmer.

"And you are pleased about it. This great man, shackled. Chained up by a woman."

I looked at him in annoyance as he continued.

"He was wild, when he was young, when he was free. The nights we have. The tour of Amsterdam, this was one to remember. Not one hooker, many. One woman is never enough for him. Are you even knowing what is on a brothel menu? You are not offering him even small part of this, I can tell." The dark eyes dared me to be shocked.

I turned my head away, willing Aleks to hurry up, and Pasha to shut up.

Shutting up was not something he was about to do. "Now he has nothing," he said. "A night like tonight? In the past we would both have been in your bed, enjoy a woman together. Is good this way. You are agree?"

I stood up. He was right. I was a vanilla crème pie, and he had shocked me.

Aleks was back. "Cold, Malphia? You shiver."

"I'm fine."

Pasha moaned about having to climb the stairs.

I took them two at a time and stood in my room trying to absorb what had just happened. My heart rate quickened as feet sounded on the step outside. What if they both came in? What should I do? What could I say? Well, no, obviously. My veins filled with ice as the door opened, and then Aleks entered the room alone.

"I'll just be a minute," I said, darting into the bathroom to compose myself.

"Okay, my sweet, sweet angel."

Sweet. Vanilla. Plain.

"I am not liking how much he is liking you," he called.

"He doesn't like me at all."

He didn't answer. He was asleep on the bed in his clothes. I undid buttons and belt, took his shoes off, found the spare blankets and tucked him in. He actually looked angelic. Aleks, who had had a wild and carefree existence, but was now shackled. The word vanilla circled, and I wondered whether I should do an internet search on brothel menus.

Chapter 36

ALEKS WAS STILL COMATOSE, but the early morning hum of electricity and water pipes had begun, so I knew other people were up. I went down to see if breakfast was available.

Will was alone at the table. "Hey, Treadwell," he said as I sat down beside him.

"Can I ask you a personal question, Will?"

He gave an intrigued nod.

"Have you ever done... had... taken part in... See, I don't even know how to say it."

"What, babe?"

"A threesome. Have you ever...?"

He laughed. "This is where I want to say 'yeah, lots of times,' to look cool. But that sort of thing hasn't gone well for me in the past. The truth is, no. Never done that. I'm not the slut you all think I am."

"Oh." I couldn't ask Justin. He might answer loudly or doomfully in the hearing of, well, everyone. Also, I thought he would have told me if he had.

"Why d'you want to know?" asked Will.

The story poured out in a whisper as the others arrived for breakfast.

Will laughed again, which was a little annoying. "You've nothing to worry about, Malph. The way he snogs you in front of us all? That's a warning-off thing. There's no way..." He paused. "He didn't even like the other one checking you out yesterday."

As if on cue, Aleks and Pasha came into the hall and made their way over to us.

"I am too old for this, everything hurts," complained Aleks. "Ah, no don't worry, angel, is just hangover. This one, he is fine. Is seven years younger, big difference is making."

Pasha's wide smile held no remnant of the previous night's antagonism. "I was always better at taking the drink," said. "You are just not want to admit in front of your girl. I could tell you some things." Thankfully he didn't, distracted instead by food and coffee.

Pasha taught our class that morning, and I grudgingly had to admit that it was good.

"You are good," he, possibly equally grudgingly, stated. "Long line."

"Wants to shag you," whispered Will. "That's what it was all about."

In pas de deux, things got weird again. Pasha joined us for the class and said that he should dance with me.

"She should have as many partners as possible," he said. "For experience?" His outstretched hand offered an 'out of the frying pan' style escape from Colin.

"If we're swapping round, I'd much rather dance with Will," I petitioned Mr. Timms, knowing that the old teacher liked our partnership.

"Sorted," said Will, hands on my waist.

"There's no point in fighting the Treadwell," Colin advised Pasha. "She's a fiery one. You'll come off the worst."

I got my way. Pasha got Simone and sulked.

"He doesn't remember," I told Will on the way into the great hall at dinnertime. "They were both drunk. But it's still uncomfortable, and I really don't want to speak to either of them right now." A hidden disquiet lurked, an undefined worry that evaded inspection.

Will put forward an interesting solution. "Let's go up to the circle. It's all dark and moonlit, nothing vanilla about it, or you."

Pulling our coats on, we were waylaid by Sun in the great hall.

"We should have gone through the back way," muttered Will.

"You're going up to the stones, aren't you?" she said. "Is it because of the Jupiter Pluto conjunction? It is a perfect night for it. I'll come too, wait for me."

Will and I looked at each other. It was bad enough to have uninvited company, but she had also attracted unwanted attention.

"Malphia!" Aleks called from the staff table.

Summoned again, we approached the table to explain where we were going and endure exclamations about the weather and the dark.

"It'll be wild," declared Will, looking at Pasha.

"Let's see if Holly will give us some food to take," I suggested, keen to be off and away.

"Vanilla pie, maybe," said Will.

A dimple appeared between Pasha's eyebrows, and he looked up as if remembering something.

"Can you please not say things like that?" I said to Will, once we were in the kitchen.

"Somebody needs to tell him."

"No, they don't. There is to be no telling, or weird references to pies. Or I won't be able to confide in you ever again."

"Something is wrong?" Aleks had followed.

"I need to get out for a bit," I told him. "Sit in the circle."

"You need space, time with your friends," he said, frowning as if he knew he was missing something. "I don't like these days when I don't see you."

It was the only day timetabled that way, but the lack of a private lesson had actually felt like a reprieve this time, and that was all wrong. I hugged him briefly before Sun arrived and the three of us headed out into the smoke-scented night.

***

Chilled and damp after an hour of meditative contemplation and torch-lit soup eating, things were much clearer. I knew what had been bothering me and what had to be addressed.

"I have to talk to Aleks."

"Openness and honesty are the cornerstones of a healthy relationship," said Sun as if spouting from a book, but meaning well, though she didn't know the details of what had happened. "You've been looking happier than I've seen you in ages; don't let a misunderstanding spoil it."

Back in the castle, the atmosphere was excited. Bekah ran up to us in the great hall. "Oh, my God! It was so—" She considered her wording as she looked at me. "Terrible. Mr. Zolotov and Pasha were fighting!"

"What?" I said.

"Shouting at each other in the office," she explained. "We could hear it all the way through here."

For the second night in a row, I took the stairs two at a time.

He was sitting on my bed holding the pink cable-knit cardigan. "I was thinking you should have wear this. Not be cold."

The bleak time when he'd given me the cardigan, and what had led to it, had to be revisited now. But how to phrase it?

He exchanged the knitwear for me, taking me in his arms gently as if I might break, again somehow reminiscent of that week. "You are thinking how to extricate yourself from this degenerate man?" he said.

"I have to ask you something."

"Malphia, he is telling me what he is suggesting to you. You must know I would never be considering such a thing. You have not been think this?"

"Not really. Not for long anyway. He talked about the past when you were wild and free, before you were shackled to me."

"Is complete rubbish!"

I stepped back and out of his arms. "He said one woman was never enough for you." I spoke over his reply. "All that stuff with Simone, when we first came here. Was that you showing me you wanted an open relationship, but I forced monogamy on you?"

He came forward and put his hands on my shoulders. "No. A complete no." He paused. "This – my behavior back then – is the stupidest thing I am ever doing. It haunts me. And you."

"No, it doesn't. I hardly ever think about it. But Pasha has known you for so long—"

"He is knowing nothing!" He shoved the chest of drawers so hard it juddered. "You are my precious girl."

"Precious. Like innocent, delicate, naïve. Vanilla."

He held his hands out in stressed confusion.

"Vanilla," I went on. "The non-flavour. Plain and nothingy. That's me. Inexperienced. So young." I looked straight at him. "Sexually, I have never done anything remotely exciting or daring. I'm dull and boring compared to what you've known in the past."

He sat on the bed. He didn't disagree. "I'm sorry," he said, voice a hoarse whisper.

"What I am is not your fault."

"You are a hugely sensual woman. I have not been satisfying you."

"What? No, Aleks, I meant I haven't had group sex or toured the brothels of Amsterdam. Things like that."

His head jerked up in horror. "How long was I gone last night?"

"Too long."

"Malphia, this, it was just..."

"I know you've had a full life. I'm not a prude."

"Is not full, was empty. You were missing. Making love to the woman I am in love with is the absolute experience. Everything else vanishes in such glory."

I went back into his arms and cupped his upturned face with my hands. "What's on a brothel menu?"

"I am want to strangle... I have say to him if he is any way threaten what I have with you—"

"Are you going to answer my question?"

He sighed. "Is so long ago I am not remembering, but I suppose... full sex, oral, anal, BDSM, various fetish..."

"Things you like to do?"

"What I like to do cannot be bought, is not on some menu." A muscle in his cheek twitched. "I like to kiss you and hold you and see you smile. Not be sad and worried like this." His thumb brushed my mouth. "I wish you had told me sooner, the ways you like to make love."

"I like to make love with you, Aleks. The rest is just details."

There was, however, great joy to be found in the details.

"Don't lose your friendship over this," I advised Aleks after he halted Pasha's apologetic approach with an upheld hand the next morning.

"How he is speaking to you is completely unacceptable."

"He thought I was ruining your life. How many times has Justin been mean to you?"

"It is not the same."

"You should talk to him."

Right as that was, I had no intention of doing so myself. Pasha had been thoroughly unpleasant and aggressive towards me. Drunkenness was not an excuse, and he needed to see my non-vanilla-crème side. Come pas de deux, he did.

"Don't." My voice silenced him as Aleks's hand had done earlier. "We're entitled to our opinions of each other. Let's get on with what we're here to do."

"You have me wrong," he started, but I walked away. He dimpled his way round Mr. Timms and soon had Sun, Will and I up on the stage of the theatre to "do something very modern, you will be liking very much." He dismissed the others, telling them they could watch if they wanted, which seemed rather unfair.

The choreography was different from anything we'd done before, technically challenging and strange. The afternoon sped by; the cold detachment Pasha wanted us to show expressed a remote sadness, and he partnered well in the discordant piece.

"Oh, Bravo!" Colin had chosen to watch. "That was quite remarkable. Miss Treadwell. You really do shine in everything you do."

"She is a surprise, this one, is she not?" agreed Pasha.

I shaded my eyes against the lights and saw Aleks sitting out there too, leaning on his hand as if gnawing his fingers.

"Have we run over?" My question was defunct. Obviously we had; even Michelle was in the audience.

"It's not a problem," she said at once. "I would love to see that again, monitored." She held up the hateful little box of tricks. "It's the most interesting thing I've seen for a while." She dismissed Will and Sun and came up the steps to affix the resented stickers to my head. They always tugged at my hair.

"You are wanting to study my parts also?" Pasha dimpled at her.

Michelle shook her head. "There's nothing of any use to me in any of your parts."

Not remotely put out, Pasha turned his attention to Aleks. "For what is she still here?" he asked, pointing at me. "The boy too." He indicated Will, who was now walking across the auditorium on his way to dinner. "They are ready for start dance. Is not Ukraine, nor is it Russia. They do not need to be absolute perfection."

"Is far more to it than that," Aleks replied. "The stronger the technique, the less prone to injury. Is more training to be done, and confidence to be found."

"Ha!" said Pasha, pointing at Aleks and taking my hand. "I had this all the wrong way turning."

"What's that supposed to mean?" I demanded, totally fed up of people and their sly digs.

"I am saying nothing," he said, and mimed zipping his lips shut.

"Good, then let's see it," said Michelle.

We performed the sequence for her, Pasha at once becoming cold and aloof through the brief embraces, though it felt more intimate in Will and Sun's absence.

Frustration grew as Michelle removed the monitors afterwards. It was difficult not to bat her hands away.

Colin came onto the stage and started discussing me with Pasha, blocking the stairs that led to Aleks who remained stock still in his chair. Eventually they made their leisurely way down into the auditorium and through to dinner, leaving me free to hug my love from behind, kiss his cheek and tell him I was sorry.

"Is nothing for to be sorry," he said. "This was good for you, new and stimulating. Everyone gets what they need, everything is okay." The flat voice belied the thumbs up gesture that punctuated his words.

"It's not, though." I stood in front of him and took his hands. "I missed my best class with you, and you're upset."

He stood up and pushed my hands away as if laying them down firmly. "You should be concerned about what is best for yourself, and clearly that is his class on stage today. You must not be worrying about others getting upset. This attitude is useless. You are wrong to think you cannot be single minded. Look at 'just us.' Sometimes, like here this afternoon, you can make it 'just this' and—"

"No, you need to stop telling me what to think." Anger flounced me out the door.

He caught up in the corridor. "Malphia, stop. I am sorry."

"Well don't be. I'm fed up of everyone being so frigging sorry. You all have a right to think and feel whatever you want, but so do I."

"Look," he said. "Lessons are over. We are not student and teacher now. Let's go out for dinner. You and me, no one else. Yes?"

"I'm too angry." I paused a second before the blurt. "I need to go to bed first."

"You want to make love? Now?" A short questioning dance took place across his eyebrows and mouth.

"Not exactly." I took a deep breath and expressed what was best for myself in the moment. "I want to have sex with you. Angry sex."

His laugh was completely infuriating.

"Is that something else I'm not allowed to say or do?" I asked through the dotted red mist that was starting to form. "Precious little Malphia, not permitted any thoughts beyond ballet? That's basically what you were saying back there, wasn't it? Well fuck you, Aleks. Fuck Colin and Michelle and Pasha, the whole lot of you."

His hands on my arms prevented another flounce. "I'd rather fuck you," he said, and I kissed him.

A clattering sound carried through from dinner, ending the rough embrace, and we sprinted for the elevator hand in hand.

But I didn't want to pause, didn't want to stand still. "I want to run up the stairs."

"So? It is a race," he declared, backing into the elevator himself.

I ran smack into Will coming down from his room.

"Hey, Treadwell," he said, annoyingly standing in the way. "What's the rush?"

"Umm..."

He stepped aside.

I reached the top of the stairs just as the sliding doors opened to release Aleks. We fell into the room, and onto the bed, in a frenzied mess of limbs and teeth and want and detail after perfect detail.

Dinner at the pub was leisurely and calm, neither of us in any hurry to return to the castle.

"You always lift me, Malphia," he told me. "Whatever is happening. And whatever is happening, you leave it outside our bed. This is very unusual."

I stared into the log fire, uncomfortable with the possible comparison to past girlfriends and the inference of strangeness.

"It is a great strength in our relationship," he said, taking my chin and turning me back to look at him.

I tried to explain. "Nothing else exists for me when we..." Explanation trailed off in the public setting.

"When we make love," he finished, with no such compunction. "It is the same for me. I don't want to lose you, angel."

"You're not going to."

"But whenever something is go wrong, we are both fearing this. I have a plan I think will help, a plan for your birthday."

"An evil plan?"

"It will give Pasha some trouble."

"Well, that's got to be good."

ele

"This is it," said Justin. "The doom. Don't go."

"We're going somewhere beautiful," I reassured him. "No doom."

"And that's all he'll tell you. Somewhere beautiful. Leaving us in the hands of madmen for three days. I'll miss your birthday; you'll be scoffing cake in some distant land without me... Oh, I know what this is. He's going to put a ring on you, a mini manacle to tie you to him forever." He clutched at my hands briefly before wringing his own.

Scepticism must have shown on my face.

"Yes, Phi, yes. And that's what you'll say too. And you're too young. Listen to me, darling. You mooned around for years about fuzzy over there." He inclined his head in the direction of Will, who was speed eating a plate of chips beside Sadie. "Then there was the oaf. Of course Zolotov is going to seem fucktabulous after all that, but he's not perfect. Think of the up/down, on/off stuff he's put you through. And, now, in this latest self-indulgent infraction, he has you writhing around on the floor with him in lieu of ballet."

"That was from Spartacus," I informed my morose friend. "I'm studying dramatic classical roles in our lessons, a different one each week." Aleks had expressed frustration with Mr. Timm's 'one ballet a term until it's perfect' method of teaching repertoire. I loved the challenge of making myself learn choreography so fast, the prize being to let go and act the character fully at the end of each week.

Justin's doom and matrimonial-laden deliberations continued all week, causing momentary daydreams of white dresses and notions of forever. But Aleks and I were actually just going on holiday to have some time alone together. Any other idea was clearly ridiculous. I would say yes, though...

Friday came at last. The thought of three days to ourselves was quite enchanting. The final lesson before departure was my private lesson in the dungeon.

"Let's really use the space," said Aleks. "Is a day for travel."

We leapt and ran and flew in the huge space of the studio and were both out of breath when Michelle arrived.

Aleks looked at her with obvious dislike. "Not tonight. We are on holiday."

"Oh, I know," she said, unsmiling.

"It's only ten minutes," I pointed out, not wanting any unpleasantness to spoil the evening. "You go and get ready, Aleks. I'll be up soon."

"You should not be wasting your time on this nonsense, Malphia."

"I'll run up the stairs," I promised, putting my hands round the back of his neck. We kissed with complete disregard for the fact we had an audience.

Then Aleks left, and I was alone in the dungeon with Michelle.

"I thought he'd never leave," she said, affixing the monitors somewhat more roughly than usual. She observed Amalgamation C, and then asked me to close my eyes and simply imagine performing it. She studied the screen. "Very good. Visualise it again, and see yourself shutting the laptop lid at the same time."

"What?"

"I want to see what your patterns do when you envisage both events at once." I really wished I had gone upstairs with Aleks. He was right, this was nonsense. But I did as requested. "Interesting," she said. "Again."

We did it again, and again, repeatedly. She started to sound cross. The computer lid slammed shut, and I opened my eyes.

"Clever girl," she said. "Off you run, then. Dirty weekend with Pasha and Aleks, is it?"

I stared at her. "No," I began before realising two things: I did not have to explain anything to this woman, and my involvement in her research was over.

Not bothering to remove the monitors – the bin in my ensuite bathroom would be the best place for them – I flounced from the studio. In the elevator I pressed the button for the top of tower, but the doors were so slow to respond that Michelle managed to join me in the small space.

"I said no when they asked me," she said. "You need to learn to say no too."

I looked away, determined not to listen to any more of her nastiness, though wishing I had, indeed, said no when she had asked me for the ten minutes a day.

"You know what I said about there being no negative stimuli in these sessions?" she said. "I lied."

There was a sudden stabbing pain in my neck, and I collapsed, bumping against the side of the lift as I fell to the floor, stunned and still.

Chapter 37

AN ICY SENSATION TRAVELLED round my body as I stared ahead, sore from the fall. I couldn't move. I couldn't speak. I could hear my heart beating in my ears. Had I had some sort of fit?

Michelle crouched, encompassing me in her perfume cloud. "Did you really think I would let you ruin the work, and oust me to a background role in my own castle?"

She stood up, leaving me to look at her shoes: the stitching, the red heels, the colours. Michelle's reds didn't match again. One shoe was much darker than the other and less shiny. They were very real, those two shoes in front of my face. The rest of this couldn't be. Any minute, something was going to happen to explain it all away. Any minute now, Aleks would wake me from this demented dream, this nightmare.

Something jangled and scraped above, and the elevator moved. Down. It felt like we were going down, but surely we couldn't go down? The basement, the dungeon, was the lowest level. There was no down.

But there was. And the sliding doors opened to it. I tried to get to my feet, but not a twitch did my muscles make. I was frozen on the floor. I tried to cry out, to scream, but no sound was forthcoming, my mouth and throat also being paralysed.

I was dragged out of the elevator by my armpits and into a darker place. I could see an old wall of large damp blocks and a low stone ceiling that seemed to sag under the weight of the castle. The hard floor hurt my face and smelled of stale, dusty earth.

Michelle moved about in unseen space. Animal fear coursed through my veins. Sweat chilled on skin. Breath was loud, rasping, sucking at the air, as I wanted to live, wanted to move. Immobility conflicted with the desire to flee, and I tried to scream again, but that was still impossible.

The light and dark red shoes appeared. I was lifted by my arm until I was nearly standing. Michelle was strong. I couldn't turn to see what she was doing, but she soon had me attached to a wall by my wrists, the top of my body hanging forward like a sad rag doll.

"Ready to begin, Miss Treadwell?" asked Michelle.

The injection in my neck burned and seared, and jolted life back into limbs. I threw myself forward and tried to struggle free. It was futile. The effort required just to move the heavy chains I'd been attached to was immense, and the pain in my wrists, extreme.

"Let me go!" I yelled. "Have you completely lost your mind? Is this some sort of joke? Or trick to see how I respond? It's not on, Michelle. You have to stop this now."

She sat on an archaic wooden chair that had roaring lion heads carved on its arms. A laptop was open on a big flat table in front of her. She laughed. "I didn't shut the lid upstairs. You've taken us to a new level. One level up. One level down. And now we're going to find out exactly what that autistic brain of yours is capable of. Can you break your chains? Can you fight me? Try." She stared at the laptop screen.

Was there anything I could say that would help the situation? Or, at least, not make it worse? My heart hammered painfully hard in my chest.

"You're not trying," she said in a sing-song voice. "I told you how to do it. Imagine Amalgamation C, and also whatever you want to happen here."

"No." Maybe if I refused to cooperate, she would give up. And we would go back upstairs. And I would find Aleks. And go on holiday. Because what was happening here, could not actually be happening, could it? I was starring in a badly made horror film, that was all. Yes, that must be it. My character started to shake convulsively.

Michelle noticed. "Oh, are you frightened? No men here to save you?" Hand on forehead, her voice an ugly falsetto, she said: "Oh, Aleks, the mean lady... Justin, make me laugh... Will, hit someone for me, maybe I'll screw you then." The play-acting ended, and she regarded me seriously. "You and Mr. Hearst should have been together, of course. My perfect mated pair. Just think what your children would have been capable of, the minds they would have had. Aleks got in the way of everything. None of you can be relied upon to do what's needed. Animals, the lot of you." She stopped speaking and stared into space.

I opted for saying nothing. The bizarre and chilling turn the day had taken was feeling less like a dream or film, the more my wrists and arms ached above me. Small sounds grew large in confinement. Breathing echoed. I was sure it echoed. Pulse became a drum, especially in my neck and my ears. I managed to take hold of the chains, wrapping them round my hands as if on some sort of insane and evil swing. They were something to hold on to, a sort of hope that I could alter and improve my lot. The carved lions on the arms of Michelle's chair stared back at me sorrowfully as if they knew there was, in fact, no hope.

Michelle came back to life. "If you're not going to participate properly, we'll have to use good old-fashioned negative stimuli. Partial to a little film show, aren't you, Miss Treadwell?" Her quick smile in my direction was a leer. "Let's head to Aleks's room first." She stopped again. She glared at me. "You weren't meant to get the top bedroom. It was all set up for my own use. The camera wasn't even wired up."

She walked over to a large flat screen that was embedded on the opposite wall. It was surrounded by lots of boxy little televisions.

"But, no," she said. "Aleks always has to know better. 'Leave that room empty,' I told him." She used a remote control to scroll through file names on the large screen. "But he installs you in it, and himself, though I didn't know about that for a long time. Ah, here we are."

Aleks's room filled the central screen, and the two of us appeared on it. Him and me. He stood naked. My back looked surprisingly bony as he pulled the shirt off me. It was like watching peculiar self-starring porn, but the sight was nothing like the experience. A range of strong emotions passed across his face as I watched the film version of myself kneel down in front of him.

She paused the recording. "When you find yourself on your knees in front of a man, something has gone very wrong. Oh, I know you think it gave you power, but it didn't. Look what you let him do. He hurt you and enjoyed it. They all have that in them, all men, they do."

The gross invasion of privacy played on and, from an observer's perspective, it did look rather brutal. But there shouldn't have been an observer. Anger muddled up with everything else: fear, disbelief, shock. I couldn't be watching this film of me and Aleks making love that night of the rebellion. The golden stars didn't show up at the end, so it wasn't real. None of this was real. It couldn't be.

She stopped the action where the stars should have been. "The rest of this is really just sentimental claptrap. Amazing what a man will say to get sex, isn't it? Especially sex like that."

"That isn't how it felt," I tried to explain. "We love each other. You can't see how it felt." Tears ran down my face, their warmth alien and yet very human in the dark home of badness. I looked at the floor, only the floor; it was better.

"See, he has you now," said Michelle. "You're trapped." The turn of her tone to tender was terrifying. As was the fact that she was now standing right beside me. "Let me show you how it should be," she said, like a kindly teacher making a correction in class. "There's never any need to demean yourself." She held my face up, forcing me to see.

The large screen was now showing another film, set in a room I'd never seen before. There were three long windows on one wall, like in my bedroom upstairs. Michelle was there, on the screen. She wore a tight red dress as she sat down on a bed and turned to someone. Aleks. He undid his shirt. She unzipped her dress. He was naked quickly. She kept on her matching red bra and thong, but took a large pendant off over her head and laid it on a bedside cabinet. A red jewel glinted in its centre, like a dewdrop of blood.

Dungeon Michelle pulled the same piece of jewellery out from under her smart cream shirt, and turned it in her fingers as she watched the film.

Back in the unknown room on the screen, the undressing seemed unconnected with the conversation. I made out the words 'choreography' and 'amalgamation.' He smiled at her. He held her face and kissed her. I knew those soft kisses. He placed them all round her neck. His finger traced a line down the middle of her body, between her breasts and down, right down. She laughed, both on film and in the dungeon. Aleks laughed too.

This was what these familiar lovers did. Smiling, chatting, laughing. The sex was straightforward, grown-up, sensible. Screen Michelle looked directly at the camera and smiled as her disgusting perfume encircled us all.

They sat back. He lit a cigarette and told her she was beautiful. So beautiful.

My eyes took pity on me and blurred with water.

"There he was," she said, still beside me. "Right where I needed him. Don't doubt he could be there again. You're just a bit of fun to him. He doesn't see your true worth. Only I do." Red claws trailed my cheek. "You'll like this next one. It's funny."

Justin's room in the tower appeared. My dear, dear friend had his back to the camera. Edward faced him and smiled. He laughed at something Justin said. It was an intimate moment between two people and, just like the first film, it wouldn't look how it felt. It was private, and I didn't want to see.

"Why did you record all this?" I asked, my voice high and shrill. "Are you completely stark-raving mad?" The question was ridiculous. If she hadn't been then, she was now.

She ignored my questions and wandered forward a little. The video wouldn't play. "You've blocked it," she said, jabbing the remote in the direction of the screen. "You and Hearst, your minds interfere with the technology. I know it. His camera rarely sent signals properly. Where is he, anyway? He should be down here too."

She pointed the remote again, and the smaller televisions sprang to life showing people moving about in various places in the castle. It was dinnertime in the great hall. We viewed it from high above. I could see Justin talking to Bekah at our table. The swimming pool: empty. The entrance hall: empty. No Will. Will was safe. That was good.

"Does this shock you, little Treadwell?" asked Michelle, back beside me, running a hateful red-tipped finger down my cheek again, her breath misting unpleasantly in my ear. "I'm only continuing a castle tradition, moving it on to its modern equivalent. My bedroom upstairs incorporates the old 'Laird's Lug.' There's a little hole for spying. You can both hear and see what's going on in the great hall. The Lairds of the past liked to check no one was plotting against them. How history repeats itself."

As Michelle spoke, Aleks appeared on one of the television screens. He was in his own room. He held a small black box in his hand. He opened it and inspected the shining object contained within.

"Aleks!" I called from my place against the hard, damp wall. He turned as if he had heard me.

"You want Aleks?" She pointed the remote at the bigger screen and the Aleks/Michelle film started up again. "We'll leave that on loop while we work. Oh, and for a little added stimulation..." She pressed some buttons, and the vile music of Amalgamation C began to play as a background track. "Shame we're not somewhere with better acoustics, but that wouldn't have been feasible today. It was hard enough getting you down this far."

She stood and watched the screen, silent and still for a moment. Big thoughts appeared in my mind. What was going to happen next? We'd walk back upstairs as if nothing had gone on? Obviously not. She wasn't going to let me run around and tell everyone about this. So... but I didn't let myself go there. Not yet. Perhaps I could still save myself. Michelle had clearly lost her grip on reality. Maybe she could be made to believe that everything would be okay. I had to pull myself together and try. I had to speak to her as if nothing was wrong.

"Michelle," I said, and she looked round at me, as if delighted that I'd said her name. "You don't have to do this here. We could go back upstairs and..." And, what? "We could have a chat. A cup of tea." She seemed to be listening intently, so I went on. "We could discuss how best to advance the research over some cake."

She laughed at that. "Now, you're the one that's sounding stark-raving mad, Miss Treadwell. I'm fully aware that the project has to be completed tonight. There will be no more ten-minute sessions. You know it too. So let's get to work."

The needle came from the side. My shoulder sockets wrenched as I fell forward and down, a limp dishcloth hung out to dry. Awake, but immobile once again. A small triangular blade was held in front of my face. "Utility knife," Michelle informed. "So useful around the home and office." She nicked my cheek with the blade and it stung.

I heard on-screen Aleks say Michelle had done well to have choreographed the amalgamations. "Condescending cretin," she said beside me, then turning abruptly. Out of the side of my eye, I saw her walk back to the table and the computer and the sad, sad lion faces on the chair. The lions were roaring, but no sound came out. I empathised.

The horror film that I was in was a bad one. My character had been chained to a wall by a maniac and was now being threatened with a knife. All to a truly mediocre musical score. Fear subsided into mental numbness. I really should walk out of this cinema. The film wasn't worth paying for, as clichéd as it was. Justin would have had something cutting to say about it.

Michelle was back. "I would have liked to have taken blood samples from you all," she said. "But that was considered a step too far, by some. Oh, well..." She zigzagged the knife down my arm.

Again, I tried to scream, but couldn't. The pain was new, different, sharp and burning. An empty vial was held in front of my face before she scraped it up the injured arm.

Michelle was laughing in two places. Aleks laughed too. I drifted and saw her as if from a distance. A lunatic. Lunacy. To do with the moon, that was. Was there a full moon tonight? I didn't know. What's for dinner? Chocolate cake and cream. So beautiful.

Back in the nightmare, there was speaking: "You respond positively to pain, don't you?" She lifted my chin and stared at my face, wide eyed, expecting an answer.

I studied the floor, all the small details, bad details, bits of dirt, lines in the earth. Her nails scratched down my face, down my neck. So beautiful, film Aleks said again.

I could smell the iron of my own blood. I seemed to smell the salt of the sea too. I wanted to throw myself into the cold ocean and swim away, far away. And never come back.

"Did your beautiful brain like that?" she asked. "Let's have a lookie-see."

She walked over to the table and gazed at her laptop. I'd lifted my head to watch her. Mustn't let her know I could move, or she might dose me again. Thoughts sped up as I dropped my head slowly back down. Could I hurt her? Stop her somehow, while chained up? I envisaged performing a sudden and unexpected karate kick. If only I were in an animé or martial-arts film. My hands could move now too. Each individual finger felt the slimy wall behind.

Michelle spoke. "What are you up to? Something going on in that head, isn't there?" She got up but didn't come near, instead leaning back against the opposite wall. I willed her to stay there. "Focus on the music," she said. "Imagine the amalgamation. Imagine touching my hand."

I shut my eyes and visualised her head bashing against the wall, knocking her out.

"Oh," she said. "Well, everyone has always hurt me. Why should you be any different?"

There was a crashing sound from above, and powdery dust fell on us as screen Aleks commented on Michelle's beauty.

"Are you trying to bring down the ceiling?" she asked. "You'll crush yourself too, Miss Treadwell." The crash noise repeated. I looked up to see a huge stone in the roof shift slightly just above Michelle. If it fell, all this would end. I willed it to fall, but the long boulder remained where it was.

"It's time for labelling," said Michelle, suddenly all bright and happy. "That's one of the first things I learned at university. Everything must always be correctly labelled." She walked over to the table, wrote something, and then affixed a sticker to the vial of blood. It was messy. Her hands were bloody. Like my arm. "And now, you," she said.

I recoiled as she approached, and shook as she knelt down beside me, knife in hand. "Thank you," she said. "I have really liked working with a whore. Especially such a neurologically enhanced one. You feel everything very deeply, don't you, Miss Treadwell?" And she stabbed the blade into my thigh.

I screamed, and it turned to vomit. Some of it got on her. She didn't notice. Too busy cutting. And crying, happy no more. Her hands rubbed dirt from the floor into the bloody mess of a wound, and I cried too. We both sobbed, great heaving, screaming sobs.

I closed my eyes, dizzy and sick from the pain. Fantasia flowers danced. Purple pansies with black centres, a ballet of congealed blood.

"Amalphia," called Michelle, voice a bit sing-song again.

Looking up, I beheld her standing in front of me holding a giant hammer. My body went weak, and my eyes cast a dark filter over the image of Michelle. Little sparks of yellow flew in and out of the picture like brightly coloured bees. And Michelle wasn't just Michelle anymore. She was a bully and an ignorant teacher, a cruel parent and a Nazi scientist. She had morphed into a personification of everyone who had ever abused anyone because of their difference.

I couldn't take any more of it. I couldn't be there. And so I wasn't.

At first there was just restful unconscious blackness. And then a fresh breeze moved gently through trees and across my face. I found myself standing on the forest path, on the way to the stone circle. It was dark and quiet, the smell of the pines calming, the earth cool and soft between my bare toes. I caught glimpses of small shapes scuttling back between the trees as I walked, bright eyes watching, curious but benign, no danger there. Bigger ones guarded, invisible beings, hidden behind the largest of trees.

In the light of the circle, the golden lady that I'd seen before held me. In love. In warmth and safety and beauty. She smiled. So did I. She held up a ring of flowers, small pink and white blooms with a sparkle on each. They made a crown for my head. White light swirled, and the lady pointed to a space in the circle of stones, a gap I had never really noticed before. She touched my brow, and I saw Aleks and Will climbing through a broken glass floor as a stone angel directed from the wall above. Will cut his arm on the jagged glass, and blood ran down. It dripped onto the earthen floor below.

The lady touched my heart and it warmed with love. So much love. Love was the way out. Love was the way back.

Back. Dark. Pulsating. Swollen. Agony.

A body mangled, smelling of ammonia and metal and sick. What had gone on here while I'd been gone? Had she finished me with that hammer? Was I about to die? My pulverised being vibrated with intense pain, except for one arm. It was numb.

Michelle sat against the opposite wall, crying again, holding the sledgehammer as if it were a baby. "I knew the chains would fit you," she said. "They were mine when I was a girl, you see. I learned to be good. You can too." She sobbed on as she crawled her way over to the table, picked up a hypodermic needle and stared at it.

I wouldn't let her harm Aleks and Will, and I knew they were almost upon us. That part of my dream was true. It had to be. The golden lady had given me a task. It would keep them safe. And if these were my last moments on earth, I could make them useful ones.

Visualising Amalgamation C proved to be a powerful pain killer as I hummed the hateful melody and mentally ordered the boulder in the ceiling to fall. The roof creaked, and the huge rock plunged in slow motion, an enormous and point-ed stone, stolen from the circle long ago. The carved lions widened their eyes in amazement. Michelle looked up and made a sound of rage before vanishing in an explosion of dust and rubble.

I was free to go again, through that restful blackness to ceiling stars and a blue sky, gentle hands and soft sleep.

Chapter 38

G LIMPSES OF LIGHT, SHORT breaks in the dark. Kind
arms: holding, lifting, taking the strain. Will's eyes, his
face dirty, streaked red and brown. A siren. An unknown man
said, "Can you hear me, Amalphia?" Bright lights. A jumble of
voices that faded away.

I blinked and breathed and took in some basic facts. The bed
had white sheets and a yellow blanket. The floor was grey. Justin
read a magazine in the distance. Aleks had a beard; his elbows
indented the bed as he rested his forehead in hands, eyes closed.

"You're hairy," I said, surprised by how my voice croaked.

He looked up and took my outstretched hand. His face was
strange, as if he'd grown much older, as if I'd been asleep for
years.

Justin stood at the other side of the bed now, also unshaven.

"You're hairy as well," I said, wanting to take his hand too,
but finding my right arm to be all tied up. "I'm hurt. How hurt?
Tell me."

"You will mend," Aleks began, sounding a bit croaky too.
"All. Your arm..."

Justin took over, cheerily, matter of factly. "Broken in seven
places. You had a long op for that. Don't you remember? No,
well, they've put pins in. We'll get you a bionic-woman costume,
cape, tights, the works. You'll look great. You've a sprained an-

kle. Don't worry, you'll dance again, blah de blah. The rest may feel bad, but it's really just cuts and bruises. Superficial is the word they keep using. As if you could ever be that, Phi." His cheeriness faded and wobbled with this last bit, and he looked like he might cry.

"Oh," I said. Missing information existed on the other side of some sort of chemical fog. "They've given me strong drugs, haven't they?"

Justin nodded. "Narcotics, straight into your veins."

It was nice there was no pain. There had been too much pain. A visual of Michelle vanishing under the stone appeared like a trailer for a film, a very bad film that hadn't really been a film.

"Is she dead?" I asked them.

They looked at each other. Aleks answered. "No. Very much injured. In other hospital. Other city. You're safe now. I should not have left you."

Justin's eyebrows assumed their annoyed position as he looked at Aleks and gave a tiny shake of his head. I didn't understand.

"Rest, Phi," advised Justin. "Enjoy the drugs while they last. They'll take them away soon enough."

"The golden lady held me," I remembered, before drifting away on a cloud, still holding Aleks's hand.

~er~

The next awakening was different. Two women – two nurses – were in the room.

"Good," said one. "We thought we would have to wake you."

They washed my unsightly body as I remembered specific things. I didn't want their hands on me. They removed various tubes and helped me walk to the toilet. My ankle hurt, but I could stand on it. Everything hurt.

They chatted on as if everything didn't hurt and was, in fact, normal. "He's a bit gorgeous, your man," remarked the older one. "The tall blond one's your boyfriend, isn't he?"

I was momentarily transfixed by her London accent. It was like a voice from long ago, from before. From somewhere I could have stayed and been safe. They changed the dressings on my battered arms and legs without reaction, not even to the large scabbed 'W' on the thigh. Correct labelling. Whore.

They talked on and on. They'd sent my friends away to get a meal. "Doesn't want to leave you, that one. Must be love," teased the nurse. "Three days, and I don't think he's slept."

"I've been here for three days?"

She nodded. "The police want to speak to you this afternoon. Your other friend's coming back for that. She brought you some clothes in. Let's put them on. You'll feel better."

I recognized the large soft jumper that belonged to Holly. It made me want to cry. It was perfect to fit over the bandages and cast, albeit terribly painful to maneuver into.

"You had a dislocated shoulder," explained the younger nurse. "It'll be bruised inside."

I sat on a chair while they changed the bedsheets. They left. I stood. I remembered more things. Impossible things. The new bedding was impossible to pull back. Everything impossible. Everything wrong and mad and, just no. None of this could be happening.

The door opened. I jumped. It hurt. But then it was so good to see hairy Will. I leant against him and inhaled. How could such a comforting aroma have ever been annoying? He turned back the covers on the bed like a superhero.

"I saw you climbing through the floor of that room," I told him. "The one we got locked in. You cut your arm."

He regarded me silently as I prattled on and on about things I suspected only he would understand or believe. The stone that had to go back to the circle, the golden lady, and the amalgamation that was evil.

We were both so tired. "Lie down, Will. Be safe here with me." I rested my head on his chest in the bed and, snuggled like children, we slept.

He was awake when I opened my eyes. "I better go, Malph. Zolotov'll do his nut if he finds me here."

"Oh." I eased tentatively into a sitting position. "Why?"

"He wouldn't let me in before, said you shouldn't be bothered by too many visitors. Had to wait till he'd gone out."

It didn't make sense. Justin had been here, so why couldn't Will be?

"Fuck," he said as the door opened.

In they all came, Holly too.

"You have waked," said Aleks, looking at Will with clear annoyance.

I shot the sentiment straight back at him, and something happened at the base of my skull. It didn't exactly hurt but it was unpleasant, a rusty grind that started the music of Amalgamation C playing in some deep place in my head. A film reel initiated: *Aleks and Michelle, the Movie*. I could do nothing to stop its surround-sound progression through my brain.

"All right?" asked Will, touching my face which was vaguely soothing but didn't change the vile inner view. I held on to his hand to make sure he didn't go. Everyone else was too loud. Holly said she would stay for the police interview, as it would be good for me to have another woman present. Aleks was determined it should be him that stayed.

"Neither," I said, way too loudly. "No one. I'll do it on my own."

My head ached. The dreadful inner film had almost finished its second playing, Aleks declaring Michelle to be so beautiful. I ignored the high-volume protestations from my friends and insisted that they all go, even Will. I didn't want any of them to hear any of it.

The police arrived in the room in due course. They knew everything. She'd filmed it all, and they had the footage. So why I had to go through every detail with them was a mystery. The cross examination from the lead detective about what Michelle had been playing on the screens was excruciating. That was the bit they hadn't seen. The internal show had stopped when the others left, but the reminder was distressing. I gave up the information in the end; battling with the man was as useless as trying to fight Michelle while chained to a wall. There was mention of trauma counselling and other so-called help that I knew wouldn't help.

Exhaustion, both mental and physical, set in properly after that. Not that I cared. Nothing mattered anymore. Aleks's presence always triggered the ultimate cinematic experience in my mind, but it didn't really upset me. After a while Amalgamation C would speed up, and my head would begin to ache. I told him I needed to be alone. Time went by in a blur of avoidance, feigned sleep and general aggravation.

Everyone and everything irritated: Holly bringing food that I couldn't eat; Aleks being in the room; not being able to lie in bed and sleep with Will because it was inappropriate, and all the get-well cards from students at the castle. They'd been told that the floor had caved in, and Michelle and I had been trapped and injured in a terrible accident. The truth about me, what had been done to me, was too unspeakable to tell.

"You've got to speak to him," said Justin, and I knew he meant Aleks.

"I do speak to him." I did, as little as possible, and mainly to tell him to go away, the look on his face touching me not at all. He'd given up trying to actually touch me.

"You don't," said Justin. "But I mean about what happened. We overheard the police saying something about weaponised assault. It's destroying him."

"Really? It wasn't that fun for me either. You know, being assaulted with weapons."

"Phi..."

"So what do you suggest, Justin? That I tell him how she cut me up with a knife to take a blood sample? That'll make him feel better, will it? Maybe he'd enjoy hearing about the film she showed me of him and her having sex? If you want him to know, you tell him."

He was speechless for a second before the door opened to admit Will and Aleks. As ever, the slow grind of cinematic spool started up inside my head. I told them all to go out to dinner.

Peace at last.

I pushed congealed and questionable food around on a plate. What was the point of eating? What was the point of anything? There I sat in a comfortable bed, all bandaged up and looked after. Somewhere, out in the world, in lots of places, assaults and beatings and cruel abuses were taking place. Some of it was happening to small children. So many vulnerable people were at risk from malevolent individuals who lurked everywhere.

The door opened. If only I could have locked it.

A young man came in.

"Who are you?" came out in a shout.

"Oh," he said, a bit taken aback. "Sorry if it's not a good time. I'm Darren, one of the police officers who was present at your interview? I'm visiting my mum, thought I'd just pop in. Couple of things." He approached the bed and handed me a box of chocolates. "You were awesome standing up to the boss like that. Everyone's talking about it."

I looked back at him, not sure what the point of this was.

He went on. "And another thing... Is it all right if I...?" He pointed to a chair.

I shrugged.

He sat. "He misled you. Always does that. It'll never get to court. You won't have to face your attacker. She'll be declared unfit to stand trial. Mentally, you know. I just thought you might be dreading it and should be told."

I hadn't been dreading it. I hadn't even been thinking about it. But this man, this police officer, knew it all and was still treating me like a normal person. I got him to open the chocolates, and I asked about his job. Drunk and drugged people were his biggest bane. I wondered if Michelle had been on something. She'd had access to drugs. Stabbed them right into me.

"You must be really fit, being a ballet dancer?"

"Not at my best right now."

It felt odd to be chatting with someone. Was I allowed to sit around and eat chocolates and chat? Hadn't everything changed in the dark? The break from my new reality didn't last long. The others soon trailed back in, and the police officer left.

"Can't leave you alone for a minute, can we, Treadwell?" Justin's attempt to make up for earlier awkwardness was obvious and annoying. "In a hospital bed, and you've still got it going on. And he was cute. Where and how? Explain."

I explained as Michelle took off her dress on the inner screen of my mind.

"Hot fuzz, indeed," Justin continued. "A police officer, good person to have around in a tricky spot, I'd warrant."

"He wasn't really," I said. "He sat and said nothing yesterday when I was made to go over everything, and they already knew it all."

"How are they knowing it all?" asked Aleks.

I accidentally looked at him. It didn't worsen the vision in my head, but it didn't feel good. He looked strained and ill and some tiny part of me, a very distant part, didn't like that. I picked up a chocolate and studied it while speaking.

"She liked to film things," I said. "They have her computers."

It occurred to me that among the nightmare of questions, there was still a lot I didn't know. So, I asked. Will sat on the end of the bed and filled in the gaps with calm and logic. He took a chocolate and held it as he spoke. It melted in his hand.

I'd been underground less than an hour. Will had somehow, and he couldn't explain how, sensed that I was under the floor of the dungeon studio and had raised the alarm. The elevator had been immobilised. They'd climbed through the glass floor and found me. Aleks had held me up, while Will located the key for the chains in the wreckage of her table.

"I saw you," I recalled, careful not to imagine the blood that must have featured in the events. Had Michelle looked like an evil witch, red shoes poking out from under the stone? If only she'd had stripy tights on. My laughter seemed to worry Justin and Aleks.

"You opened your eyes for a second," Will told me. "I was glad you weren't dead."

"You've eaten all the best chocolates," complained Justin in another mood-lightening effort. "I'm going down to the second layer. Oh, ho, ho," he said, reading what I assumed was the guide to the confections within. "Listen to this: 'If you ever want to talk, or anything,' and then there's a mobile number. Look." He showed it around to no one's amusement.

"Well, he must be some sort of pervert," I said with irritation. "If he thinks... I mean, he heard it all and sees a dating opportunity? Bloody men. And women for that matter. People, bloody people and their weird messed-up heads." Mine contained an IMAX cinema with a very limited and pornographic film schedule, but still... people!

"I'll just keep this then, shall I?" asked Justin, pocketing the note. "What? I can't have my own private database of perverts? It's not illegal if it's for personal use only, surely?"

The expected laugh didn't come. No one else filled in for me. Will had squashed the chocolate in his hand. It oozed between his fingers.

"You need to wash your hands," I told him, and he got up and went into the small ensuite. Great, people did what I asked. "You need to shut up," I said to Justin. "And you need to go back to the castle." I made myself look at Aleks, took in his bereft countenance and added automatically: "You all do. Go home and sleep, eat, relax. I'll get a taxi back tomorrow after my final checks."

I had more than enough to cope with without Aleks mooning around looking all sad. I needed to be on my own now. Totally on my own.

Chapter 39

I SAT IN THE taxi feeling cross. Aleks had not gone home as instructed which meant I had to endure over an hour in a confined space with him. He suggested we go away somewhere else together and not return to the castle at all.

"I want to get into my own bed and sleep," I told him.

I ignored his invitation to cuddle and leant my forehead against the car window as cranial pressure mounted. The sound of the amalgamation sped up the longer I was with him, causing dizziness and nausea.

I closed my eyes and concentrated my attention on the inner scene. Michelle's necklace lay on the bedside cabinet, and I was able to make it my focus. I examined the piece of jewellery in detail as if I were standing right by it, facing away from the pair on the bed. I looked at the geometric pattern of intersecting lines upon the surface of the gold disc, and I imagined becoming smaller, so small that I could stand in the etched marks of gold. I ran along the neural pathways of my brain, searching for the tiny red ruby at the centre, the place to fix it all, to unbend what had been broken.

The sound of the car driving over the gravel outside the castle shook me out of my reverie. I got out of the taxi and crunched over the small stones. The big door opened and Holly was there, talking about food and sitting by the fire and seeing my friends.

"I need to sleep," I told her, walking into the foyer. "Don't let anyone come up."

Aleks followed anyway. "Is all right, Malphia," he said on the stairs, the elevator being out of bounds, tape over the door. "I know you are wanting to be alone. I will go to my room. Wake me if is anything you need. Use phone, and I will come at once."

I didn't reply and walked on up to my room.

Crawling lopsidedly into bed, I arranged my arm how it had to be, and slept. And slept. People looked in. I kept my eyes shut and dozed on until the smell of soup enticed.

Holly fed me with a spoon as if I were a small child.

The top of the tower soon attracted a steady stream of people. There was Aleks, saying he wanted to help like he was begging. Will was just Will. We lay on the bed and listened to music. Ruaridh brought me a gentle and romantic novel to read. Sun tried to have a probing female-solidarity talk. Bekah was full of who-fancied-who gossip which was almost diverting. Sadie came with chocolate. Justin became so over-the-top funny, it wasn't funny, and time passed.

Different trays of food marked different times of day.

Aleks always triggered the same film badness, but he never stayed long. He tried to draw me out of myself, taking the less-hurt hand, saying he loved me. I touched his fingertips for a moment, the familiar square ends. In my head, one of those fingertips trailed Michelle's front, and she laughed. In my bedroom, he waited for me to say I loved him back.

Some explanation might help. "I don't feel anymore," I said, not looking at his face.

"Tell me. Whatever you are going through, I want to bear it with you."

"I don't feel love. Or much of anything. It's quite good in a way, because I can remember and see stuff." I paused and looked at the bedroom floor a moment, remembering the earthen one below the castle. "It doesn't disturb. It just is. I feel annoyed, and I feel peopled-out, and I feel physical pain, but that's it." He'd been in the room too long. "I need to sleep. My head hurts."

He left with the air of a man who had made progress in a difficult matter, and I went back to sleep.

The door opening woke me and furthered my hatred of doors.

It was the school doctor. "You were sleeping?" he asked. "You've been doing a lot of that, I hear. I've received your notes from the hospital. It seems you're doing well."

"Oh, just brilliantly," I said, looking down at my bandages-under-clothes lumpy body.

"Have you cried?" he asked.

"What d'you mean?"

"You've been through an incredibly traumatic experience, Amalphia. Do you feel sad or angry?" He'd obviously been speaking to Aleks.

"No. I'm sort of surprised to be here, you know, in one piece, able to walk around and stuff."

"Did you think you were going to die?"

"Yes." I'd forgotten that.

"You're suffering from post-traumatic stress. It would do you good to talk to someone. I can put in an urgent referral today."

"There's no point. It won't make any difference."

"Vocalising things can be extremely helpful."

"Not for me," I said. "Your counsellor types won't have experience of anything like this. She messed with my head. She's done something to me with her research. Amalgamation C is an evil thing. I need to tell Aleks he must never let it be done here again." Why hadn't I done so already? But I could tell by the doctor's face that I'd gone too far. "I know it sounds mad."

"Not mad, no," said Dr. Duthie. "Evil is a fitting word for what happened to you."

"How do you know what happened to me?"

"I know about your injuries." The following diatribe was lengthy. He knew I hadn't spoken to anyone about the details of my ordeal. The police didn't count. Friends wanted to help. People cared. I should go down and join them, get out of the room. Aleks was mentioned.

"Aleks had a relationship with Michelle," I told him, the words somehow coming out much louder than I'd intended.

"Ah." The vowel was loaded. "All the more reason to express what you're feeling to him. In fact, your anger over this issue could be a vital key. Instead of dealing with what happened, you're focusing on this. Break down that wall, and the rest will follow."

"That's psychobabble. And I'm not angry." I really didn't think about Aleks and Michelle at all. Except when my brain, and his presence, forced the visuals of them on me.

The doctor got up to go. "You'd be surprised how often the babble is right," he said and went out the door. He stuck his head back through. "And you are angry. Very."

Blasted man. I stomped into the bathroom. My leg hurt more than usual, and I removed my trousers to investigate, a tricky and time-consuming process with one useless arm. The 'label' she'd given me was redder and more inflamed than it had been. It might be infected. The doctor could have been of some actual use.

"Malph?"

"Don't come in here, Will, unless you want to see a horrific sight."

He pushed the door open slowly, and then gaped at my legs. Legs that had been hammered. Literally. The bruises and cuts looked really bad. Some were stitched. Many would scar.

"I kinda knew," he said. "There was so much blood." He sat on the floor and gently touched the biggest bruise on my thigh. I had been told it went right through to the bone. "Must hurt like fuck."

"It's all getting better," I said. "It's this that's bothering me the most, right now." I turned so he could see the scabbed mark on my thigh.

"What is that?" he asked, shock showing on his face.

"She labelled me. 'W' for whore."

"But whore doesn't start with 'w.'"

"It does, Will. A silent one."

"Well, how fucking demented is that?"

I didn't say anything. It was demented. All of it was.

"Tell you what does start with 'w,'" he said. "Will. Here." He pulled off his T-shirt and hoodie.

I sat down on the bathroom chair, and wondered if I had the energy for whatever post-traumatic madness was coming out of him.

"I'll do you a trade," he said. "I've got these." He pointed to some small round marks on his belly that I'd seen before but never really thought about. "Fag burns. Happened in care. Long time ago."

I reached out and touched them in horror.

"But see," he said. "They're in the shape of a triangle, kinda like an 'A'."

"You were just a little boy," I said, feeling a tear trickle down my face. Will had been in care. I had known that. His mum had been very young, and unable to cope with looking after a small child. Why had I never stopped to wonder what it was like for him, after that? Or before, for that matter? Why did people do these terrible and unspeakable things?

"Hey, no," he said. "Don't, Malph. The bastards can't really hurt you, you know. Not the real you inside." He smiled, snapping out of serious mode. "So how about it, then? Is your mark mine? Does it stand for Will now?"

"If you want."

He kissed the hideous wound. It tingled. And it stopped hurting so much.

"Come on then, Treadwell. Step up." He pointed to his own scars.

I kissed them, each one, and held my hand over them, completing our ritual.

"Look at me, Will. I'm like a patchwork doll." Sitting on the chair had given a prime view of the mirror. I could tell it wanted to flinch and look away.

"You could never be anything but beautiful, babe. He must tell you that."

"Umm, well..." I hadn't given him the chance to tell me much of anything. Heard him tell her that, though, every time I saw him.

"Yeah, him and the doc collared me before," Will told me. "Want me to convince you to come down for lunch. But you do whatever you want. I'll go get you something. Not sure why they sent me, to be honest. They should have known I wouldn't hassle you."

"The fact that you've never shagged Michelle was probably a point in your favour."

"He must really regret that now. 'I am very much wishing not to have been doing the shagging of Michelle,'" he said, in a horribly good impersonation of Aleks.

"Will, that's not funny."

But somehow it was. And I started to laugh. There was something of a hyena about the sound. And then it was difficult to stop, but various stitches being pulled in various ways soon forced me to calm.

"Okay, I'll come down with you," I said. "Help me with my trousers?"

The sound from the great hall was daunting. So many people. So much talking.

Simone came out into the foyer as we walked across it, and I realised I hadn't seen her since, well, everything. She scowled as she caught sight of us.

"What's that about?" Will demanded.

"Stay away from me, Will Hearst," she said. "You too, Amalphia."

I clung to Will's arm, unable to cope with the confrontation. Simone ran away up the stairs, and we were joined by curious over-hearers, Aleks among them. The wonder of the fully integrated cinema in my brain demonstrated itself as Will said Simone was a bitch, and Aleks said he would talk to her.

"No," I said. "I'd rather her unfriendliness than false simpering. Simone and I don't get on. Leave it, or I'm going back upstairs."

"Okay," said Aleks. "Is so good to see you down here, Malphia."

He smiled warmly, and we entered the hall. Every head turned. There was a collective cheer and clapping.

"Don't leave me," I whispered to Will, holding his arm tightly as well-wishers surrounded us.

"Let her get lunch without a parade," ordered Will, and the crowd dispersed.

Holly brought tomato soup over to me as I sat at the table. Aleks stroked my back. I wanted to shake him off. It was a huge relief when people exited to their afternoon classes, and I stood by the fire alone. Completely alone. For a very short moment.

"Miss Treadwell, Miss Treadwell," said Colin, joining me by the fire, Pasha at his side. "He hasn't let us visit you. We have, in fact, been forbidden from doing so. We just wanted to say..." There was a pause.

"It's hard to know what to say," I acknowledged. "Tell me about your exploits. Bekah says you both go out every night and rarely make it back in time for class the next morning."

"But this, it is not true," said Pasha, taking my hand in a chivalrous manner and guiding me to the sofa. "It is not being every night."

"And we've always made it back in time," added Colin. "Zolotov just doesn't see the funny side."

He certainly didn't. He came in to the room and sent them away. "I am sorry they are bother you," he said, crouching down in front of me by the sofa.

"They were okay. It's you that's bothering me." I glowered into the fireplace.

"This, I know. Can you tell me what to do, how to be better for you?"

"I just need to be alone," I said, finally hearing the fullness of the words. Somewhere, a disconnected part of me grieved the ending. Aleks heard no deeper meaning in the sentence and told me he would be in his new office if I needed him.

I turned my head away from him and looked at the windows instead. He left. The film in my head faded away. The windows remained. Long, pointy and Gothic. Twelve on the wall in front of me, three just like them in the most hateful movie of all time.

It didn't take long for me to locate the film set: Michelle's bedroom. I knew most of the staff slept on the second floor, above the studios, and I found her room at the very end of the corridor. It was stripped bare. The, now infamous, to me anyway, bed had no sheets, though its position in the room was

the same as it was in the film. Of the camera, there was no sign.
The white walls offered no clue to surveillance activities other
than a small triangular hole near the floor in the corner. The
traditional 'Laird's Lug' did, indeed, provide a view of the great
hall, albeit a rather limited one. I could see one of the long tables
and the fireplace through the crooked little tunnel in the wall,
but nothing else. No plotting. No badness.

I walked over to the three windows. The path through the
pines that led to the stones was plainly visible from them. Had
she watched us enter and emerge from the woods? Had she
managed to taint every part of our lives here? I opened the door
to the ensuite bathroom. Everything was white and empty there
too, but something caught my eye.

A dot of red on the white tiled floor. Shiny, round, spilled.
The tiles were cold against my cheek as I curled up on the floor
and stared at the blood. She had taken a vial of mine. This must
be hers. I reached out a finger to touch it. Would it be sticky?
How long had it been there? It was solid. A waxy flat-topped
mound. Nail varnish. Somehow that was worse than blood; I
sat up and scurried back on my bum as fast as possible, banging
painfully against the wall and causing the mirror on the opposite side of the room to shake with laughter.

I couldn't be there. So I fled to the only place I could think
of to go.

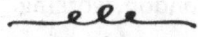

The gap in the stone circle seemed so obvious now, a sad void
like parts of me. I stayed away from it and curled up on the
flat stone. The winter sun shone low, creating long shadows of
obelisks as it must have done for thousands of years. I closed my
eyes and circled fingers round the markings on the stone, as if
they were a map that could point the way.

What to do? Where to be? How to go on?

It was windy. It was cold and damp. Even so, I could feel the
oblivion of sleep beckoning, offering a short escape from the
nightmare of life.

Different images flowed through my mind. I recognised a lengthy escalator from the London Underground. A film poster glimmered on the wall, and a well-known actor winked and held out his hand from it. I couldn't remember his name. It was something ridiculous, something to do with love. The dream version of me planned to tell Justin about the strange poster that night at home. Justin was around. Aleks wasn't, nor Will. I was on my way to work, dance stuff in a bag.

I felt a chill from the stone beneath me, and I was back in the circle, fully awake again. The light of the afternoon had faded while I dozed, but I had my answer: I couldn't stay. The thing that happened in my head, the terrible film, might send me insane in time. Aleks would be sad when I left, but he would move on. His suffering would be fleeting.

I sat up, suddenly knowing that I was not alone in the circle.

"Aye, quiney," said the old man, the person Will and I had met by the pool on our very first morning at the castle. "That's just a fair time, ye've hin."

Having become used to the way Holly spoke, I understood this to mean he knew I'd had a bad time. I nodded. It was true.

He looked at me shrewdly. "Well, fit did ye see?"

"You know about the visionary/imaginary thing that goes on here?" I asked, then just knowing: "You've experienced it."

He gave one slow nod.

"I saw me back in London, working," I told him. "It's what I have to do now."

"I wouldna be so sure o' that."

"It seemed very clear."

"Aye," he said, placing his hand on the large recumbent stone as he spoke. "But life's nay set in stone. This place disna understand time like we do. That could have been something ye'll de in twenty years, lassie."

"I don't think so. The actor I saw was looking really good for his age if that's the case." What was his name? Lovelorn? Lost love? The circle certainly had a thing about love going on. As had I in the past. I remembered saying something about 'the people and things you love' to Aleks in a conversation that had seemed oh-so-important at the time. But I'd been wrong. What difference did any of it make in the end?

"Fit aboot yer lad, yer boyfriend?" asked the old man, Jackie as I recalled his name was.

"That's over now."

"Yer hearty's still strong for him. I can see it."

"Is it?" How could that be if I couldn't feel it? Apparently my eyes felt something; they watered a little.

"Aye," said Jackie, handing me a handkerchief. "Yer affa cold, quine, and it's getting dark. Ye need a nice cuppae o' tea and a piece. I've nae ony fancy eens, mind." Biscuits, he was talking about tea and biscuits, and the idea of them did sound good.

Jackie led the way through a narrow gate at the far side of the circle glade, and down a path that ran the length of a ploughed field. He pointed out various houses and farms in the distance. The names of the owners passed me by, but it was pleasant to look at their cosily lit windows and imagine happy family bliss within.

The remaining daylight had almost faded completely by the time we arrived at the large house. It could have been foreboding and creepy, but the three-storey building felt welcoming as we walked towards it through the overgrown garden.

A stiff back door let us into an old-fashioned kitchen and Jackie made tea. It was a complicated process involving an antique black kettle and a stove that he replenished with logs. There was a mustiness about both the house and the forthcoming biscuits, but a gentle wellbeing infused our silence. He lit a lamp as it got even darker, and in the soft light he spoke of his family: eight brothers and one sister. The house had been full and noisy once.

"Ye hiv to tell him everything, quine," he said after a while, having listened to a disjointed telling of parts of my tale. "He's nae a wimp; he can take it. And he's here noo, fair anxious for ye. I've watched him coming down the circle path."

Aleks was here? I peered through the grimy window. Will stood by a great big oak tree, looking up at the house. I knocked on the glass and relief showed on his face.

"No, that's Will," I explained to my new friend.

"That's Will, is it?" he said and opened the door.

I introduced the two men, and they shook hands, which seemed dignified and fitting somehow.

But then Will turned to me. "We'd better go back, Malph. He's gone mental, called the cops and everything."

"Aleks?" I asked. "Why?"

"Babe, you've been gone all afternoon. No one's seen you, and your phone's still in your room."

"I have to go," I said to Jackie as Will sent a text to Aleks.

"Aye," the old man acknowledged, coming outside with us. "There's a way through there." He pointed to a gap in the trees at the side of the garden. "Watch out for the stream. The path will tak ye past the pool. Ye both ken it. Noo, lassie. Listen to yer haert. It winna guide ye wrong." He stopped and looked at Will. "And mind fit's important. The rest disna matter."

"Is he like, barking?" asked Will as we started into the wood.

"No. He's nice. He understands the circle."

It was so dark in among the trees that Will used his phone to light the way. It illuminated bent and gnarly branches which looked a bit like ancient arms reaching out towards us. I gasped as we came to the pool. It seemed to be reflecting the castle, all orange and smokey and on fire, the waves like flames, licking up the walls.

I pulled Will into a run, ignoring the swollen complaints of my ankle and leg, until we reached the end of the woodland path. The many thin windows of the castle blazed with yellow light that blended into a low hanging mist. But there was no fire, no disaster, no actual danger.

"Come on," said Will. "He needs to know you're all right."

"Will." I needed to say something to him, needed to make sure no one was hurt or damaged by my actions. "Everything's going to change when I go back in there. There's something I have to do, and I don't want you to feel you have to do it too. I also want to say thank you. Thank you for being my friend. Thank you for saving my life. But you must make the most of your training here. You're so very talented, and this is the best, better than college would ever have been."

He squeezed my hand, and we stepped out of the forest.

Chapter 40

W E WALKED PAST THE police car and ambulance that were parked on the gravel, and then I cringed as many people turned to look at us in the foyer. Aleks sort of sagged as he saw me. The two policemen sought assurance that no harm had come to anyone. The paramedics were not pleased to have had their time wasted, but then the emergency services departed.

"You are never to do this again!" shouted Aleks once they had gone, sagging no more. "Wandering off, no phone. I am so angry with you."

He really was. And it was sort of magnificent. Gone was the tentative, and oh-so-careful, Aleks of recent days. Here was a raging beast. I studied him as if he were a work of art which, in a way, he was. His beautiful face was etched with fury and fear and sorrow. This was very different to the man I saw in my mind, in the foul and familiar film. That man was being charming and polite and social. Had Aleks ever been like that with me? I thought back as I looked at him. Yes. When he asked me to take part in his class, that day at college. Though he had also been a bit impudent. During our day in Covent Garden? He had been rather quiet then, but honest when he did speak. Not charming. Not really.

The thought stream was interrupted by everyone else making a lot of noise. Holly berated Aleks for shouting, as did Will. Lots of people wanted to know where we had been. Will explained some of the afternoon to them as I regretted not getting to explore more memories. I had been about to recall the details of that first date, the dinner in the restaurant, where Aleks had actually been a bit rude to me. But the collective chatter dragged me back to the foyer of the castle, and the present moment. It was, frankly, annoying.

Aleks said sorry. I shook my head, because he shouldn't be sorry. I placed my hand on his chest because here at the end, I could do that. I could feel his heart beating under my palm. "You are so very real," I said, because this flesh and blood Aleks really was, and then my words reminded me of words he'd said to me. Long ago, not here, somewhere else. Before this. Before it all.

"Let's go upstairs," I said to him and took his hand.

We walked the curving staircase together in silence and then sat on my bed.

The conversation should have been simple, but it wasn't. I told him that I had to go, but he kept interrupting and, it seemed to me, deliberately misunderstanding. When he could evade my meaning no longer, he cried. I watched and felt nothing.

"I was rude to her, and then I left you down there," he said. "How could you ever forgive that?"

I shook my head. "It wasn't your fault. It was all about her obsession with Amalgamation C. It must never be done here again, Aleks. Promise me you'll never allow that to happen."

"Of course I won't."

He touched my cheek. I let him. It would all be over soon.

"Would it help you to tell me all?" he asked. "To unburden yourself of everything."

"I don't think so."

"But it might?"

I frowned. The idea was confusing. I tried to focus on facts. "You don't need that in your head. It definitely wouldn't help you."

"If there is even a small chance it could make things better, you must tell me."

His insistence was strong. The conversation had the potential to bounce back and forth for a long time. So I just told him. All of it. From my collapse in the elevator, to the stone falling on Michelle. He tried to hold me several times during the monotone narration of events. I think he needed me to hold him. But that, I couldn't do. I showed him the whore mark, the label, but then explained that Will had taken it as his own, and how that had helped.

"There's one more thing," I said, looking at the thoroughly destroyed man beside me, and not wanting to tell him. But without this knowledge, he would never really understand. The film in my head. What it was. And when it played. I stated it factually and quickly, trying to get it over as fast as possible.

He was so horrified that he didn't really look like himself anymore. "You're seeing this now?" he asked in a whisper.

I nodded. "The music's getting faster. You're going to have to go soon."

"Malphia," he said, and stopped, finally lost for words.

I studied the joint between the carpeted part of the room and the wooden floor by the barre, the thin metal divider, a tiny hole in the wood shaped like a keyhole, and the scratches made by shoes and feet.

"I loved you so fast," he said. "From the first moment I saw you, there has been only you."

I couldn't cope with declarations of love. Or memories of it. I couldn't cope with any more of this talk we were having. So, I just spoke the simplest of truths. "You have to stay away from me now, Aleks."

Looking like I'd hit him with a sledgehammer, he started to speak again, but I curled up on the bed and covered my ears. He was gone when I unfurled.

My belly felt hollow. But I wasn't actually hungry. I couldn't even feel that anymore. My mother would be pleased. Her daughter would finally be properly thin. She could direct her bile toward my various new disfigurements instead.

Everything ached. Sleep wouldn't come. Something odd and itchy was occurring. It was a bit like how I'd felt when Aleks had been ill, how I'd sensed that. But it wasn't quite the same. This was a sort of swollen rage that needed to burst, something unfinished and wrong, and – against my better judgement – I had go to him.

⌒ell⌒

He sat on his bed wearing an outdoorsy jacket that I'd never seen before, and he was in the process of lacing up what looked like walking boots.

I watched him. The film played.

"Is happen now? The thing?" he asked.

I nodded and asked my own question. "What are you doing?"

"I am going to kill her."

"Oh." I sat beside him on the bed, and we looked at one another. "No," I said. "Don't do that."

"Why not?"

"You would go to prison."

"Does it matter?"

I didn't feel anything, so what were the facts around this? "You're not a killer. You shouldn't become one."

"She should suffer, feel pain and fear, and then die."

"I don't think she feels things like normal people." Michelle and I had that in common. Pushing the thought aside, I became more forceful. "Promise you won't do it. It won't change anything. Whether she's alive or dead makes no difference now. I want to sleep, and this is stopping me. Say you're not going to do it."

He sighed. "Okay." There was a pause. "Malphia, I need... I just... I can't..."

He leapt to his feet and switched to fast and loud Ukrainian. He then punched the wall several times, making little impact on it. His hand was bloody as he leant back against the door, still and silent after the storm.

The blood drew me across the room. I took his hand and inspected it, knowing how it was going to swell and bruise. It was much worse than that time he'd hit Gavin. Flecks of white plaster were embedded in the raw flesh, and that might lead to infection.

"I need to clean this and put a dressing on it," I told him.

He let himself be led into the bathroom where I found the first-aid kit. "It might hurt," I warned of the antiseptic fluid.

He observed me in silence.

"I would make a good nurse," I mused. "I have no emotional involvement, and I'm experienced with wounds." A tear dripped off my chin and onto his hand. "Sorry, did that sting?"

"No."

I dressed the grazed knuckles. The obscene film show was easier to ignore with a firm focus. Or maybe I was just getting used to it.

"I'm going to bed," I told him, once I was finished. "You should do the same. I'll leave tomorrow, Aleks. It'll be better then."

He brushed the back of his non-hurt hand down my cheek. "You need to give yourself time."

I shook my head. "Time won't help. I'm a different person now."

He started to argue, his face all twitchy. I turned and left. There was only so much drama someone incapable of human emotion could take.

Back in my room, sleep remained elusive. A distant sadness wanted to make noise but couldn't. I was actually glad when he burst in, put the lamp on, and climbed onto the bed. He made no sense, talking fast about different people.

"Look at me, Malphia. I need you to see me. You are not the one that is a different person. That man she is showing you, he is not me, is idiot." He tapped his forehead with his fingers. "Does not exist now. He is dead from the second of seeing you. Is like spiritual awakening? Being born again? This is me. I fell in love with you. Am new person, never before been. Look at my face. Is changed, no?"

I examined him. It was interesting. My fingertips explored cheeks, eyebrows, nose, mouth, and returned to the cheekbones. He was right. His face was certainly different; it was less angular than the face of the man in the film. That man was much thinner. I closed my eyes to study the film man for a moment. The segmentation of his ribs was very clear through his skin.

So, what about the man who sat in front of me on the bed? I tugged at his shirt. He pulled it off. I felt his ribs, and his collar bones, and his shoulder blades. There was more flesh on them. This Aleks was much healthier.

"Something's happening," I realised. "The film. And the music. They're slowing down. Talk to me, Aleks. Tell me things. True things."

"I found you," he said. "Find me now. See me. I am yours. Only yours."

I pressed his cheeks back and gazed into his eyes. They were deep and brown and full of love. That wasn't visible on the face of the other man, the film man. It wasn't a film about love.

"It's stopped," I said.

I waited for it to resume. It didn't. A musical echo faded away into an abyss.

I touched the dip on Aleks's nose. I touched his mouth. It hurt to sit up on my knees, but I did it to kiss him, to remember what it was like.

I stated a fact. One that I'd just become aware of again. "I love you." The truth of the words was huge. Feeling love once more, after the strange hiatus, was like being warmed from within by a great big pink fire. My body felt all melty and relaxed. I was so happy that Aleks was right there in front of me, loving me back. How blessed was I?

Something was happening. Something that hadn't happened for a long time. I was crying. Properly crying. It was difficult to breathe as my storm hit. Huge and convulsive, it howled. He cradled me, and rocked us both, joining me in the great crying.

The deluge finally calmed, and we lay in the bed together. A huge tiredness washed over everything like a wave, and then pulled back, clearing sharp shingles away, leaving only golden sands in its wake.

Chapter 41

THERE HAD BEEN A loud sound. "You're okay," he said. The words seemed to be both a statement and a question to which I nodded, tightening my grip about his waist and snuggling closer to him in the bed. The noise came again.

"Who is it?" he called.

It was Holly. She came in, saw us, and immediately backed out, saying, "Oh man." The rest of the conversation was conducted through a thin crack at the side of the door. There were two 'affa important-seeming' men to see us, yes both of us, and it was nearly lunchtime.

"I will go and deal with this," said Aleks.

"No!" Panic rose at the thought of his going, quickly followed by a specific fear. "Did you kill her? Did you kill Michelle?"

"No, angel. I stayed here with you."

"Oh, yes." I felt muddled and confused. Here I was, looking at Aleks, and it really was all okay. Nothing terrible was happening. My head was just my head, my mind my own again.

"I will get rid of whoever it is, and come straight back," he said.

"I'll come too. If it's the police again, I'd rather get it over with. And I don't want you to go out the door and come back in. It's been bad..." I slapped my hands over my eyes. How bad had it been for him, to see my reaction, to be so rejected?

Hugging was gentle. Everything was gentle. I made him turn away as I got dressed, though he'd already seen. He forbade more apology, telling me that I had done nothing wrong, and then that love transcended any need to say sorry. Such an idea seemed poetic to the point of silliness, and I surprised us both by laughing which hurt my stitches. And he said sorry.

It was a dishevelled pair that sat down in the new office across the desk from two imposingly smart men in dark suits. I didn't take in who they were and just sipped Holly's sweet tea. With Aleks's hand in mine, these strange men could talk about an educational trust and funding and liability all they wanted. The piece of paper that was passed across the table had a very large number on it. Aleks got angry. He suspected they'd known Michelle was unstable. He said what they were offering me was an insult.

Two more bits of paper appeared before I understood. And really, it was so simple. "You're going to give me money to never talk about any of this, and never sue."

I was right, but there was a bit more to the meeting than that. Aleks was being offered complete control of the school and a virtually unlimited budget in the first year to turn the castle into a centre of excellence for dance in Scotland.

That was good. It would be so very good. For him. For me. For everyone. "I'll sign," I said. "I accept."

Aleks shook his head. "You have the right to seek proper compensation. And not be gagged in this way."

"You won't get more than this," said one of the suited men. "Take it to court, and you may get nothing."

I smiled at him, a remembered task in mind. "I have an extra condition, something I want you to arrange for me."

"Yes?" the elder of the suits asked, and I made the deal.

Emotions returned. Physical strength too, a little more each class as Aleks's hands guided and corrected. I worked hard to perfect my tendu and really began to understand the importance of the seemingly simple stretch of the foot. I was wary of the other therapeutic exercises, worried about a connection to Amalgamation C, though he assured me there was none.

We had a conversation about the peculiar nature of the sequence. Aleks told me that the stone in the roof had been dislodged by the piano foot when it went through the floor. I had not made it fall. Of course I hadn't. The idea that a combination of movements could cause telekinetic effects was nonsense, springing as it did from the obsessed and deluded mind of Michelle. I'd been subjected to an extreme form of aversion therapy, and the result had been terrible, but that was all over now.

The fact that I had almost walked away from Aleks was a frequent source of horror to me, and I held on to him whenever possible.

"Can you at least put each other down at meal times?" moaned Justin.

"I think it's lovely," said Bekah. "The mum and dad of the castle should always be together."

"I am liking this thought," said Aleks.

I liked that he smiled.

When he wasn't teaching, I often sat in his new office with him, the room we'd nearly gone into during the Christmas party. I loved the patterned tile by its door, the one that looked like Jackie's house. I loved the wide window that overlooked an old shrubbery garden behind the castle. I loved Aleks's enthusiasm and ideas about how to make the school great. I loved him.

Holly coming into various rooms and saying "Oh man," became a farcical and common occurrence. It always seemed to take place mid-embrace.

"She thinks we're having sex all over the place," I said.

"I know," he replied, laughing into my neck. It was good we could laugh about it, the fact that what Holly thought was happening everywhere was, in fact, not happening at all.

February turned to March. The nights grew lighter, and the days longer. I returned to teaching, preparing Bekah's class for their first exam. The syllabus was exactly the same as when I'd done it myself as a student, and I found it just as robotic and boring as I had back then. I asked Aleks if I could do a freestyle class for my pupils as well, and he said yes at once, making me suspect he would refuse me nothing after all that had happened.

I sat in his office one morning, while he was teaching, and used the big computer to register my students for their exam. I had to verify my email address and waited impatiently for my mail to load. It had been a long time since I'd bothered to check email; I'd barely done it since being at the castle. The mail page was colourful as it displayed an animated logo in front of me. It had two reds that didn't match. Images flowed through my mind as I stared at the jarring and offensive colours. I remembered Michelle leaving for Christmas. I remembered Michelle returning after Christmas. The first Michelle had been happy and friendly, telling me she'd email me. The second one had morphed from warm to cold as she'd observed Aleks and me together.

Was I about to face that promised Christmas email now? What was it about? Aleks. The therapeutic work. Something she'd wanted me to see to make him look bad or unattractive? Had she known about us, back then? No. The transformation to bitter and mean had been too instant, too extreme.

My heart hammered as the slow rural internet started to open the page properly. My fingers were sweaty on the keyboard. And then it wasn't there. The email. The Michelle email. There was the new registration message from the exam board, and marketing from various places where I'd bought clothes and theatre tickets. That was about it. I scrolled up and down, desperate to find the dreaded communication. I searched all the folders from spam to trash and back again. Nothing. Maybe she'd forgotten to send it. Maybe she'd already been beginning to break down then. She'd been unbalanced all along. A damaged person. I knew bad things had happened to her. She'd said as much in the lower dungeon, the real dungeon. That day. That night. While that film was playing.

The film of her and Aleks. And it had been Aleks in the film. Of course it had. The concept of a 'different man' had fooled the broken part of my subconscious, but it wasn't actually true.

Aleks had made love to Michelle. Aleks had kissed Michelle. He'd given her those soft kisses that I knew so well. Lots of them.

The door opened and the man himself came in, happy for a moment before seeing my face. He transformed from positive to negative as he regarded me. His smile faded away completely as I stood.

I pushed the chair back. I leant forward and put my hands on the desk to steady myself, to brace for the emotional tempest that approached. I looked up at Aleks, and the air around me turned to a brilliant and violent red, little yellow sparks dotted through it.

"It was you." I didn't sound like myself, as if I was the one who was a different person. But I wasn't. And neither was he. "You kissed her." That was the worst thing. I didn't know why, but somehow it was.

He didn't try to deny it. "I'm sorry," he said. "If you could know how much I wish I had not."

"Stop," I said. I didn't want to hear his wishes or regrets. Things were as they were. And they had to be dealt with. "I'm so angry."

"Lay it all here," he said, holding his arms wide. "I can take it. I want to."

The anger was so intense that I could have shoved him, hit him, bit him, cut him. My body shook with rage, and it had to be released. But not onto him. Because: bad things. Bad things happening and being repeated, harms inflicted, passed on. Michelle. Me. The violence had to stop with me.

So I didn't touch Aleks. I smashed up the office instead. It started with the computer and its slow internet. The large screen then lay on the floor, blinking up at the ceiling, as I flung every book, ornament, object and thing from every shelf, desk and windowsill. The pictures came off the wall. The comfy chairs were too heavy for me to upend with my hurt arm. So Aleks helped. I glared at him. I didn't want his help.

And then Holly walked in. "Oh ma—"

I spun round. "If you don't like what you see, learn to knock!"

She backed out, hands held up.

The energy in the room, in me, changed. The anger wasn't gone, not completely, but it had receded somewhat. For now.

I touched Aleks's arm. He covered my hand with his. But it was too soon to talk. I couldn't talk. So I left him there, in the mess, and walked through to the kitchen and Holly.

It was too soon to talk there too. But there was cake. And hot chocolate. And Holly squeezed my shoulders as I sat at the big table.

Lunchtime soon came, and I went through to the great hall to join my friends. But I couldn't settle, couldn't eat. Anger might have calmed, but a feeling of disquiet sat with me at the dining table. It had to be addressed before it grew into something dark and distressing.

"Justin," I said. "Would you teach Aleks's class this afternoon for him?"

"Ballet?" he replied, looking doubtful. "Phi, it's really not my thing. I certainly couldn't teach it."

"I'll do it," said Will.

That sorted, I returned to the scene of my earlier rage. Aleks stood at his desk, having restored the computer to its proper place, but not any of the chairs or other things. I stayed near the door, rather than picking my way through the detritus of the room.

"I've calmed down," I told him, not that he'd looked worried. "And I have to speak to you."

He almost smiled. "I would say 'have a seat,' but…" He glanced at the upended chairs.

I almost smiled too. It was time to put my natural blurtiness to good use.

"It's about our relationship," I said.

"Okay." He looked less sure of himself. There was no smile now, almost or otherwise. He walked round to the front of the desk and sat against it, bracing himself for what was to come, perhaps.

"Sex," I said, "or making love, as you would say, has always been a big thing for us."

"Mmm," he said, tilting his head to one side. "You find these words humorous? Making love?"

"Not when you say them. But I think I understand what's happening with us, part of it anyway." I paused, making sure to get it right. "You're afraid that you might hurt me."

"Yes," he admitted. "And you are afraid that I will be repelled by the appearance of your body."

"Yes." It was a shock to hear him say it, but it was true.

"You have hurts," he said. "Scars. But you are as beautiful as you ever were. And not only to me. It is just a fact. I am as attracted to you as ever. Have you not noticed the number of cold showers I have been taking?"

"No," I said, almost laughing as I thought about it. "Or, I didn't realise they were cold."

We looked at one another across the mess of fury. "We could take a warm one now," I suggested.

"Test the waters?" he said with a small smile.

Unfortunately the word 'test' travelled with us up the stairs, circling like the stairway itself, and making us both nervous.

"It's not an exam," I said, trying to lighten the mood as we arrived in my room.

"No," he agreed. "But you must not take points off me if I cry. Because I might, Malphia. You know I do this."

"Yes," I said. "And I should get to go into the shower first, and let the water make it all steamy so you can't see me so clearly."

"There is no need for you to do this for me. But if it makes you more comfortable, yes, of course."

Annoyed with us both for being so very, very polite, I went into the bathroom, got undressed quickly and stepped into the shower cubicle. I turned the water up hot, and the air steamed up.

"Are you even in here?" he said, joining me moments later.

"I'm here."

Here. Just us. Nothing in between. We stood. I looked up at him. He looked down at me. Then he put one of his hands round my waist, and took my hand with the other, as if we were going to waltz. And that's what we did, right there in the shower. Lovely slow dancing like at the Christmas party. I rested my head on his shoulder. He kissed my ear, and that changed things.

We kissed under the shower head, the water running down over us both, washing us clean, waking us up, like some sort of strange hot baptism.

"We did this in your flat," I remembered. "Our first morning together."

"With the chocolate pudding," he added, lifting me up against the tiled wall as he had then.

We avoided nothing. He touched my scars. I didn't draw away. He cried. I cried too. For everything, and then nothing. Because we were happy now. Bad things had gone on, but life went on too. We went on. Sex went on. And it was good. So good. So very good.

I had become so used to experiencing unpleasant physical sensations, I'd forgotten how wonderful my body could feel. And this, with the hot water and the steam, and Aleks, Aleks, Aleks. This was sublime.

I forgave him for being too gentle with me because how could he be anything else? He forgave me for immediately wrapping myself up in a towel after we got out of the shower. It didn't really make sense anyway. My arms weren't hidden.

Back in the bedroom, I dropped the towel and got into bed.

Aleks got dressed. "I want to stay, but I have class," he explained.

"Will's going to teach it for you."

"Will?" he said, frowning. "You arrange this?"

I nodded, smiling.

"Malphia, Will does not know the specific limits of each student. You were given these notes before you started to teach them. I have to take the class myself."

I sighed and sat up. "You've become a totally responsible teacher. I have to say, it's not much fun."

He smiled and came over to kiss me. "I am so happy that we are back in this place together. I love you so very much. And there can be more fun later. Tonight."

"But what am I supposed to do in the meantime?"

"Well," he said, as if about to make a daring suggestion. "You could take part in the classes on your own timetable. Pasha's workshop in the theatre? Is usually good, no?"

I shrugged, feeling no enthusiasm at the idea of doing such a thing. But Aleks left, and I was all alone and a bit bored. Or something like bored. Unsettled. Antsy.

I got out of bed and opened my leotard drawer. So far, since everything, in Aleks's classes I'd only worn trackies and long-sleeved T-shirts. I took out the red leotard, that audacious and offensive item of dancewear. I put it on and pulled knitted warm-ups, tights and a short ballet skirt over the top. There. I could be audacious if I wanted now. No one was going to chain me to a wall for it.

I interrupted the workshop, being very late indeed, but didn't apologise. Everyone seemed pleased to see me anyway.

"He didn't go for me teaching his class," Will told me.

I nodded.

The choreography they were learning on the stage was complicated. My brain felt slow and stupid, unused to complicated. My legs were stiff and sore. My feet didn't like the pointe shoes. And the unsettled feeling was still with me, brown and grey and blue. It was hot and stuffy in the theatre, and I pulled off my top warm-up. Everyone looked. Everyone stared. I'd forgotten they hadn't seen. How could I have forgotten that?

So I walked out, ignoring the barrage of soothing words that started up behind me.

"Amalphia, don't go," said Sun. "We didn't mean anything by—"

But I was gone. Down the corridor, and out into the foyer. I looked up at the stone angels of the ceiling. They looked down at me. One of them blew a trumpet, heralding what exactly? Some event in the distant past? Or a new one, yet to come?

The stony visages of the angels called to mind other stones. I'd been avoiding many things in this post-dungeon life of mine. One of those things was a stone. Still wearing the uncomfortable pointe shoes, I pulled my knitwear back on and headed out the big front door of the castle.

It was frosty outside, but bright and sunny, the air fresh and clean. I walked over the gravel, and the grass, and took the forest path to the stones. The bustle of the world, of the castle, ceased to exist in the quiet and muted light of the forest. I found myself running up the hill, between the high trees, hurrying to see the change that had taken place.

The overnight frost had been harder in the circle. Everything was white and crispy, which lessened the shock of the mess that had been made. A digger had obviously come in from the field, its tracks now dusted with white, like icing sugar on chocolate cake. Lots of people in big working boots had walked about and churned up mud, their footprints now frozen and hard. The ground of the circle was lumpy-bumpy. Like me. Injurious things had happened here. Some were already fixed, and the rest would heal in time.

I stood in front of the new stone, the old stone, the freshly planted and put back stone. The tall pointed megalith had a thick layer of frost upon it. Tiny spikes of ice stood out all over its grey surface. I brushed a finger across them, and everything turned red again.

"Why?" I demanded of the stone, my voice loud, the words echoing round the glade. "Why didn't you fall earlier?"

I shoved it. It didn't shift. The workmen had done a good job. That condition of my compensation package had been well met.

"It's because you would have just lain there, isn't it? You needed me to see you, to recognise what you were, and arrange to have you returned to the circle."

My new friend Jackie had been pleased about the return of the stone. He'd told me that its theft was probably part of some hate crime in the past, and that it had been put right now. He claimed this would help lift the dark energies that hung around the castle. I didn't know if there was any truth to this, but I liked visiting Jackie and listening to his ideas. I walked to his house once a week, armed with home bakes from Holly, who had been dismayed by the tale of the stale biscuits.

I walked round and round the stone now, pacing in my pointe shoes, pushing the wretched boulder every so often. "How dare you use me like that?" I said to it. "Look what happened to me." I stood, arms wide, as if to show my scars. "You could have fallen the day you got dislodged. Then there wouldn't have been a dungeon for us to go down to! All those televisions would have been crushed and ruined, maybe even discovered; she might have been stopped then." I kicked the stone with the hard toe of my shoe. It made a nice plunk noise. It was rather satisfying. I did it again, and again. Both feet. Both shoes. The satin tore. The pink fabric turned brown from the frozen mud on the base of the rock. And then I hammered on the stone with my fists, which really hurt, and the anger faded to dark blue. Grief. I sank to the ground, leant back against the stone and cried. And cried.

The tears tasted salty. My hands were red and raw. The stone remained quiet. Well, of course it did. What was I doing anyway? Shouting at an inanimate object? Blaming it for all that had happened? How ridiculous had I become?

I thought back over the events of the day. I'd smashed up an office, tried to rearrange my boyfriend's work schedule to my own liking, and then walked huffily away from people who had only meant to be kind. Back near the beginning of term, Aleks had told me that the diva was part of a dancer's make-up. Well, it didn't have to be part of mine.

I stood up. I had a whole castle of people to apologise to. I had a whole life to live. But first – I looked down at my muddied and inadequate outfit – I would put on some warm clothes and have some hot chocolate.

Full Circle

T HE END OF TERM arrived, the Easter break, and with it came partings.

Simone was the first. She left early one morning, pausing only to request that Sadie wish us all 'good riddance' on her behalf.

Then Pasha handed me a note bearing his number. "Aleks is having years of fun. You too must experience life, all its many joys."

"Pay for those in Amsterdam, do I?"

He was suitably abashed, and we hugged a farewell.

Colin was straight as ever. "Any chance of a goodbye shag?"

Then came the one that really mattered.

"Are you sure this is correct and respectful, having a picnic up here like this?" asked Justin, helping himself to a sandwich.

"Absolutely, it is," I confirmed. The food was beautifully laid out on the flat stone of the circle on this wonderfully warm and sunny spring day.

"Amalphia knows these things instinctively," said Sun. "If she says it's okay, it's okay. Look, I know you lot have your secrets, but is anyone going to explain the new stone?"

"It's not new, it's old," I said, then telling her that the stone had been embedded in the ceiling of the deeper dungeon, that I'd seen it fall while down there, and how I had dreamt about it while unconscious.

Her face showed horror and amazement as I told an edited version of the story. "That wasn't a dream, Amalphia," she said. "It sounds like astral projection into a different realm."

"You do have the best experiences here, Phi," said Justin. "I mean, spiritually, not, obviously... Oh, you know what I mean."

I did. I lay down on the grass, the heat of the sun blissful in its intensity. The season was in full bloom. Tiny pink and white flowers had started to appear round the base of the stones, and their heady scent made me think of fairies and magic. I held Will's pink stone aloft and smiled at the inner rainbows the sun revealed.

"All I want to do is take my clothes off and lie here," I said, feeling a pull a little like that first time Will and I had found the circle. I smiled up at him now. He was being very quiet today, sitting on the stone, possibly experiencing similar sensations in this ancient place.

"Well, maybe we should leave you to it," said Justin.

"Yes," agreed Sun, looking at her phone. "Time's getting on."

"I'm not actually going to strip," I said, sitting up. "You don't have to go."

"Look," said Justin. "Hearst has something to tell you. He's frightened to do it. We've all known for days. I'm surprised Zolotov hasn't let it slip. So, you know, have fun."

Sun and Justin got up to go, Justin helping himself to some small cakes on the way, and then the two of them disappeared into the trees.

As my oldest friend slid off the stone to sit by me, I knew. Aleks had mentioned that it would soon be time for Will to stretch his wings. I hadn't thought about what that would mean.

"When?" I asked.

"This afternoon. I've been trying to tell you, babe. I've a week's tryout for the company, you know the one everyone from college always wanted to get into? He arranged it."

A tear ran down my cheek.

"Don't, Malph. I'll be back if I don't get it."

"You'll get it. Of course you will. I'm just being selfish because I'll miss you."

"You'll be fine. You're going to marry him and live happily ever after in the castle, aren't you?"

"I don't know about that."

"Kind of obvious to the rest of us. He barely lets you out of his sight. I thought he'd be here today."

"He doesn't come up here."

"And are you really happy, just teaching?"

"Yes." I had discovered great satisfaction in helping others be the best they could be. I was perfectly content. No one had voiced the fact that my disfigurements would be an impediment to a career in ballet – Aleks still insisted on my studying repertoire – but I knew. "In a way, it's a relief," I told Will. "No more stage fright."

He frowned. "That might fade in time."

I shook my head. Deep down, I had always suspected it wouldn't. I changed the subject and stated a fact. "I don't want to say goodbye to you, Will."

"So, don't. Come and see me. Bring Zolotov with you, if you want. He's got that fancy flat, hasn't he? You might stay there sometimes?"

There was a fast hug, a quick promise of lots of communication, and he was gone.

I stood in the centre of the circle. Alone, in stillness, eyes shut, heart hurting. The sun shone and time wavered. It felt like the stones were spinning around me until warm hands on my face stilled them.

Will was back. "Not married yet, though, are you?" he said and kissed me on the lips. We stared at each other for a second before our mouths came together again. Soft. Warm. The completion of a story. His hair sprung back under my fingers. His tongue tasted the same as mine. He picked something out of my hair, face serious: a small pink flower of the circle. Then, he really was gone.

Hand on buzzing mouth, I smiled. Fourteen-year-old Amalphia had just had all her romantic wishes granted. The past was fixed, wiped clean of resentment and sorrow.

And the present was clear. I ran down the woodland path in my bare feet, back to the castle, and home to Aleks.

Next Up...

DON'T MISS THE NEXT exciting instalments of Amalphia's journey:

CABRIOLE: Dancing in the City
FOUETTÉ: Dancing with the Past

And look out for a new series – Castle Dancers – set in the same world, and coming soon!

Acknowledgements

HUGE THANKS GO OUT to my husband and children for their never-ending support. The three of you are always there to help me, whether I'm curled up on the sofa in the midst of an autoimmune flare-up or desperate to discuss a diabolical new plot twist. I love you so much.

And to the friends who were there for me during difficult times in my life, times that inspired some of the events in this novel: thank you so very much.

I've written more about the inspiration behind this series of stories on my website at ailishsinclair.com

About the Author

AILISH SINCLAIR TRAINED AS a dancer and taught dance for many years, before working in schools to help children with special needs.

She lives in Scotland beside a loch with her husband and two children where she dances (medical conditions allowing) and writes and eats rather too much chocolate.

More Ailish

Online

- www.ailishsinclair.com

- @AilishSinclair on X/Instagram/Threads

- Sign up for the newsletter at ailishsinclair.com

Visit the castle and stone circle in the past:

- Sisters at the Edge of the World

- The Mermaid and the Bear

- Fireflies and Chocolate